D1003931

STICKING TO THE SCRIPT

CIPHER OFFICE BOOK #2

STELLA WEAVER

SMARTYPANTS ROMANCE

COPYRIGHT

DEDICATION

To two incomparable TREASURES.
Linda, without you, I would have never started writing.
Brooke, without you, I would have never kept writing.
Your love and encouragement made me believe this was possible.
Thank you. XO

PROLOGUE

Tonight, was *Do or Die.*
Make or Break.
Ride or Get off the Horse.

Even though I wasn't sure that last one was a real idiom, I knew it was apt. I felt as if my entire future happiness hinged on how tonight played out.

I wanted to roll my own eyes at the melodrama of it all, but really, it was warranted. Honestly. And unless you were a gay man looking for love in Chicago in the 21st century, you couldn't comprehend the level of *done* I had reached.

But, as dramatic as that all sounded, I *was* optimistic. I hadn't lost all hope. I had exactly one fuck left to give. Figuratively. Well, maybe literally too. I didn't know what the night would bring. I just hoped it was good. It didn't even have to be great. All I needed was *not terrible*. Just. Not. Terrible.

I had my cab driver drop me off a block from my destination, preferring to walk off the nervous energy coursing through me. I was in Boystown, in East Lakeview, heading down Halstead Street to meet my date, King.

Two weeks ago, in another bar here in Boystown, he'd leaned into me, put his lips to my ear—presumably to be heard over the loud music, but probably it was just an excuse to generate sexy vibes—and said, *"I'm King."* To which I replied—not so cleverly, *"I'm sure you are, big stuff."*

I'd been slightly drunk because my friends and I were smack dab in the middle of a bar crawl to celebrate Ernesto and Paulie's bachelor party. I'd bumped into the stocky ginger and said something to him that I couldn't remember now, but I'm positive was witty and cute in the moment. He'd been charmed enough to buy me a drink and chat me up the whole time we were there.

When it came time for a change in venue, I said my farewell, gave him my number and left the beefcake behind. The night's revelry had been about Ernesto and Paulie, not me. And besides, I was drunk and didn't want to make an impaired decision that could backfire in my face.

If there was one thing I had plenty of experience with, it was the backfire.

Backfire? More like dumpster fire, I thought with a snort.

The idea of doing the bar crawl and looking for a guy hadn't occurred to me because I was already in the mindset of being off the horse, ready to hang up my lasso and call the rodeo finished.

My year in the romance department had been so spectacularly bizarre and disheartening that I felt a break from the insanity was necessary.

The nightmare had started with James, the choir singer. He was a tenor and had the voice of an angel. I met him at a holiday party where his choir performed, and their rendition of "Hallelujah" had given me goosebumps. When he winked at me from the first riser, I was smitten.

But when we met up after the New Year, gone was the angel, replaced by Satan's minion. He loudly and vulgarly berated the Uber driver *and* patrons in line for the movie we were seeing. I suspected he was high on something. I stuck it out through the film, but later at dinner, when he called our waitress a stupid cunt, I had to get the hell out of there.

Next had been the other James—James the Second, as I referred to

2

him. He had kept his left hand in his pants pocket almost the entire night, letting loose occasional, low, sex moans. The moans had been the majority of his contribution to the conversation. And, even then, would annoyingly interrupt my witty dialogue. I became fed up, confronted him about it and he admitted he had been tugging on his scrotum ring.

Sure, that hadn't been the *worst* thing a guy had done on a date with me, but I wasn't looking for quick, kinky sex. Those days were fading fast. Sex was cheap and easy. I knew I could get on Grindr and have a face full of dick in a matter of minutes if I wanted. Cheap and easy wasn't appealing. Honestly, it never really had been.

Don't get me wrong, I wasn't uninterested in getting laid. Oh, I wanted it, but I wanted *more*, so I kept trying the dating thing.

I went out with Ben, who I dubbed Bennet the Bandit. Our date started with a lot of promise. He had been engaging, flirty, and he managed to lull me into a sense of false hope when he went in for a deep and heady kiss. His hands found their way to my ass, squeezed and kneaded. Then, hope was dashed suddenly when he broke off the kiss, snatched the wallet from my pants and took off at a breakneck run.

That had really sucked.

My most recent dating disaster had been Travis. Tragic, tragic Travis. An interesting thing about Travis was that he raised umbrella cockatoos.

In general, I found animal lovers to be great people. I imagined anyone who loved large, loud, and ill-tempered cockatoos was probably a laid-back, kind person. Travis and I had two nice dates. No fireworks, but they were, *by far*, the best dates I'd had in a long time.

However, before the third rolled around, he'd shown up at my apartment with four nearly bald birds crammed into an undersized cage. He'd demanded I take them as a gift. When I politely declined, stating I couldn't be a responsible pet owner due to my work schedule, he flew off the handle and said he was going to go home and wring all their necks.

All of them.

He had *fifteen* birds at home!

I calmed him down and listened to him complain about the noise and the dust and the droppings. I thought by the time he had left, I'd done a good job of convincing him to find a sanctuary for them, but I wasn't positive. So, I called the ASPCA on him. To this day, I don't know how it all ended, but I really hope those birds made it out of his house alive.

July was fast approaching, and so far, all I had to show for my troubles was a new wallet and driver's license. *Thank you, Bennet.*

Sure, my tales of tragedy kept my friends entertained, but it was wearing me down. These situations I found myself in played out like scenes from slapstick rom-coms. Except from my vantage point, nothing was remotely romantic or comical. Not even a little bit.

I didn't want to go into work Monday morning and regale Janie with another failure. It was tiresome to pretend it didn't matter, and it was getting harder to sell.

Unless I was self-sabotaging—which I absolutely was *not*—a date eventually had to go well. There had to be someone in this city who clicked with me.

The odds were in my favor. They had to be. No one could have the year I'd had and not see the tides change. I was long overdue for a date that wasn't going down in Crazy Town.

King seemed like he could be the one to bring my losing streak to an end. We'd been texting here and there and blessedly he hadn't been pushy. He hadn't sent any unsolicited dick pics or tried to engage me in sexting. What he had sent me was an intriguing picture of himself from the neck down, shirtless, tattooed, and kilted. He told me his interests were lifting and bagpiping.

With all of that in his favor, he still managed to earn Strike One. He hadn't wanted to meet for a daytime or early date. He wanted to meet at a bar. At *eleven PM.* It was an unholy hour to meet up and indicated to me that he didn't want to get to know me too deeply. The sting of that was soothed a bit by his choice in venue.

Rather than meeting at any number of loud and boisterous clubs along Halstead, he'd chosen Jimbo's. Jimbo's was a pub geared toward an older crowd who wanted to enjoy drinks and company without competing with ear-busting music. I reasoned that maybe he had a job where he worked late, that maybe this wasn't going to be just about sex.

Like I said, I was optimistic.

But I was gun-shy enough to arrive slightly later than our agreed upon time so I could spy on him. I wanted this guy to ride the line between fascinating and ordinary—fun but not *too* fun. What I absolutely needed was to make sure he was fully dressed and not re-enacting scenes from *Braveheart*. I swore, if he so much as whispered the word *freedom* with even a slight hint of a Scottish accent, I was out.

As I approached Jimbo's I silently begged, *Please, please, please, you pipe-playing hunk of ginger, don't let me down.*

I peeked through the pub's pristine window and let out a sigh of relief when I spotted him. Seated at the bar, dressed in well-fitting, casual clothes, he looked just as I remembered him from a couple of weeks back, if maybe a bit bigger, more muscular. His short sleeve was pulled tight around his bicep and a scrolling tattoo was visible, teasing. His short red hair, though receding, was gelled into a stylish sweep. At first glance, he seemed unapproachable, almost brutish. I continued to spy as he spoke to the barman and owner, Jim.

Jim had been running his pub since the early nineties and he knew people. He knew how to deal with troublemakers, too. I watched as he laughed at something King said, then stuck his hand out for a shake.

That sealed the deal for me. If Jim was cool with him, I was game.

Steven Thompson was back in the saddle.

CHAPTER ONE

STEVEN

"I promise we can leave as soon as Botstein cuts the cake," Elizabeth whispered into my ear.

I patted her hand reassuringly. "No worries, my little Belieber. We'll stay as long as you need to be here."

When we arrived, Elizabeth had been dismayed to see that of the dozens of people in attendance, she only recognized a few. To top it off, the party was a definite yawner. I was sure it was going to wind down early.

"Steven!" she hissed. "If you're going to air my private shame, at least get it right. I don't listen to Bieber."

I laughed at her faux outrage. She was too cute. I enjoyed spending time with Elizabeth. She had a sardonic wit and a forthright way of speaking that was at odds with her tiny stature, gorgeous face, and demonstrably affectionate and compassionate heart. Elizabeth was my kind of people.

She also had a not-so-secret love of pubescent boys singing in harmony. Truly, it was endearing.

Leaning down to whisper in her ear, I said with mock accusation, "I call *bullshit*. I heard it last Thursday when you pulled your earbuds out." I straightened and shook my head. "You're going to go deaf if you keep listening at such a high volume. Aren't you a doctor? Shouldn't you know this stuff?"

Elizabeth was an emergency room physician and tonight was a party celebrating her mentor's retirement. Apparently, he was an excellent doctor and was held in high regard. She hadn't wanted to attend the party alone, so she begged me sweetly and I gracefully acquiesced —because that's the kind of friend I was.

Giving.

Supportive.

Available... Always available.

She needed me to be her plus-one tonight because her husband, Nico Manganiello, aka Nico Moretti, the famous comedian, was working out of town and couldn't make it home in time to join her.

A few years ago, my co-worker, Janie Sullivan (or rather, Janie Morris, as she'd been back then), introduced me to Elizabeth and Nico when I moved into the East Randolph Street building our boss owned. I hit it off immediately with the couple and found they were no hardship to know. Nico was not only hot as hellfire, he was one of the most friendly people I'd ever met. Plus, the hand-delivered homemade apple fritters he brought to me on Sundays meant he had my undying devotion.

Never underestimate the power of fried dough, folks. Never.

"Thanks again for coming with me," Elizabeth said for the fortieth time. "It shouldn't be too much longer."

The party really was abysmally boring, but there was one true bright spot in the whole, dull shebang. Dr. Ken Miles.

DKM, as I now referred to him, was by far the most entertaining person here. He was blond, blue-eyed, square-jawed, and dressed in a suit and tie, the cut of which accentuated his athletic build. The hue also paired nicely with his light coloring, which told me he knew how to dress himself for maximum effect. He was *Handsome Level: Corn-Fed Meets Trust Fund.*

I smiled to myself at this label. I loved to assign people into arbitrary categories based on characteristics. It wasn't a scientific or useful thing I did. It was simply fun. For instance, my boss at Cipher

Systems, Quinn Sullivan, was *Handsome Level: GQ Meets IQ*. Once, in the early days, after a painful one-on-one limo ride, I assigned him a *Personality Level: Mute Meets Rude*. I respected the man, but after that display of moodiness, it was wholly deserved.

Corn-Fed Meets Trust Fund was certainly appropriate for DKM. He had reached the level of handsome that was a turn-off. To the untrained eye, he appeared to be a calm and confident yuppie snob.

But my eyes weren't untrained. Oh no, I was a pro. I could spot a faker. I knew pretense when I saw it. He was only *pretending* to be relaxed. I could see it in the overly casual stance, the flashes of tightness around his mouth, the laugh that seemed forced.

He glanced around the room, passing his gaze over me, only to clock back immediately when he noticed I was looking at him. I didn't bother to avert my attention.

His brows drew inward, and he acknowledged me with a brief lift of his chin. Then he immediately pulled his eyes away and rubbed the back of his neck.

Just as I suspected. Totally uncomfortable.

Everyone else was chatting quietly in little groups, but not him. He spent most of the time on the fringe, by himself until someone, an acquaintance or stranger, approached him with a handshake and a "how-do?" I noted that the only people he had deigned to approach so far were Elizabeth and Dr. Botstein. But that probably had more to do with the possibility that there weren't many recognizable faces for him, rather than any anti-social tendencies.

Earlier, when Elizabeth had spied him walk through the door, she'd stepped up on her tiptoes, elongated her neck for a better view and said, "Oh, there's Dr. Ken Miles!" She'd given him a wave when he noticed her, and he made his way toward us.

"Good lord, I must be desperate to see a familiar face in here if I'm happy to see him."

"My, my," I said, arching an eyebrow. "Isn't he a pretty thing." And he was. So very, very pretty.

When he approached, he slid his left hand into his pocket and gave Elizabeth a smirk. His indolent, relaxed stance came off as completely affected. I was repulsed and intrigued. The conversation that followed did not disappoint.

Without any greeting, he said, "Dr. Finney, let me guess, your husband's conspicuously *out of town* again? You should probably get a private investigator to look in on that."

Oooh, I thought. *Ass. Hole.* His satisfied smile displayed a row of perfectly aligned teeth. Teeth so vibrantly white, I suspected they were professionally bleached.

Bleached Asshole, I amended.

The implication that Elizabeth and Nico had marital troubles rankled and I felt the need to jump to her defense.

"Yes, well, even with talent and a hot bod," I said coolly. "It takes a lot of hard work to earn his level of success. And that just means I get the pleasure of being Elizabeth's arm candy for the night."

I glanced down at Elizabeth and she gave me an approving smile, so I gave her a wink. The asshole, however, assessed me for a moment with a blank expression and pale blue eyes.

"So, are you her new bodyguard or something?" he asked, and Elizabeth huffed.

The idea that I was her security detail was pretty funny, given that my body mass was well below the average guard's, but aside from that, I still thought it was a strange question. She *did* have a security escort tonight, but he was most likely patrolling the perimeter of the banquet hall. He wouldn't be mingling in the party with her.

"Dr. Ken Miles," she began, making an obviously begrudging introduction. "This is my friend, Steven Thompson." She swept an arm down along my torso as if presenting a prize on a game show. "Steven, this is Dr. Ken Miles." To him, she simply issued a slight flick of her finger.

Still expressionless, and with his free hand, the doctor reached out for a firm-but-sweaty handshake.

"Be careful with this one," he said to me, releasing my hand. "Could be dangerous and I didn't think to bring a six-shooter with me."

Elizabeth tsked in disgust as he dropped his mask and issued her a triumphant smirk. "Enjoy the party."

The bizarre exchange seemed to have ended with some victory for the man—one I clearly didn't understand—but as he walked away, I saw him smooth his hair and straighten his (already straight) tie in a nervous gesture. I knew the exchange had made him uncomfortable.

Not long after he left us, he was forced to circle back, as it was announced that dinner was being served, and the seating arrangement put him directly across from us at the large table.

Throughout dinner, Elizabeth and I chatted between bites and I kept one eye on the young doctor. He ate his meal with a bored, vacant expression, only altering it when someone spoke to him or he clandestinely checked his watch. For a brief moment, his lip would curl, and his nostril would flare as he discovered how excruciatingly slow time was progressing. *Same, bro. Same.* If he would have bothered to glance in my direction, I would have given him a comical look that conveyed an understanding and kinship in our shared boredom. But he didn't look across at us. Not once. His avoidance of us—or Elizabeth—seemed pointed and deliberate.

His avoidance was perfectly fine with me, as it freed me up to watch him as closely as I wanted to. Considering how dull the party was, and how fascinating he was, it made the time pass pleasantly.

And now, I found myself curious. Dismissing Elizabeth's reassurances and talk of pop music, I broached the topic of the intriguing and strange DKM. "Never mind that," I waved my hand impatiently. "I'm watching your buddy over there. And I think there's something off about him."

She snorted. "Ya think? He's an ass, that's what he is. I knew he'd make some crack about Nico. He never misses an opportunity."

"Oh, he's an ass, no doubt about that," I agreed. "But what I want to know is, what's all that weird six-shooter talk about?"

Elizabeth's eyebrows lifted. "He's *Dr. Ken Miles.*" The emphasis clearly indicated that I was supposed to get her meaning, but I didn't.

"Yeeeaahh, that part was clear," I tilted my head and gave her my squinty-eye scrutiny. "But what does it *mean*?"

"You know how before you and I met, Nico's stalker attacked me in the hosp—"

"He shot Fancy Nancy!" I gasped.

"Fancy Stalker," she corrected. "That's how I refer to her, but, yeah, he did."

"And the plot thickens," I murmured. I'd heard the story in bits and pieces over the years and knew the doctor who had interrupted and ultimately stopped an attack on Elizabeth by a crazed, jealous fan of Nico's, was the same guy who had been making a play for her when Nico was.

It all made so much sense to me. The snide comments about Nico, the jibe about guards and guns. He was the hero of the scenario and *still* came out the loser. Poor, Corn-Fed Hottie.

"I guess I can't blame the guy for being bitter about getting dumped by an amazing woman for the Hotshot Italian Stallion," I reasoned.

She gave a half-hearted chuckle but was quick to correct me. "We never dated. We talked about it, made plans to…meet up," her blue eyes darted away from mine for a moment before returning. She smiled widely as she continued, "But Nico happened. Nico obliterated everything. My fears, my plans. I couldn't date Ken when Nico was taking over my heart and mind."

"Oh, aren't you just disgustingly cute?" I teased. "But really, back to DKM. Is it stress-related, do you think?"

"What are you talking about?"

"Look." Using the hand holding my wine glass, I extended my finger in what I hoped was a subtle point in the doctor's vicinity. He was standing next to a wall, underneath a sconce that shone down and made a golden halo around his already light curls. The effect was startling, and like a flame seducing a moth, his visage had lured in a pretty brunette.

"Okay, I'm looking," Elizabeth replied, unimpressed. "He's talking to someone who I think works in administrations at Chicago General. I don't know her name."

"He is trying so hard to be Mr. Suave—*excuse* me—*Dr.* Suave," I quipped. Elizabeth was not arrogant in the least about her degrees, but

I still liked to tease. "He looks like he's trying on poses for a modeling shoot."

"He does," she agreed, as we watched him first lean one forearm at shoulder-level on the paneling of the wall, then quickly straighten to push one side of his coat back to slide a hand in his pocket, then decide abruptly to cross his arms over his chest. He lifted one hand to scrub his jaw while he nodded at something the woman said, then he smoothed his hair.

To anyone else, he probably looked like he was trying to maneuver himself into the most flattering position for this attractive woman he was talking to. But I saw agitation. Discomfort.

The woman said something to him that made him break out his megawatt smile. When she walked away, he watched her for a moment, then let his smile slip.

What happened next, shocked me. It shocked me and confirmed my suspicion that he was one odd duck.

DKM started to turn his body in toward the wall, obscuring his front from my view.

But he wasn't quick enough, because I saw. I saw what he did.

Slowly, I turned to Elizabeth, a gleeful horror radiating through me. "Did I just see that? Did he really just do that?"

"Yes, you did," she answered flatly. "Yes, he did. Dr. Ken Miles is a nose-miner."

CHAPTER TWO

DKM

I t was *him.*

Steven Thompson.

Why did he have to be in *this* cafe, *this* morning? Weren't there a thousand coffee places in Chicago? How was it that the night after meeting him, he was sitting in my regular Sunday stop?

I started and ended my Sunday lakefront runs at East Randolph and always popped into Buzzy Bean afterward. I'd never seen him before, and I was positive about that because I would have certainly noticed him. As it was, I recognized him immediately when I stepped inside.

It was the glasses. His horn-rimmed, hipster glasses were designed to be eye-catching.

And caught my eye, they had. They suited his face, highlighting his hawkish nose and intense gray eyes.

The night before, those eyes had made me very uneasy.

I debated for a moment before joining the line to place my order. I needed my caffeine fix, and a quick assessment of him told me I could probably get in and out without being noticed. He was sitting at a two-seater across the room, his face in profile. On the tabletop sat a tall-sized beverage, a large muffin—really, these portion sizes were out of control—and a messenger bag. He wasn't eating or drinking anything, but instead, scrolling on his phone, not looking up. Not once. It irritated me.

The fact that it irritated me, irritated me. I wanted to get my coffee in peace, didn't I? To not be dissected by his intense gaze? I didn't need his scrutiny.

He had made Botstein's party a strange experience. It was already going to be awkward and uncomfortable, with so few familiar faces, plus, I had been exhausted. We'd been short-staffed with both an intensivist and a nocturnist on vacation and I'd been working long shifts up until yesterday. I wanted to skip out of the party, but as one of Dr. Botstein's former Chief Residents, I felt it was only right to attend his retirement bash. He'd been my research mentor, and if it hadn't been for his encouragement and tutelage, I doubted I'd be in the same position I was in now at BKC Memorial. I owed him a lot, so I downed some coffee, donned a suit, and put in an appearance.

When I spied Elizabeth, my first reaction was to be happy our residency group had been invited. But as I made my way toward her, I couldn't see anyone else. A cursory inspection told me we were the only ones.

That struck me as strange. I understood inviting *me*, but Elizabeth? I guessed Botstein (or his wife) was hoping to get Nico Moretti to attend.

Ugh, Nico.

A flash of irritation hit me at the thought of seeing the man, but the feeling had been quickly replaced with petty triumph when I saw her companion was not her husband.

Mr. Thompson had been with her instead. He was bold with his gaze and his words, sticking up for Elizabeth when I picked on her. In my defense, she made a terrible mistake when she married Nico and I wasn't above an *I-told-you-so*. Even though his interference was annoying, I respected his loyalty.

But he just wouldn't stop eyeballing me. From the moment we made eye contact, to the moment they left, I felt his eyes on me—and not in a sexy, appreciative way, either. I knew *those* looks, I got them all the time, and I wouldn't have minded if he'd sent me a few. But, no, his were probing and assessing and *knowing*.

It made me nervous and pissed me off.

The more I thought about it, the more I was sure Elizabeth had brought him with her for the express purpose of annoying me. It was just like her to have such an off-putting friend.

As I paid for my iced coffee, I considered saying something to Mr. Thompson. Our previous interaction left me at a disadvantage, and the competitive side of me always wanted the upper hand. I knew it probably wasn't a good thing, but I didn't care to do any introspective digging.

What I could do was walk up to Mr. X-Ray Eyes and compliment him on something. Put him in a position to be polite. Show him I wasn't bothered by his intimidation tactics last night.

Whatever I did, I needed to do it soon. I couldn't stand around the shop staring at him and his stupid, big muffin all day.

I squared my shoulders, set my expression into one of practiced coolness, and walked over to his table. He didn't notice my approach until I was standing next to him.

He glanced up, then set his phone on his bag. "Well, well, Dr. Ken Miles," he said, smiling broadly. His eyes gave me a sweeping once-over and he sat up straighter in his seat.

"I like this rumpled, sweaty look you have going on." He gestured briefly to my running shorts and T-shirt. "It suits you."

Damn him. He sounded sincere. *I* was supposed to be the one saying nice things, disarming *him*. I struggled to find the right words. *Your glasses are sexy.* What? No, Jesus, I needed to think quickly. *I like the way your shirt matches your eyes.* Creepy...something not creepy.

My window for an appropriate duration of silence was shrinking fast, and I was on the verge of losing this match without having said one thing, so I blurted loudly and with unintended derision, "Nice messenger bag."

There was a beat of silence in which Steven arched one blond eyebrow over the rim of his glasses. His smile didn't dim. If anything, it grew broader.

"Your tone confuses me, but the words were phrased as a compliment, so I'll take it as such and say, thank you, it *is* a nice messenger bag."

"I-it was," I stuttered. "Meant as a compliment, I mean. Excuse me if I was terse." I gave myself a head tilt to crack my neck. I felt the need for movement, but what I really needed was to turn the conversation around. I forced myself to relax and issued him what I hoped was a charming grin.

He pocketed his phone, grabbed his bag, and hung it on the back of his chair. "Well, in that case, please have a seat and tell me more." He pointed to the chair across from him. "I love compliments. More so if they're spoken as insults. Maybe if I get to know you better, I'll let you verbally abuse me in a pretty sing-song voice. It will be psychologically thrilling and completely unhealthy. I'll love it."

His statement shocked a laugh out of me. Uncharacteristically, and probably because Steven's comment struck me as so funny, I started to sing low as I sat in the chair. "You're a weird, little freak of a man, Mister Thooooomp-son."

I could feel a slight heat rise to my cheeks as I did it, but Steven didn't make fun of me. Instead, he said, "Hold up there, DKM, we need to be in a very special place in our relationship before you start with the head games."

The heat in my cheeks intensified as the implication of us in a relationship planted itself in my mind. It unnerved me because Steven, with his messy hair, lanky build, and prominent proboscis, was just the type of guy I went for. Except, ideally, he wouldn't be looking at me like I was an oddity or a specimen under a microscope.

Steering the conversation away from relationships, I asked, "DKM?"

Smile still in place, he nodded.

"Dr. Elizabeth Finney's influence, I presume?"

"Oh, no," he chided with a strange wobble-shake of his head. "Give it up, it will never catch on. You can't out-Finney Finney."

Elizabeth always called me "Dr. Ken Miles." Never "Dr. Miles" or "Ken." At one time it rankled because I knew it was her way of keeping me at arm's length. Now, it just seemed oddly petty, like she was going out of her way to take me down a peg. Steven obviously didn't think my attempt at turnabout was working.

I sighed. "Well, if you're going to call me that, I should get to call you MST."

"M?" Steven furrowed his brow and adjusted his glasses with the knuckle of one finger. I liked it.

"For Mister," I clarified.

"Yes, of course. Hmm, it's *okay*." Steven took a sip of his coffee and then made a show of pondering the nickname. He tilted his head to the side, squinted, and tapped his lips with a forefinger. "If you tack on 3K to that, I'll approve. But it will have to be a private, pet name."

"MST3K? What does that mean?" I asked, genuinely confused. I was also—again—hung up on the suggestiveness of his comment. *A private, pet name*? I was beginning to suspect he was making these comments to rattle me. I'd felt from the start that he knew me, knew every thought, flaw, and vulnerability I had.

"Gasp." He said this with an odd lack of inflection but wore a comically horrified expression. "I *knew* it. You were raised on corn, football, and textbooks, weren't you?" His assessment wasn't far off, and it set me on edge again. I wanted to fidget, but instead, I smoothed my hair.

"An adolescence without *Mystery Science Theater 3000*," he continued, "is a joyless one." He bit his bottom lip in a way that I supposed was to convey pity, but the truth was, it only served to draw attention to his mouth. *Hot*.

"I'm afraid I missed it. Was it a cartoon or something?"

"It was—or *is*, I guess, since they have a reboot now—a television show with poor production value, robots, and horrible B movies narrated by a funny and sarcastic cast, who were being held hostage in space by a mad scientist."

Oh, man, he was a nerd.

A *Hot. Nerd.*

I didn't have a ready response, so I was honest. "Sounds like a colossal waste of time."

"I suppose it is if you don't much value entertainment and humor." He said this with a friendly and calm tone, but his gray eyes caught mine with an intensity that contradicted his careless persona. I broke the contact and took a long pull from my straw.

"I didn't mean to rain on your nerd parade." The slight reproof I detected bothered me, so I said the word 'nerd' as if it were completely repugnant. As if a nerdy man wasn't my personal, potent Spanish Fly.

"My parade's impervious to your rain." He waved off my words. "But seriously, check it out. You might actually enjoy it."

"Even if I did have a desire to sit around watching old TV, I really don't have the time."

"Ah, yes. Elizabeth mentioned you were running an ICU or something."

I cleared my throat and briefly met his eyes. "In rotation, yes. I do switches between the ICU and inpatient and outpatient pulmonology." I shrugged. "It's what I trained to do," I said modestly.

Normally, I wasn't modest about my position. I took a lot of pride in my job and the work I had to do to get there. I'd finished my fellowships and was an intensivist double boarded in critical care and pulmonology. I found my niche in the ICU and was suited to it.

But I didn't want to come off boastful or cocky to Steven. Clearly, Elizabeth had been talking about me and I didn't want to sink to whatever low opinion she'd given him. I knew the residents under me had never appreciated the standard of excellence I'd required of them. I'd been seen as a hard-ass or Botstein's sycophant, but neither of those things were true. I just wanted everyone to do their best. We had immense responsibility, needed to be cognizant of that fact, and act accordingly. Elizabeth and I had not only disagreed about behavior on shift, but we also had a near-brush with romance. So, I didn't hold out hope that Steven heard much that was positive about me.

Imagining all manner of skewed embellishments, I became increasingly agitated. I placed an elbow on the table and propped my chin in one hand, letting my fingers graze the tip of my nose. I hoped the move looked casual. I wanted to fidget. I wanted to leave.

I also wanted to stay.

There was a protracted silence during my woolgathering, and Steven watched me with an amused glint.

"See, this is the part where you say, 'Oh, yes, Steven. I have grand plans to do such-and-such and so forth and make a difference in this terrible world we live in,' and then I say, 'Good for you, Dr. Ken Miles!'" He said this last part with such exaggerated happiness and an energetic fist thrust, that I couldn't help but laugh again.

"Good, relax. You need to relax," he encouraged.

"I am relaxed."

"No. No, you're not," he said with a small shake of his head. "You look perpetually uncomfortable. It couldn't be me, I'm a delight."

"Yeah," I muttered. "A real *delight.*" I made air quotes with my fingers, and, I swear to God, I never hated myself more than in that moment.

His assertion pissed me off. Generally, I was a confident person. My ego was very healthy. But in those times when I felt unsure or off-kilter, I faked it. I knew how to disarm with a smile, speak with author-ity, and keep completely calm when chaos was happening around me. I took great pains to never let anyone see me falter or experience stress. If someone took me by surprise or I didn't immediately know the best way to react, I had a mask. A set, blank expression that gave nothing away. It usually worked like a charm. At least I thought it did. No one ever accused me of being 'perpetually uncomfortable' until now.

This only confirmed what I already suspected about Steven: He was too astute. I wanted to admit that it *was* him, that his propensity for examination was something I didn't think was particularly delight-ful. But that admission felt like giving him power over me, so I choked down my irritation as well as I could, stood up slower than I wanted to —because I really just wanted to fly out the door and jog out my frus-tration all the way home—and made my excuse to leave.

"I'm not high-strung, Mr. Thompson. Just busy." I could hear the stiffness in my voice, and I hated it. "I need to leave, but I appreciate you letting me interrupt your breakfast."

I held my hand out for a shake.

Steven opened his mouth and glanced from my face, to my hand.

Then he closed his mouth and looked again, from my face to my hand. He made a small whimper in the back of his throat before muttering, "Oh, what the hell," and giving me a firm shake.

It was a bizarre moment, but I didn't take the time to ponder his behavior. I released his hand, left the cafe, and headed back to the trail for another run.

CHAPTER THREE

STEVEN

I examined Janie's face from across the table. She was seemingly oblivious to my scrutiny, so intent was she on glaring a hole through the wall her husband, Quinn, had just passed behind.

I heard the front door of their penthouse close as he left. Janie fumed at the spot a full twenty seconds before she growled and brought her eyes back to me.

"Let's eat." It sounded less like a suggestion and more like an order, so I dutifully mirrored her movements and lifted my fork. Their part-time housekeeper had presented us with a beautiful lunch of couscous salad with chicken and vegetables. It smelled divine. I was happy to eat it, but Janie was angry that when I'd arrived for our meeting, my contribution to lunch—Italian beef sandwiches with extra giardiniera and fries—had been confiscated by her husband.

"Sodium," had been his only explanation or greeting as he'd taken the bags from me.

Janie was over seven months pregnant and had recently been put on bedrest by her doctor. Quinn, who'd already been grouchier than normal, had become insufferable.

I tried to be generous with my thoughts and not take his attitude personally. I knew he was in a constant state of worry over his family and I knew him well enough to understand that he wasn't going to allow himself to be out of control of the situation. Micromanaging Janie was his new full-time job, and probably the only thing that kept him from going crazy. But throughout the pregnancy, I felt like I couldn't do anything well enough to please Quinn. It might not have been personal, but at times, it sure felt like it.

I was determined to not let him ruin my good humor, so I dug into work with Janie, all the while trying to stay upbeat.

It was *not* easy.

Quinn hovered and Janie seemed to chafe at his behavior. Despite all of that, we worked quickly, reviewed expense reports and discussed projections for the Schmidt-Fischer Group proposal Dan and I would be presenting in Hamburg the week after next. When we broke for our Dr. Quinn, Medicine Meany-approved lunch, I was a little relieved Quinn decided to step out. But he took the offending take-out with him, and I bet my next year's salary that he'd taken those sandwiches to eat with Alex down in the data center.

Once we'd taken a few bites, I tried to draw Janie into conversation and into a brighter mood. "I haven't given much thought to pregnancy since health class in junior high, but I wasn't aware that the parasite could actually imbue the host with the personality of the father."

She frowned. It was an intentionally stupid statement, and a gamble. I wasn't sure if she'd humor me, as she'd always done before her pregnancy, or if she'd go full Sullivan and tell me to get the hell out of her space.

Luckily for me, it was the former. "A fetus is not a parasite. A parasite is defined as an organism that lives in or on an organism of another species—its host—and benefits by deriving nutrients at the other's expense." She rubbed her distended belly. "The baby and I are of the same species."

I smiled, probably my first genuine smile since having the beef torn from my hands. Janie was a gem. A rare and beautiful gem. From the moment I met her, I was captivated. She towered over me when she wore heels, which pre-pregnancy, was almost always, and she wasn't afraid to accentuate her height. The clothes she wore, the shoes she chose, they all complemented and highlighted her statuesque physique. She looked stunning and didn't seem to concern herself with the fragile egos of shorter, lesser men. Add to all of that a thick and lustrous mane of red curls and, I don't care who you are or what your sexual orientation is, you can't help but watch as she passes by.

When she was hired on with Cipher Systems, I was relieved to have such competent help. At the time, our company was small, but beginning to expand rapidly. Being in charge of accounts management and accounting for Cipher's private and public security branches, I knew the rate of our expansion meant I needed another set of eyes and hands. I wasn't going to be able to do it on my own for long. We needed to find someone as soon as possible.

And what a find Janie Morris had been.

To my absolute delight, in addition to her brilliance with numbers, she had an insatiable curiosity about everything and, what I suspected to be, a photographic memory. What she learned, she remembered. Like her husband, I found her knowledge of factoids and data fascinating.

"There is such a thing as a parasitic fetus, but that is referring to an incomplete minor fetus attached to a larger, more completely developed fetus, called an autosite," she explained.

"See." I pointed to her with my fork. "Those fetuses are the same species and one is a parasite to the other. I stand by my opinion that they are all parasites."

She narrowed her eyes in suspicion, further strengthening my theory that the baby was making her more like Quinn each day. "Are you…well?"

"What?" I asked, confused.

"Your moods have been off the last three times we've spoken," she declared. "It's unusual for you to have mood fluctuations."

Before I could respond, she took the conversation off on another tangent.

"This morning I read an online article from the *Tribune* that said that using your hands meaningfully triggers healthy engagement and activity in about sixty percent of your brain, and the rhythmic, mathematical nature of knitting and crocheting keep the mind absorbed in a healthy way, providing escape from stressful thoughts, but allowing for internal reflection."

I didn't know why she was talking about this, but I was glad to go on the ride—grateful she was abandoning talk of my moods.

Or so I thought.

"I think you are suited to such a pastime and could also benefit from its meditative and therapeutic qualities."

The image of myself perched on a tiny stool, furiously knitting baby booties flashed into my head, and I had to laugh.

"I'll email you a link to the article. Also, I could teach you how to crochet."

I took a bite of my salad and pondered what she said. Janie usually didn't comment much on my life or offer opinions, rather she liked to listen, observe and ask relevant questions. But she never meddled. Not that I thought offering to teach me crochet was meddling, but for her, it was as close as she'd ever come to it.

"Is this your way of luring me and my sparkling conversation into your knitting group, or are you saying I need therapy?"

Janie was part of a knitting group that met every Tuesday evening. She crocheted rather than knitted—apparently, they were different things—and she seemed to really enjoy the craft.

Janie blinked, giving my question thoughtful consideration. "Neither. Though Nico might like another man to commiserate with." Elizabeth was a part of the knitting group and Nico had learned to crochet in order to infiltrate the weekly meeting and spend more time with her. It was sweet, really. Bizarre, but sweet.

"Ha! One." I held up my index finger. "Nico doesn't need to commiserate at all. He's living the dream. And two." I extended my second finger, frowned and shook my head in mock sadness. "I doubt he would like my testosterone invading his sacred space. I'm magnetic and I would be a usurper of all of the adoration you ladies bestow on him every week."

Janie smiled and shook her head like I was ridiculous. It was funny, the idea that I could out-shine Nico. I was friendly, and knew I had a fair amount of my own charisma, but he was a force of nature. Everyone liked Nico. *Everyone.*

Nico was currently the only male yarn-crafter in the group. Aside from Elizabeth and Janie, there were five other women. Two of them— Marie and Ashley—I didn't know very well. I'd only been in Marie's presence a handful of times. Ashley, I had only ever seen on the screen of a laptop once, since she attended the meetings via Skype from her home in Tennessee. Fiona, the eldest of the group, now worked for Cipher Systems and Sandra, a psychologist who worked with Elizabeth at Chicago General, was part of the CS family too, as she was married to Alex Greene, our Chief Information Security Officer. Alex and Sandra happened to also be my neighbors across the hall.

Lastly, that left Kat. One might think that with Kat's shy demeanor and lack of affiliation with Cipher Systems, she would have slipped past my radar. But, oh no. She was my favorite.

There was something about Kat Tanner that drew me in. We had become fast friends, and since she worked in the Fairbanks building, too, we met up often for lunch. Though recently, not often enough.

Thinking of Kat, I asked, "Has Kat been making it to knit-night? She's so busy lately, we can't make our schedules mesh for anything."

"She's been there," she replied. "But she had finals, work and…" She averted her eyes. "Boston. You know."

Janie mentioned Boston hesitantly, probably unsure of how much I really knew about Kat's family situation. It was a closely guarded secret that she was Kathleen Caravel-Tyson, heiress to the Caravel Pharmaceutical fortune.

Kat had been living life here as Kat Tanner. Working full-time as the executive assistant to the CEO of an architectural firm and going to school part-time at the University of Chicago. Her destiny as a woman who'd inherit controlling shares of her family's empire, meant that sooner or later, she'd have a monstrous amount of responsibility on her shoulders. She was working very hard to be prepared for this eventuality, even though it hadn't always been what she'd wanted. So, in addition to getting an education, she was also flying to Boston two weekends a month to learn all she could about Caravel Pharmaceuticals. I admired the hell out of her for it.

"Well, I think sweet, stinky German cheese is in order," I announced. "I'll pick some up on the trip. I'm positive a few wheels will help lessen her burdens."

Kat's favorite thing in life was cheese. She adored it, craved it, fantasized about it. If I had to go abroad for a business trip, the least I could do was bring back her drug of choice.

"I also like cheese," Janie stated, rather pointedly.

I gave her an indulgent smile. "And cheese you shall have, darling. I'll bring you back a suitcase full."

"Thank you. But we've gone off topic. Back to my point," she said, and I sighed. I didn't want to get back to the subject of me.

"The thought occurred to me that you might be stressed. You're taking on more work because I'm on bedrest and you've stopped talking about your weekend escapades altogether."

"No!" I said quickly—and probably too forcefully. I lowered my voice to assure her, "It's not the work. Work is fine."

Her concern that the bedrest was causing me stress was off base. She did quite a bit of work remotely from the comfort of her bed, though Quinn did limit her. We lived in the same building, so it wasn't hard to meet if we needed to do so. For me, the worst and most inconvenient part of the pregnancy was her husband's cranky ass. The last thing I wanted was for her or Quinn to think I couldn't handle the workload. Things were already stressful enough for them without worrying I wasn't giving the accounts the attention they needed.

But she hit close with the 'weekend escapades' comment, though she might not have realized it. Too close for my liking. I didn't want to do it, but sharing a bit about it would at least, hopefully, assuage any concern she had about my problems being work-related.

I widened my eyes in feigned surprise and excitement. "You mean I haven't told you about King?"

She shook her head. "No, who or what is King?"

I rolled my eyes dramatically, trying to convey that this story didn't end well. "King is the name—first, last or nick, I have no idea—of this guy I met last month. Red hair and gorgeous eyes. He sent me a picture of himself in a kilt and boots. Shirtless, of course. We'd been texting back and forth, and I asked him what he liked to do, what his hobbies were because, you know how I am, I like people who are offbeat and interesting."

Janie nodded. She knew this about me. I collected an interesting bevy of friends and dates because people and all their oddities fascinated me. I always imagined when I found someone to be my perfect match, he wouldn't be the sexiest guy or the handsomest man, but he'd be captivating and fun and there would never be a dull moment in our relationship.

But now I knew *Unicorn Level: Eccentric Meets Lovable* didn't exist. It was a deluded fantasy I held on to for too long. I was sick and tired of wading through assholes and freaks. If someday in the future I decided to pick up the dating gauntlet again, I'd battle with someone who didn't qualify for the circus. Or prison. Or a mental hospital. For now, Steven Thompson was off the horse.

Instead of voicing those thoughts, I continued with my story, pretending it was just another funny, wacky Steven anecdote.

"He told me he was into bagpiping and I thought, 'That's different, that's fun.' So, when we were making plans to meet up, I floated the idea of going to the Scottish Festival and Highland Games that was happening at the time. I thought it would be something he'd like to do, but he said he'd rather meet up for drinks in a pub. At *eleven*."

"Oh," she said knowingly.

"Yeah, it looked like he only wanted a hook-up." I shrugged. "But that was fine, I knew I could weave a charm spell over drinks. I didn't need a whole afternoon date for that. So, I met up with him, we talked and flirted. I tried asking him about his kilt and bagpipes, but he made everything into a dirty, double entendre."

That had been Strike Two against King.

"He was wearing his kilt?" Janie asked around a bite of the salad.

"No, he was dressed in regular clothes. Unfortunately. I thought I might get a little William Wallace cosplay entertainment," I fibbed. "But anyway, I was buzzed enough that taking him home seemed like a good idea." Another fib. I had been stone-cold sober when I invited him home. He'd been angling hard for the invitation and I stubbornly held out hope for a connection even though he wasn't giving me much that seemed authentic. That should have been Strike Three, but I was an idiot.

I leaned forward, indicating that 'the good part' was about to happen. I exaggerated my expression and said, "As soon as we were in the apartment, King tore my shirt from my body." I mimed a tearing motion with my hands and continued. "He ripped the damn thing, pushed me against the wall, pinned my wrists above my head and… and…" I paused for effect, enjoying Janie's rapt attention. "*Licked my armpit.*"

She barked out a laugh and sighed, clearly relieved that it was something funny and not frightening. *Little did she know…*

I usually enjoyed dramatizing my dating misadventures—as long as the impression I left my audience with was one of amused astonishment. I turned the tragedy into humor, flipped the bland into colorful and most importantly, diverted any possible pity the listener might have felt for me into a sense that I was living my fullest, best life. Today, I wasn't embellishing or dramatizing to simply deflect from work concerns, I was downplaying to make sure that the story—if it got back to Quinn—wouldn't send up any red flags or cause my boss to lose his shit on me. I didn't need him knowing what really happened in my apartment that night.

"It's a fetish called maschalagnia," she said. "I confess, I haven't read much about it."

"Janie, he *licked* it," I emphasized. "I'm the last person to kink-shame or yuck someone else's yum, but I am extremely ticklish and I. Couldn't. Get. Away! He was strong and I was wiggling like a worm, laughing even though I was being tortured."

Fib number three. I hadn't been laughing. Not even close.

Though I was giving the story a light spin, I felt disgusted at the remembrance. I pushed my plate away, appetite gone.

"To cut to the chase," I continued. "He didn't mind giving up the licking because the real show, apparently, was the bagpiping."

Seeming bewildered, Janie asked, "He brought... bagpipes?"

"No. No, he did not," I issued three rapid staccato shakes of my head. "I learned something new. See, when a man and an armpit love each other very much, they engage in an act called bagpiping. Google it. Or don't. It will ruin the pipes for you. All I know is that I am scarred for life. I'm ticklish and have sensitive skin, we would have never worked. I told him to hit the bricks." With a small sigh I said, "*C'est la vie.*"

In reality, the experience had been disturbing. I hadn't simply told him to 'hit the bricks.' He had used his strength and weight to try to strongarm me into cooperating. We scuffled, which, in retrospect, could have easily ended a lot worse for me than the few bruises on my arms and back. But I had kept calm throughout the short altercation— more incredulous and angry than scared. I was scrappier than I looked, and I had been bolstered by the knowledge that I had back-up.

I knew he noticed the high-level of security: the thumbprint scanner the doorman used to let us in, and the watchful, black-clad guards in the lobby. I knew he noticed and so, with delusional confidence, asked him if he was stupid.

You think your face hasn't been recorded since before you set foot in this building?

You think there's not at least eight elite security team members ready at a moment's notice to take you down?

Fuck you.

Somehow my tactics worked. He pulled away from me and released my arm. For a moment, I didn't think he'd leave.

Shaking with rage, he pointed a finger at me. The tendons in his neck bulged.

Through gritted teeth, he said, "I don't give a *shit*," spittle fell from his mouth, "about Obama!"

He turned from me then and stormed for the door. Before he left, he yelled, "I'm not afraid of Obama!"

The crazy asshole thought Barack Obama, 44th President of the United States of America lived in my building.

I locked the door, leaned against it, and said with heartfelt sincerity, "Thanks, Obama."

CHAPTER FOUR

DKM

I loved my sister, I really, really did. But sometimes… Sometimes I wanted to be an only child.

I was on my third call of the week with her. She was in a flurry of wedding plans—all of which she felt the need to discuss and complain about. And, it was fine. Really. Because I loved her.

But this week's calls were morphing into something different.

Now, her sights were set on me.

"You need to text me your measurements," Kari said impatiently, by way of greeting.

The demand annoyed me greatly. Not only did I not know my measurements off the top of my head, but I was very busy settling into my new position at BKC Memorial. She knew this. Also, the wedding wasn't until the end of October. It was now the beginning of July. I didn't feel like my measurements were a pressing issue at this stage.

What really set my teeth on edge was that she assumed I was going to be part of the wedding party. This was never discussed until now. For the record, if my sister wanted me in her wedding, I'd be there in a heartbeat. But she had a terrible habit of making unilateral decisions for people and not discussing it with them beforehand. This part of her personality was the source of most of our, admittedly few, arguments.

I couldn't let this stand.

"Hello, and good afternoon to you, too, grump," I said, giving the grumpiness right back to her.

"Hi," she said quickly. "I need those measurements very soon, Ken. Brandon and I have decided on the style of suit we want the groomsmen to wear."

"I don't recall ever being asked to be a groomsman, Kari." She made a choking sound and before she could launch into a tirade, I continued. "Being a groomsman in your wedding is going to require a commitment and responsibilities. Don't you think we should discuss this?" I imbued my tone with a slight chiding.

It was true, after all. Her wedding was going to be a weekend event on Mackinac Island in northern Michigan. I was looking at fittings, a bachelor party, a rehearsal dinner, and an entire weekend of being bossed around and forced to endure nonsense like riding in horse-drawn carriages, fudge tasting, and probably pumpkin picking, all for the sake of photographs. The least she could do was ask.

"Kenny," she coaxed, using my childhood nickname. I could hear the edge in it though, and I smiled, perversely enjoying her struggle to keep cool. "Would you please be one of Brandon's groomsmen?"

"I don't know, I hardly know the guy." At this point, I was being a dick and she knew it.

"Shut up. You're my only sibling. You're in my wedding. This is one of those unspoken rules and I'm not going to grovel. Send me the measurements," she demanded again, but this time with a laugh.

"It's an unspoken rule?" I asked. "I must love you more than you love me, because when I get married, I'll just do it and not cause stress and inconvenience for all of my loved ones."

"I swear to God," she grit out in warning. "Whatever Barbie doll you marry had better include me or I will *cut* her."

I laughed heartily, enjoying my sister's pretend anger. She'd started calling my girlfriends Barbies when I was in high school. My first girlfriend, Rachel, kind of looked like Barbie, so the Barbie and Ken coincidence was something Kari never let slide. It didn't help that I had a type, and my type was blue-eyed blondes with great smiles.

"Speaking of Barbies," Kari continued, sliding back into her drill sergeant alter-ego. "Are you bringing one?"

I sighed and rubbed my free hand down my face. I was tired, and not in the mood for this conversation. My mother and sister acted as if my single status meant I was playing the field fast and hard. I think Kari assumed I had someone different in my bed every night. This was probably because I never talked about anyone specifically. Mostly that was because there wasn't anyone to talk about. Apparently, my father had reasoned to my mother that residency and fellowship left me little time for relationships. But since I had completed it, Mom had been suggesting I should settle down and "find the right lady."

It irked me for several reasons. I didn't like how marriage was treated as another box to tick off my Success Done Right Card.

College: Check. Med School: Check. Residency and Fellowship: Check. Practice: Check.

Wife and Kids: Pending.

I didn't want the person I spent my life with to be a checkmark on my list. I wanted them to be the reason I had a list to work on. I wanted my spouse to be my partner, my motivator, my cheerleader. And I wanted to do the same, be the same for someone.

It also bothered me that my parents completely discounted my sexuality. When discussing *Kenny's future*, the suggestion of a boyfriend or husband was never mentioned. My mother never so much as acknowledged my bisexuality, and my dad... Well, he acknowledged it. Briefly, loudly, and angrily—but only once. Since then, it's not been spoken of.

Another point that was frustrating was despite what my mom thought, I didn't find it easy to meet people and talk with them. My face, my form, my job, these all helped, but a man had to be more than that if he wanted to find something real. I wanted *real*. I wanted *lasting*. Casual relationships never felt right for me. Unfortunately, I hadn't been able to find what I was looking for. But, then again, I hadn't been looking very hard.

"Put me down for a plus-one. I'll either show up with a date or I won't. We're over three months away from the wedding, Kari," I said, trying to appeal to whatever sanity she had left.

She sighed and went silent.

"Kari?"

"I'm just excited," she said quietly. "It's been a long time coming, and I'm so happy. I'm getting the wedding of my dreams with the man of my dreams."

Her words caused a pulling sensation in my chest.

"I'll get measured this week," I promised.

After we hung up, I pondered the wedding date problem. I needed to bring one. It was going to be an issue if I didn't. By 'issue' I meant lots of annoying questions from the family and offers to set me up with random women they knew in Chicago.

Bringing a date to a three-day, multi-event wedding over four hundred miles away, came with its own set of headaches. The more I thought on it, the more ridiculous it seemed to bring a date. I was nowhere close to being in the type of relationship where a couple could endure that mess. The likelihood of meeting anyone who would fit the bill to go with me was slim.

The easiest place to meet people was at work. My social life outside of the hospital was almost non-existent. But I knew firsthand that using the workplace as a dating pool was a recipe for disaster.

There was the gym, and I did, from time to time, engage in light flirting. That's all it ever was, though. Superficial. *Maybe* occasionally, there were half-hearted attempts to cast a net. But, there again, I didn't particularly want to shit where I ate. What I needed to do was spend my time off trying to meet new people. Thinking about the difficulty I found in that task made me sweat. It meant leaving my comfort zone and extending myself.

Unbidden, images of Steven Thompson came to mind. I had, in a way, extended myself last week in Buzzy's. So much of that interaction had been cringe-worthy, yet… Yet, I'd nearly enjoyed myself. His perusal felt invasive and intense, but, as I reflected on it, I realized I liked it, was excited by it. He was attractive. Smart, funny, self-assured. I thought, maybe if I spent time with him, he'd rub off on me.

Oof, I wiped my hand down my face and nearly groaned aloud. Mental images of Steven rubbing off on me in the literal sense were too alluring. He may have been kind of hot, but I didn't get the sense he liked me all that much. I didn't really give him much to like, since I started out on the wrong foot, but the truth was, I wasn't going to go out of my way to change his opinion or chase him. I wouldn't chase anyone.

In a flash, a hard truth sprang to mind. *Maybe that's why you're still single.*

* * *

"Uh, hey." Dr. Sweet greeted from somewhere behind me. I glanced over my shoulder to see he wasn't addressing me, but Dr. Menedez instead. "Hey, Nat."

"Morning, Colin," she replied. "How are you today?"

I returned to my coffee prep, uninterested in whatever awkward exchange was about to go down between Colin and Natalie. I hadn't been on the job long, but I'd been here long enough to witness more than a few cringey exchanges.

"Doing well." He lapsed into a long pause before continuing in a rush, "So, I was thinking, I mean, I was checking the listings for the Music Box last night, and I noticed that they're playing *The Sound of Music.* I remembered you said you liked old musicals."

Colin routinely launched into spontaneous conversation with Dr. Menedez whenever he could get her attention. It was hard to watch. He never seemed to have a plan for the conversation, and he had no game.

In fairness to him, he did seem to have a particular plan this morning. I just didn't think *nervous, insecure,* and *desperate* was the way to play it.

The best plan was to fake it 'til you make it. Plan your words and actions carefully, take plenty of time to sow the seeds of attraction. Glances, smiles, banter. Above all else, we men had to come across as confident and not invested in a yes. More often than not, it worked.

Dr. Sweet was definitely coming across as invested. The pressure was on Dr. Menedez. She was going to ruin his whole day and she knew it.

And, of *course,* she was. My opinion of her was that she was smart. Not just intelligent, but wise. Wise enough to not bring needless drama into work. Colin wasn't wise. He was thinking with his eyes and his dick. Besides, she was a surgeon and he was an anesthesiologist, for God's sake. There were lines people just shouldn't cross.

I capped my coffee cup, eager to leave before I had to bear witness to the crushing of his dreams. But before I stepped away, he said something that caught my attention.

"If you didn't want to see *The Sound of Music*, they're also playing *Akira*, *The Gremlins* and *Mystery Science Theater 3000* this week." He said this all hurriedly as if to prevent a premature refusal.

Before I thought better of it, I interrupted. "The Music Box plays television shows?"

Colin twisted toward me, his eyes widening a fraction with incredulous surprise. "What?" he asked sharply.

"*Mystery Science Theater*. That's a TV show, right?" I asked.

At this, he narrowed his eyes, plainly annoyed with me for the interruption. "They made a movie too," he said dismissively, turning back to Natalie.

"Oh, okay. Thanks." I left the cafeteria quickly, unconcerned that Dr. Sweet was most likely plotting my murder. I had thought to invite him to play racquetball, but that was probably a non-starter now. Oh well, it didn't matter and was totally worth it, because he'd just handed me a plan. And a man always needed a plan.

CHAPTER FIVE

STEVEN

Tuesday afternoon, my cell phone rang out the tune of *NSYNC's "Bye Bye Bye," alerting me that Elizabeth was calling. A glance at my screen showed that she'd called twice before. I'd been too busy for the entire morning to take any calls. First, I'd had a brief meeting with Carlos Davies, Cipher Systems Chief Operations Officer, to talk about the payroll budget for a second receptionist and an accounts manager position he filled the day before to help with the tasks Janie was unable to do.

I went into that meeting slightly peeved and defensive, still unconvinced we needed to hire a new accounts manager. I was handling Janie's job—and my own—without issue. When I said as much to Carlos, he gave me an exasperated look and replied, "You're VP of Financial Operations, Steven. You don't need to spend time fielding customer relations calls. And I don't need to tell you how fast we've been growing. We need more help. According to Quinn, we shouldn't hold our breath for Janie returning any time soon. There's no reason for you to do it all."

I knew he was right, but the conversation I'd had with Janie made me worry that there were some behind-the-scenes concerns that I wasn't able to hold down the department in her absence. I didn't like that it bothered me, and I needed to get used to the idea that we needed more help.

Then, later, because Dan had other appointments, Quinn came in to sit in on a call with the Schmidt-Fischer Project Manager. When our receptionist, Keira, sounded the Code Pink alert over the intercom, warning everyone of Quinn's imminent arrival to the office, I had a Pavlovian urge to flee to the break room. But, alas, as everyone else tried to make themselves scarce or invisible to avoid exposure to our boss' foul mood, I was left to hole-up with him in his office for the call. The meeting, though productive, lasted longer than usual. It was now past lunchtime and I was ravenous.

I shoved a potato chip in my mouth as I answered Elizabeth's call. "I'mna eat wil wuh tck," I mumbled in greeting.

"Busy day?" she asked with a laugh.

I swallowed. "Yeah, so far. How about you? I see you've called a couple of times. You must not be too busy."

"I am, actually, but I've been calling you every chance I had because I need to talk to you."

"Okay, shoot." I grabbed my bottle of green tea and took a long swallow.

"Why is Dr. Ken Miles calling me for your number?"

I choked on the tea. *What in the world?* DKM wanting to talk to me seemed unlikely. For one thing, I got the impression that having a conversation with me was distinctly distressing for him. And by all accounts, he was straight, so there couldn't be an element of attraction. I was also a friend of someone he disliked. What could he possibly need with me? Maybe…

"Maybe he wants me to help him get back in your good graces," I proposed.

Elizabeth snorted. "That's not a possibility. He and I are both fine with the way things are. If he wanted to use you to get to me, he wouldn't have come to me to get to you."

It was sound logic, I supposed. "I'm out of ideas. What did he say?"

"He was his charming self," she said with faint sarcasm. "As soon as I called him back, he answered with, 'Elizabeth, I need to get in touch with your friend, Steven Thompson.'" She affected a decent impression of Ken's deep voice and tone, even if his haughtiness was exaggerated. "No, 'Hello, how are ya.' That annoyed me, so I asked him why. He said it was a 'private matter.' I told him your number was a 'private number.'"

I laughed, imagining DKM's annoyance.

"But," she continued. "I told him I'd give you his number and you could do what you wanted with it. So, call him, then call me back. I'm perishing from curiosity."

I heard noise in the background, and voices speaking close to Elizabeth.

"I need to go, but I'll text you his number right now." She clicked off.

True to her word, within thirty seconds, I had Dr. Ken Miles' phone number displayed on my screen.

Though I was curious too, I had lunch to eat and two reports to finish before I'd let myself call him. But even then, when the afternoon became slow and I had ample time to make the call, I delayed.

I told myself it was because he was likely busy and then we'd have to play phone tag. I would rather call when we both had time to talk. My reasoning made no sense, considering I had absolutely no idea when a good time would be for an ICU doctor. Was any time a guaranteed opportune time?

I was being uncharacteristically hesitant. It wasn't like me to put off tasks—even unpleasant ones. When things needed to be done, I did them. If things needed to be said, I said them. Putting things off always made them worse, I reasoned, so I never dilly-dallied. Weirder still, was that I didn't anticipate the conversation was going to be unpleasant for me. I imagined it was going to be rather amusing. No, my problem was that I wasn't sure how I felt about DKM, nor could I imagine a plausible reason for him reaching out to me.

He was hot. There was no denying that. He was handsome, muscular, and athletic. Seeing him last week in his running shorts with his shirt and brow damp with sweat had been a mighty fine way to start my morning. But…he was a little bit of a jerk, and a little bit of an odd duck.

I was now in the phase of my life where I was actively avoiding weirdos. My weirdo-meter had been pegged, and no matter how much delight I found in conversing with and observing him, the voice in the back of my head wondered if he was calling because I had some sort of kook-magnet or Bat-signal that made these people gravitate toward me. *Ha, Bat-Signal. More like Batshit-Signal.*

I gave myself a shake. Ken wasn't crazy or even that strange, and he might very well have been calling me about something as mundane as my messenger bag.

Decision made, I called him, telling myself that if he threw up any red flags, I'd simply block his number, just as I'd done with King a couple of weeks ago. Simple. Elegant. Efficient.

The phone rang a few times before he finally picked up with a breathless, "Dr. Miles."

It was six PM and he was panting. Clearly, I'd caught him at a bad time.

"Hello, Dr. Ken Miles, this is Steven Thompson. Elizabeth relayed your message. I'm sorry if this was a bad time to call."

Two more panting breaths. "No, no, it's fine, I'm at the gym, but I can talk." He inhaled deeply and let it out slowly. "Thanks for calling me back."

"No problem."

There was a lengthy silence and I smiled to myself at the immediate and predictable awkwardness. It looked as if I were going to have to pull the information out of him.

"So…" I began slowly. "What did—"

"Did you know that there was a movie made of *Mystery Science Theater*?" he blurted loudly.

I pulled the phone away from my ear and made a confused face at the screen. *What?*

"Uh, yeah," I said, returning the phone to my ear. "Yeah, I guess I did know that. But I don't think I ever saw it."

"A colleague of mine mentioned that it will be playing this week at the Music Box Theater. Do you know the Music Box, over on Southport?"

I couldn't help myself. I was grinning from ear to ear. I knew the Music Box. Everyone knew the Music Box. This guy was too much.

"Sure, it's where I see *Rocky Horror* every year," I answered, not certain if he knew what *Rocky Horror* was.

"Good. Well, I thought I'd go see it, since it was on your recommendation, but I don't really know if anyone I know would like to watch it with me. I thought maybe you'd like to join me."

His words sounded slightly rehearsed and it went far in softening me toward him. If he were nervous about asking if I'd like to see a cult movie with him, he was probably in need of a friend. The thought made me sad for him and annoyed at myself for being judgy. If he were looking to me—someone who clearly made him twitchy—for someone to hang out with, then he must be lonely.

Poor, handsome weirdo.

CHAPTER SIX

DKM

I was running behind. I *hated* running late.

I was lucky Steven agreed to see me. I knew I hadn't made a very good first impression, knew he probably thought I was an asshole. So, I figured this date was my one shot at changing his perception of me. I needed to get my shit together, be charming, and engage in conversation without becoming self-conscious. If I didn't, I was sure there wouldn't be a second chance.

I had it all worked out in my head. The movie's one evening show-time was at seven-thirty, so I was going to shower and dress at home—take my time getting ready, then arrive early and purchase our tickets. When Steven arrived, I was going to issue him a devastating smile, tell him it was great to see him, then give him a sexy perusal. I'd tell him he looked nice—which I was positive he would, he appeared to always dress smartly and tastefully—then, when he thanked me and recipro-cated, telling me how great I looked, I'd give him a playful wink because my winks always seemed to net positive results.

But, all of that was probably out the door now. Toward the end of my shift, a patient was brought in from the emergency department with respiratory failure secondary to pneumonia and needed to be intubated.

It didn't necessitate the cancellation of the date, but it did mean that I had to leave straight from the hospital to the theater.

I was still going to work my moves in if I could, but mostly, I was going to have to wing it. This date felt a little too important to wing, but I didn't want to cancel. I couldn't cancel. I really wanted to see him again, see if that alluring, prickly heat I felt when I was with him could be explored further.

As the cab approached the theater, I opened the selfie mode of my phone camera and took stock of my image. My hair was messy, the waves sticking up slightly. If I had showered, I probably would have tamed them with some gel or something, but as it was, it fell in a way that looked deliberately mussed. I checked my teeth for any specks, and popped a breath mint, satisfied with my appearance.

Before exiting, I unbuttoned the second button of my shirt and fanned, taking a deep breath of my scent to make sure I didn't stink. The weather was hot and balmy, but the hospital was always cool, so I was fine. All deodorant and laundry scents. Good enough.

Going down this checklist in preparation didn't soothe my aggravation at my tardiness. I still felt rushed and unready.

As I walked up to the theater, I saw Steven standing under the marquee, looking at the lights. Dozens of white bulbs overhead illuminated his tilted face. There was a glare shining from his glasses, but the rest of him looked almost ethereal. Lean, fair, and unearthly. I snorted, giving myself a mental shake. I was romanticizing him, painting him as an angel, when I knew he had a bit of the devil in him. The temptation I found in him was proof enough of that.

He hadn't noticed my approach, so I called out, "Good evening, Steven."

His head whipped toward me, his toothy smile glinting in the lights. *He has a great smile*, I thought, beginning to relax. *This is going to be fine. I'll be fine.*

"Hey, DKM!" he greeted. "You're looking good. Nice to see you."

Shit. I was supposed to compliment him first. He got the jump on me *again*. Not wanting to let the moment pass, I hurriedly improvised. "The lights," I gestured stiffly. "They're glowing like aliens in your glasses." The horror of what I said registered and I immediately, frantically backtracked. "No, what I mean is, not—" *Don't say angel, don't say angel, you freak.*

Steven's eyebrows rose in bewilderment above his glasses, but he kindly, blessedly, interrupted my stuttering with casual ease. "I get it." He pointed to the lights above us. "This definitely looks like a UFO hovering above, ready to teleport us on board."

I smiled, sure it wasn't the underwear-dropping, devastation-bomb I'd planned earlier. At least it wasn't a grimace. I felt like grimacing.

"And, you know," he continued, not devastated *or* dropping his pants. "It's fitting, as we're about to see a cheesy sci-fi." He waved the movie tickets in his hand.

I felt my face fall. I'd wanted to buy our tickets since I had invited him. My disappointment, which I was trying to mask, must have been evident on my face, because he hastened to add, "I got here first, and I started to think about the show and how I've never seen this movie and how there's a very good chance you'll think it's crap. So, I thought if I paid for the tickets, you couldn't be too mad when it went south."

Any annoyance I felt evaporated, and I laughed. I was positive I wouldn't like the movie. It sounded idiotic. But I liked that Steven seemed unsure of his own recommendation, like he cared about my reaction to it. Warmth bloomed in my chest.

I cleared my throat. "Oh, no worries. It's a cult movie, right?" He nodded. "I assumed it was bad, but also that it needed to be watched with an open mind and low expectations."

"Exactly!" he said, pointing an index finger at me.

As we proceeded into the building, I let myself take in the atmosphere of the old theater. Each time I visited, I was impressed by the decor, which was reminiscent of a sumptuous and lavish age. Thick, red drapes, gold accents, and soft lighting emanating from Tiffany and art-deco styled fixtures, perfectly complemented the 1920s architecture of the building.

The theater itself was large, and its ceiling was lit with twinkling stars and a moving cloud formation. It felt like watching a movie in an open-air courtyard. I thought this was an ideal spot for a first date, and as I watched Steven glance around the lobby appreciatively, I gave myself a pat on the back for thinking of it.

Steven brought his eyes to mine and smiled. "I love this place. I feel compelled to wear a fedora and smoke cigarettes."

We were standing in the concession line and I was absorbing the features of his face, mainly thinking how much I liked the way his smile transformed him. His resting face was hawkish in its angularity —not unattractive but giving a false impression of severity. When he spoke, when he smiled, warmth and friendliness exuded from him. I liked the dichotomy. I liked the face, the voice, the easy kindness. I wanted to make him smile at me again.

As the line moved forward, I realized I'd spent too long staring without replying. I didn't want to come off as a fawning creep, so with a manufactured sternness I said, "Do not start smoking."

"Yes, okay, Dr. Bossy," he said as we stepped to the counter. His voice was teasing, but as we ordered our snacks, I worried I had missed the mark with my reply.

To make it all worse, when I noticed Steven pulling out his wallet, I nudged him aside. "No. No, you will not pay," I declared.

"Oh, thanks. Thank you."

By the time we made it into the theater and found seats, I was positive I'd already screwed myself. There was no way that in those few minutes I'd managed to make a better impression. If anything, he was probably sure I was the biggest dickhead in Chicago.

The previews started and Steven held his soda cup toward me. "Here's to lowering our expectations."

It took me a beat to realize he was waiting for me to knock my drink into his. I did, hastily, and said, "Cheers, mate," complete with an atrocious Australian accent. I was glad for the mostly dark room, because my face filled with heat. Steven smiled, but made no comment. Not for the first time, I had to ask myself what in the hell was wrong with me.

Suddenly, I felt stiff and perturbed. My neck felt tight, so I rolled my head. My shoes felt constrictive, so I flexed my toes. I started to get hot, so I pushed my sleeves to my elbows. I tried to do this all casually, subtly, but of course, he noticed.

"Are you okay?" he whispered. The movie had begun, and he'd slouched down a bit, his posture completely relaxed. His eyes, though, they were piercing, knowing.

I smoothed my hair and rubbed the back of my neck, averting my eyes from his. "Yeah, just settling in."

I forced my muscles to relax, mimicking his position and facing the screen. I could still feel his eyes on me.

"Ken," he called for my attention. I turned my head to see him smiling at me. "It's fine, okay? I'm happy we decided to do this. Don't worry so much."

For a moment, I was stunned—surprised that he was enjoying himself, but also that he knew what I needed to hear to be put at ease.

The idea of being with someone who could pull back the curtain and see my inner workings, was both thrilling and frightening. But knowing he liked what he was seeing, meant more to me than if he were enamored with the best, polished version of myself.

An internal weight lifted from me and I smiled.

I smiled through the entire movie.

CHAPTER SEVEN

"Well, I'm embarrassed," I said once we were seated at our table. After the movie let out, Ken suggested we walk down to a nearby sports bar for a bite to eat. I readily agreed, and we walked in companionable silence.

The movie hadn't been great. It hadn't lived up to the magic of what I'd remembered of the old TV episodes. Ken had laughed several times—more than I had. And there was one joke about Harvey and Claude Rains flying a pilotless plane that he apparently thought was hilarious. I would never have guessed that he'd have understood a *Harvey the Rabbit* or *The Invisible Man* reference. But his laugh was hearty and contagious, so I found myself laughing along.

Ken looked up from a drink menu in surprise. "Are you really embarrassed?"

I huffed out a laugh. "Only mildly. It's not like I *wrote* it. But I *am* the reason you wasted your night watching it. I've learned my lesson. I'll be more sparing with my recommendations."

Ken took a long drink from his water, then shrugged. "I found it amusing. I can see the appeal of taking an old, bad movie and trying to make it funny by adding sarcastic commentary over it. But it was a little absurd."

"'Open mind, low expectations,' right?" I reminded him. "You know, that seems like good advice for all aspects of life. Maybe you've stumbled upon the key to happiness, Ken."

He grinned. "Should I write an inspirational book?"

"Nah, trademark it and sell merchandise," I quipped.

Chuckling softly, he said, "Somehow, 'Open mind, low expectations' doesn't have the same ring to it as 'Live, Laugh, Love.' We'll just have to keep the key to happiness our own little secret." He issued me a conspiratorial wink, and I was charmed.

Ken was surprisingly funny when he relaxed. The night started with him being slightly irritable. He seemed overly concerned with making an impression on me, and when I assured him that I was having a good time, he completely transformed. He loosened up, enjoyed the movie and was now engaging in witty banter. At Buzzy's, I thought I started to see that side of him, but he'd shut down when I remarked on it. He was self-conscious but had a lot of potential.

His apparent irritation with his less-than-smooth conversation and eagerness to pay for things, struck empathy in me. I didn't like the idea of him feeling as if he needed to buy my friendship or view tonight as an interview or audition. Friendships needed to happen organically. Was it possible he didn't know how?

I believed I was starting to see the real Ken, see his quirks and attitude for what they were—coping mechanisms and armor for his vulnerabilities. Sure, he had more going for him than the rest of us average folk. He could be a supercilious dickhead when he felt like it, but I wanted to see what he looked like without his shell. Was he playful? Was he sarcastic like me? Was he passionate about anything?

Not only was he evoking empathy in me, he was spurring my curious nature—and that was my weakness. I loved people who surprised me, people who weren't what everyone assumed they were. At first glance, Ken appeared to be another snotty, privileged white guy. He looked like getting laid and making money would be his primary goals. Those types were boring. But DKM was shaping up to be anything but boring.

When our waitress approached, I ordered fish tacos.

Ken ordered the check to be given to him at the end of the meal.

And a cheeseburger.

I shook my head in amused exasperation and decided to employ my special brand of subtle interrogation. "So, DKM, got any hot romance there at the new hospital?"

His eyes widened in surprise and he made a sound that was most likely a swallow-misfire. Did I say *subtle interrogation*? I lied. Not much was subtle about me.

"Uh…" He blinked rapidly.

"Are you seeing anybody?" I asked. "If television drama is to be believed, hospitals are rife with beautiful, horny singles ready to mingle." An amusing thought struck me, and I veered into a tangent. "If you were on that show, they'd call you McPretty. But only because McDreamy was already taken."

Ken's eyes narrowed. "What are you talking about?"

"That doesn't offend you, does it? Calling you pretty?"

"You think I'm pretty?" His expression, rather than appearing offended, seemed pleased.

I scoffed. "Don't fish. It's beneath you, McPretty."

His smile widened, dimples appearing in his cheeks. "I'm not completely sure I know what you're talking about. But to answer your question, no. You don't need to worry about that. I'm single and I absolutely do not use the hospital as a dating pool." He shook his head emphatically. "Working alongside someone you're romantically tangled with is a disaster waiting to happen."

"Ooh," I said, infusing my voice with exaggerated curiosity. "Is this a lesson Elizabeth taught you?"

"Is this your roundabout way of pumping me for the backstory?"

"That wasn't my intention, but since we're here, go ahead and spill the beans. Or, I could just ask her…" I let the threat hang, knowing he'd take the bait.

His brows lowered. "And, I'm sure the story would be entirely accurate and not at all biased," he said snidely.

"So, give me the straight version, no embellishments."

He paused, seeming to weigh his words. "I wanted to date her and thought she wanted the same. But after I gave her some career advice, that she needed to hear, by the way,"—he held up his hands as if defending himself—"she told me that she would rather we just…" A flash of distress crossed his face.

"Just what?" I prompted eagerly.

"You don't mind hearing about this? Are you sure this is okay?"

"Uh, yeah!" I exclaimed. "I'm nosy as hell, Ken. Just don't disrespect her. She is my friend and I care about her."

"I guess you probably *should* know."

I really didn't *need* to know. What went on between them wasn't my business in the least, but my gossip-loving heart was positively giddy that Ken seemed to think I had a right to the information.

He cleared his throat and continued. "She told me she just wanted to have a sexual relationship, rather than dating."

"Did you play hide the salami?" I asked, trying to inject some levity.

His gaze bore into mine. His eyes were a vivid cornflower blue and they seemed to be trying to convey some meaning to me I couldn't decipher.

"No."

His eye-contact had me rattled, so I filled the silence. "Why not?" It was stupid of me to ask. I knew the answer and could feel that he didn't want to talk about it.

His nostrils flared, and he leaned toward me. "She and I made plans to…hook up. And when the night finally arrived, she stood me up for Nico." He spoke rapidly like he was trying to get the details out as quickly as possible.

"My pride was dented," he continued. "My opinion of her lowered significantly, and work became tense when we were on shift together. She brought with her drama I didn't need. I'm in a different hospital now and I'm certainly not going to put myself in a position where I dread going in every day because I had the urge to screw someone."

His words were slightly heated, and it seemed like he had strong opinions on the matter. I wondered if those feelings were due in part to the role he had played in the shooting of Nico's stalker, or if Ken just couldn't get past the way Elizabeth had rejected him.

As nosy as I was, I did have some boundaries, so I abandoned all talk of Elizabeth and turned the conversation.

"Do you like your job?" Asking a man about his job was usually a sure-fire way to get him to talk about himself. It also came in very handy as a deflection technique. I wasn't allowed to divulge much about my own employment, as I had a non-disclosure agreement to adhere to, but I didn't enjoy explaining even the basics of my job. As exciting as Cipher Systems was, and as challenging and rewarding as I found the work, no one really understood the thrill I got from maximizing profits. The quickest way to get someone to tune out was to talk about cost analysis.

"I do," he replied, nodding. "I love my work."

The arrival of our food halted any elaboration as we said our thanks to the waitress and dug in.

The silence was easy and contented, but mid-way through his burger Ken cleared his throat. "I'm an excellent doctor."

I glanced up to see his face had morphed into a sour expression.

"That sounded arrogant as hell. Sorry." He shook his head as if to clear it. "What I mean is, I know I've given you the impression that I'm an uptight, rude asshole." Out of a sense of courtesy, I started to shake my head in immediate denial, but Ken held up one hand and gave me a rueful smile. "And," he continued, "you might not think a decent physician should be uptight and rude. You're right. But when I'm attending—when I'm treating people and diagnosing them—I'm not either of those things. I'm capable and compassionate. I do well under pressure and thrive on responsibility. I go in and rely on my training, my intellect, my instincts, and I excel. I have a sense of confidence and competence when I work that I don't have in any other aspect of my life. So, yeah, I enjoy my job."

I smiled, entertained by the show of emotion in his sudden speech. I was also delighted by his passion. "It sounds perfect. We should all be so lucky to have a career that is so singularly suited to us," I said. "By the way," I hastened to add, "I never questioned or doubted your abilities as a doctor. It never occurred to me to think you were anything other than an excellent physician."

"Oh." He looked sheepish. "I didn't need to spew all of that out, did I?"

"Don't apologize, it was great. So much better than, 'Yeah, being a doctor is cool.'" I said this with a dopey voice, hoping to pull a smile out of him.

It worked. He smiled broadly and said, "Being a doctor *is* cool, Steven."

A laugh died in my throat as I glanced over Ken's shoulder toward the bar. Standing in profile was a man who looked identical to King, the psycho from my ill-fated date at Jimbo's Pub.

I ducked my head, hoping that Ken's broad shoulders would obscure me from King's view.

"*Shit*," I whispered. The last thing I needed was for King to recognize me and make a scene. His last contact with me was through texts, and he'd sent two before I blocked him.

KING: your pit taste like dog ass
KING: got nothin to say 4 eyed BITCH?

In retrospect, I found it hilarious, but at the time, I hadn't thought it so amusing.

"Steven, are you okay?" Ken asked, much too loudly.

I hunched down further and tapped my forefinger frantically against my pursed lips in the universal sign for *shut the fuck up*.

Ken, concern and puzzlement etched on his face, reached over and laid his hand onto mine. He gave it a light pat and caress before whispering, "What is it? What can I do?"

I glanced down at our hands and thought, *I bet he's kind to his patients*. I appreciated his concern...and the fact that he'd lowered his volume.

"There's a man by the bar with red hair and tattoos—no!" I grunted, as he began to twist toward the front of the restaurant. "Don't be obvious. This guy has some marbles loose and I *really* don't want him to recognize me, *capisce*?"

"Alright," Ken agreed. He put his left elbow on the table and leaned slightly into it, obstructing King's view of me further. As he slowly turned his head to see him, I bent over to the right, pretending to tie my shoe.

"There's no one with red hair at the bar," I heard him say.

I popped my head up in surprise, abandoning my concealment. "What?"

Sure enough, King, or the someone I thought was King, was gone. I glanced around the dining room and didn't see him anywhere. He must have left.

"Am I going to have a jealous boyfriend angry with me?"

He asked the question seriously, with no hint of humor. He didn't appear annoyed or particularly worried, only desiring to know what his situation could be if King approached.

"No," I assured him. "I went out with him once, but he's not right in the head. Kept yelling about Obama." I knew it was an oversimplification and a distortion of King's motives, but I'd only just met Ken, and attempted armpit sexual assault didn't feel like something I wanted to share this early into our friendship, if ever.

"Ah," Ken replied knowingly. "I've seen my fair share of those poor souls in the ER. I hope he gets help."

And with those words pulling on my heartstrings, befriending DKM didn't seem like the one-sided charity act it had on Tuesday.

CHAPTER EIGHT

DKM

I woke up the morning after my date with Steven feeling lighter than I had in…well, since undergrad, probably. It was a great feeling. It felt like the skies had parted and the heavens were singing, infusing me with peace and purpose.

I was officially ridiculous, but I didn't care. I couldn't stop smiling. I smiled while I showered, I smiled while I made coffee, I smiled while I ate breakfast. It made chewing a little difficult, but there was no stopping it.

I knew what I wanted, and I wanted Steven Thompson.

Though the date started rough, it exceeded my expectations. It seemed like Steven had a knack for putting people at ease—effortlessly smoothing over any potential awkwardness and keeping up a flow of engaging conversation. His whole demeanor allowed me to relax and let the night progress exactly the way I hoped it would.

Well, not *exactly*.

Once we decided to share a cab, I began to hope for a kiss at the end of the ride. But just as we pulled up to his building, his phone rang.

He checked the display and said, "Oh, this is Dan, I have to take this." When he answered the call, he connected his eyes to mine.

Seeing the obvious confusion—and let's face it—disappointment on my face, he mouthed, "Boss."

I nodded and gave him a thumbs up. I knew all about taking work calls at inconvenient times.

He opened the door of the cab. *"Hang on a sec, O'Malley."* Covering the mouthpiece, he said to me, somewhat distractedly, *"Thanks for dinner, McPretty. Let's do it again sometime,"* and exited the car.

It hadn't been the ideal ending for the date, but I sat back, satisfied with his encouragement.

Let's do it again sometime.

He wanted to see me again. I felt electric with anticipation and edgy from the knowledge I was heading into—or attempting to head into—previously uncharted waters. I'd never been in a relationship with a man before, not a serious one, at least.

In college, I'd had the occasional fun with a few guys, but it had never been exclusive or even romantic. We'd basically been friends who made out and sometimes gave each other head. It had been exciting because they weren't shameful, closeted, hurry-up-so-no-one-suspects blowjobs.

It had been liberating. No one cared what we did, and it was eye-opening and fun. A lot of fun. But none of it had been love or even serious.

My experience with women far outweighed my experiences with men. But, honestly, that wasn't saying much.

With the exception of the first couple of amazing, confidence-and-alcohol-fueled years at OSU, I'd never been comfortable going out of my way to pursue people I found attractive. I always preferred to play it safe and long—to test the waters, see if attraction was reciprocated without putting my neck out there. Then, when I thought my chances were good, I'd make my move.

This style worked for me. It might mean I went long periods of time without dating or sex, but it suited, not just my personality, but the insane lack of personal time I've had since I began med school.

Plus, there had been Angie. Angie was my only adult, long-term relationship. If it wasn't love, then it had been damn close. We were together almost two years, finally calling it quits when it became clear long-distance wasn't an option. She stayed in Columbus and I left for Chicago. Our lives were going in different directions, and though I was sad to lose her, I knew we had to move on.

Being with Angie made me realize how much I loved being in a committed relationship. I loved the certainty, the familiarity, the trust, and friendship. Not to mention the regular sex. I did especially love that.

It felt good to end the day with soft touches and sweet words, knowing there was a special person that was all mine—who cared about me. Casual dating and sex hadn't ever been exactly ideal for me before Angie, but *after* her, it almost seemed abhorrent.

Angie and I found each other at a time when I needed someone. She'd been a miracle, really. When I met her, I had been at my lowest. I felt alone. Not just alone but demoralized.

I spent the first two years of college high on the freedom to be myself—happy exploring who I was away from home and family. And, as far as my sexuality was concerned, I never warred with myself through adolescence. I never thought my feelings were shameful or greedy.

Growing up in a fairly liberal and close-knit family, I didn't think my bisexuality would cause anyone to bat an eye. Since I felt like it was a non-issue, I assumed it would be for everyone else, as well.

I was wrong.

Over-confident and naive was what I was. I hadn't realized being anything other than heterosexual was fine and dandy for other people, but when it was me—when it was Robert Miles' son, things looked a little bit different. Suddenly, all the liberalism went flying out the window.

My dad had been my idol growing up. He'd been the perfect role model. Educated, wise, and kind. He always had time to explain social and political issues to me and Kari, never talking down to us or making us feel less-than because we were kids. He groomed us to be thoughtful, confident, and ambitious.

He and my mother set a great model for marriage. I always knew I wanted to have the type of relationship my parents had. They listened to each other, made time for each other and were physically demonstrative. They showed a united front to me and Kari. There was no playing Mom against Dad to get what I wanted, because they were always on the same page, always in agreement. Looking back, I'm sure they disagreed, but if they did, they didn't make it obvious to us. Our home was warm, our family a perfect, safe haven.

Which is why, when my Dad showed up unannounced to visit me and caught me making out—like, hardcore making out—with Harry Deluca outside my door, I was shattered by his anger.

It had been awful. To this day, when I remembered it—remembered the look on his face, I felt sick.

A lot of young people expected the worst when they came out to their parents. I hadn't. I thought maybe someday I'd possibly bring a boyfriend home for Thanksgiving and they'd say, *does he have any dietary restrictions we need to know about?* Like it was nothing. I honestly didn't think it would matter.

But it mattered. He stood stunned. And in that moment, worried about the look on his face, I blurted, "I'm bisexual and that's Harry. Bye, Harry." Harry ran off. Dad gritted out that we should go inside. Then…he'd raged.

He told me no one would ever take me seriously. No one was going to trust me, no one was going to want to be with me long-term if they knew. I was on a long road to a successful career and it was important that I seemed like a steady character, that I appeared to be decisive and not a "waffler."

He told me that if I had the desire to be with women, it was beyond foolish to pursue relationships with men. I was choosing a difficult career path, didn't I want the rest of my life to be easy and smooth? Didn't I want respect and a family?

He said, "No one respects or wants someone who lets their dick call the shots. You need to get yourself together and grow up." With that parting shot, he had left, and our relationship was forever altered.

That day was the only time I'd ever felt heartbreak. He let me down in a way I never imagined he would. Needless to say, my relationship with my father had since been strained and distant.

I'd been deaf to his arguments. They were ignorant. I was the only one who knew what or who could make me happy and I was the only one who had to live my life. He had it all wrong. He was wrong. My perfect father was completely, utterly wrong and I was determined to live my life just as I had been—on my own terms.

A month or so after my fight with Dad, I got my shot with Trisha Banks.

I met Trisha late freshman year. She was gorgeous, funny and had a body made for sex—all curves and smoothness. She loved wearing dresses, even in the cold Ohio winter. Her legs were always on display and I couldn't help but watch her whenever we were in the same room together. She always seemed to have a boyfriend, so I contented myself with glances here and there, the occasional conversation.

I hadn't bothered to see Harry again after that night. He was tainted. I didn't think I could look at his face without my heart hurting, so I wasn't seeing anyone. As it turned out, neither was Trisha, finally. I made sure to find myself in her path a couple of times a day, I asked her to dinner, and we had a great time.

But when I tried to kiss her, she pushed my face away and got very angry. "Oh, no," she'd said. "I don't want any of your confused bullshit screwing me up."

"What in the hell are you talking about?" I asked, my own anger rising. I hadn't liked the sudden shift, her tone or what her words were implying.

"You know what! I'm fine being friends with you, Ken, but I don't want to be used." She had her hands on her hips in exasperation.

"I like you. I have no intention of using you," I replied honestly.

"Suuure," she let the word drag with sarcasm. "We've known each other for almost two years and right after your dad shows up and screams at you, you're suddenly straight and interested in me? Seems legit." Her attitude seriously pissed me off. Everything she said pissed me off. That I'd been the subject of gossip, really pissed me off.

"For one thing, I've always been interested in you, but you've always been with someone else. Now, you're not. Second of all," I went on heatedly, "I'm bi and nothing that went on between my dad and I is any of your business."

Trisha had screwed her face into a grimace. "Spare me. Every girl knows what it means when a guy says he's 'bi.'" She made angry, exaggerated air quotes and I was repulsed. Air quotes? What had I ever seen in this girl? Air quotes? Really? "What he really means is he'll be officially gay when he finally gets the balls to come out. Bisexuality isn't a real thing, Ken. Quit using girls to work through your personal problems!"

With that impassioned speech, she fled into her dorm and left me with a sour stomach and a lot to think about.

I realized I had been too idealistic and naive about myself and the world. I had been walking around for my entire life completely comfortable in my skin, sure that all I was and all I would become would be perfect—sure that my hard work and dedication and brain and heart would get me where I wanted to go. I hadn't banked on everyone being so damned judgmental—or the possibility that their judgment would affect or hinder me.

Even though my bliss-bubble had been well and truly popped, I knew my life was mine. And if I had to live without the approval of assholes, then so be it.

My resolve didn't take the pain away—didn't lessen the absence of the comforting illusion I'd had of a supportive and loving father. His loss hurt and I felt alone.

I had Kari. She was great and helped me through it as much as she could. But at the time, she had been home in Cleveland working on her post-grad, and still felt too far away for real support.

A few weeks later, when I met Angie, we clicked, and I was smitten. I couldn't see anyone but her, no one could turn my head. I was happy and contented. She erased the loneliness and made life fun again.

Until now, I hadn't been ready, I hadn't settled—and there sure as hell hadn't been any guys—or women for that matter—to stir me up like Steven did. I hadn't felt this excited to see anyone since Angie. If he could make me feel this way again, then he was absolutely worth chasing.

CHAPTER NINE

STEVEN

Sunday morning, as I was wheeling my suitcase into the living room, there was rapid, insistent knocking.

Approaching the door, I said, "Alright! Alright! I'm coming!"

I heard Elizabeth say, "Don't think about ignoring us, we have fritters."

I laughed, delighted with her ploy. She was adorable and smart. She wanted information and knew Nico-delivered apple fritters was the perfect way to persuade me to give it to her.

I opened to find the couple grinning at me. Nico's was the dimpled grin of the happy and contented, eager to spread joy to fellow man. Elizabeth's grin, however, had a more pointed message that said, *I'm going to work you over and you will succumb.*

I hadn't called her back after I'd talked to Ken on Tuesday. Nor had I responded to the two voicemails she'd left since then. She was here for the scoop.

"Please, please, do come into my humble abode." I made a broad, sweeping gesture toward the living room then made a motion to relieve Nico of the fritters as he passed.

But Elizabeth, the tiny, evil ninja, inserted her body between me and the treats. "Hold them high, Nico. Don't let him have them!"

For his part, Nico did her bidding, raised the plate as high as he could and continued into the apartment.

I sighed in exasperation. "So, you're here for an interrogation, I see. Determined to bring torture into it, hmm?" I squared my shoulders and smoothed my T-shirt, as if readying myself for battle. "While I applaud your cunning, I'll have you know that you are a *monster* who is in direct violation of the Geneva Conventions."

Nico laughed. I always felt a sense of accomplishment when I made him laugh. "I'm nearly as tall as he is, I could have them in an instant," I boasted, snapping my fingers.

"Ah, but he's wily and plays dirty," she said. "You'll never get them."

"Ugh. Alright. I have not had my coffee yet and I'm *starving*, so I'll acquiesce this time and tell you whatever you want to hear," I capitulated. "Just please give me the doughnut."

As I prepared our coffees and dished up the fritters, Elizabeth spied my suitcase. "Going somewhere?"

I nodded. "Tomorrow Dan and I are going to Hamburg for meetings with a client for potential expansion."

"Who's watching Wally?" Nico asked.

Wally was Dan's dog. He was a four-year-old black lab mix, and, in my completely unbiased opinion, the best dog on the planet. Dan had been doing a lot of traveling—more than his normal amount—due to Janie's bedrest and Quinn's need to be home with her. That meant Wally needed a dog-sitter. Alex and I were the usual sitters.

"Alex and Sandra are taking him," I replied.

"I'm home this week. If Alex needs a break, I'll take him," Nico offered.

"I'm sure he'll appreciate that," I said as we sat on the couch. "Now, for the house rules," I announced.

"*Don't spill, or I'll have to kill,*" we three said in unison. Nico said it loudly with a smile, while Elizabeth's recitation was delivered in a robotic monotone.

My couch was a large, white, curved sofa that meandered in a lazy, reverse S shape. One end had no backrest, but instead, spread into a wide, circular cushion. It was soft, but firm enough that it retained its sleek shape after use. It was furniture art and fit the space of my apartment as if it were perfectly created to inhabit it. Also, it was obscenely expensive.

Did I mention it was white?

It was white. *Snow* white.

Elizabeth rolled her eyes and said, "You're the one who's going to be spilling. So, spill."

"It was no big deal," I explained. "I called him back, he wanted to see a movie," I said the words plainly, casually, and sipped my coffee. I hoped she'd be disappointed in Ken's mundane motivation and lose interest. I didn't know whether it was because she knew him and apparently didn't like him, or because maybe at one point, she more than liked him, but whatever the reason, I didn't feel like sharing the story with her. I felt oddly protective of my time with DKM.

"He asked you to a movie?" She blinked, nonplussed.

"Who are we talking about?" Nico asked, leaning around Elizabeth to look at me. His green eyes held a mischievous twinkle, no doubt eager to hear a new chapter of farce and lunacy in Steven's Big Book of Dating Disasters.

"Ken Miles," I replied.

Nico's twinkle and dimple disappeared. Whether Elizabeth disliked Ken or not, I was sure Nico loathed the man. I couldn't blame him; it was his prerogative to hate men who used to lust after his wife. He arched one raven eyebrow and asked, "How'd that come about?"

"Yeah," Elizabeth said. "How, Steven?" Her tone was curious, but I thought I detected a little tinge of disapproval that I didn't like.

Not wanting to make an issue of anything, I replied with an easy nonchalance. "I ran into him at Buzzy's. We started talking about *Mystery Science Theater 3000*—"

"That show's a riot," Nico asserted, reaching for his fritter. "The reboot is pretty good, too."

"That's what I told DKM." I took Nico's lead and grabbed my own heavenly pastry. "Then, when he found out the movie was playing at the Music Box, he asked me if I wanted to see it. So, we went." I shrugged.

"There's a movie?" Nico asked. "How did I not know this?"

I mumbled around my fritter bite, "You're not missing much."

"Stinker, eh?"

"Little bit." I shrugged again. That had been two, overly casual shrugs in just a few seconds and I worried I was playing it too cool. Elizabeth's powers of observation surpassed my own. If I wasn't careful, she'd have me giving her every last detail of the evening.

"So," she broke in. "Are you thinking this might have been like, you know, a date?" Her brows were drawn together in concern, her words tentative.

I tilted my head in stern exasperation. "Puh-leeze. The man didn't know who McSteamy was. I got the memo that he's straight."

"Who's McSteamy?" Nico asked.

I pursed my lips together, raised my eyebrows and gestured to Nico. "I rest my case."

Elizabeth laughed. "I'm sorry, I just didn't want you getting the wrong idea or anything. He's"—she looked at her husband in apology—"he's very good-looking, and I could see how asking you to a movie could get your hopes up."

"Nah," I waved dismissively. "I know what's up. But I think we could hang out," I volunteered without thinking. I instantly regretted my slip.

"Good luck with that," Nico said with a laugh.

"We had a good time. He's kind of funny," I defended.

"Not possible," he declared. Nico was a comedian, and a very successful one at that. He knew what was funny and wasn't about to give the odious Dr. Miles any benefit of the doubt where humor was concerned.

Inexplicable annoyance spurred me to continue. "I think I might make hanging out with him a regular thing."

"I don't think a stiff like that knows how to have fun."

Elizabeth grimaced at her husband's uncharacteristic snark, then issued me a sympathetic smile. "Well, it will be good for Dr. Ken

Miles. He's not the most colorful person in the city, that's for sure. Maybe you'll broaden his horizons."

After breakfast, I said my thanks and saw them out. When I closed the door, I let my smile drop, feeling suffused with irritation. I knew they had their own history with Ken and were allowed to have feelings about him. But that was all wrapped up in romantic drama and had nothing to do with me. I didn't want that negativity souring my enthusiasm for our budding friendship.

I got the feeling there was so much more to Ken left to suss out. His dispassionate demeanor and model good looks didn't immediately evoke imaginings of depth or warmth. But it was there. And when I returned from Germany, I was going to learn more about the intriguing Dr. Ken.

CHAPTER TEN

DKM

ME: Hi. How are you doing today?

Ugh. The text sounded stilted. I deleted it and tried again.

ME: Hey, how's it going?

Better. More natural. But *how's it going*? That wasn't a great way to word a greeting. What was 'it?' *How's it going* was starting to look wrong, the more I stared at it.

Delete.

ME: Hey, how are you?

Cripes. Why did every word look and sound stupid? *Just say it, Ken. Man up.*

ME: Hi Steven, it's Ken. Do you like jazz? There's a jazz trio playing on Friday night. I was going to check them out. Would you like to come along?

There. Done. Sent. No more second-guessing.

It was the Monday following our Friday night movie date, and I had spent the weekend trying to think of things Steven and I could do together that we'd both enjoy.

I loved jazz, and Club Tremolo was the kind of place where you could dine and see a great performance any night of the week without having to purchase tickets in advance. I thought it seemed like the perfect place for a low-key date. I only hoped Steven liked jazz, too.

I pocketed my phone and started my rounds. For the first hour, I obsessed about a call back from him, reaching in my pocket several times to touch the phone, imagining I could feel a vibration. But the morning became busy with clinics and two transfers from the emergency department, so I didn't get a chance to check my phone until after two.

I had one missed call from Steven. I stepped into the lounge to call him back. Thankfully, there was no one inside.

"Well, hel-lo, McPretty MD," came Steven's chipper greeting.

"Hi, sorry I missed your call."

"No problem," he assured. "I just wanted to tell you that I love jazz, but unfortunately, I'm going to be busy with work this week and by Friday, I'll be tuckered out from riding Manuel. Any chance we can do this Saturday or any other day next week?"

Riding Manuel? What the hell? Who was Manuel and what exactly was his job? I was taken aback and couldn't hide the reaction.

"Who's Manuel?" I nearly growled the words.

Steven laughed. "Ah, Manuel," he sounded wistful. "Manuel is gorgeous. Sleek and posh. He's ruined me for all other planes."

Now I was confused. "Planes?"

"Yes, Manuel is the name I've given to the company jet. We've been parted too long. But this afternoon, one of my bosses and I will be headed to Hamburg for a few meetings. Manuel and I will have ample time to become reacquainted."

Relief coursed through me and I laughed. "Of *course,* you'd name the plane. Why Manuel?"

"I have a thing for Spanish men. It seemed fitting."

And just like that, I was irritated again. I was demonstrably *not* Spanish or of Spanish descent. The idea that I maybe wasn't physically attractive to Steven hadn't crossed my mind until this point, and I felt my confidence waning.

"Oh," I said quickly, ready to end the conversation. "I hope you have a good trip."

"Wait, wait. Don't try to hang up," he insisted. "That is, unless you have very important doctor business to do, then, of course, hang up on me."

"I'm not busy just now, I can talk." When I realized I was smiling again, I had to shake my head at myself. Steven had the unnerving ability to make my emotions vacillate wildly.

"I'd love to listen to some jazz," he continued. "But I really will be tired on Friday. We'll be back in Chicago sometime Thursday, but I'll have to go into the office on Friday and probably stay a bit later than normal. Does Saturday work with your schedule?"

"Yeah, no, that's fine!" I said too loudly, flinching at my over-eager reply. I lowered my volume and continued. "I'll be off, so it will work out great. The club has performances every night and this trio is scheduled for the entire weekend. I checked."

"Sounds good. I'll get in touch with you later this week and we can iron out the deets, okay?"

"Okay, have a safe trip. Talk to you soon." I disconnected the call, Manuel and Spanish men forgotten. He wanted to see me again, so I took that as a very good sign.

I realized, with some shame, that I didn't know much about Steven's life. He was a great conversationalist, skilled at getting me to talk, but he hadn't volunteered much about himself.

I should have been more attentive and asked questions instead of letting him lead. I had no idea that his job necessitated traveling by plane to far off places. I didn't have a clue what his job *was*. I needed to dig deep with Steven and know all about him. Saturday, I was going to find out what made him tick.

CHAPTER ELEVEN

STEVEN

"He flies in beauty, through the night," I improvised, stroking the butter-soft leather backrest of my seat.

"In cloudless climes and starry sk—" My phone chimed with a text message. It interrupted my ode, which was rude, but also convenient, as I had no idea how to work the next line.

"And soars the best…?" I questioned quietly, pulling out my cell. "Whether dark or bright." Fully cognizant of my lack of creative talent, I facetiously boasted to the empty cabin, "Boom! Poet Prowess, right here." Somewhere, Byron was tossing in his grave.

QUINN: Do not bring back any cheese that is over 175 mg sodium per ounce.

"Oh, for Thor's sake," I snarled at my phone. "I get it, man. I get it."

Dan, just coming aboard the plane, asked, "Quinn?" He wore a similarly frustrated expression and waved his phone.

"Listen to this shit." He shook his head and scrolled his screen until he found the message. "If Steven attempts to bring any unpasteurized cheese home for Janie, I'm ordering you to 'lose'"—Dan held up his free hand to air-quote *lose*—"his luggage."

I felt a slight heat rise to my face. I was embarrassed that Quinn felt the need to enlist Dan to police me. He already laid out the rules of the cheese in explicit detail. "Gee, I'm beginning to think he doesn't trust me or something," I said lightly, unwilling to allow the sting to bleed through.

"He doesn't," Dan retorted. "Not where Janie is concerned."

My phone chimed again, and as I glanced at it, Dan's chimed as well.

In unison, we read aloud, "*I'm serious.*"

"Jesus, Mary, and Joseph," he muttered as he dropped his laptop bag on the seat. "All my life, I've never seen him this way. He's lost his goddamn mind."

Daniel O'Malley was Quinn's business partner and best friend since childhood. As his business partner and best friend, he'd been picking up all of Quinn's slack since Janie had been put on bedrest. So, in addition to his position as Chief Security Personnel Coordinator, he'd been doing Quinn's more public tasks, like the traveling and meetings.

Unlike Quinn, who seemed to have shed some of his street-tough upbringing, becoming a more urbane and polished businessman, Dan's previous life was evident by his thick, south Boston accent, frank manner of speaking, and neck tattoos playing peekaboo at his collar.

His daily uniform consisted of an expertly tailored black suit and black tie. My initial impression when I met him six years ago, was that he was *Tough Guy Level: Federal Agent Meets Mob Enforcer.* You wouldn't know it at first glance, but Dan was laid-back and funny.

At the moment, he didn't appear laid-back. He was clearly frustrated with his friend.

"I know he's worried about Janie and the baby, but she knows —*better than he does*—what she can and cannot eat."

"It's my fault," I admitted, sullenly. "I should have never brought up the cheese."

"You dumbass," Dan said lightly. "Why'd you say you'd bring her cheese? Why not yarn or thread or whatever the hell she knits with?"

I sighed and settled into my seat. "I mentioned that I wanted to get Kat some cheese as a present. It snowballed from there."

STICKING TO THE SCRIPT

At the mention of Kat, Dan stilled. After a moment he said, "Yeah, she likes cheese, that's a good idea. But don't get her any of that shit with maggots in it."

Horrified, I said, "What the hell? Why would I give her maggoty food?"

"It's a thing. I swear." He raised his right hand. "Some black market shit. I heard Janie tellin' Kat all about it, how the larvae can do damage to the stomach. She wrinkled her nose all up and said she'd take a pass on that one," he gave a shrug. "So, no maggots."

He selected a seat in the row across the aisle from mine and busied himself by digging in the side pocket of the laptop bag. I debated for half a second on whether or not to give him shit about Kat. I couldn't let it pass. My inner devil was strong, my angel, weak.

"Ooh, eavesdropping, huh?" I issued him a meaningful eyebrow wiggle once he turned back to me. "I know you security guys love to get your information on the sly, but I could, you know, just give you her number and you could ask her about herself."

"Hey, you try bein' in the same room with Janie talking about cheese maggots and see if you can ignore it," he deflected. The expertly executed way he so completely sidestepped the implication about Kat, made me want to give him a standing ovation and slow clap. *Bravo, Bro. Bra-vo.*

I didn't entirely understand the dynamics of what was happening between Kat and Dan or why they avoided each other when both clearly wanted to do the horizontal mambo. Despite our friendships, it really wasn't my business. But that didn't mean I couldn't mess with them once in a while, right?

"Maybe *you* could buy Kat the cheese, since you know *so* much about her." I shrugged, then began buckling my seatbelt. "Nothing says love like a wheel of cheese. I'll just get her yarn."

"It's a long flight, asshole," he said. "How about you don't bust my balls, okay?"

I took pity on him. "Ugh. Fine. This is going to be one boring trip," I joked.

Dan got up, presumably to use the bathroom, and just as he returned, my phone chimed with a text.

"Oh, great," he said from behind me. "What's it going to be this time? We gotta grind up vitamins and rub them all over the cheese?"

He leaned an arm on my headrest and bent down, eager to see Quinn's next edict.

I opened the text.

"Ahhgghh!" we both yelled, rearing back.

It *wasn't* an edict and it *wasn't* from Quinn.

It was a dick.

Full frame of cock, balls, and pubes.

I jerked the phone away and laid it screen-side down on the seat. *Fuck my life.* I could feel the heat rising in my cheeks, the sting of mortification slapping me across the face. Dan, if you wanted to get technical, was my boss. *A* boss. We joked and had an informal relationship, but dick pics in his face was a bit *too* informal, if you asked me.

I wouldn't put it past some of my friends and acquaintances to send dick pics, but they wouldn't be sending them to *me.* Likely, I was simply an accidental recipient. Friend or not, accident or not, I was going to tear them up just for the embarrassment. It was beside the point that the cock in question was impressively large. I didn't appreciate it in this circumstance.

As I lifted the phone, careful not to flash the sausage at Dan, he said, "Well that will teach me not to read over anyone's shoulder again, eh?"

I glanced at the sender information. It wasn't a saved contact and a number I didn't recognize. I did also give the picture a thorough examination, you know, in case I recognized it. I didn't.

"It's a wrong number," I said, heat increasing in my face. "I don't know this person."

Dan, facing forward, avoiding eye contact, shook his head. "Hey, you don't have to explain anything."

"I'm serious," I insisted. I got the feeling he didn't believe me, and I wanted him to know I didn't want or encourage random dicks popping up at four PM on a workday.

"Yeah, no, I know," he said, turning toward me. "What I mean is, it doesn't matter. That's your b—" He halted mid-sentence, his face split into a joyful, radiantly happy smile. "Hold up. Are you *blushing*?" he asked. "Ho-ly shit, you *are*."

I closed my eyes.

"Oooh!" he hooted. "This is the best day of my life."

Deciding to ignore his chuckling, I tapped out a reply to Mr. Pushy Penis.

ME: You have the wrong number and you need to groom. Tidy that shit up.

"You know what this is, Steven?"

"Hmm?" I asked absently, my phone chiming with a reply.

"You thought you were being funny before, bustin' *my* balls…"

I opened the message.

UNKNOWN: We're going to be friends, Steven. Don't block my number again.

King. My ears buzzed and it was a wonder I heard Dan's words.

"…but you just got slapped by Karma."

CHAPTER TWELVE

DKM

Wednesday, I arrived at the gym after my shift for leg day. In the summer, I preferred to do my cardio outside as much as possible, but I had to utilize the gym when I needed to lift. Just as I started step-ups, my phone chimed with a text.

STEVEN: Hey, DKM. I can't sleep and feel like a chat. Want to talk?

I hurriedly typed my reply.

ME: Sure. Give me 5 minutes?

In the lobby, I approached the desk attendant. "Hi, I need to make a call for an emergency consultation, is there any chance you have an empty room I could use?"

The guy was at the desk regularly and I knew he'd seen me in my scrubs before, so I figured I could possibly get away with my lie.

"Sure," he agreed easily. "The daycare room is closed tonight because Lena is out sick. I'll unlock it for you."

"Thank you."

He led me into the daycare room and flipped on the light. "Take as long as you need, Doc."

I smiled, not in the least repentant for my lie. I found the only chair in the room that was made for an adult and sat down.

ME: I can talk. Should I call you?

My phone rang almost immediately, and my heart kicked up in anticipation.

"Hello?"

"DKM, did I bug you at work? What time is it there?" Steven asked. He sounded subdued, tired.

"I'm at the gym, so it's fine. I think it's like a quarter to six," I checked my watch. 5:48. "What time is it there?" I asked.

"I don't even know. Late. After midnight. I can't sleep, my rhythm is off." He yawned quietly. "Friday is going to suck. Just when I'm accustomed to German time, I'll have to go back to normal. It's the only thing I hate about traveling."

I wanted him to tell me more about his work, so I asked, "Do you have to travel often?"

"A bit. We have a lot of business in the Midwest, but many of our newer clients are overseas, so I get to travel mostly when we're courting new or prospective clients."

"What do you do?"

"I'm the numbers guy," he said, offhandedly. I got the feeling he didn't really want to talk about it, but I was interested, so I pressed on.

"What does that mean, 'the numbers guy?' Are you an accountant or something?"

"I'm VP of Financial Operations." He paused but seemed to sense I was poised to ask more questions, so he added, "With the exception of my title, I'm legally required to keep my trap shut about my specific duties and company services. I can only tell you what information is available on our website." There was a hint of apology in his voice, as if he didn't want me to be insulted that he couldn't elaborate. I wasn't bothered by it in the least. I was bound by confidentiality laws every day, so I understood.

"Okay, so what's the website say? What's the company?"

"Cipher Systems. We do surveillance, physical and cybersecurity for corporations. In rare cases, we'll do personal detail, but that's not what we specialize in. You won't find that on the website, but it's something you already know, after all."

"I do?" I asked confused. I didn't know anything about his job and couldn't understand how he figured I did. "You're talking about bodyguards, right?"

"Um, yeah," he answered hesitantly. "Like Nico, for example. He's one of our few clients with personal detail."

"Nico," I said flatly. I knew about Nico's need for a security detail and didn't enjoy thinking about it. A thought struck me. "Wait. Was that guy with Elizabeth one of yours?"

"I had to open my big mouth," he muttered softly. Then, louder, he said, "Yes, sorry. I shouldn't have brought it up. I know it's probably unpleasant for you to think about. Elizabeth told me what happened with you and the Fancy Stalker."

I grimaced. *Fancy Stalker* was Elizabeth's flippant, cutesy name for the woman who'd attacked her, and I hated it.

"Well done, though," Steven continued. "You saved the day."

Without thinking, I emitted a disgusted scoff. I'd once been flippant about the reality of the situation, too. I'd arrogantly thought the presence of a bodyguard was somehow a power play by Nico in response to me. The timing had been convenient, after all. He'd shown up at the hospital, sized me up, then practically pissed on Elizabeth's leg right there in the CRU. Before I knew it, she had a bodyguard.

Total. Power. Play.

I hadn't imagined Elizabeth was in any real danger. The media had been a problem. Mostly I thought it was complete bullshit that she was allowing his baggage to infiltrate her life. At the time, she was a resident in a large, downtown hospital. She didn't have time for bodyguards and paparazzi. The way I saw it, Nico was a detriment to her, professionally. I was sure he, in the long run, would be no competition for me.

But I'd been mistaken. The fan that had been causing a ruckus, ended up being an unhinged stalker. The threat had been real, and Nico never needed a power play because Elizabeth hadn't really wanted me. At least, she hadn't wanted me in any way that mattered.

Even after she left me at the start of our first date to chase down Nico, I stupidly thought I could talk some sense into her.

I sought her out, intent on telling her what a huge mistake she was making. When I found her in the doctor's lounge, I had been startled and horrified to find myself facing down the barrel of a handgun.

Normally, I have a very good grasp on time and space during stressful situations. I would go so far as to say my focus was heightened in emergencies. I could be presented with a screaming, flailing gunshot victim, aware of their loved one hovering near, blood-soaked and weeping. Within moments, I could decide what needed to be done. Blood draws, scans, IVs, or surgery. I made rapid-fire plans that saved lives. I did it every day. In the ER, I was a rock.

But that afternoon in the doctor's lounge, space and time warped and slowed, skipped, and sped. What transpired in less than a minute, felt like an hour of panicked deliberation accompanied by strange gaps.

Elizabeth's quick action allowed me to gain possession of the gun but being disarmed hadn't been a deterrent for the woman. She continued her attack on Elizabeth despite my warning and my warning shot into the corner of the lounge. Seeing her rear back to punch Elizabeth in the face spurred me to make the decision to shoot her.

Pain will stop her.

I aimed for her knee, pulled the trigger and felt the kickback. I watched in horror as she pitched to the side from the force of the bullet striking her in the abdomen. Again, time crawled as I saw her fall to her knees.

I missed her knee.

She slumped and collapsed to her side.

I may have killed her.

Elizabeth recovered with amazing speed, tearing off her lab coat and pressing it against the woman's wound.

Why did I shoot her? I probably should have pistol-whipped her or something.

I looked down at my hand and tested the weight of the revolver. *So small. So terrible.*

People were in the room with us after that. Elizabeth's guard, nurses, and physicians—they took control of the situation. I could see the wound in the woman's side, hear her crying.

At minimum, I perforated her colon.

And I had. The woman was rushed to surgery where a portion of her damaged intestine was removed, and a colostomy was performed.

Her name was Menayda Kazlauskas and my actions meant she was defecating into a bag for the rest of her life.

I didn't like thinking about Menayda because I didn't enjoy the self-recrimination I felt. My reflexes and responses hadn't been working efficiently. I'd made a fear-based, impaired judgment, took action, and caused irreparable harm. It didn't matter that I *saved the day*, or managed, despite my ineptitude, to not kill the woman. I knew I'd meant to shoot her leg and missed. I knew that if I'd been thinking clearly, I would have found another way to stop her.

But none of this was Steven's fault. It wasn't even Elizabeth or Nico's. I just couldn't allow myself to feel good about the outcome. Nor did I want the conversation to move from Steven to me, so I cleared my throat and asked, "Do you like your job?"

He hummed with evident disapproval at my blatant evasion. There was a moment of silence where I wondered if he'd change the subject, wondering if we were at a standoff where neither of us wanted to talk about ourselves. Luckily for me, he capitulated.

"I do. I make a lot more money than I did working for the insurance company, benefits are better, and I get to travel. I'm kept reasonably challenged, which is a *very* good thing for me. I work alongside a few supremely intelligent, amazing people who I respect. But, the coolest thing about it, honestly, is that in this company, I was able to discover what I'm best at, then given the encouragement and trust to do it the way I saw fit." His voice dipped low when he said, "It's like a family. I don't know where I'd be without it."

"I'm impressed," I replied. "Sounds like you have a lot of responsibility."

Steven laughed, ending his moment of seriousness. "It's not impressive. I make bottom lines bigger and I do it well. But it's not like I go into work and save lives or improve the quality of life for dozens of people every single day."

Realizing he was referring to my work, I felt a burst of pride.

Steven liked to be sarcastic sometimes, but he seemed sincere and not at all stingy with his compliments. He made me feel like how I felt mattered to him.

There was a lull in conversation while I wool-gathered, and I realized that if I wanted to keep Steven from hanging up, I needed to open my mouth and say something. So, I did.

"You're nice." I shook my head at my own lameness. *Ken, you are an idiot.*

He let out a huff of a laugh and said, "I have my moments." Before I could say anything else, he announced, "I did have an actual reason to call you besides insomnia."

"Oh?"

"Yeah, I promised Dan—he's one of my bosses—that I'd dog-sit for him on Saturday. He's probably going to be working late and I don't know that I'll make it to jazz."

My heart sank. "Dog sitting?" It sounded like a thin excuse and I suspected he just wanted to cancel.

"He's my neighbor and sometimes I watch Wally if he has to work long hours," he explained. It was on the tip of my tongue to just say, *cool, whatever, bye* and end the conversation, but Steven surprised me by asking, "Do you want to hang out with us?"

"At your place?"

"Yeah," he replied. "We could watch a movie—your choice, obviously, since my movie was last week."

"I chose the movie last time," I reminded.

"Pffft. Would you have picked that movie if I hadn't made you think it would be awesome?"

"Not in a million years," I said happily.

Steven hooted a laugh. "At least you're honest. I love that about you." My smile grew so large, my cheeks and jaw started aching. "So, see? That's what I mean," he continued. "I'll make it up to you by letting you pick. You like Chinese? We'll order in."

"Sounds great."

"It's a plan, then. Look, I'm going to let you get back to sculpting that bod of yours and I'm going to try to catch some sleep. I'll talk to you later."

We said our goodbyes. I hopped out of the chair, did a victory fist-thrust and said, "Fuck yeah!"

The obscenity was loud and felt a bit criminal spoken amongst all the child daycare paraphernalia, but I didn't care because Steven had just given me the green light.

Dog-sitting, my ass.

CHAPTER THIRTEEN

STEVEN

Late Saturday afternoon, Wally and I took a walk around Millennium Park to get a little air and exercise before Ken arrived.

When we returned to the residence, Lawrence, the concierge caught my eye and gestured to me. As I approached his desk he said, "Mr. Thompson, I have the mail that's been accumulating since your trip."

I accepted the small stack, issuing him a smile. "Thanks, Larry. I wanted to let you know that I'll be having a guest in an hour or so. His name is Ken. You can just send him up, okay?"

"Sure thing, Mr. Thompson."

I started to take a step when Wally whined, attention on Lawrence.

"Oh, Wally! I have something for you, too." He slapped his forehead and walked out from behind the counter. Wally wagged his tail and started dancing in anticipation for the treat he knew the concierge would give him.

"You're a good boy, you are," Lawrence said, kneeling. "How's about a shake?"

Wally dutifully sat down and offered a paw to the man.

He laughed heartily, enjoying the routine he had with the dog. One treat and several pats and praises later, we made our way toward the elevator.

My cell rang, Ernesto was calling. Not wanting to trap anyone in the elevator with me while I carried on a conversation, I backed away from the elevator doors and answered the phone.

"So?" I asked without preamble. "How was it?"

I hadn't heard from Ernesto since the day he and Paulie left for their honeymoon in Arizona. Ernesto was a photographer who worked primarily in fashion. Fashion photography paid well, but Ern's heart was in nature photography. Their Arizona honeymoon had come about because Paulie was able to give Ern the wedding gift of permits for them to hike the North Coyote Buttes in Vermilion Cliffs National Monument. These permits were hard to come by, but Ernesto had always wanted to photograph the beautiful waves in the Navajo sandstone.

"Oh! Steven, it was *breathtaking*," he gushed. "As soon as I saw the waves, I began to weep. Paulie, he too, was so overcome with the majesty of the land, he cried as well."

I smiled, imagining Paulie, who was, despite being a fashion model on display in magazines and on billboards in all manner of undress, not given to revealing his emotions openly for anyone to see.

"Wow," I said. "I can't wait to see the pictures. If Paulie's crying in front of your guide, then it had to be spectacular."

"Yes, yes," he agreed dismissively. "But I wanted to tell you about something. We need to plan a night out because we went to see Paulie's *abuelita* yesterday and, you know, she is just a sweetheart, always trying to be so…" He paused. "She just tries to show him that she's supportive of us. Anyway, she says to Paulie, 'Come meet my new neighbor he's a gay, just like you!'"

I laughed, "*A* gay, huh?"

"Paulie said, 'Nonna, we don't have to meet every gay person you come across.' But she said, 'No, you will love him! So fun! So interesting!' And like the good grandsons we are, we went next door and met him."

"Uh-huh," I said, suspicion developing.

"He's forty-one, single, kind of cute. He's got salt and pepper hair."

"Oh, boy," I muttered.

"And, get this! On the weekends, he's a clown!"

Aaaannnnd, there it was.

"A clown. Seriously? You think I should date a clown?" My friends were now actively trying to set me up with circus people. This might have been an all-time low.

I saw a nearby guard, Damon, flash a grin at my words. I decided to take the elevator. As I waited for the door to open, Ern continued.

"Yes! He's got a trunk full of costumes and magic trick stuff. He does balloon animals…" he sing-songed, cajoling—as if the ability to shape dogs out of balloons was peak bangability.

"Oh, my!" I said, sarcasm dripping from my lips. "Balloon animals? Why, it's more than I ever dreamed."

"Oh. Excuuuse me," Ernesto drawled, offended. "Sorry I didn't read the rule that said mimes were fine, but clowns weren't."

"It was *one* mime, *one* time!" I defended. And because I knew Damon was listening, I added for shock value, "Turned out, he was a screamer. Who woulda thought?"

Damon coughed.

The doors to the elevator opened, but before Wally and I stepped in, I covered my mouthpiece and playfully admonished the guard, "You get more than you bargain for when you eavesdrop on me."

The doors closed and I turned my focus back to Ern, who was still making his case.

"Also, did you, or did you not tell me that in college you let a fire-eater blow you?" he demanded.

I combed my hair with my hand and let out a sigh. Ernesto only meant well. He didn't know I was on a penis hiatus, and I wasn't about to go into it with him, either. He'd only accuse me of being melodramatic and redouble his efforts to find me a man. It was best if I simply thanked him and gave a reasonable excuse for not meeting Bozo.

"Yes, Ern, that's all true," I agreed. "I appreciate you looking out for me, but I just got back from Germany and I'm wrecked. I'm dog-sitting for Dan so I'm really not down to clown this weekend, alright?"

"That's fine. But I want you to come out with us soon. Whether Scooter is there or not."

"His clown name is Scooter, huh?" I asked, imagining a guy in full clown regalia, cruising up, honking the horn of a brightly colored Vespa.

"No, Scooter is his real name," Ernesto replied. "His clown name is Charlie."

I shook my head, exasperated. "Okay, we're done. Talk to you later."

Before I clicked off, I heard Ern yell, "Tell Wally I love him!"

When I entered the apartment, I dropped the mail and keys onto the side table and asked the dog, "How do you do it? All the boys are falling over themselves to get a little tail wiggle from you."

Wally kept silent.

"Oh, secrets. I get it."

I unfastened his leash and he trotted over to make himself comfortable on my brand-spanking-new, spacious, gray area rug. I cringed. There was a reason I usually watched Wally in Dan's apartment. Wally was certainly a good boy, housetrained as well as a dog could be, but I didn't love fur and dog smell on my furniture and accessories.

But Ken was coming over for dinner and I couldn't host him in Dan's place, so I decided to allow Wally to make himself at home all over my beautiful rug.

"You just keep your paws off the couch, mister. Got it?" I warned.

Checking the time, I decided to place our dinner order and jump in the shower.

I was strangely nervous about Ken coming over, and I didn't think it had anything to do with him, necessarily. I'd felt off all week. Getting that ominous message from King, then having to focus on meetings and proposals had resulted in little sleep. When Dan asked if I'd watch Wally, I nearly refused, remembering Ken and I were supposed to listen to jazz. But the thought of going out felt exhausting, so I agreed to dog-sit, thinking I'd beg off and see Ken another day.

But simply talking with him on the phone reminded me of why I wanted to hang out. I regretted that I was going to cancel, so I impulsively invited him here.

The food arrived before Ken and I eyeballed the array. I'd gone a little overboard, worrying about what he'd like to eat. I made the assumption beef was okay, since he'd eaten a burger at the sports bar last week, but I wanted to make sure he had a selection, so I ordered six dishes. Broccoli beef, sweet and sour pork, shrimp chow mein, General Tso chicken, orange chicken, and something called Vegetarian Paradise. All the bases were covered. I surmised that if he couldn't find something he liked, then he just didn't like Chinese food.

When he arrived, I opened the door to find him looking very handsome and dapper. His blond hair, which was longer on the top, usually had some unruly waves that looked haphazard and adorable. Tonight, those curls were subdued with product. I suspected they wouldn't stay put for long, but it was clear Ken was going for a tidy look. It was equally adorable.

He was also wearing a tie and blazer. His blue shirt matched his eyes, making them glow. The effect was startling. His attire seemed an odd choice for hanging out in my apartment and eating out of cardboard boxes, but I couldn't deny that he looked great. No one hated eye-candy and I wasn't about to look a gift horse in the mouth.

"Well, good evening, McPretty MD," I said happily, moving aside to let him in.

"MST3K," he greeted, smiling widely.

"Did you just come from a modelling convention? Because you look dashing as *hell*." I wanted to acknowledge his efforts. It was hard not to remark on his epic levels of handsome, but I didn't want to make him uncomfortable by lacing words with sexual innuendo. I was trying *very* hard to keep it neutral. I had no idea at this point if he could take any teasing flirtation from another man without being uncomfortable.

Ken's wide smile turned sheepish—more adorableness—and he said, "Thanks, you look good, too." He lifted a bottle of wine. "I brought this. I didn't know if you liked wine, but it seemed like a good choice to go with dinner."

It was a good choice, as it was a Chenin blanc, and would pair nicely with most of the dishes I ordered.

"I do like wine, thank you. I bought beer just in case you were a beer drinker."

"I enjoy both," he said, glancing around the apartment. His eyes took in the art I had displayed, my furniture, and the large windows that showcased a spectacular view of Lake Michigan in the waning sunlight. After a moment, he brought his eyes back to mine. "But I rarely drink. Between years of working long hours, and special occasions being few and far between, I haven't been a regular drinker since my first couple years of undergrad." He grinned. "I'm probably a light-weight at this point."

"Meanwhile, I could drink you under the table," I quipped, walking to the kitchen.

Ken trailed behind me, and I gestured to the many take-out boxes littering the granite countertop. "There's lots to choose from. I hope you're hungry." I reached into the cabinet and grabbed a few plates, determined not to let Dr. Dapper McPretty eat from the box.

"Steven, you didn't have to buy dinner—or order so much. I would have gladly bought the food."

I waved away his protest and started to open the wine. "I'm the host."

"But I asked you out first," he argued, brows drawn in annoyance.

"Ken," I began, my tone serious. "Let's get real here for a moment. I make a good living. So do you. Neither one of us are trying to get a free meal out of the other, right?" He nodded. "The more we hang out, the money will even out." At that, he seemed to completely relax. He was back to smiling. I liked his smile. I also kind of perversely liked his hair-trigger annoyance. He was fun.

"My friend Janie is the same way," I continued. "And it occasionally sucks the fun out of lunch for me. We'll be having a great time; good food, pleasant atmosphere, fascinating conversation…then, BAM!" I clapped my hands. "The check arrives, and we have to argue about things. It's a mood killer. Don't kill the mood, DKM."

He patted my back and said, "I won't. Thank you for dinner." He reached for a plate and started to dig through the boxes.

It was then that Wally let out a loud bark from the spare bedroom, reminding me I needed to set him free. I always locked Wally up when people came in and out of the apartment, as he was excitable.

Ken's bent head shot up at the noise. "You *are* dog-sitting."

"Yeah, I told you," I reminded on my way out of the kitchen. Halfway down the hall, I called out a warning, "He's going to be excited, watch out!"

Wally took off out of the bedroom, no doubt as interested in the new person as the smells of the take-out.

"Oh!" I heard Ken exclaim. He sounded as excited as Wally looked. "Hello there! Aren't you a good boy?"

When I entered the kitchen, Ken was bent over Wally, giving him vigorous pats on his flank.

I began pouring our wine and said, "God, Wally, quit hogging all the men. Leave some for the rest of us, wouldya?"

Ken laughed and crossed to the sink to wash his hands. "He's a friendly pup, isn't he?"

"Yes, he is," I agreed. "But please don't fall for any begging. He doesn't get table scraps on my watch."

I proceeded to the living room, set my wine and plate on the glass top coffee table, and settled on the couch, ready to give Ken my rule of the house. But when I looked up, his brows were furrowed with concern.

"What is it?" I asked.

"Your couch is really nice. And white. Should we eat here?"

I was touched—on a soul level. I laid my hand on my heart as if I were overcome by emotion. "Ken, I think we should get married," I said with faux solemnity. "You *get it*. I've finally found someone who *gets it*." I rubbed my hand reverently along the soft material of the sofa. "I trust you to be careful. After all, doctors have steady hands, right? I'll just keep my eye on your wine intake." I patted the seat forcefully and ordered, "Come and eat."

He stood for a beat, hovering with his plate and glass before joining me.

"Any ideas what movie you'd like to watch? We could rent anything, or you could choose from what I have already." With the remote, I accessed my movie library and began scrolling.

"Wow, that's a lot. Have you watched them all?"

"Of course. Most of them several times. I liked them, that's why I bought them."

"You watch movies more than once?"

"Uh, yeah. Doesn't everybody?" I asked. But I knew the answer. Ken didn't. Ken wasn't like everybody.

"I don't," he replied. "I mean, I've seen some movies more than once. When I was a kid, I watched *The Wizard of Oz* every year. But as an adult, I guess I don't see the point of revisiting a story I already know the end of. The thrill of a book or movie," he continued, "is to work up to the climax. It's nearly impossible to feel the same things the second or third time around. My time would be better spent watching something new and different."

I took a sip of my wine and mulled over his words, thinking about why I watched my favorite movies time and time again. I decided that Ken was both right and wrong. "I agree that watching a film or reading a book for the second time won't produce the same emotion and anticipation it did initially," I said, nodding. "But, for me, I've found new things to love and enjoy about them the second or third time. Jokes I've missed, clues I hadn't realized were important before—or just enjoying the nuances of a great performance that I only cursorily noticed, rather than savored or appreciated the first time around. Second and third views, especially with films that completely blow your mind, can reveal some surprising layers."

Ken took a drink then nodded thoughtfully. "I guess I can see that. Maybe I've just never had my mind blown or finished a movie thinking I missed an aspect or didn't get to appreciate all that it had to offer." He twisted his torso toward me, setting his wine on the tabletop. "What movies have you loved that made you come back for more?"

"That's a hard question, because so many have."

"Off the top of your head," he prompted.

"Well, I do really like movies that are thought-provoking or confusing. Those are mostly dramas or thrillers, but I do have a soft spot for comedy. I guess the first few that come to mind are *Memento*, *Pi*, *Eternal Sunshine of the Spotless Mind* and um," I struggled to think of one that wasn't so weird. "And maybe *The Red Violin*. Those were all great."

Ken's face broke out into a smile and he said, "I've seen *Memento*! Yeah, that was confusing. I'd agree that a second watch would not only be useful, but maybe even necessary."

I laughed, inordinately happy that he'd agreed with me. "Exactly right! I've seen it a few times and I'm not totally convinced I know what the hell happened."

Ken held out his hand for the remote and asked, "Do you mind if I look through the movies?"

"Not at all," I assured him, handing it over. "Pick anything that you want. I'm easy."

While he searched, I pulled out my phone and sent a text to Dan to let him know Wally and I were at my place. He responded almost immediately.

DAN: Thanks, I'll be back soon. I'm in the data center with Alex and Quinn. Q's bitching in my ear about archival capacity.

I shook my head at my phone. If Quinn was raising a fuss about the surveillance parameters, I knew my next task was going to be figuring out how much it was going to cost to make an upgrade. He'd archive the data for an eternity if he could.

"How about this?" Ken asked, pulling my attention from the phone.

"*Eternal Sunshine of the Spotless Mind*. Excellent."

We started the movie and dug into our dinner. Early on, Ken shed his jacket and tie, and when he finished eating, he leaned back and draped his arm over the backrest. His position prevented me from leaning back without some awkwardness, so even after I'd finished my food, I continued to watch the movie with my upper body pitched forward, forearms on my knees. I didn't mind too much, though. A glance at Ken's relaxed posture gave me a sense of accomplishment. I loved that he was at ease with me.

About midway through the movie, there was a knock at the door. Wally bounded up from his spot on the rug and started wagging his tail. I paused the movie and said, "That's likely Dan." I stood up, grabbed Wally's leash and answered the door.

Dan stood at the threshold, a tired smile on his face. "Thanks again. Sorry it took so long. I finally had to say, 'Look, this is Chachi's problem, not mine. I'm going to bed.'" Chachi was the nickname Dan used for Alex when he was particularly irritated. I had no idea why he called him that, but he used it with regularity.

Dan, thankfully, didn't appear eager to stay for any longer than it took to fetch Wally. I was prepared to put him off if he had, though, because I didn't relish Ken and Dan recognizing each other. Dan had been Elizabeth's shadow in the hospital when the attack occurred. No doubt both of them had some opinions about the other. Not only did I want to avoid Ken disparaging Dan, I really didn't want to give Dan any further ammo for "busting my balls."

When I returned to the living room, Ken was standing next to a shelf, examining the trio of framed pictures I had of my sister and her family.

He glanced over his shoulder at me and asked, "Sister?" He had obviously deduced our relationship easily, as Sophie and I looked eerily alike.

"Yes, that's my sister Sophie, her husband Tom Thumb, and their girls Amalia and Ophelia."

"Tom Thumb?" he asked.

"His name is Thomas," I said, trying to keep my voice light. "But he's short, like *really* short, and a total asshole to boot, so I call him Tom Thumb." I didn't like Thomas, and I was pretty sure he hated me.

Ken fully faced me and asked, worry lacing his tone, "Is he mean to your sister? Your nieces?"

"No, no," I assured him. "He's kind to them, from what I can tell. He just doesn't like me."

"That sounds like it could make the holidays rough. Why doesn't he like you?" He flashed me a meaningful grin. "How could he not love a *delight* such as yourself?"

I laughed, remembering when I told Ken I was a delight. "I know, right?!" I sobered a bit and replied, "If you ask my sister, the reason is because I'm too outspoken and I get on his nerves."

Ken tilted his head and narrowed his eyes in suspicion. "But what do you think?"

I paused, a little reluctant to continue. Thomas wasn't a sore spot, necessarily. But his dislike of me was rooted in his intolerance for my obvious homosexuality. Sophie wasn't much help in that respect, preferring to mimic our dad's advice that if I were just a little less conspicuous about it, people like Thomas wouldn't dislike me so much. Whenever I was bullied in school Dad made a point to not give me any sympathy about it, saying I brought it on myself—that if I was smarter, I'd know how to keep these things from happening to me. I'm sure my dad and sister thought they were supportive and had my best interest at heart, but Thomas was a reminder that they thought I needed to be different to keep others from actively hating me.

The result? I didn't lay my problems out for other people. I kept them to myself. I didn't want well-meaning, shitty advice, didn't want anyone knowing I had problems, or to hope for help when no one really cared. Which is why Ken and I had a stare-down before I finally capitulated.

"I think if I were straight, he wouldn't mind my *outspokenness*."

He frowned. "That's…really fucked up. I'm sorry you have to deal with him."

I shrugged. "He's not important, it's fine. I don't see him much and when I do, the worst of it is that he either ignores me or gets a few passive-aggressive digs in."

Ken looked angry on my behalf, and it felt…nice. Unnecessary, and slightly uncomfortable, but nice. I didn't want to talk about me, or Thomas, so I suggested we take an intermission.

"Do you want to grab seconds? There's so much food."

"No thanks," he answered, stretching his arms to the ceiling. "I will have another glass of wine, though, if you don't mind."

We took our dishes into the kitchen and did a quick tidy before taking our refilled glasses back to the couch.

"As it turned out," I remarked, "we probably could have made it to jazz after all. Sorry about the change in plans, but I've been so tired this week, I'm glad we stayed in."

I made sure to sit farther over to the left so I could sit back, and he could still spread out. He placed his wine on the tabletop and asked, "Do you mind if I switch off the overhead light?"

"No, no, not at all," I assured him. It was a good suggestion as the room was a bit too bright for watching TV. "The switch is right there." I pointed to the fixture on the right wall.

He switched off the light, leaving only a glow from the television and a faint illumination coming from the kitchen area. It took my eyes a moment to adjust, and Ken settled himself next to me, closer than he'd been before, so I resolutely kept my back pressed against the cushions, unwilling to forfeit my space if he felt like manspreading into my territory again.

"You've been having trouble sleeping?" he asked quietly.

"Yeah, sometimes I do." Since meeting King, I had, anyway.

"Can I show you a technique I use?"

"Sure," I replied.

"Sleep is very important, and when I was a resident, I needed to maximize my sleep time. I needed a way to fall asleep quickly to catch as many minutes as I possibly could." He angled toward me, touching our knees together. "This is a breathing method called cardiac coherence. You inhale deeply for four seconds," he drew in a large breath, ticking off the seconds on his finger. Then he began exhaling slowly, ticking off six seconds.

"The exhale extends a bit longer, for six seconds. It activates the parasympathetic nervous system, slowing your heart rate, decreasing blood pressure, and relaxing your muscles," he explained. "Doing this for five minutes will not only help with insomnia, but stress management and anxiety. Try it."

He sat up straighter, so I mimicked his position and inhaled at his lead. I watched as he flared his nostrils at the inhale, his chest rising with the breath. The light from the television starkly illuminated one side of his chiseled face, leaving the other in shadow. His one eye exposed to the light seemed colorless, radiant. He flashed a smile as we finished our second exhale. I couldn't help noticing the dark couldn't obscure the brightness of his even, white teeth. Returning his smile, and feeling very relaxed I said, "We only did it twice and I can already feel the difference."

"There's another one that you might like better. It works best if you lay down." Without waiting for a response, he dropped his knees to the floor and turned to gesture for me to lay out on the sofa. I obliged.

Ken leaned over me, his features barely perceptible in shadow. "This is abdominal breathing. When you inhale, first inflate your belly, like you're filling it up with air, then do the same with your chest. Exhale the same; first the belly, then the chest." He grasped my right hand, which had been dangling off the sofa, and set it on my stomach. He kept his hand on mine.

"It works best if you feel the rise and fall of your abdomen. Deep breath," he instructed, softly.

I took a deep breath and distended my belly. "Good," he said, sliding his hand up my torso to my chest. "Now the chest."

As I exhaled, he slid his hand slowly back down to my stomach, and whispered, "How do you feel?"

The words, combined with the almost-caress of his hand, sparked goosebumps. I swallowed hard, my Adam's apple rippling in my throat. "G-good," I stammered thickly.

A knock sounded, effectively—blessedly—ruining the one-sided, sensual charge that was happening, and I all but flew off the couch. I raced to the wall, flicked on the light and said, "Oh, Jesus, it's like Grand Central Station here tonight. Hang on."

Rising from the floor, Ken blinked against the glare of the overhead light and said with a sigh, "Don't worry, it's fine."

When I opened the door, I found Ernesto waiting with a broad, happy grin. In lieu of a greeting, he called out, "Wally! Papa Ern is here to see you!"

He was holding a large package, wrapped in brown paper. I assumed it was one of his photography prints. I loved gifts, loved Ernesto, and welcomed the interruption, but I didn't want to let him in. He'd meet Ken, make some assumptions, and my stupid face after that near-boner I just had, would betray me. I could feel a slight blush creeping already.

"Sorry, Wally's not here. Thanks for coming by, but I'm busy right now. No time to chat." I made a motion to shut the door.

"Why are you so rude, Steven?" he asked, holding the door open. He slid the package through the gap and said, "I have a present for you and you're tossing me out!"

I backed away, allowing him entrance. I knew the more I protested, the bigger stink he'd make, so I gave in.

"You are acting weird," he remarked on his way through the entrance hall. "What's going—" He stopped short when he saw Ken. "Ooh," he cooed, turning to give me a knowing look. "I get it now."

Ken approached his hand extended. Ernesto switched the print to his left hand and met Ken's shake. "You must be Wally," Ern said sarcastically.

"No," he replied. "I'm Ken. Wally's a dog." His face was slack, expressionless. In that look, I thought I detected annoyance, but couldn't be sure.

Deciding I needed to take control of the situation, I said, "Ernesto, this is Ken, Ken this is Ernesto. Dan already came by for Wally, so you're out of luck."

He turned away from Ken, issued me a gleefully conspiratorial stare and mouthed *Oh my God*. Being newly married to a model didn't mean Ernesto couldn't be dazzled by Ken's good looks. I issued him a nearly imperceptible nod which I hoped he'd interpret as, *So hot, it should be criminal.*

Aloud, he said breezily, "It's fine, I really came to bring you a thank you present. Paulie and I appreciate all your help with the wedding. You were a lifesaver."

With sincerity I replied, "No thanks are needed. I was happy to help." Running errands, hosting the bachelor bar crawl, and helping two of my best friends celebrate their commitment and love had been an honor. And, I was always a sucker for love. But I was also a sucker for gifts, so I said, "I do love your presents, though. Gimme." I playfully made grabby-hands at the package.

I tore the paper open to find, as I expected, a framed photograph from Ern's trip. What I didn't expect was the reaction it evoked. I gasped in wonder and awe.

The vivid striated waves of reds, oranges, and whites, illuminated by the desert sun and captured so close as to have no orientation with the sky or perceivable ground, didn't look like a photograph of sandstone. It appeared abstract.

It was bright, hypnotic, and absolutely stunning.

No wonder Paulie cried. I felt near to it myself and I was only looking at it from the perspective of a camera lens.

I felt Ken sidle close to me for a look at the print. He bent his head near to mine and I felt his breath on my cheek as he said, "It's beautiful."

The combination of his low timbre, scent, and proximity mixed with the earlier confusing stimulation, put my dick on alert.

Mayday! Mayday!

With rapid, jerky movements, I hurried to the far wall and made a show of pondering where I'd mount it.

"So, Ernesto," I heard Ken say. "Are you Spanish?"

I lowered the picture and whipped around in surprise. What kind of question was that to ask someone? Ernesto had an obvious accent and dark features which were indicative of a mix of native and Spanish genetics. I didn't know why Ken would bring ethnicity up in conversation, unless he was uncomfortable with Ern. *Fucking. Great.*

Ken's face still bore that vapid blankness, and for a moment, I thought I was going to have to intervene on Ernesto's behalf, but then Ernesto replied suspiciously, "Somewhere down the line, yes. But my family has its roots in the Yucatan. Why do you ask?"

Ken seemed to realize he was bordering on giving offense and laughed in a self-deprecating way. "I'm sorry, Steven said he liked Spanish guys. I was just thinking you two had a thing." He appeared to be apprehensive about that prospect. Maybe, again thinking I was bringing him into an uncomfortable misunderstanding.

With heartfelt relief, I laughed at his awkward fishing. Ernesto laughed as well and gave Ken a pat on the shoulder. "No, no! I am married and Steven and I are only friends. You have nothing to worry about from me."

I inwardly laughed at Ernesto's implication that Ken and I were involved, and I waited for Ken to catch it and deny it, but he apologized again for being rude.

Ern waved him off and said his goodbye. I walked him to the door, and when we reached the threshold, he started excitedly punching my arm.

"Ow!" I whispered, rubbing my smarting bicep.

"I want every detail. Do you hear me?" His voice was hushed, but emphatic. "Call me."

I closed the door behind him, not bothering to disabuse him of the idea that I was about to get into Ken's pants. I'd 'fess up later, but for now, I was just going to let him think what he wanted.

I stood in the entryway for a moment, giving myself time to shake off the confusion of the last few minutes. I spied my neglected mail sitting on the table and noticed a small manila envelope amongst the junk. Curious, I tore it open. Within were two standard sized papers folded in half.

My stomach flipped when I saw what was printed on them. Grainy, blurry photos taken from several yards away, showed me talking with Ken at the sports bar last week. They were terrible pictures, printed on regular paper from a home printer, but I could still decipher that I was the subject.

"King," I whispered.

CHAPTER FOURTEEN

DKM

As soon as Steven came back into the living room, I perceived a radical shift in mood.

I'd screwed up.

My intention with Ernesto hadn't been to come across jealous or worse, *racist*. I was sure Steven would have understood the reference to Manuel the plane and laughingly given me the story of whether he and Ernesto had history. They *did* laugh and *did* assuage my curiosity, but not before they both issued sharp looks, alerting me to the fact that my intentions were perceived as suspect.

But even after the laugh and apologies, Steven looked pinched. He wouldn't make eye contact with me as he settled himself back on the couch. He left the overhead light on and sat a full cushion away from me.

"Let's finish this movie, okay?" He restarted the movie and crossed his leg away from me. His body language told me there was no going back to where we were a few minutes ago.

I had been so close to kissing him. Poised above, ready to lean in. My hand had felt the clenching of his abdominals and the uptick in his breathing in that brief moment. Then it all had been shattered by the knocking.

Frustration didn't begin to describe what I was feeling.

I allowed myself to focus on the film, hoping that by the end Steven's demeanor would change. But when the credits started to roll, I scooted closer to him and he seemed startled, like he'd been deep in thought.

"How were you getting home tonight?" His brows were drawn, voice sharp.

I felt my face betray my perplexity, but I caught myself and let my expression go slack. "I hadn't decided. I usually take the bus from Michigan and Washington on Sunday mornings, but at this time of night, I'll probably call for a cab."

"I don't like that," he muttered softly, as if speaking to himself. Then, louder for my benefit, he said, "Hang on a second."

He looked at his watch, grabbed his cell phone from the coffee table and rose from the couch. Dialing a number, he left the room with purposeful strides.

I tried to hear the conversation over the movie score, but all I could make out was "Damon."

When Steven returned, he said, "Damon, one of the guards, will be here in a minute. He's going to give you a ride home."

I was dumbfounded and embarrassed. I slid on my blazer and said tightly, "That's not necessary, I'll leave now and request an Uber."

"No! Don't do that." His words were rushed. "This will be easier. You'll get home faster. The car will leave from the underground parking garage and it has tinted windows…"

How nice, I thought. *I'm being thrown out by security, but at least it'll be in luxury.* I couldn't help my derisive snort.

My snort didn't seem to register with Steven. He was looking at his watch again and chewing on his lip, so I shook my head and walked to the door, determined to leave immediately.

"What are you doing?" he asked in alarm as I started to open the door. "Damon's coming."

"I don't need a ride," I said as I pulled the door open.

Poised to knock was a tall, beefy man in a black suit. He smiled at Steven and said, "Good evening. This the guy?" He gestured to me with a slight tilt of his head and a twist of his lips. "He doesn't look like a clown."

Steven bared his gritted teeth and opened his eyes wide. "Not. Now. I know I'm asking you for a favor, but that doesn't mean you get to mess with me."

So, I'm a fucking clown now, huh?

Damon laughed, clearly enjoying Steven's reaction. "Fine, fine," he said, sobering. "But, seriously, I do have to fill out a VCO form for the rig, just so you know."

"Yeah, I know," he replied. "Fill it out however you need to. If Dan or Stan need to know why, send them to me."

I was angry at this point and didn't appreciate being talked around like I was some inconvenience that needed to be dealt with. "I'm leaving," I announced. "No forms or cars necessary. Good night, Steven."

I made a move to pass Damon when Steven grabbed my forearm. "Please just go with him. It will be much safer if you do and I'll worry if you don't."

His gray eyes were beseeching, pleading. I didn't understand what was happening.

"I don't understand."

"I know, I know," he nodded. "But just do this for me, please. And call me as soon as you get back to your place."

His face and tone softened me some, but I still bristled at his treatment. Ungraciously, I capitulated. "Fine."

When Damon and I left Steven's apartment, he led me down to a subterranean garage where a fleet of shiny, black Mercedes SUVs sat in an orderly row, each having been backed into their spaces with precision.

As we approached the first vehicle in the line, he unlocked the door with the fob in his hand, preceded me to the back passenger-side door, and gestured for me to get inside. I situated myself in the seat, gave him my address on West Taylor and spent the next ten minutes alternating between anger and hurt.

Entering my apartment, I was currently in the anger phase, and in a childish pique, I closed the door harder than I should. It made a slam that was both satisfying and regrettable. I sighed.

Well, I was 0 for 2 in that building. Last time, I'd been ditched by Elizabeth, and this time I'd been thrown out by Steven. Both were humiliating, but this one hurt more. Not only did it hurt, but I bore some responsibility. With Elizabeth, there was nothing in my power I could have done to change the outcome, but tonight, I'd clearly blown it. We'd been in semi-darkness, whispering, and inches away from kissing. If his friend hadn't shown up, I'd probably be rolling around naked on that giant, shaggy throw rug, touching every inch of his skin.

I scrubbed my hand over my face and growled. With embarrassment, I replayed my words in my head.

I'm Ken, Wally's a dog. What a moron.

Are you Spanish? Who asks someone if they're Spanish?

Gah!

Steven was done with me, I could feel it. He tried to pretend like he was concerned for my safety or something but that felt like bullshit to me. Why would he worry about me? I planned on exiting his building, getting into a cab, and going home. I was a grown-ass man who took trains, busses, and cabs all over the city all the time. It didn't make sense.

But when he'd finally made eye contact on my way out…he genuinely seemed distressed. I couldn't understand what his game was. I would have preferred if he'd been honest with me instead of putting on a show of fake concern.

Call me as soon as you get to your place.

That had been a nice touch, but I was sure if I dialed right now, he'd let it go to voicemail.

The more I thought about the night, the more I wondered if what I said to Ernesto was even the problem. Maybe I'd misread him, maybe my come-ons weren't doing it for him. Yeah, I thought I detected a flash of something, but up until then, nothing had been working. He wouldn't relax into me even though I'd tried to get close. And the dog-sitting had clearly been real, not an excuse to get me to Netflix and chill.

I had to face facts. Steven was just not that into me.

But the thing was… I really liked him. He was generous and easy going and so damn cute. I got him to open up a bit about his family and allowed him to turn the conversation when he didn't want to talk about it anymore. Pushing wasn't what I wanted to do, but I had felt relief that he shared.

I'd learned quite a bit about him tonight. The apartment decor was a big tell. If I had to come up with adjectives for his style it would be elegant and eclectic. The color palette of the apartment was neutral with its starkly white couch, heather gray rug, and glass tables. At first, it would seem like it was designed to allow the view from the large windows to be the focal point, but one look at the walls told me it was all to showcase the art.

It ranged from charcoal sketches to bright pop art. Abstract to realism, prints and originals, photography and sculpture. Each was beautiful, eye-catching, and placed in such a way that seemed fluid and harmonious despite the mix.

The reaction Ernesto's picture elicited on Steven's face had been pure thrall. He'd been utterly absorbed in it for a moment, appreciating all that it had to offer, and it cemented what I'd suspected earlier when we talked about movies. Steven loved having his mind stimulated.

His film choices were ones that were thought-provoking, confusing, and of such quality that he wanted to delve into them again and again.

Looking around at my apartment, seeing the lack of consideration I'd given to my surroundings, I felt boring and listless compared to Steven. Unvaried and bland. Maybe I was too boring for him. Maybe I couldn't stimulate his mind enough.

Maybe if I'd just kissed the hell out of him and run my hand down to his dick like I'd wanted to, I could have proven that I could at least have given him one hell of a genital stimulation.

I groaned and flopped down on my couch. I shouldn't have been this upset about a guy not liking me. We'd only been on two dates, but I'd already started fantasizing about lazy Saturdays in bed, runs in the park, and bringing him to Kari's wedding. He was so magnetic and had a deceptive openness to him that invited taking him into confidence. He broached topics like money and Elizabeth—which felt slightly taboo to me at such an early juncture—with such an easy candor that I wondered why I'd ever thought it was taboo.

But I say *deceptive* because I'd seen, in his conversation about his brother-in-law, that his openness wasn't total, nor was it enthusiastically given. He'd been honest, hadn't dramatically or harshly shut me down, but his voice had gone lower, the words pulled reluctantly.

And I wanted to know him.

Still.

God, but this chasing thing sucked. Dusting myself off after setbacks was hard. I wasn't used to working this hard or putting so much hope into someone. Calling him now, after the insane way we'd ended the night, felt like an act of desperation, and I wasn't going to do it. I wasn't a glutton for punishment, nor was I a desperate man.

But…maybe I could text him. I mean, I *did* promise him I'd let him know I was safe. I needed to keep my promise, right?

Having talked myself into it, I dug my phone out of my pants and typed out a text.

ME: I'm home. Thank you for dinner.

I threw my phone down on the cushion next to me and stood up to undress, stripping off my jacket and shirt. I felt tired; in need of a hot shower and some solid sleep. Just as I unbuttoned my pants, my phone rang. It was Steven.

My heart kicked up and I took a deep breath, annoyed with myself for being so nervous. *Calm down.*

"Hello," I answered coolly, as if I weren't on the verge of tachycardia.

"You said you'd call," he said, sounding peeved.

His peevishness ticked me off, and without thinking—because if I had given even a fraction of thought beforehand, I surely would not have said this—I said, "Being thrown off the premises by a thug didn't exactly fill me with joy, Steven. If you were pissed, I wish you would have just said so instead of calling security on me like a criminal."

I rolled my eyes at myself. Maybe I *was* a glutton for punishment.

Steven let out a sigh that sounded more like a growl and said with force, "That's *not* what that was."

"Then what was it?"

"It was a chauffeured ride home," he said softly, a note of defeat lacing the words.

"Talk to me, please." Not only did I want to know everything about Steven and encourage trust, I also had little patience for grown people deflecting and dodging important and difficult conversations.

The silence stretched so long, I worried we'd been disconnected. "Steven?"

"I'm here," he said, but didn't continue.

"You can tell me anything. I'm a doctor, you know," I cajoled, trying to sound cute. "I've heard it all."

"I bet you have, McPretty MD," he replied, and I could tell he was smiling. He paused before continuing. "I'm...exhausted."

His words were an admission, a confession, said with reluctance rather than offered as an excuse.

I opened my mouth to ask if he was under a lot of stress, when he spoke up. "Did you ever make a decision that was so hasty and stupid that when you close your eyes to sleep, you could only lie there and castigate yourself?"

His question surprised me. It was much more revealing than I'd expected, and I felt sympathy for him. I knew those feelings. I *hated* those feelings.

"Yes," I answered. "When I think of shooting that woman, even now, years later, I still feel sick to my stomach, like a pit of fear and regret has lodged itself in me and wants to drain all the blood from my head."

"Damn, Ken," he laughed softly. "That's exactly how it feels."

"What's keeping you up?"

He paused again. "Did I tell you that I had a guy steal my wallet earlier this year?"

"No."

"And another guy threatened avian mass murder."

"Um, what?"

Instead of clarifying, he continued. "Then, there was that guy I told you about at the restaurant," his pitch altered, as if he were going to continue, but instead he huffed a curse. "Shit. At some point, I have to examine the possibility that it's not bad luck and these things aren't just happening to me, but that I'm subconsciously making poor decisions that put me in these terrible situations."

My feeling was that he was being too hard on himself. I loved Steven's usual confidence and ease, and the regret I heard in his voice spurred me to reassure him.

"Hey, we all make mistakes. We don't get through life without them. But sometimes, being averse to risk, is a mistake itself." I deliberated for a moment about whether to admit this about myself. *No risk, no reward, Ken.* "As someone who hates risk and loves overthinking everything, I have to say, life can be lonely when you don't take chances on people."

"Hmm." He seemed to think about it for a moment before turning the conversation. "DKM, I just realized something," he said with exaggerated surprise. "You hoodwinked me tonight!"

Amused, I asked, "Hoodwinked, huh? How'd I do that?"

"You tricked me, and I'm ashamed that it took me the whole night to figure it out." Then, softly, with mock disgust—almost as if he were speaking to himself, he said, "It's the quiet ones you have to watch out for."

This set off a round of laughter for me. I didn't know what he was talking about, but his reaction was hilarious.

"How could I have tricked you?"

"I chose the movie! Again!"

It had been an intentional choice to watch a movie he said he liked to re-watch. I didn't feel like I was there to enjoy a film, I was there to learn about Steven. I wanted to know his likes and dislikes, wanted to know what made him who he was.

"I chose both of the movies we've seen," I pointed out.

"Well, next time, I'm not saying a word. You are on your own. I'll have my poker face on, and my body language will reveal *nothing*!"

Next time. He wanted a next time. I still didn't grasp what happened at his apartment tonight, but he'd opened up and seemed to want to continue dating me. I wanted the *next time* to be as soon as possible and I wanted to help him feel better.

A plan hatched, so I asked, "What are you doing tomorrow morning?"

CHAPTER FIFTEEN

STEVEN

This morning I was giving a lot of thought to my poor judgment. Mostly because I was outside in the early hours, meeting Ken at Millennium Monument for a jog.

A jog.

Talk about poor judgment.

Who was I trying to kid? I didn't run, I didn't lift. My lean, mean body was one-hundred percent thanks to genetics. Could I have been a little more mean and a little less lean with some gym time? Yes. Was I going to probably pass out a half-mile into this run because my endurance was non-existent? Also, yes.

So why was I here? Why had I agreed to this madness? I'll tell you why. Because that sexy weirdo said all kinds of things like, *stimulation, physical release, deep breathing.*

He suggested, in that low voice of his, that I consider physical release as an escape from stress or boredom. The words, and the connotation I'd imagined (because I'm a perv), evoked images of sweaty, straining bodies, heaving breaths, and Ken's handsome visage contorted in orgasm.

He'd continued on casually, as if I weren't on the precipice of a full-blown erotic fantasy, and said, "Running is an excellent way to burn off energy. It releases endorphins which can feel like a high. I love it. You should come with me tomorrow."

He presented the idea as if it would be so much fun. At his usual time, there wouldn't be too many people on the trail, and we'd get to see the gorgeous, morning lake vista. I didn't bother telling him that I got to see the morning lake view, unimpeded by tourists and joggers, whenever I wanted from the comfort of my living room. I knew he was trying to help.

His desire to help me feel good, share his love of running, and the promise of seeing him all sweaty and windblown again spurred me to agree.

Okay, it was like ninety-five percent *sweaty and windblown*. I was a red-blooded man, after all. And just because he was straight, didn't mean I was blind. I was aware though, that this was a slippery slope. I shouldn't allow myself any time to think about Ken in a sexual way. It wasn't a big jump to go from, *Gee, he's pretty*, to *I wonder if his ass feels as tight as it looks*. And I knew I was skirting a little too close with some of the thoughts I had last night.

I'd gone to bed, set to do breathing exercises like I promised him I would do before we hung up, but kept imagining his hot hand on my body sliding sinuously up and down my torso. First, it was simply the remembrance of him feeling my abdomen rise, then my imagination started taking it further with him sneaking in a caress of my nipple on the pass and going a smidge lower—past my waist—with each breath. He'd do that several times, each time being bolder, going lower. I imagined I couldn't see his face at all, just feel his breath on me.

I finally had to shake myself out of it and give up the exercise because I'd been fully hard and disgusted with myself for going there with Ken in my brain. If I thought I'd made bad decisions about men before, those would be nothing compared with the shattering, consuming, and futile choice of having feelings for a straight friend. *That's* stupid. *That's* a disaster.

I should have begged off the run, I thought as I made my way to the monument. But as soon as I saw him standing there waiting for me, energetic and happy and so stinking handsome, I felt glad I'd come.

He was in a lightweight zip-up sweatshirt and basketball shorts, his toned, hairy calves on display. His hair was blowing in the breeze and his grin was contagious. As soon as I stepped next to him, he reached out and gave me a brief hug. The hug took me by surprise, but I managed to issue a few pats before it broke.

"I'm glad you made it," Ken said, stepping back.

"I think you have mind control powers or something because I can't believe I actually agreed to this."

He laughed. "Why, because it's early, or do you not run?"

"Both!"

"I'm sorry for the hour." He twisted his lips in sympathy. "Later on in the morning and afternoon this place"—he gestured around the park —"and the trail gets a little too packed for my liking. But it's my favorite place to run in the city. The lake at dawn and in the early hours is beautiful. Plus, it's supposed to get hot today, and I'd rather exercise while it's still cool," he explained.

"I'm glad you invited me to join you, really." And I was. In that moment, I was stupidly happy to be there with him.

"As for the jogging, we don't have to go hard. We can walk if you'd rather. Your company is a bigger draw to me this morning than the workout."

Aww, I was touched, and I appreciated the out he was giving me, but I didn't want to look like a wimp, so I said, "I'm up for it! Let's do this!" Even knowing I was probably going to be regretting that enthusiasm, I still said, "I'm ready for the cardio."

We did some stretches, where I intentionally avoided looking at Ken while he did his, just in case my eyes caught something my dick couldn't ignore. I didn't need that embarrassment. It was going to be hard enough to get through the morning without feeling self-conscious about my lack of athleticism. If I made it a mile without stopping, I'd be surprised.

We set off at a pace I was sure was too slow for Ken but was confident I could maintain for a good while. He guided us through the park and down to an entrance to the Lakefront Trail, where the view *was* beautiful, and the breeze cooled the sweat on my rapidly heating face.

Every now and then, Ken—who wasn't breathing hard in the least —would ask, "Is this pace too quick?" or "Want to go farther?" I appreciated that he didn't talk other than to check in. By the time we turned around at the Shedd Aquarium, I was sweating so profusely, breathing heavily, I couldn't have talked if I wanted to.

He stopped us once we reached the point of the trail where we'd entered. He said we'd gone over two and a half miles, and I felt elated. "That was great," I panted, removing my glasses to swipe the sweat from them. "My legs probably won't work tomorrow, but I really enjoyed this, Ken."

"I'm glad. I did too. You kept a good pace. I figured we'd use this last half-mile or so back to the monument as a cool-down." He raked his hands through the curls at his forehead. The hair at his temples looked slightly dampened with perspiration, but that was the only indication of exertion I could detect. He still looked fresh and energetic.

I was sure I looked like a shriveled tomato in comparison.

"This is my regular Sunday morning routine," he continued. "If you ever want to join me, feel free. I always start at the same place, same time. Most of the time I'll turn around at the Shedd and make my way to the river and backtrack here, but if you come with me, we can do this shortened route until you build up your endurance." He made the offer with a smile, but then seemed to check himself. "No pressure, though! Don't feel like you have to come."

I chuckled at his quickly worded assertion. "Let me see if my legs will work tomorrow, and I'll think about it."

"The offer's open."

We walked in silence for a bit, then he said, "The movie we watched last night...I've been thinking about it."

I had hoped Ken wouldn't talk about last night, because I didn't want to discuss my paranoid behavior or make any more excuses. He graciously let me off the hook with hardly any explanation, and I counted myself lucky for it. But the movie was a safe topic, and one I was interested in exploring.

"Oh yeah? Did you like it? I wondered what you thought of it."

"I liked it. I mean, it was entertaining throughout, and I was able to suspend my disbelief enough to really get absorbed in it. But…" he trailed off, deliberating his next words.

"But?" I prompted, eager to hear his takeaway.

"But the *end*," Ken breathed. He looked at me, blue eyes wide. "I was surprised by the level of emotion I felt. I realized I hadn't known what I wanted for them until it happened."

"You didn't know you wanted them to be together?" I asked. That he hadn't been automatically rooting for the lovers the entire time was surprising.

"I felt sad for him," he explained. "I wanted him to be able to preserve his memories of her and be able to move forward from there because those memories were precious. But when those were gone and all they had were recordings of themselves saying horrible things about each other, I thought, 'This is your future self—or past self, in this case—telling you the other person is a path to unhappiness.'" He shook his head as if exasperated. "I know people don't ever take good advice, especially where love is concerned, but if they couldn't believe *themselves*, then they were idiots, in my opinion."

"Isn't that the truth!?" I exclaimed in eager agreement. "People never take good advice. They always do what they're compelled to do. Which should mean you couldn't have been surprised that they chose to do it all over again, right?" I asked.

"No, I wasn't surprised that they chose each other," he gave another shake of his head. "I was surprised that when they did, I was happy and relieved and hopeful. I didn't know I wanted that for them until my eyes started welling up."

I stopped in my tracks on the sidewalk and looked to Ken's face. He was wearing a rueful, almost shy smile, like he was embarrassed by what he'd admitted.

"Wow," was all I could say.

He let out a self-deprecating huff and said, "Yeah, I guess I'm not immune to feeling sappy about love, even when the evidence is clearly showing heartache and doom."

"You're a romantic," I declared as we resumed walking.

"Yes," he said after a moment. "I guess I am."

My insatiable curiosity and unrepentant nosiness, wasn't going to let the opportunity to dig into his love life pass, so I asked, "Are you constantly in and out of love?"

"No," he answered readily. "As a matter of fact, I've not been remotely close to being in love since college."

"Oh, no," I said, anticipating a sad story. "Was she the One That Got Away?" Strangely, I didn't like the idea of Ken pining away for some college sweetheart. It seemed sad and wasteful. Not sweet or romantic in the least.

He snorted. "No nothing like that. Angie and I had deep feelings for each other, but we were young, and our paths were going in different directions. We'd known it from the start. If we'd been able to stay together, if things could have been easy, I think we would have fallen in love and made a good go of it," he explained. "But it didn't get that far and that was fine, too. Everyone else…well, they've just been possibilities. Possibilities that didn't pan out."

I was relieved there wasn't any big heartache in his past. Still, I wanted to know more.

"What would you say makes you a romantic?"

"I think it's because I'm not very interested in casual relationships. I want commitment and a true partnership. I want to put work into something meaningful, not into transient, shallow relationships."

I was surprised by his candor. He didn't strike me as the type of person who would lay his most personal dreams out for anyone to hear, and I was warmed by his trust in me.

"And no relationships since Angie?"

He shook his head and shrugged. "I've dated here and there, but things always fizzled fast. Honestly, up until now, school and work have taken up too much of my time to put in the required effort it takes to foster a relationship, so I've been single."

We nearly reached the fountain of the monument when he stopped to face me. His expression was one of sheepish hopefulness. He was back to being too adorable.

"But now," he announced. His eyes boring into mine. "I'm finally in the perfect place to make it happen." His voice was low and earnest. "I want it. I'm ready."

My stomach flipped. I felt like I was going to puke up a swarm of butterflies. *God damn it.* I was suddenly intensely jealous of whichever woman got to be the recipient of all his attention and dedication and love.

I hated her, whoever she was. I hated myself in that moment, too, because I knew I was feeling things for Ken I had no business feeling. *Never, ever, ever fall for the straight ones.* That's the best advice, and woe betide anyone who ignores it.

But, as Ken pointed out, no one ever takes advice contrary to their heart's desire.

It seemed I was well and truly fucked.

CHAPTER SIXTEEN

STEVEN

"Schultz wants to have that conference call on Tuesday, three PM Hamburg time, so that means eight AM for you," Carlos said.

I could see in my periphery that he'd only cracked my office door and poked his head inside. I acknowledged him with an "Uh-huh," unwilling to break my concentration and halt the report roll I was on. But when his words registered, I snapped out of my trance.

"Wait, what?" He'd already shut the door behind him, but thankfully heard me and came back in.

"Tuesday. Eight AM. Schultz. It's in your inbox."

Schultz was the Project Manager with the Schmidt-Fischer Group we'd presented to last week. "Who's on the call?" I asked.

"On our end, looks like you, Dan, Betty, and Rian," he said, and a lightning-quick grin flashed across his face. *Interesting…*

Rian was the woman Carlos had recently hired as an accounts manager, and I thought I detected a bit of interest on his part. Honestly, when I saw them together before her interview, I thought I was imagining things. Carlos' taste in women ran to more of the *stone-cold fox* variety. I'd never seen him give a second glance to anyone who wasn't a ten. I thought maybe he had some interest in Dan's ex-girlfriend, Tonya—I'd seen him check her out more than a few times—and gave thought to setting them up. Rian was gorgeous, to be sure, but she wasn't exactly built like his usual type. Damn, if he didn't look alert and happy whenever she was around. *Very interesting…*

"I thought it would be a good thing to let her sit on a call with one of our large, corporate accounts—just to get a feel for it," he continued. "She won't be saying much, only listening."

"Quinn's not coming in?"

"No, he's said Betty could take notes and he'd confer with Dan later," he replied. "It's just contract finalization, you know how these things go."

I bit back the urge to tell Carlos I didn't need Rian *getting a feel* for contract finalization calls. He felt we needed more manpower around here, and he was right. Getting territorial over these tasks wasn't constructive in the least.

"Yeah, thanks."

"I'm leaving for lunch, you wanna grab something with me?" he asked.

"No thanks, I'm going to work through and get this finished so I can call this week O-V-E-R." I was ready to go home and veg out. Normally, I'd be calling Kat for a movie date, or seeing what Ernesto and Paulie were up to, but the week had felt interminable and I was tired.

The good news was, there had been no further contact this week from King. No cock and balls, no vaguely sinister texts, and nothing via the postal service either. The bad news was, I'd started obsessively thinking about Ken. If I wasn't completely absorbed in work, I was either thinking about how sweet he was, all eager and weird, or wondering if his dick would be so big I'd choke on it. Then I'd descend into a pit of regret and engage in what I called *self-loathing/self-loving*. Everyone was familiar with hate-fucks, but this…*hate-yank*, was a new level of depravity for me.

To make matters worse, he'd called the night before to chat and hint around about going to the jazz club. I managed to be noncommittal, steering the conversation to how busy work was for me and before I knew it, his deep timbre was guiding me through another slow, heavy breathing session. It was like Pornhub and ASMR decided to come together to create an unholy, erotic blend that both calmed and excited simultaneously. It was absolute torture.

Once I discovered my hands unconsciously wandering into my promised land, I'd cut him off, shrieked that my toilet was overflowing, and hung up.

It was not my proudest moment.

Not long after Carlos left, my office phone rang. It was Keira at the front desk. "You have a delivery, Steven. And it looks like it's something yummy."

"Ooh, I do like things that are yummy," I replied. "I'll be right out."

The corridors of Cipher Systems were nearly empty, as most everyone had gone to lunch.

Keira was sitting at her desk and gestured to the box in front of her when she saw me. It was a familiar gray and white polka-dotted box from Plaisance Patisserie, and the smell emanating from it was heavenly. "Somebody must really like you," she teased.

"I keep telling people I'm delightful." I swept my arm down from my head to my knee and said, "It's nice to know *someone* out there appreciates all of this."

Just as I reached out for the box, a booming voice startled me. "Step AWAY from the box, Steven!"

I jerked my hand away and saw Dan moving into my space. He put a hand to my chest, his expression dire.

"You need to move back," he directed with a gentle shove. Without taking his eyes off me, he ordered, "Keira, take your lunch break now, we have reason to believe this package is suspect. It might be best if you left."

Keira scrambled to grab her purse, a flash of fear crossing her pretty features. She speed-walked down the hall toward the elevator.

I felt the blood drain from my face, "Are you serious?!" *We have reason to believe...* My heart started galloping in my chest. I hadn't told anyone about King—at least, I hadn't told anyone about his threatening behavior. But if there was a possible threat, I had no doubt Dan could have gathered the intel. His extensive experience with physical security meant his instincts could and should be trusted.

What if this is real? What if this is King?

"Did you order the delivery?" Dan questioned, pulling his phone from the interior chest pocket of his jacket.

"No." I shook my head. "But—" I began, wanting to impart that I did have some idea that this was from Ken. Dan cut me off with a swift raise of his hand to silence me as he put his phone to his ear.

I'd told Ken the night before that Plaisance Patisserie was my favorite bakery in the Loop, so this had to be from him. I didn't know why he'd send them to me, though. It was nice. Really thoughtful. But it was too much. Again, I suspected he was trying to buy my friendship. *Who would have thought a guy like him would have such terrible self-esteem?* I thought. *It just goes to show that—* My musings were cut off by Dan's words.

"Stan, I need you to bring Anzo up to the office. Now."

Oh, God, Anzo. Stan Willis was the Assistant Security Personnel Coordinator for this division and our most senior lieutenant. He'd adopted Anzo, a retired TSA bomb-and-drug-sniffing shepherd not long ago. If Dan thought we needed Anzo up here, he must either be paranoid, or have genuine reason for this level of vigilance.

No, this was crazy. The box was from Ken, it was full of tasty bites of heaven and there were no drugs or bombs hidden inside.

"Dan, smell it," I said, scoffing. "It smells exactly like the sweet treat it is."

He scowled. "Yeah, well, DNT smells like sweet treats too, Steven. Do you think we should risk the whole floor blowing up?"

Shit. I didn't know what the hell DNT was or how powerful it could be. I opened my mouth to agree that utilizing Anzo was probably a good idea, but Dan interrupted, obviously assuming I was going to argue with him again.

"You know what?" he said testily, his Southie accent thickening. "Why don't you go stand your ass around the partition and let me do my job?" He pointed to the left hallway which was about twenty-five feet away from Keira's desk.

"Fine," I grumbled and walked to the other side of the room.

We stood in tense silence for a minute or so when I had an idea. "We could call the bakery and verify they delivered it."

I thought it was a simple solution, but Dan got snippy again. "Steven! I got this, alright? Stay calm!"

Just then, Stan emerged from the elevator with Anzo on a lead and trotted toward the desk. He issued a few sharp, unintelligible grunting commands to the dog, along with some hand gestures. Within seconds, Anzo rose up on hind legs, sniffed the box, and dropped into a seated position, his eyes never leaving the box. He gave one loud bark and Dan yelled, "We need to evacuate the building!"

He waved his arm, urging me to move quickly. Stan and Anzo broke out into a sprint toward the elevator. I caught up with them and we all got in. My heart was racing in panic, but I suddenly had the presence of mind to shout, "Wait! We need to make sure everyone is off this floor!"

I made a move to exit the elevator, intent on pulling the fire alarm, but Keira stepped in front of me, appearing out of nowhere.

I gaped at her. She lifted her phone and I could hear the clicking of her camera taking frame after frame of my face.

They all began laughing uproariously. Bewildered, I looked around the elevator at their smiling faces. Even the damn dog looked pleased with himself.

A joke.

A fucking joke.

"You should see your face right now, man," Dan said, hand on chest, struggling to catch his breath. "I-I told Stan you'd never fall for it. I was sure you'd tell me to go fuck myself. Oh my God. I love bustin' your balls."

Without a word, I gave them each a glare—scathing and promising retribution—and made my way back to the desk to collect my box, all the while feeling their eyes on me and hearing their snickers of waning mirth.

I lifted the lid and discovered an array of—what I estimated to be —fifty, gorgeous, colorful macarons. They were courtesy of one

McPretty MD—the name made me smile despite myself—who said he hoped these would make my Friday sweeter.

This fucking guy, I thought in exasperation as I scooped up the box. I turned to head back to my office when Dan spoke up from the end of the hall.

"Hey, I forgot to tell you something." His smile was as large as I'd ever seen it. He was maniacal with glee.

This fucking guy…

"What?" I asked impatiently.

"Quinn wants to see you in the data center ASAP." I dropped my head in exaggerated despair, which sent Dan into another fit of laughter. "Good luck, man."

"That's it!" I yelled, half-serious in my anger. "No macarons for you! Any of you!"

* * *

"Those better not be for Janie."

I'd taken two steps into Alex's Lair—AKA, the data center—when Quinn started in on me.

Confused, I looked at the box of macarons in my hands and then back at him. I probably should have taken them to my apartment before I made my way here, but that would have taken me longer, and I was eager to get the meeting finished.

The fact that he'd gone on the attack because he assumed these were for her, ramped up my already simmering anger. I bit my tongue because, not only was he *Boss Man Level: Mute Meets Rude* and kind of scary, but he was also going through a very difficult time. I liked and respected Quinn and I adored Janie, so I felt a lot of compassion for what they were going through at the moment.

However, if I were honest, this version of him was wearing on my last, raw, exposed nerve and didn't inspire much in the way of openness. I'd come up here toying with the idea of talking to him about King—thinking I needed to rip off the Band-Aid and let him lambast me.

After Dan's practical joke, I'd gone back to my office completely rattled. It had been a shitty thing to do to someone, but I knew if Dan had known about King, he wouldn't have subjected me to that fright. That thought forced me into some introspection I'd been avoiding. For a moment I'd considered that I had received an explosive package, and it wasn't out of the realm of possibilities.

I wasn't an alarmist, by any means. A dick pic and a couple of Kinnears did not a terrorist make. But I *was* more worried about the situation than I allowed myself to admit. If I was worried and I thought in that one moment I was in real danger—danger, that was going to have serious ramifications for others in my sphere—then I needed to admit I had a problem.

I wasn't the only one in those pictures. Yes, I was the focal point and no mention had been made by King about Ken, but he was there. He saw him. If there was even the slightest chance Ken was in danger, I needed to tell him.

Not only did I owe it to him out of simple decency, but I also needed to stop this thing that was happening between us. I was being wooed and pursued for friendship and it was strange. It was also confusing because my heart and my dick wanted it to be something else entirely.

The madness had to end. I needed to tell him about King and get him out of my life, no matter how much I wanted him in it. It was for the best and any other course would be selfish and destructive.

With that decision made and this terrible task on the horizon, I was in no mood for Quinn's neurosis and acrimony. His immediate criticism and censure slammed the door shut on any confession. I wasn't going to give him more reason to dislike me.

Plastering on a smile, I held the box higher. "Don't worry, these were not en route to the penthouse. They're mine," I explained, lifting the lid. "Would you care for one?"

Without answering or sparing a glance at the cookies, he said, "My goal is to upgrade data retention from the cameras to 120 days. I want you to figure out what that's going to cost."

Out of some perverse sense of defiance, I turned to Alex. "Would you like a cookie?" Alexander Greene was Cipher's cyber genius, and in my opinion, the biggest asset the company could have. Cryptography and cost-analysis didn't co-mingle very often, so I wasn't privy to his day-to-day activities, but I did know that our ability to provide superior cybersecurity to our clients was because Alex was one of the most talented and intelligent hackers in the world.

"Yes," he responded plainly, and pulled a green one from the box. He examined it.

"Pistachio," I said. "Classic."

He took a bite and appeared to be thoughtfully assessing the flavor. Aware of Quinn's silent seething beside me, I prolonged the cookie-tasting by asking Alex what he thought of it.

"It's unusual. I've never had a cookie like this."

There were a lot of things Alex never had growing up. From what I knew of his childhood—foster homes and detention centers—I figured macarons weren't ever on his menu. He always struck me as being a delightful dichotomy. He was, if it was even possible, both guileless and cagey. Eager and reluctant. Young and old. It was hard to come up with a label for Alex as he was layered and fascinating. But as his attractive level, he was a *Hipster Meets Rebel*.

Setting the box on the desk next to him, I said, "Have as many as you want."

To Quinn I asked, "Do you want this for future clients, or are you doing this for every camera we run?" I furrowed my brow, thinking of the exorbitant cost of upgrading every licensing agreement. We oversaw thousands and thousands of cameras, some of which monitored low-traffic areas. Those cameras already archived ninety days.

"Every camera," he replied.

I turned to Alex and asked, "Is this difficult to do?"

He swallowed what was in his mouth and shook his head. "No. It's a simple call to the company and changing the agreements. We use the option for full-footage redundancy with storage both on the device and in the cloud. Each camera can be set to archive for different durations."

"Which means all of our cameras that aren't currently retaining 120 days will get a cost hike?"

"Yes."

I scrubbed my hand through my hair and thought about the added expense. It wasn't an insignificant hike. This company that Alex had us using was innovative, integrative, and *expensive*. He could view live feeds of any one of our thousands of cameras at any time, from any of his devices. He'd been impressed with their cyber protection and knew they offered state of the art technology for facial recognition. Another bonus was that the per-camera licensing meant we could save money on some cameras and use others to their full potential.

I didn't say what I was thinking, which was that it was an unnecessary expense. I wasn't hip to the day-to-day surveillance needs, but I couldn't imagine that four months of archival footage was ever going to be necessary. I didn't say it because surveillance wasn't my area of expertise.

What *was* my area of expertise was money, so I asked, "So are we going to eat it in the short term?" I shook my head. "This has to get passed on to the clients as soon as possible. I can't let this screw with my bottom line," I quipped.

Quinn didn't appreciate my input. "It's not *your* bottom line, it's Cipher's," he snapped. "If I say I want full-footage redundancy on every last camera, then that's what I'm going to get."

I flinched. I hadn't said we shouldn't do it. Yes, I *thought* it. But I hadn't said anything about not doing it.

"I'm just trying to do my job, Boss Man," I defended.

"Then do it. Make it work." He strode to the door, and without looking back he said, "Figure it out, it's what I pay you for."

This fucking guy.

CHAPTER SEVENTEEN

STEVEN

Not long after I'd walked into my apartment, my phone rang with a call from Kat.

Without so much as a hello, I whined, "Honey, darling, love, I can't bear to go out tonight, let's stay in and watch something." Kat and I often took in a movie on Fridays and we hadn't seen each other in weeks. Truth be told, I didn't relish company, but it was preferable to going out. It would have been perfectly fine with me if I didn't step foot out of my apartment for the entire weekend—I was that drained.

"I wasn't thinking about a movie," she said. "I'm coming to visit Janie for a while. Elizabeth said Quinn's driving her crazy and that she'd enjoy some company and distraction."

"Oh, that's a good idea," I replied, relieved. I loved Kat and she was an easy companion. I never felt like she was here for mental gymnastics or energy vampirism. I didn't have to be 'on' for her and I appreciated that. Even so, basic conversation felt too much for me. If she wanted to spend her Friday night up at the Peevish Penthouse with the Surly Sullivans, that was fine with me.

"I'm on my way up, would you like to join me?"

I'd rather stab myself in the eye with a rusty fork. "Thanks, but I've already had the pleasure of Quinn's charming company today. I'm good." An idea suddenly came to me so I asked, "Will you stop by here on your way up? I have something for you."

I still hadn't given Kat or Janie the cheese I'd brought back from Germany last week. Not only was this the perfect moment to give Kat hers, but I was going to be a sneaky sneak and get Kat to deliver Janie's.

It was a slightly crappy thing to do to my poor angel. As soon as she walked in, Quinn would subject her to an interrogation and a parcel search. It was fine though, because A, Kat was a tough cookie, B, Quinn would be so much nicer to her than he would me, and C, everything in Janie's box was up to the standards he had set, and had been double checked by Dan.

So, no big deal, see? Kat would be fine.

Even so, when I opened to find said angel, her big, gorgeous eyes blinking so trustingly at me, I felt a twinge of guilt.

"You need a drink first," I said quickly, taking her hand and leading her to the kitchen.

"But—" she started to protest.

"Believe me, you really, really do," I insisted. I led her to the granite-topped island where the round, wooden gift boxes of cheese sat.

"Oh!" she breathed. "Is this what I think it is?" She reached out and caressed the top, lovingly tracing the faux-burnt logo of the cheese shop.

"It is," I confirmed.

With both arms, she pulled the stacked boxes toward her and embraced them in a hug.

I laughed, enjoying her exaggerated worship, but I warned, "Only one is yours. The one on the bottom is Janie's."

"That's nice, she'll love it."

"Your mission, should you choose to accept it, will be to deliver that cheese to Janie this evening."

She eyeballed me suspiciously and drummed her fingertips on the box. "Why don't you do it?"

"'Cause I don't wanna!" Petulantly, I thrust my chin forward and stamped my foot. I could only hold the ridiculous expression a mere second before we both laughed.

"That bad, huh?" she asked. I nodded slowly. "Okay, I'll do it."

"God bless you, child," I kissed her hand then proceeded to pull out two shot glasses from the cabinet.

"I don't need a drink, Steven."

"Yes, you do." I poured two shots of tequila and slid one toward her. "Think of this like a Kamikaze pilot taking his meth right before flight." I gave an inward wince at my wisecrack. Kat wasn't a teetotaler by any means, I knew she and her knitting posse enjoyed their Tuesday cocktails, but Kat had a past with reckless drug use I knew she regretted. I didn't want to bring up any painful memories for her or make her feel bad.

Luckily for me, she laughed, unoffended. "Gotcha." She tilted her head back and sucked the shot down. Her face screwed up into a grimace and she said, "Oh my."

Following suit, I said, "Yeah, that's the stuff," and banged my fist against the counter. "Care for another?"

Once the heat of the tequila hit my insides, I felt keen for more. *Maybe I'll get shitfaced tonight.* Maybe I'd put on some acoustic emo music and let myself wallow in maudlin longings. I'd eat macarons, shoot top-shelf liquor, and have a few hate-yanks in order to avoid dealing with Ken. Yeah, I wouldn't deal with him, I'd just sit and obsess about him all night. *Great plan, Steven.*

"No thanks," she replied. "I'm headed to Boston in the morning for a meeting with the board. The last thing I need is a hangover." Kat's grooming for her eventual inheritance and responsibilities meant she had to prove to the powers that be within the company that she understood all aspects of the business. She had a lot on her shoulders, and I didn't envy her one bit. "Besides," she continued. "Janie's expecting me, so I should probably head up." She adjusted her purse on her shoulder and hefted the boxes up. "Thank you for the cheese, you are the best!"

She held the boxes somewhat awkwardly and I worried they might be too heavy for her. "Do you need help?"

"No, it's fine. I got it."

"Are you sure? Because I bet Dan wouldn't mind helping you carry them." I winked. "I could call him…"

She shook her head quickly, "Don't do that! I'm fine. It's one floor." She sounded a little panicked by the idea. I hadn't been serious, only trying to joke with her. The way those two acted when either one was mentioned was like they'd been zapped by a cattle prod, especially since Dan had broken things off with his girlfriend a few months before. I didn't get it, but I held out hope they'd stop pussyfooting around.

"Calm down, nervous Nellie, I'm just kidding with you." I opened the door and said, "Give Janie my love and tell Quinn Dan inspected the cheese."

As we said our goodbyes, my phone chimed twice.

UNKNOWN: stop blocking me i miss you lets have fun
UNKNOWN: answer me when i call

My heart kicked up, startled because just as I finished reading the second message, my phone rang. The same number from the texts flashed on the screen. This had to be King.

"What do you want?" I answered angrily. I *was* angry. I was so pissed that he'd laid his hands on me and so livid that he'd made me afraid for myself, and for a few moments, my friends and coworkers. It didn't matter that he'd had nothing to do with the prank, but just knowing that the real and palpable fear of that possibility wouldn't be in my mind if he hadn't started doing this—whatever *this* was—to me, was infuriating.

"Please don't be mad," he said, his voice even. There was no hint of the menace and rage he'd been emanating when he'd been here. He sounded…*jocular*, and that was more enraging than if he'd answered with obscenities. Who the hell did he think he was, trying to be friendly? *Fuck this guy.*

"Fuck. You."

"Give me another chance, okay?"

Chance? Chance to what? Beat the shit out of me? Rape me? Kill me? "Call me, text me, or send me one more thing and I'll go to the police," I threatened.

"But you didn't even give me a shot. I know we'd be good together. I know I was too rough, but you had me so *hard*, baby." He spoke low and rough, infusing intimacy into his voice, no doubt hoping to take this into obscene caller territory.

"Not happening. Again," I asserted, "if you contact me, I'm getting the authorities involved. Piss off."

"Don't—" he began, tone angry. I disconnected the call and blocked this new number of his. How many times could he change numbers? Or phones? I needed to change my number, that's all there was to it.

Standing in the quiet stillness of my apartment, with the echo of his voice in my head, I felt the memories of King flooding back to me. He'd kissed my neck as I'd unlocked the door, his hands digging into my quads, all the brimming impatience cresting. I'd hardly got the door shut before he'd pushed me against the wall and knocked the keys out of my hand. I hadn't been alarmed by that point, just excited. But his kiss had been painful, almost a grinding of our faces and I hadn't liked it, I turned my face to the side. "Whoa," I cautioned, intent on slowing his roll. He stepped back a fraction, but immediately tore my shirt, causing the buttons to fly. The movement jerked me, angered me. "What the hell!"

The disturbing memories were interrupted by the sound of a text alert.

DKM: I've been thinking about you. I know you've been busy, but I'd like to see you. Maybe a few drinks and some jazz would be a great way to unwind. Are you free tomorrow?

I felt a sharp pain behind my eye. *Maybe I'm having an aneurysm,* I thought. Ken was going to be the sweet and shiny cherry on the stroke sundae I was eating.

This fucking guy. Those fucking macarons. That fucking jazz. Ken was like a damn mirage. *Unicorn Level: Look But Don't Touch Meets Completely Fictional.* I'd done something extra heinous in a past life, I was sure. Karma was really bending me over this time around. *Oh, you're trying to escape man-troubles? Too bad sucker, we're sending you a kind, smart, sexy heterosexual to torment your ass with artless benevolence and buns of steel.*

I downed two more shots, discarded my shoes and flopped down on the couch, letting the alcohol work its magic. *Oh, magical agave, give me strength!* I needed to call him. I had to tell him about King—at least, what was important for him to know. There was no getting around that. Maybe if I embellished, maybe if I made it sound like there was imminent danger to me, he'd bail. Then I wouldn't have to try to extricate myself from him. If I did, I'd fail. Even now, I wanted to hear his voice and tell him that I'd love nothing more than dinner and jazz and drinks and conversation with him.

With frustratingly sluggish movements, I dug my phone out of my hip pocket. My mind was clear, I knew what I needed to do, but my body felt like moving my weight to the side took herculean effort. *So damn tired.* All I had going for me right this moment was liquid courage and an obligation to be honest about potential dangers. I just hoped it would be enough to scare him off.

CHAPTER EIGHTEEN

DKM

I didn't always shower at the gym, but when I did, I missed phone calls. It was just the way life worked. My phone could be silent all day long, but as soon as I step in for a five-minute shower, it blows up.

I had four missed calls and three voicemails from Steven's phone. My first thought was *emergency*. It wasn't like Steven to repeatedly call when sent to voicemail. There was nothing about his personality that was anxious or demanding, so my instincts told me there was a problem.

I wanted to dial him back immediately but decided it would be for the best if I listened to the voicemails. There was the possibility that he wasn't in a position to talk and I needed information.

Still wet and naked except for a towel around my waist, I stood in front of my open locker, intently listening to the first message.

"DKM, I'm going to leave this as a message, which I suppose is really for the best. I mean, if I talk to you, I'm going to say all sorts of weird shit that I didn't mean to say, so…"

He trailed off, his voice subdued. His tone and his lead-in were a bad sign. This had all the markings of a break-up call. I lowered myself to the metal bench behind me. After a short pause, he continued.

"Oh! I need to say thank you for the macarons. They're soooo

damn delicious, I'm eating one right now. It's the one with the choco-late ganache in the middle. Those are my favorite."

The garbled way he said 'favorite' indicated that he was, in fact, eating. I smiled in spite of myself.

"So, the thing is, you know how I told you about all the really bad dates I've had and how I was worried that the one crazy guy was at the restaurant with us?"

"Sort of," I said aloud, like an idiot. He'd briefly mentioned a couple of strange men but hadn't gone into enough detail about them to suit me.

"Yeah, well, he was and I—"

The voicemail beeped and cut him off.

"Shit," I said softly, playing the second message. My takeaway from his slightly rambling message was that the red-haired, mentally disturbed man *was* at the restaurant with us, as he'd suspected. I didn't feel good about that, and clearly Steven didn't either.

"Shit, sorry! I guess I need to speak faster. IHaveAVeryDangerous-StalkerAndYouShouldn'tBeFriendsWithMeAnymoreBecauseHeCould-HurtYou."

He took a breath and continued.

"He's batshit crazy, muscular, and mean as hell. Run far! Run fast! You don't want another Fancy Stalker situation, so shoo! I'm changing my number tomorrow. Have a nice life."

He clicked off, and I sat in stunned silence as the automated voice prompted me to delete the message or listen to the next. Numbly, I selected the last of his voicemails, my naked skin developing goose-bumps despite the oppressively humid air of the locker room.

"Wow, I'm such an asshole, I just realized how panicked you might be. Ugh, fine! I don't really think you're in danger. At least not yet. But it's only a matter of time before he gets the wrong idea about us. God, Ken, I have the wrong idea about us! You need to find other straights to hang out with, because if you think you can hang with gays and not make all of us crazy for you, you're out of your damn mind. Take your fun jazz nights and chiseled jaw and hit the bricks, mister."

There was a brief rustling sound, then his voice sounded far away. *"There, that oughta do it,"* and he disconnected.

"What the *hell?!*" I boomed, my voice echoing through the room. Several men murmured and cast me annoyed glares, but I was too stunned to care.

Other straights? I have the wrong idea about us?

Everything about those messages was alarming. He wasn't speaking with his normal ease, he'd been genuinely distressed. That he suspected he had a stalker, was chilling. That he thought he needed to push me away to spare me the danger, was both infuriating and sweet. That he thought I was straight, and we were just friends? That was the screwiest part of all of this.

We were *dating.*

I made a big, embarrassing, *I'm ready for love* speech on Sunday.

I sent him fifty macarons for god's sake!

You should have kissed him, asshole. Youshouldhavekissedhim, youshouldhavekissedhim, youshouldhavekissedhim.

Go! Kiss! Him!

With haste, I put my shoes on, grabbed my bag, and made to leave, intent on going to Steven. At that moment, my loosened towel fell to the floor. I looked at it in astonishment, then huffed out a self-deprecating laugh.

Show up buck naked, Ken, Steven will think he has two crazy stalkers.

Given how I felt in that moment, how unhinged and fixated I was, one could think, *maybe he does.*

Maybe he does.

CHAPTER NINETEEN

STEVEN

I woke to my phone emitting a low, irritating, clacking judder on the glass top of the table. My eyes popped open, glasses still on my face. It took a moment of disorientation before I comprehended that I'd dozed sitting up. The waning daylight in the apartment was proof I'd lost several minutes, but not much. From my laptop, the sounds of Foxing crooning, *I swear I'm a good man, I swear I'm a good man,* meant I was only a few songs into my playlist of heartache.

I grabbed my phone and flailed a hand to my laptop beside me, slapping the space bar to cease the music.

The front desk was calling.

"Hello," I rasped. My dry mouth tasted of cookie, tequila, and regret.

"Mr. Thompson, this is Lawrence. I have Dr. Miles down here to see you, should I send him up?"

I opened my mouth to answer but stopped myself. Did I want him here? Did I want to have this conversation face-to-face? No and no. But did he deserve that much after the train-wreck of voice messages I left him? Yes, he did. I hadn't handled it very well, said some mean, and downright embarrassing things, and I needed to be an adult about it. Still, I hesitated.

"Mr. Thompson?" the concierge prompted.

"Yeah, Larry, sure," I replied. "Send him up."

"Will do. Have a good night."

I closed my laptop and switched on the lamp in the corner. I wasn't ready for the glaring light of the overhead fixture and figured a little dimness for this conversation would serve me best. I estimated I had, at minimum, forty-five seconds until Ken showed up, so I busied myself by erasing the evidence of my pity party. I stowed away the macarons and laptop and chugged a glass of water so hurriedly, the liquid overflowed the cup and ran in rivulets down the sides of my chin and on to my button-up. "That's just great," I muttered, swiping at the dark spots.

Expecting Ken to knock at any second, I stood in the entry. Resigned and determined. We'd talk honestly, no histrionics, no alcohol-fueled rambles, just the straight dope. I needed to keep my resolve when I was staring him in the eyes—in those hypnotic, glittering orbs of temptation. *Dammit! Don't be swayed by the sexy eyes, ignore the cleft in his chin, and whatever you do, do* not *get side-tracked by his Adam's Apple.*

When the knock came, it was loud and impatient. As an indicator of his mood, it was accurate. He stood on the threshold just long enough to connect his eyes to mine, then barged past me into the living room.

He had a gym bag slung on his shoulder, which he dropped with a *thunk* onto the floor. He was wearing black track pants, sneakers, and a white undershirt that fit over his muscles with obscene adhesion.

I took my sweet-ass time following him the half-dozen steps. *If his nipples are showing through, you're a dead man walking, Thompson.*

As I faced him, I was surprised to see his slack expression had turned turbulent. His chest was rising and falling rapidly, nostrils flaring. He unclenched his jaw to speak, but no sound emerged. And damn, that goozle in his throat decided to do an alluring, little dance, rippling with unspoken words. His body told me he was angry and agitated, but his eyes, they were…beseeching? Tormented? I couldn't say.

"Ken, I," I began, but he closed the distance between us quickly, and brought his chest flush with mine. When the soft warmth of his hand and slow advancing of his face registered, a new frisson of aware-ness suffused my body. But for the millisecond between our chests touching and his hand cradling my jaw, I thought this was aggression and I jerked back instinctively.

Ken noticed my jerk and seemed to quickly change tactics. He pressed his forehead to mine and whispered, "Kiss me."

Without a thought, I closed the small space between our mouths and placed my lips on his. It was the permission he needed, and he tightened his hand on my head, pulling me deeper into the kiss, which turned hot and forceful.

And praise be Thor and his giant tool—it was *delicious*. We ate ravenously at each other's mouths for a moment before my brain came back online.

How is this happening!? My hands, which had found their way to his hips, floated up and hovered in indecision near his biceps.

Ken slowed the kiss, pulled back slightly and grasped my wrists. He guided my hands to his chest—*I knew those nipples were poking out!*—and took the kiss deeper. His tongue slid against the seam of my lips, demanding entry. When I relented, he groaned, wrapped both arms around me, and pulled our bodies together.

The slide of his wet mouth on mine, the invasion of his hot tongue, the insistent prodding of his rapidly thickening cock against my own, spurred me into action. My blood pumped fast and my breathing became shallow. I gave a sinuous grind of my hips to feel the friction —to show him I was as hard and eager as he was.

Ken's mouth separated from mine to let out a deep groan of anguish and delight. Gratified, I gave another slide of my groin and was rewarded again with a low moan. He attempted to bring his mouth back to mine, but I grabbed a fist full of his hair, and pulled his head back gently. Staring into his desire-hooded eyes, I kept up my grinding, driving us both crazy with the motion that was nearly too much plea-sure, but not coming close to enough.

In the quiet dimness of my apartment, the rhythmic swishing of track pants pumping against trousers and our labored, choppy breath, created an erotic soundtrack. The sensations and the sounds must have been swamping him because he groaned again and slid his eyes shut. I didn't want him to break the contact, so I tugged harder on his hair and demanded, "Look at me, Ken."

When he did, I asked, "What the hell are we doing here, huh? This is insane." My words might have seemed like I was second-guessing, like I wanted to stop and parse this all out, but my tone was rough and raw, and my hips were grinding our cocks together harder. I didn't want to stop. I didn't want Ken to stop either. I wanted words, though. Any words. Dirty words, sweet words—even angry words would have been fine. I needed to hear how affected he was by me, to have spoken evidence of how much he liked what we were doing. I wanted to know he was engaged in this act with me.

His lip curled in a sneer as his hands found their way to my ass. He squeezed and said, "What's insane is that you're so clueless."

My hand loosened from his hair and he took that opportunity to reconnect our mouths in a blistering, carnal kiss. Without breaking contact, he walked me backward to the nearest wall. When my back touched the solid surface, he pulled away, reached an arm behind his head, and stripped off the T-shirt in one fluid motion.

I marveled at the smooth expanse of his torso. His erect nipples and flexing pectorals were as dangerous as I suspected. *You're dead, Thompson. His nipples killed you and now you're in heaven.*

He set to work rapidly undoing the buttons of my shirt. When he opened it, he grasped my undershirt roughly, "This goes too, damn it, I need your skin."

I quickly divested myself of the shirts, eager to press our hot skin together. When we did, we moaned in unison.

"Steven," Ken whispered as his mouth met mine. We kissed for minutes? Hours? Days? I had no idea. I was swept up in the need for more. More heat, more friction, more Ken. His smell was enveloping me, his taste was infusing me, the radiating passion was making me lose touch with time and space. We were hovering, suspended in sensation.

Eventually, he pulled himself away slightly and said breathlessly, "Take your cock out for me."

I felt my shaft get impossibly harder with the demand. I couldn't move fast enough to get my belt and pants undone. Just the thought of his big hands on me had more excitement escaping from my tip. I shoved my pants and underwear down just low enough to expose me.

Ken groaned again, his eyes transfixed on my jutting dick. He rubbed himself through the material of his pants as he reached for me with his other hand. I hissed at the contact, my eyes shutting of their own volition. Again, it was too much and not enough.

"You're so hot, so smooth and hard." With a squeeze and a pull, he marveled, "You're *long*." He twisted his grip as he reached my head, smearing the precum partway down my shaft. I let out a curse, pumping my hips for more.

"Show me yours," I ordered, chokingly. I could hardly speak through the pleasure that was consuming me. Any other time I would have cringed at the lame words. *Show me yours*. But in that moment, it was what I wanted, plain and simple. I needed him to let me have him as he was having me.

Without breaking his hold on me, he pushed the front of his waistband down under his balls, causing them to jut upward. I reached out and smoothed my palm up and down the underside of him before squeezing the shaft tightly.

Ken moaned and watched my hand for a moment before repeating in a raspy tone, "I need your skin." He adjusted so that our cocks touched. He pulled mine down, rubbing our heads together, blending our silky fluid.

"Look at us, Steven," he said. "Nothing has ever looked so fucking hot as my cock rubbing on yours."

I silently agreed. I was on the brink of coming from the combination of sensual assaults. It was incredible. He was incredible.

He shifted again to line up our undersides and gripped our cocks in his right hand. We pumped our hips in earnest then, both of us chasing our orgasm. With my hand, I explored our heads and parts of the shafts he wasn't touching.

I glanced up to see his face screwed into a grimace, signaling he was close. I was close too and wanted us to come together.

"Fuck, Ken, come," I spurred, reaching lower to tug on his sac. "I want to see you shoot all over me." He grunted, my words clearly having the right effect. "Yeah," I encouraged. "Make a mess of me, of both of us." That did it. With a shout and firm jerky motions, he was letting loose. The sight and the sound sparked my own, and I spent myself.

I was glad the wall was to my back because I would have lost my balance. I was wrung dry.

Ken released his hold and panted out, "Are you up to speed now? Because if not, I've got more where that came from."

CHAPTER TWENTY

DKM

Huh, I'd rendered Steven Thompson speechless. *Well done.*
He was leaning against the wall, his mouth agape and his softening cock still hanging out of his pants. His glasses were slightly askew, his hair messier than normal.

He looked beautiful. I wanted to burn this memory into my brain and never forget that I'd had this effect on him.

I tucked myself back into my pants and said, "Let's get cleaned up a little. Then I want to talk to you."

He swallowed and nodded. "Yeah, let's, uh, do that." He raised his arm and flicked his thumb toward the hall. "The bathroom is back there on the left."

Once we had tidied, I made myself at home on the couch, slouching and spreading, conveying an unapologetic confidence I didn't feel. It was important to me that Steven understood what my motives had been from the start—that I had no regrets and hadn't blown my load all over him on a whim. How *he* felt about all of this was a mystery, therefore my confidence was pretty shaky.

When he joined me, he had two opened beer bottles in his hands. He'd put his undershirt back on and buckled his belt. He still had a slightly dazed afterglow. *Again, well done, Ken.*

"Here," he handed me the beer and sat. "I don't know about you, but I could use a drink, McPretty." He sighed.

"What happened to the 'MD?'" I asked, infusing my voice with humor. "I didn't spend thirteen years of my life to be just a regular McPretty."

Without looking at me, he smiled. "Yikes, sorry. Let's blame it on the hand-job, okay? My thought processes have been temporarily compromised."

I wasn't sure how to segue into conversation, so I opted for bluntness. "So much is making sense now," he nodded slowly in agreement, still looking forward. "I guess my dating attempts were too subtle, huh?"

Steven huffed out a rueful laugh and shook his head. "It's pretty damn obvious now." He was pensive for a moment, then whipped his head to look at me, his eyes wide. "Hey! You were so totally coming on to me with that breathing shit, weren't you?!"

"Absolutely," I agreed. "If Ernesto could have waited five more seconds, I would have had my tongue in your mouth."

He muttered softly, "What a cockblocker."

"And you thought what? We'd just be friends?"

"Well, yeah. I thought you were straight." He laid all his splayed fingers on his chest and said, "I'm clearly *awesome*—"

"A *delight*," I interjected.

"And I thought you could use a friend—that you needed some help socializing."

I felt my face bunch up. I didn't bother smoothing it over or keeping the rancor from my voice when I said, "I have friends, you know. I'm not completely pitiful." I was stung by the thought that I'd been a pity project for him. I might not have had a lot of close friends in Chicago, but I had casual friends I met up with when I could. For instance, there was Jeremiah and Mike. I met up with them occasionally, mostly for racquetball. Of course, they'd been residents at Chicago General and I hadn't played with either of them in months. Alright, so I didn't surround myself, every spare minute, with people. So what? I was busy.

I was also lonely. And Steven, with his stupid x-ray vision, saw all of that. Of course, he had.

"Whoa, hold up," Steven said, raising one hand. "Don't take that the wrong way. *You* called *me*. Romance didn't occur to me as one of your motives. What else was I supposed to think?"

I didn't want to fight, I just wanted to know we could move forward. "Alright, fine. But you don't want to be only friends, right? That's what you meant in your message?"

He shook his head, his gray eyes sparking with feeling. "I can't be just friends with you. It's not possible."

Relieved, I set my beer on the table and twisted to kiss him. It was intended to be quick, but as soon as our lips met, the kiss turned hot. Steven fumbled to set his beer on the table without breaking contact. When he did, both of his hands found their way to my hair, gently tugging with every swipe of tongue.

I pulled back after a moment, intent on finishing our conversation. "Wait, wait, we need to settle some things."

Breathing hard, he said, "If you want me to focus on conversation, you need to scoot back." He turned his head away from me and held his palm out. "Your face in mine short-circuits my brain."

I smiled. And rather than scooting back, I raised my hand to interlace our fingers. "I'm not moving, and you're going to jazz with me tomorrow night," I declared. "It will be a date, I will pay." At this he snorted. "Maybe if I'm lucky, I'll get a good night kiss."

Still facing away, he muttered. "You'll get a kiss all right…"

I hated to turn the conversation, but we had to talk about the other thing.

I brought our laced hands down to rest on his leg and rubbed my thumb on his. "Tell me about this stalker."

CHAPTER TWENTY-ONE

DKM

W hen I arrived at Steven's apartment on Saturday, I felt nervous in a way I hadn't before. For one thing, I had a fantasy build-up of this jazz night, to the point where I almost wished we'd scrap it and do something else. For nearly two weeks, the imaginings of it had been playing on a loop in my head—soft lights, entwined fingers, the air charged and swirling with heady promises fueled by music and alcohol and physical awareness. I was afraid I had too much invested in this night playing out exactly that way.

That Steven opened the door and surveyed me with an open appreciation and hunger he'd never shown before, helped to strengthen those expectations and fantasies. His bold assessment of me and languid movements were seductive. It drove home just how off-key we'd been before now. He'd *never* communicated attraction so blatantly, so invitingly to me. Seeing what I'd been missing, what he was like when everything was open and possible, cemented to me that I'd been too guarded in my communications as well.

No wonder he hadn't a clue I was into him. Had I ever looked at him and said what was passing through my mind? *You look sexy. I want to kiss you.* Or, *Let's hold hands for the movie.* Had I ever given him brazen, lustful looks of appreciation all the times I noticed how well his clothes fit or at how disarrayed his hair was, or even how his sarcastic quips fired me up? No. I'd stupidly been too guarded and worried about being judged.

Well, that was over. Starting now, I was going to make my intentions crystal clear.

"Damn, you look so hot, I can't wait to peel you out of those pants."

Or I could be a creepy perv. Nice move, asshat.

Without missing a beat or acting at all shocked, he chided, "Now, now, you promised you'd buy me dinner first."

I felt a blush heat my cheeks and he laughed. "You're too fun." He grabbed the lapels of my jacket and pulled me in for a quick kiss. As he retreated, he said, "You look nice, too."

Steven was wearing snug, dark-wash jeans, a belt, and a gray, fitted button-up. The color highlighted his eyes, and his long, lean frame was accentuated by the cut and fit of the outfit. It was an understated pairing that did its job to perfection.

Seeing how simple and effortless his attire was, I rethought my choice of tie and blazer. I was trying too hard and it showed. The tie had to go.

"I'm going to take this off," I announced. I shoved the tie in my jacket pocket and undid the first two buttons of my shirt.

"Either way, you look gorgeous," he said with a wink. "Should we go?"

* * *

Though Club Tremolo didn't require reservations for dinner, I hadn't wanted to risk loitering in the bar for an hour waiting to be seated. So, after I left Steven's the night before, I called to request a table away from the stage. I wanted to make sure we could converse and enjoy our company without too much interference from the music.

When we arrived, the hostess led us to a small table a good distance from the stage. Ambient light shone down, and the scheduled quintet was playing an upbeat number. I watched Steven as he took in the atmosphere of the club.

I wondered if his scanning of the room was purely out of appreciation for the club, or if he were trying to spot this 'King' douchebag in the crowd. I hoped it was the former, because I wanted him to enjoy himself tonight and, if just for a few hours, leave his enormous stress load behind. But there was a part of me that wanted to know he *was* concerned and using some vigilance. The conversation we'd had the night before about it had been him warning me of dangers, while simultaneously trying to convince me there was no threat.

He'd shown me texts from three different numbers—one of which was a picture of a dick—and some out-of-focus pictures of Steven when we'd gone to dinner together.

So, see, it's just been some texts and pictures. No threats.

I didn't feel nearly as calm or optimistic about this as he appeared to be. I was scared for him, honestly. Someone in their right mind, and with good intentions didn't change their number or switch out phones to keep contact with someone who blocked them. Sending pictures to prove he was following, *wasn't* benign. These were fear tactics. Fixation and intimidation.

When I asked what had happened when they went out, he told me that when he'd brought him to his apartment, the man wasted no time in being rough and impatient. Steven tried to slow him down, get him to ease up, but that only resulted in going from rough to violent. Apparently, his building's conspicuous security gave the man pause and was enough to deter him from taking his plans further.

Steven's building *was* obviously secure, even to someone who wasn't paying much attention. The doorman allowed entry via thumbprint, the lobby had several guards stationed at various points, and the concierge was anything but lax in his own duties. Upon leaving last night, I'd made it a point to scan for cameras. There'd been dozens of domed fixtures that could have been concealing cameras. Knowing that Steven was falling asleep in such a well-protected place, made it easier for me to leave him.

I just wished I'd been able to convince him to alert his boss about it or go to the police. But he'd adamantly refused, saying there was nothing anyone could or would do at this point, so there was no reason he needed to spill his private business to anyone, least of all, his employer.

He'll murder me and toss me in the lake himself! No thanks.

I didn't like it. I didn't agree that there was no danger. I'd seen firsthand what could happen when fixation turned violent—how someone could shut out the entire world and just give over to a focused, intense rage. I'd yelled, I'd fired—neither of those had penetrated her mind. She wanted to hurt, she wanted to kill, she wanted to release all her psychosis and hurt and jealousy and hatred right on to Elizabeth. And nothing was going to stop her.

I had to shoot her.

Thinking of Steven in the same position, imagining him at the mercy of anyone who was as single-minded in their destructive rampage as Menayda Kazlauskas was, terrified me.

I'd do it again.

Looking at his face, watching his eyes dart around the room, I felt a peace about the shooting. I grabbed his hand resting on the table and held it, causing him to direct his attention back to me.

"Have you ever been here before?" I asked.

"No, have you?"

"Once, probably two years ago. I liked the food and the trio that was playing was sensational. I told myself I'd come back again, but never managed to. I'm glad I could be here with you."

He flashed me a genuinely happy smile. "Me too." He opened his mouth to say something, but then looked over my shoulder and pulled his hand away.

A waitress stopped alongside the table and greeted us. She took our drink orders and stepped away. We smiled at each other across the table and I prompted, "What were you—"

I was going to ask what he'd started to say before the waitress appeared, but she whirled around and stepped back to the table, interrupting again.

"I forgot to get your starter order. Would you like an appetizer?"

We hadn't looked at a menu or barely had a chance to say a handful of words to each other, let alone decide on a starter.

She was looking at Steven, so he said, "What do you rec—" but I didn't appreciate the rush so I put the brakes on.

"We just sat down and haven't looked at the menu. We need more time to look over the selection." What I said wasn't rude, but by Steven's arched eyebrows, I could tell my tone was less than pleasant. I quickly checked my manners and said, "Please."

"Sure, I'll get your drinks and give you a few."

When she left, Steven said, "Grumpy Ken returns, huh? I'd wondered where he'd gone to."

"Sorry, I didn't intend for that to come across as rude, but I didn't want us to be rushed. I'd like to draw the night out if I can," I explained, leaning in on my forearms. "I've been thinking about this date with you and, well, when I get something built up in my mind, I can be a prick when it doesn't work out like I planned."

He laughed sharply, as if he were surprised by my admission.

"It's a defect that runs in my family," I continued. "My sister is the *absolute worst*." I rolled my eyes, then smiled in a way I hoped was inviting and charming. "Feel free to give me a reality check whenever I get too unbearable."

"Ooh, I look forward to it." He rubbed his palms together in exaggerated anticipation. He then rested his forearms on the table and mimicked my forward posture. "So, do you just have the one sister?"

"Yeah, Kari," I replied. "She's thirty-five."

"Hey, our parents all love alliteration, it seems. Ken-Kari, Steven-Sophie," he pointed out. "Sophie is older than I am, too. But just by a year. I'm thirty-three. How old are you? I know you can't be as old as thirty-five."

"Thirty-one."

Our server came back with our drinks and Steven picked her brain for recommendations, being extra nice and animated with her, most likely trying to make up for my earlier snappishness. We ended up ordering a bacon and brie starter and when she left, I decided to sow some seeds for later down the road since we were on the topic of siblings.

"My sister is getting married the last weekend of October."

"Here in Chicago? Are you from Chicago? I can't believe I haven't asked you that yet."

"No, we're from Cleveland, but she's getting married on Mackinac Island up in Michigan."

"In the Hotel?" he asked excitedly. I nodded. "Before you go, we'll have to watch *Somewhere in Time* with Christopher Reeve. You'll hate it."

Ignoring the movie comment, I said, "Maybe by then, you'd like to be my date?" I inwardly chastised myself for the unintentional inflection I put on the words. They weren't meant to be a question, but rather, something for him to consider later. I didn't want to put any pressure on him or make plans for us so far into the future that I could get hung up on or build outrageous expectations around. The truth was, I had a lot of hope that three months from now, we'd still be seeing each other. And if we were, it would be weird *not* to bring him. If I felt this way after a month of knowing him. I could just imagine what I'd feel after four.

"You're really a go-getter, aren't you, DKM?" He sounded a bit bewildered.

"When it comes to dating, no, not really. But for other things, yes," I explained. "The wedding is going to happen. I have to be there. I thought I'd present the possibility to you so you could think about it."

"Oh, I'm going to think about it, alright," he muttered.

"I don't mean to pressure you or anything," I quickly added, sensing I'd crossed a line.

He raised one hand to stop me. "It's fine. I knew you were an intense guy. I just didn't realize what it would feel like to have that intensity focused on me."

His heated gaze locked with mine in unspoken awareness, revealing his own simmering ardor. It was a look rife with earnest intent and eager reciprocation. I could almost hear him thinking, *Bring it on, Dr. Miles. Bring it on.*

I was definitely going to bring it.

* * *

Okay, what am I bringing, exactly?

Climbing into the cab broke the spell of the club and dissipated a lot of the easy confidence I'd been luxuriating in throughout the night.

We'd enjoyed the jazz as background music through dinner, so engrossed as we were in the fluid conversation. It wasn't until our plates had been cleared away, that we lapsed into a natural lull to focus on the entertainment. The night had so far been all that I'd hoped it would be and more.

But, with the coolness of the outdoors and abrupt cessation of our soundtrack and rhythm—the absence of murmuring diners, clinking dishes, cymbals and trilling saxophone—I was hyper-aware that *next* was *now*.

As the car pulled away from the curb, Steven examined me. "You have that thing going on with your face again."

"What thing?" I asked.

"The thing where you look like a cyborg or android whose switch is in the off position."

"That's…I don't know what to think of that."

"Think about this," he said, and leaned into my ear to whisper. "You. In my bed. All night."

I felt heat rush to my face and my dick twitched. He pulled back to smile at me. "Yes?"

"Yes," I rasped. I wanted that. Wanted it so much, but I was afraid to get my hopes up.

Did I want hours and hours to lick and suck and explore? Did I want to know his every bend and bulge, ticklish spots, and erogenous zones? Did I want to spend the evening in orgasmic bliss? *Hell yeah, I did.* I had a pocket full of flavored condoms at the ready for just such a fortuitous occasion.

But all of that meant I was going to have a discussion with him I was apprehensive about starting. It needed to be done, I just didn't know what his reaction was going to be. Would he be annoyed or irritated by my lack of experience? It's not like I couldn't navigate my way around a penis or anything, but I knew I was in uncharted territory and hoped he had the patience for it.

Steven pulled me from my musings with a soft curse.

"Shit." He was looking ahead to the front of his building as we approached the circle. Nico and Elizabeth were exiting and walking toward an idling black SUV. "Don't pull up close, wait until they pull away," he instructed our driver.

"I've got other fares, you know, I don't have all night to wait around," he complained, but still stopped the sedan just inside the circle.

Steven dug cash out of his wallet and laid the bill on the man's shoulder. "Here's a twenty. It will be two seconds."

"Steven." I issued him an incredulous, wide look, momentarily taken aback by his behavior.

As the cars started forward, he explained, "Do you really want to have the night interrupted with awkwardness and glares from Nico? Because I don't." The car stopped and he opened the door. "Let's not make this weird."

I followed him out but stopped on the curb. Ready to tell him I didn't give a shit what Nico thought, he stepped to me and brought his mouth to mine. The kiss was hot and brief, ending when I tried to take it deeper. He pulled away and asked, "Can that be the reality check I give you when you get all cranky?" Without waiting for my answer, he said, "I look forward to your bad moods and might deliberately provoke them."

"I think that's a good plan," I agreed, pacified.

We made our way through the lobby and into the elevator and when the doors shut, my earlier concerns rose again. "We need to talk about some things first," I blurted.

"Of course," he said readily, unsurprised by my loud declaration. "This talk is what had you suddenly uptight in the cab?"

"Yes." I rubbed my hair, then my eyes, frustrated with myself already. "I-I just don't…I'm not great at segueing from 'I had a great night' to 'Let's get naked.'"

Steven scoffed. "You seemed pretty sure of yourself last night when you were demanding I take my cock out for you."

I flushed at the memory, heat suffusing my body. "That was different." And it *was* different. I'd come to him full of anxiety and urgency then. There had been no real forethought, no planning. Dates were a whole other ball game from spontaneous passion.

"Besides," I said as the elevator doors opened. "It's not just the segue that I'm not sure how to navigate, it's the conversation about…expectations."

Steven's brows pulled down in confusion. We didn't move for a moment, each of us staring into the other's eyes. Him trying to make sense of my words and me trying to wordlessly communicate. But nothing was getting solved that way, so I walked out of the car and stepped into the hallway of his floor.

"Let's go inside. I know I'm not making sense, but we can't talk about it here."

After we entered the apartment, he flipped on a lamp and said, "Tell me what you meant by *expectations*." He crossed to the couch, sat down, and rested his elbows on his knees. "Are you talking about establishing a no-strings thing, or is this about whose penis goes where?"

I joined him on the sofa. "I think you know I want more from you than a hook-up," I huffed out a rueful laugh. "No, what I meant by *expectation* is that I know you probably think I have some set rules about what I like or what I was going to do, but my experience with men has been limited."

His face and body seemed to still, absorbing my meaning. "You haven't been with a guy before?"

I couldn't tell if that was a pause of disappointment or surprise or what, but I needed to lay the cards out. "Not…fully," I ended on an exhale.

Understanding dawned and he relaxed. "Oh. Okay, so you've been with men, just not penetrative sex, right?"

"Yes, so, I'm not set on any certain way or anything. I'm open to experiencing all of it with you, but I might need your patience."

"Holy shit," he whispered, shaking his head.

"Is that okay? Is that a *good* holy shit?" I honestly couldn't tell.

"Oh, the sexy unicorn wants to know if I mind showing him the delights of man-love," he muttered to himself, staring toward the inky blackness of the windows.

"I take it we're cool then?" I smiled expectantly, even though he wasn't looking at me.

"Life is really bizarre," he continued in a whisper, blinking hard.

"Steven." I raised my voice a bit, hoping to penetrate his ruminations.

He stood suddenly, grabbed my hand and hauled me up. "We're going to the bedroom. Now."

"Oh, good, I was worried I wouldn't get a chance to *Bring It*."

Without looking back at me, he said, "You're such a weirdo sometimes, DKM."

CHAPTER TWENTY-TWO

STEVEN

"I can get us out of this, if you want," I said, looking past my own reflection in the mirror to Ken. He was standing slightly behind me, fiddling nervously with a few errant curls on the top of his head. The man looked gorgeous, and I couldn't find fault with his hair or his outfit, both of which seemed to be causing him stress.

How he could fret about his appearance was a baffling mystery to me. His tall, hard, frame meant clothes—off the rack—fit like they were made for him. It didn't matter what they were, either. Scrubs—sexy. Preppy polo and slacks—sexy. Suit and tie—sexy. Jeans and T-shirts—sexy. Sweatpants and compression shirts—sexy as fuck.

Don't even get me started on his birthday suit...

Standing next to him, examining both of our reflections side by side, I felt a twinge of insecurity. Usually, a disparity in physicality wouldn't bother me. A few inches in height or even several pounds difference in either direction, was never anything I cared about. But with Ken, it wasn't just a matter of a couple of inches and a couple of pounds. It was also brighter eyes, stronger jaw, straighter teeth, fuller lips, shorter nose. And—god damn it, something I did not want to think about—*thicker* hair.

For a couple of light-eyed, blond men in their thirties, we couldn't have looked more different.

Discordant.

These were feelings I didn't have on the regular. When I looked at him, I felt happy. When I looked at myself in the mirror, I felt content. I loved how Ken looked and I recognized my own unusual assemblage of features were attractive in their own way. Plenty of men—Ken included— let me know the sharp face and lithe body was a turn-on. No, I had a good grasp of my own appeal.

I just wondered if, to the outside, we seemed mismatched.

In the mirror we did.

From the inside, we didn't. From the inside, we felt harmonious.

Ken stopped messing with his hair and connected his eyes to mine in the mirror.

"Babe, for the seventeenth time, I want to do this. I want to know your friends."

I smiled at the use of the pet name. He, unlike me—who barely ever called him by his real name, preferring a multitude of cutesy and bizarre terms—didn't feel very comfortable using them. *MST3K* was abandoned after the first attempt, and he said *Honey* reminded him of his grandmother, so he only busted out the *Babe* occasionally.

In the three weeks since our official first date, he'd only really used it as a softener to preface a slight scolding. *Babe, I don't care which one is McSteamy or McDreamy. Babe, we don't have time for round two, I'm going to be late for work. Babe, I'd rather contract bacillary dysentery than watch this dancing show.*

His use of the word now meant he was tired of me overthinking our night out tonight. We were meeting Ernesto and Paulie for drinks. I hadn't been keen on the idea, but Ernesto had been insistent, and Ken had been enthusiastic. My reluctance was obvious, and I suspected it was starting to annoy Ken. I didn't want him to think I wanted to keep him apart from my friends, but... I kind of did.

We were in a bubble of awesome right now. Exploring each other, learning how to navigate this new relationship, feeling giddy twenty-four hours a day—these were things I didn't want to alter.

I didn't want Ern planning group nights out yet, I didn't want them to grill us or put pressure on us to admit or confess things, and I sure as hell didn't want any judgment.

I sighed. Ken looked miffed, like I'd hurt his feelings. I didn't want that. It was the opposite of what I wanted.

"Okay, McPretty, but you have to promise me something." I turned to face him.

"What?"

"You have to promise me that when Ern gets all presumptuous and obnoxious and asks you what your intentions toward me are, or if you make enough money to keep me living the lifestyle to which I'm accustomed, you won't get offended, angry, or scared off."

His annoyance evaporated and he laughed. Shaking his head, he said, "I promise."

"It's only been three weeks," I pointed out. "Getting the third degree from friends seems like something for later down the road. Much later."

"I disagree. The sooner I meet them, get to know them, and let them get to know me, the better for all of us." He kissed the tip of my nose and gave my ass a light slap. "Now quit worrying and let's go."

* * *

Reason #564 of why I was less-than-thrilled about Ernesto's plans: We were meeting in the same club on Halstead where I'd first met King during the bar-crawl. For all I knew, I was walking into one of his regular haunts.

Something told me, though, that the venue didn't matter. If he had decided to continue following me—because I *knew* he had to have followed us after the movie last month—he could show up regardless of where we went.

Those last three weeks of July had several, closely-spaced contacts from King—from the dick pic and text, to the photos, to the phone call. But after I'd threatened to involve the police and I'd changed my number all had been silent. Crickets for three weeks and it had been fantastic.

Between the silence from King and the dizzying heights of being with Ken, I'd almost forgotten that I was ever concerned about the man. And it wasn't until Ernesto texted me a couple of hours before that I'd thought about risk.

ERNESTO: Paulie wants to dance. He wants to go to The Magnificent Male.

I almost mentioned it to Ken but decided to let it go because I figured King was a thing of the past. Besides that, I didn't want to argue with Ern and Paulie over where to meet, and I could tell Ken was already taking my reluctance for this night personally.

So, I sucked it up and hoped for the best.

As the cab pulled up to the club, I scanned the sidewalk, checking for King lurking around. Ken exited the car and stared up at the sign of the club which was a giant replica of the street sign for The Magnificent Mile on Michigan Avenue, but with the I on Mile switched out for an A.

"This is awful," Ken said pointing to the sign. "I'm embarrassed for them."

I laughed, "Don't be. See how busy they are? They're doing fine. It's we who have to look ourselves in the mirror and ask the hard questions like, 'where was my self-respect?'"

He smiled and patted my shoulder. "It's not that bad once you get past the cringey sign."

"Wait, what?" Was he implying he'd been here? This place was a total meat market.

"It's nice inside," he said, shrugging.

"*I'm not very interested in 'casual,'*" I mimicked with sarcasm, playfully throwing his words back at him. "Have you been putting me on with this whole Innocent, Corn-Fed Choir-Boy persona?"

"I never said I was a choir boy." He smiled impishly, then became serious. "I *don't* want casual, but sometimes, that's all that's on the table." I nodded, understanding exactly what he meant. "Besides, it was only a couple of times. I don't love the air of desperation that bars have. And when I go, I'm in this space where I'm flattered and given a lot of attention that's a complete lie. No one is truly interested in *me*.

After the third guy who couldn't be bothered to learn my name, I stopped going to bars."

It was tough out there for those of us wanting relationships, and I sympathized. I was just about to say that those men didn't know what they were missing, when he stepped into me and gave me a hug.

His hug was long and sweet, and slightly awkward there on the sidewalk, where people were having to swerve around us. But I didn't break it or speak, instead letting him have his moment. When he finally pulled away, I asked, "What was that for?"

"Because I know how lucky I am to have you. I almost didn't go to Botstein's party. I almost skipped it." He took a deep breath and exhaled slowly. "I almost missed you."

I wasn't often at a loss for words, but Ken left me speechless. He was always so….*sincere*. He was standing outside of a busy, raucous, ridiculously named club where no one was taking anything but fun seriously, and he was effortlessly exposing his heart. It was a weird spot to have this kind of moment—or for him to have this epiphany or whatever, but maybe it *was* completely appropriate. Maybe standing still on this dingy sidewalk, the calm center of a storm made up of manic revelry and shallow connection was the most impactful situation to say, to realize, something special was between us. Something that almost wasn't.

I opened my mouth to say something—because I always had something to say—but nothing was appropriate, nothing was good enough. If I made a sarcastic joke like, *almost only counts in horseshoes and hand grenades*—which was on the tip of my tongue—it would spoil the significance, and I didn't want to do that. I didn't want to ruin it, but I also couldn't think of anything that could come close to being as sweet or honest. I didn't know how to preserve the moment, so I kissed him.

I used my mouth to convey all the feelings I couldn't put into words, I used my arms to squeeze him tight to show him I was relieved —relieved he'd gone to Botstein's, relieved we'd met. I hoped he understood, I hoped he'd feel me saying *I know, I know this is rare and special and could just as easily have never been.*

I kept the kiss going for long moments until I felt a tap on my shoulder and heard a loud throat clearing. Ken and I separated to find Paulie standing next to us expectantly.

"Oh, hi, Paulie," I said, giving him a smile.

"Ernie wants me to tell you that if you don't want to have to sit on the sticky floor, you'd better get in there. He's having a hard time saving your seats."

Imagining Ernesto in there fighting tooth and nail for four in-demand chairs, spurred me into action. "Yes, right! We'll come in now."

We made our way to the ticket window, paid the cover, and had our hands stamped in rapid time. As soon as we walked through the door, Ken linked his hand in mine. I gave it a squeeze.

When we found Ern, he was draped across three chairs, yelling at a guy who looked to be tugging on one of the backrests. I couldn't hear what anyone was saying, but Ern was pointing his finger, first at the man, then at the seat, then at Paulie, who had taken his own seat next to the one Ern's feet were occupying.

Paulie stood up, the man turned around and disappeared. Yikes.

As soon as Ern spotted us, he sat up and exclaimed, "Thank *fuck!* I almost had to use Paulie as a *weapon!* He's a *pacifist!*"

Paulie sat down and shook his head, a small smile playing on his lips. He was a quiet guy, reserved. To anyone who didn't know him, they'd probably label him as shy. But he really wasn't shy, he just didn't talk a lot, preferring to let Ernesto fill the silence. It was no surprise that Paulie was a model and Ern, a photographer. They'd met and Paulie posed quietly while Ern kept up a monologue of instruction, praise, and natter. In that way, they were perfect for each other. Really, they were perfect for each other in a lot of ways.

I introduced Ken to Paulie and he shook hands with both of the men. He was wearing a big, happy grin, and for a split second, I felt guilty for trying to weasel out of this.

"I'm going to get us all some drinks," Ernesto announced. "Now, you guys get to guard my chair." He rose, took two steps, and a man hovering nearby, turned to us. Ern saw the movement and yelled,

"Paulie!" Paulie lifted his booted feet and plunked them down on Ernesto's vacant seat, deterring the man from approaching.

"Geez," I shouted over the music. "It's like the last round of musical chairs at a kid's birthday party in here."

"I know," Paulie said. "I came to dance, but I don't think I'll be able to get Ernie to leave the table. He's like a bulldog tonight."

"We'll get you out there, don't worry," I promised.

And, we did, eventually. It took a couple of rounds of drinks and some seriously hardcore puppy dog eye communication from Paulie to Ernesto for the latter to relinquish his hold on the conversation and the possession of the chairs.

While they were gone, Ken and I managed to lose one of the chairs. In fairness to me, it happened when my attention was turned to the *third* man who'd come to ask Ken to dance. How was I supposed to protect Paulie's chair when I needed to guard my man, too? I could only do so much.

When the would-be man-stealer walked away, Ken turned to me with a half-apologetic, half-smug smile. "It's going to happen," he shrugged.

"Conceit isn't a good look, McSmuggy, I—" I lost the thought when I noticed the missing chair. "We're dead meat!" I shouted. "Look! Paulie's chair is gone!"

"Oh, shit."

"Yeah," I agreed. We were in for it.

As soon as I saw Ernesto's face register the missing chair, I threw Ken under the bus. "It's his fault!" I pointed at him. "His face made the chair disappear!"

Ken gaped at my betrayal.

Ernesto, who seemed to comprehend my meaning, didn't let me off the hook. "You need to learn how to multitask! Do you see who I'm married to?" He pointed to Paulie, whose tight, sweaty T-shirt was clinging to his ripped abs.

"Calm down," Paulie said, dragging the remaining chair closer to him. "I've got something you can sit on."

Ern gasped, pretending to be scandalized. Paulie sat down with his own smug grin and pulled Ernesto to his lap.

"Whoa," I held my hands up. "That is my cue to go fetch another round. Feel free to use this time to chastise Dr. McPretty for his substandard chair-guardianship."

I stood, and Ken grasped my hand. I thought I might find irritation from my jokes etched on his face, but he was grinning widely, clearly enjoying the banter.

"I just want water, please. I'm running tomorrow," he reminded me, rubbing his thumb along my knuckles. Ken had a half-marathon in September he was conditioning for and wanted to spend tomorrow morning running a 15K.

Impulsively, I bent down and brushed my lips against his. When I straightened, Ernesto had a gleam in his eye, "I'll come with you."

When we made our way to the bar, I tried to get the attention of a bartender, but neither of them acknowledged me. Ern, unconcerned with the lack of service, dove into conversation.

"He's really into you, I can tell."

"I'm really into him, too," I replied absently, still trying to flag down a server.

"Damn. Everyone is, it seems. We can't leave those two alone for a second."

I tore my eyes away from the bartender closest to me to glance back at our table. Sure enough, two men were chatting up Paulie and Ken. I couldn't see Ken's face, but I could tell he was shaking his head. Smiling, I refocused my effort on getting us some drinks. "Excuse me, barkeep!" I was ignored. Again.

"That's probably going to happen a lot," Ern warned. "I have to deal with it all the time."

I looked at him, and not for the first time wondered how he managed to cope with the attention Paulie received. It wasn't only that Paulie was startlingly handsome and fit, it was also that Ernesto wasn't what most people would consider good looking. He was on the shorter side and slightly paunchy. I personally thought he was a cutie, but I conceded that I mostly felt that way because I was drawn to his magnetic warmth and engaging personality. Ernesto didn't get second looks—not like Paulie did. I never asked because it wasn't my business, but now he seemed to be wanting to impart some of his wisdom to me, so I took the bait. "Is it a problem?"

"At first? Yeah, I broke up with him like five times over it."

"What?" I was shocked. I didn't know any of that had happened.

"Okay, so the break-ups lasted like twenty minutes," he admitted. "But the point is, I made so much drama over shit Paulie couldn't control. He finally said, 'You either want to be with me, or you don't. What do you want?' I decided I couldn't let my fear keep me from being with him. So here we are."

"Married," I said pointedly.

He laughed. "Yes, Paulie is persuasive. But I'm just trying to tell you not to worry about the men."

"And the women," I added.

He waved his hand. "So, he's passing? Big deal. Paulie is too. Who cares about the ladies?"

"Ken does. He's bi." I watched as Ern's face fell.

"Oh, well," he said after a moment. "There's nothing wrong with having fun then." The words had a forced breeziness, and I kicked myself for opening my mouth.

The bartender chose that moment to take our order and when he walked away, Ern faced me, his mouth turned down at the corners. All breeziness gone. "Look, I don't need to tell you why this is a bad idea. I can tell you really like him, just make sure he's not using you to experiment with, okay? You deserve better than being toyed with by some confused frat boy."

I opened my mouth to defend Ken against the accusation. He was a grown, professional, honest person, not some immature coward and didn't deserve to be reduced to that when Ern didn't know him at all.

Ernesto didn't let me say my piece, instead, he cut me off. "I know, he's not a frat boy, but my point is that even if you do have a relationship with him, eventually…" he shrugged, letting the sentence hang.

We stood in a silent eye-war until the moment was broken by the arrival of the drinks.

"Here," I said through clenched teeth, thrusting two of the drinks at him. "Take Paulie his shot." The bartender had forgotten the water, so I had an excuse to separate myself from Ern for a few moments. He took the drinks, his frown deeper than before, and walked off without a word.

Eventually... I knew what he meant. He meant that someday a woman would come along with her boobs and womb and Ken would accept that invitation happily, ready for a picture perfect, heteronormative life.

I shook my head at this. What was I supposed to do? Live like Ern had before Paulie gave him his come-to-Jesus talk? Scared and suspicious? No thanks.

I looked at the bartender, made eye contact, but he turned away. God damn it! "What's a guy gotta do to get a fucking water around here?"

"I'll get your water, baby," a voice rasped in my ear, lips touching the shell.

I flinched away from the contact, but the man pushed in closer.

King.

King whatever-his-name-was, stood against me, his groin to my hip, his legs nearly straddling me. I could smell the alcohol on his breath, but underneath the alcohol, I could smell his scent, which flooded me with flashes of memory from the night in my apartment.

Reflexively, I shoved him. "Get the fuck off me!" He budged, not by much, his groin was still pressed against me, but his chest was no longer touching me. The people nearby looked curiously at us but didn't seem concerned.

"I know you came here to see me," he said, happily, smiling like a lunatic. "As soon as I saw you walk in, I knew you wanted me to see you."

"You're crazy, I—" I attempted to step away, but he crowded me into the bar, the edge pushing into my ribs.

His smile dropped. "Trying to make me jealous with that guy wasn't smart," he cut me off, voice low and menacing. "Don't try to hurt me unless you want me to hurt you back."

CHAPTER TWENTY-THREE

DKM

When Ernesto came back to the table, he plunked down two shots next to Paulie. "Here." His voice was tight, threaded with irritation.

I looked at him and found his eyes fixed on me in a glare. *What the hell?* Was he mad about the guys at our table? We sent them along without issue. I felt bad for Paulie if Ernesto was this jealous.

Except, he wasn't glaring at his husband. All his ire was aimed at me. Confused, I turned around to see if I could gauge Steven's mood. What I saw was his face stamped with anger as he shoved a man away from him.

I stood up quickly and made my way to him. The man, who was practically on top of him, crowded him into the bar. A flash of distress crossed Steven's face, galvanizing me to all but tear the man away from him.

I pulled his collar roughly as soon as I was within arm's reach. "Back *off!*"

The man stumbled. A good look at his red hair and stocky build, and I knew this was King. If anything, this realization enraged me further.

He followed him here.

He *touched* him.

I took advantage of his stumble and inserted myself between Steven and King. "Stay away from him," I shouted. I wanted to be heard over the music, but also to show I wasn't messing around. I didn't know if it would work. If my brief encounter with Nico's stalker was any indication, forcefulness didn't always work as a deterrent. I braced myself for an unhinged attack.

For one moment, the man's face screwed up in rage, but the second his eyes connected to mine, his demeanor changed. The transformation from tense and confrontational to subdued and apologetic was light-ning fast, and it confused me.

My own muscles stayed bunched, ready for a fight, even when he stepped backward and lifted his hands in a pacifying, defensive gesture.

"I don't want trouble, I just thought he might want a drink," he said, taking another step backward.

I felt Steven's face next to mine as he leaned over my shoulder. "Fuck off," he snarled.

King looked from me to Steven, and his surprised expression turned sad. "I just wanted to be friends with you." His eyes came back to mine and he repeated, "I don't want trouble."

"Then get the hell out of here. Now." I gestured to the door and took a threatening step toward him.

He hesitated, his eyes flicking from me to Steven. He seemed to be weighing his choices and measuring the two of us. After a moment, and without a word, he walked away.

I watched his back, making sure I saw him leave. Once he had, I turned to Steven, who was watching his exit as well.

He sighed, bringing his eyes to mine. I couldn't tell what he was thinking but we held contact for a long minute, until he reached over to the bar, downed a shot he'd ordered and said, "I'll order us a ride."

* * *

We didn't say a word to each other until we got back to the apartment.

I wanted to talk in the cab, but too much eye-contact from the driver in the mirror, too-little eye-contact from Steven and the rigid set of his jaw, put me off any conversation. After accidentally looking in the rearview mirror and getting a wink, I turned my attention out the window and stewed in silence.

But as soon as we walked into the apartment, Steven laughed bitterly. "Well, that was a barrel of laughs, wasn't it? I'm so glad we went." He tossed his keys on the side table and walked through to the bedroom without so much as switching on a light. I was hot on his heels.

"I think you need to talk to your boss now," I said as he turned on one of the bedside lamps.

"DKM, you were so magnificent. Such a knight! My strong protector!" His voice held such an exaggerated enthusiasm, it could have only been pure sarcasm.

I bristled. "Are you seriously pissed at me for coming over?"

His shoulders slumped. "No, no. I would have done the same if the situation were reversed. But, I'm not helpless, I'm not weak, and I sure as hell wasn't afraid of him."

I knew he wasn't helpless or weak, but he'd looked afraid, I'd seen it in his face. I didn't know if he was trying to convince me or himself.

"I know you're not, Steven, but I'm not going to stand by and let you fight your battles alone."

"He's not even scary," he continued, as if I hadn't spoken. He wasn't looking at me, but instead, busying himself by pulling the comforter down on the bed. "Did you see how he just cowed down as soon as you put yourself between us? He's a pussy." He tossed one sham to the floor and grabbed another. "He was a pussy when he was here, and he was a pussy tonight."

I took the pillow from his hand and stepped in front of him, encouraging eye contact. "But he followed you tonight. That's not okay."

Steven raised his eyes to mine and chewed on his bottom lip. "No," he said with a sigh. "He didn't."

"How do you know?" I didn't believe him. I thought he was trying to downplay the threat again.

"Because..." He swallowed. "Because he said he thought I came there to see him. He was already there." Steven grimaced, shutting his eyes tight, then peeking at me out of one, like he was going to confess something terrible. "It's where I met him."

"What?!" My voice boomed, echoing in the quiet room.

"Shh," he demanded, grabbing the front of my shirt. He pulled me in and pressed our lips together. I didn't pull away, but I didn't want to let him deepen the kiss. It was a blatant ploy to shut the conversation down and I wasn't having it.

But then he swept his tongue against my lips as his hand grazed my cock. I groaned and he took that opportunity to slide in. The synced strokes of his tongue and hand felt so good.

One kiss, I promised myself. I'd let him have one kiss, then we'd talk.

But the kiss never ended, it turned into neck sucking and belts unbuckling. When my brain came back online, we were naked, lying in his bed and Steven was partially on top of me, licking the crease of my upper leg.

He's really good at distraction. I made a mental note. I'd need to remember this someday. His lips and hands and skin had me operating on a basic, primordial level that was wholly centered around sensation. But I needed to wake up my higher brain functions and bring us back to reality.

"S-Steven," I choked out.

"Hmm?" He hummed in question as he nuzzled my balls with his nose.

"Wait, we," I let out a groan when he licked the puckered skin of my sac. "Shit, Steven, we really need to stop and talk about this."

He raised his head and looked at me. His eyes, without his glasses (which I had no memory of him removing) had an obvious lust-fog quality to them, like he didn't quite comprehend what I was saying. They looked soft and sweet. But then my words penetrated, and he shook his head. "What's to talk about? The blowjob you're about to get?"

I huffed out a laugh, but my traitorous dick twitched eagerly at his words. "Not the blowjob. Your boss."

He growled, put his face down into my groin and let out a muffled, "No!"

The sound vibrated my balls. I moaned and grabbed my shaft. *That felt good.*

My moan encouraged him. He took one of my balls into his mouth and applied a gentle suction. I gave another firm pull on my cock, reveling in the heat of his mouth.

Minutes later, I tried again, fighting the libidinous pull. "Steven." He hummed again, this time making my entire body jolt. "N-nothing," I rasped. "Continue."

He lifted his mouth from me and laughed, the lines around his eyes and mouth crinkling adorably. He rose up on his knees and made a show of stroking his own shaft. His hair was in need of a cut and messier than usual and I loved it.

"I'm glad you're finally onboard, DKM."

"Oh, yeah, I am," I moaned. I was fully onboard. Conversation could wait. I watched him work himself with one hand while tugging my sac with the other. I loved his body. He had an abundance of light, springy hair. His pubic area was trimmed short, and the hair continued in a trail up his torso and across his chest. I loved it. I loved the natural hair, the unashamed masculinity of it. My own was sparse compared to his, and lighter, too. I'd wondered what he thought of my smoother chest, whether he liked it or wished I was hairier like he was, but those thoughts disappeared quickly because he was always touching it and looking at it and telling me he was dead from it. Or maybe that was just my nipples. I've been told my nipples have killed him.

Steven stopped the motion of his hands, then used his considerable reach to lean to the bedside table. He grabbed a bottle of lube, laid it next to us then rose above me for a deep kiss while he ground his cock into mine, his gyrations quickening.

I groaned in delighted frustration. I wanted more friction. Needed more.

Steven stopped his movements, rose to his knees again and maneuvered my legs farther apart. I heard the *snick* of the lube lid opening and tensed. *Was he going to fuck me?*

We hadn't done that yet, hadn't talked about it. But as soon as the thought came to me, I was excited. *Yes.*

It was on the tip of my tongue to say, *Yes, do this. Give it to me.* I was ready for possession, especially after what happened tonight. I didn't care that I'd never done this before, didn't care that I wasn't the one doing the fucking. I just wanted all of him. Wanted to be together in every way we could.

But Steven felt my stiffness and said, "Don't worry, we're not doing that yet. Relax, and trust me, I'm going to make you feel so good." He slid to his belly, bringing his face back to my aching dick.

"I know you will." Steven always made me feel good. I propped myself on my elbows for a better view but ruined the effort by falling back to the bed and closing my eyes as soon as he took me into his hot mouth and swirled his tongue.

I let myself get swept away again, losing all thought, focusing on the wet heat of him. His mouth and hands worked me, slowly at first, then with a faster rhythm. He pulled on my sac and massaged my taint, all the while keeping up that glorious suction. I felt like I was going to levitate from the bed, when suddenly I felt a cool, slick finger massaging lower on my hole.

I briefly stiffened. Steven didn't take his hand away, but kept up his firm, circular massaging. He lifted his head and asked, "Do you play with your ass?"

I looked at him, felt my cheeks heat inexplicably, and answered, "Yeah."

"Has anyone been here but you, Ken?" His voice was gruff and low, his finger exerting a slight pressure on my ring of muscles.

"No."

"I'll make it good, I promise," he vowed. "Slow and easy and so very, very good." I knew he would. I'd done this to him before, several times, and he'd always come hard. I'd thought a few times that it would have segued into sex, that I was preparing him for me, but it didn't.

I was eager now to feel what he'd felt. I was eager for everything.

He bent his head and took my cock back into his mouth and I chanted, "Yeah, yeah, yeah." Multisyllabic words weren't in the cards for me tonight, I guessed.

Steven took his time with his hands, he also lightened up on the rhythm and pressure of his mouth, too. It was obvious he had a plan, because his mouth and his fingers were working in tandem, first light and tentative, lulling me into a semi-relaxed state—or as close to relaxed as a guy could get while he was being sucked and fingered—then more bold and exploratory as my ardor grew and my muscles started to tense. When he repeatedly bumped my prostate in time with the downward stroke on my cock, I knew I couldn't last long. I felt every muscle in my body tense, the hair on my arms stand on end, and I roared my completion.

"Damn," I huffed, barely able to catch my breath. My whole body was covered in a sheen of sweat and my hard exhales were cooling my chest. My muscles, which had all been clenched so tight seconds before, had become loose and languid.

I was wrecked in the best way.

CHAPTER TWENTY-FOUR

DKM

Monday nights sucked.

They didn't suck because it was the start of the workweek or because I was any more tired than normal. It was simply because Mondays were one of the nights Steven and I didn't stay together.

We'd fallen into a pattern in the last three weeks where I spent Tuesday, Friday, and Saturday nights with him.

So really, it wasn't just Monday nights that sucked. Sunday, Wednesday, and Thursday were also equally terrible.

But today was Monday, and I'd gone to the gym after work, come home to my drab little apartment, showered, and ate dinner. I contemplated going to bed, but eight felt a little too early for that. I tried to talk myself into it by saying I was tired, but the truth was, I was just bored and lonely.

I wanted to be with Steven. I didn't want to be sitting here on my brown couch staring at my bare walls listening to the clock tick. I wanted to be tangled up with him, listening to him chatter on about... anything, everything.

But I guessed we were taking things slow, in a way. I think Steven thought three nights together a week wasn't slow. At first, he seemed reluctant to have me spend the night during the week, but I was persuasive and hated waiting until the weekend to see him. He also thought introducing his friends to me after three weeks together was near-disastrously premature. I didn't feel the same, obviously. I was eager for all of it.

I had to remind myself that Steven was a little behind me. I had jumped into the deep end with both feet, and he hadn't even known he was in the pool. I'd been falling in love with him for weeks before he knew I was interested.

Love.

Yes, love. That's what was happening here, what this had become for me. Everything felt both tentative *and* passionate. Fragile *and* powerful. I felt like I was on the cusp of forever—a hairsbreadth from having everything I ever wanted. But also like I was one misstep away from ruining my whole life.

I was just getting ready to call Steven, wanting to hear his voice and wish him a good night, when Kari called. I hadn't heard from her in a couple of weeks and felt, in this lonely moment, stupid-happy to talk to her.

"Happy Monday, Dr. Miles." She sounded cheerful.

"Dr. Miles," I greeted in return. Since we were both doctors, we'd occasionally play this game that almost always ended with me joking that it was unfair I had to address her as such when her doctorate was in educational policy and I was an MD. She played like it pissed her off, but we both loved the game. "You sound happy. Everything going according to plan with the wedding?"

"I'm so glad you asked!" she exclaimed. Then, with an about-face, she went into full-blown drill sergeant mode. "I need you to come home for a fitting. ASAP. Like, this weekend."

"Ah, God, Kari, I can't do it this weekend. I have plans." And I did. I had plans on Saturday to do a long run rather than doing it on Sunday because Steven wanted to join me for the short version. I also planned on spending both days with him.

"Plans." She sounded pissed, which aggravated me.

"Yes, plans." I mimicked her tone. "I'm conditioning for the half-marathon in a couple of weeks, and I have a date."

"A run? You're putting me off for a run? You can't find a few hours to hop on a plane, hug Nana—who's been on my ass about you by the way—get fitted, and get back on another plane to go home? We're talking one afternoon, Ken."

Her attitude that my very limited personal time should be devoted to her and her plans annoyed the hell out of me.

This could not stand.

"Why is Nana on your ass about me?" I dodged her other questions, perversely stoking her ire.

She scoffed. "She says she wants you to go through Pop's stuff and take what you want before she dies so that, and I quote, 'the rest of the vultures don't screw Kenny out of it.'"

I shook my head in exasperation, but I couldn't help but laugh. Our grandmother had been talking about her imminent death for decades. I was sure she used it as a way of getting her busy and ungrateful family to show her some attention, but at this point, we were all immune to the guilt. Plus, I kept abreast of her health and knew her to be doing exceptionally well.

"So why is she on your ass about it? She has my number. She can call me."

"That's what I told her, but apparently, you're a very *busy* and *important* big-city doctor and can't be bothered all the time," Kari groused. "As if I'm not busy enough, I have to be her go-between."

"Well," I drawled, tsking. "You do only have an EdD, and I'm an MD," I teased. "She knows what's up."

"Screw you, buddy," she laughed, but it was thin and tinged with irritation. "I'm working fifty-hour weeks *and* planning a wedding." She was quiet for a moment then said, "Doug, Brandon's best man, is going on vacation and won't be available for a couple of weeks either. Justine just informed me that she's pregnant and will probably be showing by then and she's freaking out about the style of the bridesmaid gowns. I'm feeling very impotent right now and at the mercy of everyone else's schedules."

I wanted to say, *So, elope if you don't want to deal with everyone else's pesky lives.* Instead, I tried to remind her that it would be fine. "You have two months. Everything is going to work out perfectly."

"And now you're leaving me high and dry for a jog and a piece of ass. Nice."

I felt a little bad. I would have liked to take Steven with me and introduce him to Kari, but meeting family could possibly be out of his comfort zone. And the truth of it was, I didn't want to be away from him after King had approached him on Saturday. On Sunday we'd talked about it. I'd been angry that we'd gone to the same club where Steven had met him. But it did seem as if the meeting had been accidental, and not a case of stalking. Steven assured me that the man wasn't a threat and I made him promise that if King contacted him in any way, he'd involve his boss. He wasn't happy, but I said either he would, or I would.

Despite that promise and all his reassurances, I didn't feel comfortable leaving town without him by my side.

"I really can't this weekend but let me see what I can do next weekend. Otherwise, I won't be able to come until after the run in September."

"Fine," she moaned. "This date…is it a first date or…"

"No, I'm seeing somebody."

"Ooh, do tell," she cooed. "Blonde?"

I laughed. I knew where this was headed. "Yes, but not as light as mine."

"Uh-huh. And blue eyes, right?"

"More of a gray, but yeah."

"Thin." This was a statement and not a question.

"I'd say 'lean,' not skinny," I clarified. "And to answer your next question, no, he's not short, he's only like an inch or two shorter than I am."

"I swear, you are such a narcissist. Why you choose people who look like you is—" She paused, awareness infiltrating her brain. "Wait, *HE?*"

"Yes. His name is Steven, and even though it's still kind of new, I'm certain I'm in love with him." It felt great to say that aloud. As soon as I said the words, I knew it was the truth. I loved him. And, god, it felt good to talk about him with Kari. She was the only person in my life who I felt close enough to unburden myself. She'd seen me through my rift with my dad, adjusting to life in Chicago, and stressful times during med school.

There was an unexpected stunned pause. Alarmed, I said, "Kari?"

"What, so you're gay now?" Her tone was sharp, derisive, and I was taken aback.

"Um, no. I'm bi and you know that." She did know it. After the shit show with Dad, I'd turned to her for consolation and she had stepped up. All pep talks and love. I couldn't understand this dismissal or selective amnesia.

"What I know is that you went through an experimental phase in college but that you got over it when Dad set you straight."

I gripped my phone so tightly it made a cracking noise. *Not Kari.* I could feel the blood pounding in my ears. She'd been sympathetic to me back then. Had she been lying to pacify me? Hoping I'd *get over* it?

"Being bisexual was never a *phase*," I spat, standing suddenly. "It's been my reality before, during, and after college and it will continue to be my reality for the rest of my life! What's so hard to understand about that?" I yelled.

"Whatever," she said coolly. "Tell me, when you haven't mentioned anyone but women over the last *decade*, what was I supposed to have assumed. Dad talked to you and you continued with women. Experiment over."

Her calm, snide tone enraged me. "Name *one* woman, other than Angie, who I've referenced since Dad *set me straight*?" My voice rivaled hers for snideness.

"I don't keep up with your revolving door of ass, Ken. What's your—"

"You can't," I interrupted. "You know why? Because Steven and Angie are the only people I've been with in all this time who lasted more than two weeks. No one else, *male or female*, have been worth even a passing mention to you."

"Fine. You're bi and you're in a homosexual relationship. The whole family thinks you're this straight, handsome, brilliant, young doctor. When you show up with this guy on your arm at *my wedding*, what do you think is going to happen, hmm?"

I was silent. Silent because she was making this about her now, and I was shocked. She was my one real confidant and she didn't know me —or at least didn't want to know who I really was. I felt adrift and lonelier than I had before she called.

"It won't matter," she continued. "It won't matter that I look amazing in my dress that I've starved myself to squeeze into. It won't matter that Mom and Dad shelled out tens of thousands to make my wedding perfect. It won't matter that you've finished your fellowship and now have an enviable position at a top-notch hospital. The only thing anyone will be thinking about is which of you is the woman in the relationship."

I growled, "What the fuck is your problem?" Who was this person? Maybe I didn't know my sister, either.

"You know it's true. Even the ones who are completely supportive will find the gossip too fun to ignore. You'll be a *spectacle*."

Our family and their circle of friends were mostly kind, accepting people, but they were nosy. What did it matter? Why should we care? Was she saying all of this because she imagined that a fraction of attention will be moved from her to me? That was stupid.

"And, Dad. He'll lose his shit on you again. Is that what you want?"

I ignored her. I decided to stop living for his approval a long time ago. His feelings about my relationship with Steven were irrelevant. But there was one thing I needed to know.

"If I decide to bring Steven, am I disinvited?" I asked the question quietly, knowing that our relationship was hanging by a thread.

"If the only way I can get you to come to my wedding is to allow you to ruin it, I'm not left with a great choice, am I?"

We were both silent for a long moment until she sighed wearily. "I can't deal with this right now. When you can find time to come home for a fitting, give me a call and we can talk about this. We will both have had time to calm down and think rationally."

I opened my mouth to say that time wasn't going to erase her self-ishness, but she'd already disconnected.

CHAPTER TWENTY-FIVE

All month I'd been working a few days a week from Dan's apartment. At first, the change had been boring and annoying. I enjoyed the bustle of the office—of busy people, the interaction, and ambient noise of ringing phones and humming electronics.

But I enjoyed watching Wally too, and as the weeks went on, I didn't mind hanging out in Dan's apartment so much. It was clean and nicely decorated—if you liked dark wood, leather, and the let's-retire-to-the-study-for-cigars-and-whisky vibe—and, best of all, Wally's doggy butt stayed far away from my new rug.

Today, I hadn't been getting much work done. I'd spent the morning half-heartedly reviewing expense reports, but I couldn't stop thinking about Ken and his strange behavior from the night before, so I decided to take the dog out for a long walk. I felt safe taking Wally out, he had a very protective nature and could be intimidating when he felt like it. Plus, the weather was sunny and warm, which meant the park was teeming with people, even on a weekday. I really needed the walk, the air, and the time to think about Ken. He was being weird again.

Just when I thought Weird Ken was gone, replaced by the confident and sexy McPretty MD, he'd shown back up to keep me on my toes.

Weird Ken, Prickly Ken, Fidgety Ken—I still adored him, but I didn't like that he seemed troubled. He seemed distracted and restless. He was chewing gum like a madman and hardly ate any dinner. More than once I caught him staring blankly at nothing, like he was deep in thought.

When I asked him if he wanted to talk about whatever was bothering him, he said for me not to worry, that he was under a lot of 'bullshit stress' and it wasn't my problem. I knew he hadn't meant for it to come across rudely, but it sure sounded like he told me to mind my own business. So, I had, and I did my best to not take it personally.

When we went to bed, it was the first night together where we hadn't fallen, tangled and suctioned to each other, racing toward orgasm. Instead, we turned off the lights, stripped off our clothes and Ken pulled me to him, laying a sweet, chaste kiss on my lips.

Can we—can I just hold you tonight? I just want to feel your heat. I'm tired. And cold.

Something was definitely going on with him, and it was all I could think about today.

Not long after I had returned from the walk, there was a knock at the door. I hurriedly corralled the dog into a bedroom to avoid any undue excitement and was surprised to find Kat waiting in the hall. Her expression didn't change at the sight of me answering Dan's door, but still I asked, "Are you here for me?"

"Yes. Dan said you were here."

I perked up at this news. Dan and Kat rarely conversed with each other, and for her to have had a conversation with him meant she had to be having some big feelings right now.

"You spoke to Dan?" I motioned her inside. "Tell me everything."

"It wasn't like that," she said. "You know he doesn't think of me that way."

Like hell.

But I could understand why she thought so. "Maybe because you avoid him," I chided. He couldn't really show interest when she made herself invisible.

"You know why I avoid him," she replied.

I really, really don't, I thought. She had a huge crush on Dan, and he was no longer involved with anyone, so I didn't see why these crazy kids couldn't at least get their flirt on. There must have been something that went down between them, something that presented more of a hurdle than just her shyness. But what it was, remained a mystery to me.

"I needed to speak to you and Dan told me where you were, that's all."

I watched her take in Dan's displayed photos with a rapt expression. She looked as if she were trying to absorb every detail. It reminded me of the way Ken examined my place the first time he'd come over. It hadn't been critical, but more like the art and decor was my coded diary and he was scoping out my secrets.

Thinking of Ken made me wonder if I should tell Kat about him. I hadn't talked to her since I'd given her the cheese, and uncharacteristically, I wanted to burst out and confess, *I have a boyfriend and he's smart and weird and sexy and thinks my hairy chest is a thing of boner-inducing magnificence.* But there was always the possibility of Ken's reputation preceding him. I didn't know what Kat knew about him or what she thought of him. Did she think he was an uptight, superficial asshole? Or did she think of him as the guy who saved Elizabeth in the hospital? I didn't relish seeing any disappointment in her eyes over him. Not now. I also had to face the possibility that Ken's distance last night was an indication that he was unhappy in this relationship. Maybe this was the beginning of the end. Why would I want to gush to Kat about him today, only to have to confess he's left me in a couple of weeks. *No, thank you.* I'll keep my heartache and misery to myself.

Wally barked and pulled my thoughts back to the present conversation.

"You've been here less than thirty seconds and you're already bursting bubbles," I huffed. "Come on in, Debbie Disappointment. I need to let Wally out of the bedroom."

"Why is he in the bedroom?" she asked, following me farther into the apartment.

I explained why it was better for Wally to be shut in when people came by and walked down the hall to release him.

"Alright, buddy," I cooed quietly to the dog as I approached the door. "Go give Kat some love. Convince her to be your new mommy."

"I brought you lunch," she called out. "Sushi from Mai Tai."

I opened the bedroom door and watched Wally haul ass toward Kat.

"Okay, then," I yelled back. "You're forgiven."

When I entered the living room, Wally The Very Good Boy was doing his utmost to follow my instructions. Jumping, dancing, licking, he was pulling out all the stops. Kat was not immune to the dog's affection and excitement.

Giving Wally ear rubs, she asked, "Forgiven for what?"

"Forgiven for not asking Dan out. He's been single for something like two months. The time has come to stop avoiding The Security Man."

It was time to get real. She needed a push, and not just suggestions or jokes. She needed a friend to tell her she had to finally take the Boston Bull by the horns and ride him into the sunset.

She straightened from Wally. "Steven," she said, mild censure in her voice.

I wasn't having it. I crossed my arms and issued her a look that I was sure told her I was not going to drop this subject. "Kat."

Like Dan, she was excellent at deflection, and she turned the conversation. "I need—I need you to consider a request for your help." She took her coat off and approached me, her large, doe eyes sober and searching. Grasping my hand, she said, "I received a call today from Uncle Eugene, you know, my father's lawyer? And, Steven, this is serious."

My heart clenched. Kat's mother had been institutionalized for many years with severe schizophrenia. Her father was also very ill with Alzheimer's. If this Uncle Eugene was calling her with something serious, it might very well mean one of her parents had taken a turn. I squeezed her hand, "Tell me."

"You remember my cousin Caleb?"

"Yes," I answered, disgust edging into my tone. "The pharma bro who is one evil deed away from becoming a real-life portrait of Dorian Gray?" This guy was always so rude and cruel to Kat, I hated that she was forced to deal with him—he wasn't just family, he was the CEO of Caravel. The stories she told about him always pissed me off, but she admirably ignored him and refused to give him the satisfaction of getting a reaction from her. She was amazing.

"That's the one," she affirmed. "Well, you know how my dad is getting worse? Caleb is trying to obtain guardianship of me—and my property."

What the hell? "Why would he do that?"

"He wants control of the family's shares, which—if he succeeds in his bid for guardianship—would be his as soon as I inherit."

I was taken aback. Her cousin's plan to obtain guardianship over her seemed preposterous, but as she explained the hows and whys, I understood the real threat to Kat. Her life in Chicago, though respectable, was highly unusual for an heiress and someone who would soon have the responsibility of owning a large stake in a multi-billion-dollar company. Add in her less-than-pristine rebellious teenage years, and the fact that both of her parents were incapacitated with mental disorders and Caleb, as her closest relative (not currently institutional-ized), had a very real shot at winning that bid for guardianship. And if he were to obtain guardianship, Eugene warned that she would be insti-tutionalized herself and Caleb would control all finances, essentially making her unable to seek legal recourse. Her father still being alive wasn't the protection and the time-buffer she hoped. Caleb was making his play for control now.

I watched as Kat sat on the couch and crossed her arms over her middle in a protective gesture. She was obviously close to crying, but valiantly trying to keep control. My heart broke for her, my mind whirled. *How could this be happening?*

"Eugene thinks the best way out of this is through marriage. If I marry, that person will have rights to me that will surpass Caleb's. He will most likely contest my marriage, but Eugene seems to think that will be a losing battle."

I was relieved there was an easy and perfect solution to the prob-lem. Marriage would certainly cut that Machiavellian douche off at the knees. I'd love to see his face when he got the news that Kat had thwarted his plans by hitching her wagon to…*Oh my God.* "Oh my God," I blurted, the thought striking me suddenly. "Are you going to ask Dan?"

What a gift from the universe! Ask and ye shall receive! This was much better than locking them in a closet together or pretending I was ill and calling them both to my bedside to hear my dying request that they make out.

Yes, I had considered both options.

By the confused look on her face, I knew we were not on the same page. "What? No!" she insisted vehemently.

"Not Dan. *You.*"

CHAPTER TWENTY-SIX

STEVEN

An aneurysm was imminent.

The past twenty-four-plus hours had been an emotional rollercoaster.

When I walked out of Dan's apartment last night around six, I'd made sure Kat had my new phone number and left her with Wally, a smile, and all calm positivity.

"It will all work out, Lambchop. Don't worry."

But as soon as I shut that door behind me, my brain went haywire.

Fuck, fuck, fuckety, shit, fuck, fuck!

I convinced her to ask Dan. "You ask Dan, today…If he doesn't immediately say yes, if he hesitates at all, then I'll marry you."

The pain behind my eye got sharper.

What the hell was I going to do?

I told her I was seeing someone, let her know that it wouldn't be okay for me to do this…then I gambled.

I gambled because Kat needed help. Kat needed someone to protect her. I knew Dan was the man for that job—not me. But she'd been so sure that Dan wouldn't say yes, so sure that if he did, it would be dangerous to her heart.

I worried for her heart. I did. So much. *But what about Ken's heart?* How could I marry her and expect to not cause carnage in my own life? I couldn't.

I had to make her be brave. Dan was the perfect candidate for this. He was a white knight, impervious to bribes or threats, connected and powerful in his own right.

And he cared about her. I knew he did.

At least, I *thought* he did. Kat's re-telling of their history *did* confirm their mutual lust, so I knew I wasn't without hope here. But she also told me about a side of Dan I didn't know and never would have suspected in a million years.

Dan casting off his attraction for an amazing woman because of her former promiscuity? I was honestly confused and disappointed by the revelation and yet something about it didn't ring true. Something wasn't right, so I still took a gamble on him and asked her to consider me her back-up plan to Dan.

She'd looked so lost and terrified I couldn't do anything *but* reassure her I'd be there for her.

God damn it, Daniel O'Malley, you'd better take your head out of your asshole and make the right choice.

That Beantown Bozo was going to be dead to me otherwise.

He had to say yes. There was no way he was going to turn down an opportunity to help Kat. Especially if that opportunity put him in close contact with her. Even if some part of him didn't think a relationship with her was a good idea, he still wanted her. And just like Ken and I had discussed, people don't take their own good advice. When they *want,* they *do.*

Dan was going to *do.* He had to. He would be the stupidest sonofabitch if he didn't. I knew Dan wasn't stupid.

My perception of my ability to understand and predict human behavior had shown itself to be a bit skewed in recent times. And, honestly, that's why I couldn't feel as confident about this as I appeared to Kat. If he said no, I was in a world of trouble.

Maybe I *was* sabotaging myself. Otherwise, how could I just blithely say, *then I'll marry you,* like it was nothing?

"What about your boyfriend?" she'd asked.

"I'll talk to him tonight. He'll understand, or I'll make him understand. I hope. Don't worry about it."

But Ken wasn't going to be okay with this, and I *wasn't* going to talk to him about it unless it was abso-fucking-lutely necessary. Even if there was a chance he'd feel sympathy for Kat or anger at the cruel injustice of her situation, I didn't know if it would be wise or prudent to explain the entire situation to him. He'd be another person who'd be in on a conspiracy to commit marriage fraud. It would put him in a bad position.

I stayed up late into the night, popping ibuprofen and fretting. I'd started to call Ken half a dozen times, wanting to hear his voice, wanting to know if he was feeling better than he had the night before. I wanted him to be here, but at the same time, I needed to wait for Kat's call alone. I had to ride this out alone.

I considered the fact that maybe he was already thinking about breaking up with me. That maybe the events of Saturday night were too much for him. Maybe he thought he couldn't handle my baggage or being in a relationship with a man.

We'd yet to have sex, and part of me worried that he was hesitating taking that step with me because he wasn't sure he wanted to go that far. Maybe he *was* confused, maybe the novelty of being with a guy was wearing off and he wanted out before it went any further. I hadn't pushed. He asked for patience and I wanted to give that to him. I'd honestly been enjoying the slow explorations and didn't feel like fucking was an immediately necessary act for lovemaking.

His words, his eyes, his body, mouth, and hands conveyed nothing but eagerness. Never in my life had I enjoyed intimacy so much. He made it exciting and fun and sweet. The sweetness was what set him apart from everyone else I'd been with. He liked to savor and praise and cuddle. He loved pillow talk, loved to continue caressing and whispering long after we'd come and our bodies had cooled. Nothing about his behavior before Tuesday would have made me think he was unhappy with the way we were in bed.

Nothing except not asking to fuck me.

I can tell you really like him. Just make sure he's not using you to experiment. Ern's words replayed in my brain, but I batted them away. Ken wasn't using me, and he wasn't treating our time as temporary. He talked about introducing me to his sister and taking me to her wedding. For Thor's sake, I brought Wally home one evening and he sat playing with him musing about what kind of dog we could adopt when we were ready.

This wasn't a man who was playing around.

Still, Ern's mini-lecture mirrored some of my own fears and Ken's entire demeanor on Tuesday had been worrisome.

I finally fell asleep sometime around three with my cell clutched in my hand.

At 6:38 AM my phone buzzed, startling me awake. It was a text from Kat.

KAT: He said yes. We're getting the license today.

My whole body slumped in relief. "Oh, thank you God, and thank you, Daniel O'Malley," I breathed.

I hurriedly typed out a couple of texts to her.

ME: OOOHHHHHHHHHHHH MMMMMYYYYYYYYYYY GGGGGOOOOOOOOOODDDDDDD!!!!

ME: I want all the details. Call me. And pics or it didn't happen.

I wanted her to think I was excited and happy for her—not so relieved I was on the verge of tears.

Tossing my phone aside, I fell back to sleep until just after ten, then called Keira to inform her that I would not be coming into the office.

I spent the whole day thinking about Ken and how I had just been given a get-out-of-jail-free card. I wanted to know we were okay, know he wasn't doubting us, or angry with me. The more I thought about it, the more I was sure it was King that had been upsetting to him. He'd told me that the situation with Nico's stalker had been traumatizing for him, that he regretted the force he'd had to use on her. Saturday probably gave him pause and made him wonder if he should subject himself to a situation that could possibly escalate to that point.

I didn't think that it would, and I didn't want to lose him. I knew I needed to talk with him and straighten everything out, so I sent him a text around four asking if he'd spend the night with me tonight.

At five-fifteen he replied, and my heart dropped.

DKM: I'm going to stay home tonight. I'm still not feeling well. I'll see you tomorrow. X

By eight o'clock, my nerves were shot. I'd imagined all sorts of scenarios where Ken arrived tomorrow to dump me. In one, he said he didn't want to spend any more time with me because he knew he wasn't interested in men anymore. In another, he said King had started threatening him and he blamed me. Then, there was one where he admitted he just didn't find me attractive.

I couldn't take it anymore, and frankly, I was pissed off at the imaginary Ken for all the things he'd said, and I was pissed at the real Ken for making me wait for a resolution. I decided to call Damon and enlist his help.

"Can you give me a ride to Ken's place?"

"Who?"

"Ken. My boyfriend." *I hope he's still my boyfriend.* "You gave him a ride home about a month ago."

"Oh, yeah, the clown?"

"He's not a clown!" I snapped. "He's a doctor." I softened my voice when I admitted, "I don't know where he lives, and I need to stop by." I cringed. How did I not know Ken's address? How had I never been to his apartment? I knew he lived on Taylor—I'd heard him say that much, but I should have taken the time to visit his place. "Will you help me, please?"

"Sure. Let me do my eight-thirty rounds, then I can get Amid to stand post while I'm gone. Nine, okay?"

"Yes, thank you," I said sincerely. "I'll be in the garage at nine."

I could have avoided inconveniencing Damon and Amid by simply asking Ken what his address was, but I didn't want to run the risk of him talking me out of it or refusing to let me come over. I had to have this settled tonight.

The ride didn't take long, and Damon double-parked in front of an old grey stone in the UIC medical district. The building wasn't big, only three stories, and the facade was of a neo-classical design with bay windows and columns flanking the front entrance. It was well-lit on the outside and the windows facing the street all had lights burning inside.

Four college-aged people emerged from the entrance. They were talking and laughing loudly. Ken had once said his building was always busy, and it seemed like he was right.

Neither I, nor Damon knew what apartment was his, so I had to call him.

"Hi," he greeted. He sounded sleepy.

"What is your apartment number?" I asked.

"Why?"

"Because I'm there. Here. I'm outside of your building and I don't want to knock on every door trying to find you."

"Are you alone out there?" His voice held a tinge of alarm and I heard rustling.

"No, Damon drove me, but I'm sending him away now." I said thank you to Damon and exited the car.

"I'm coming down," he said and disconnected.

I walked up the steps and as I reached the top, Ken opened the door. My breath whooshed out of my lungs at the sight of him. He was dressed in a white T-shirt and flannel sleep pants. On his feet were bright white socks—no shoes. He looked so sexy…and tired. His hair was disheveled, and his eyes were heavy, like he'd just woke up.

"Hey." He gave me a smile and reached his hand out to me. As soon as I took it, he pulled me closer to envelope me in a long hug. I let out a ragged breath, relief replacing tension, and I melted into him.

"I'm glad you're here," he said into my neck.

"Me too. I've missed you."

He broke the hold and led the way up one floor to his apartment. As I walked inside, I noticed immediately a distinct lack of decor. Ken had furniture and a TV set up, but that was it. No art, no knick-knacks, no throw pillows, or even photographs. There was, however, an abundance of textbooks, which overflowed a small bookshelf to stack on the floor. The apartment looked clean, smelled clean, but was blank and sad.

Ken looked sad, too. It made my heart hurt.

"Why didn't you come over tonight?"

He sighed and scrubbed his hand over his face. "Because I didn't want you to have to deal with my shitty mood." I followed his lead to the couch and sat. "I know it bothered you on Tuesday, so I figured I'd spare you."

"If I was bothered by it, it's because you were obviously upset about something," I clarified. "I wish you'd talk to me about it. It is King? Are you angry with me?"

"Oh Jesus." He closed his eyes briefly, then turned to fully face me. "No. But I meant what I said the other night, if this escalates any further and you don't tell your boss, I will."

"So, it does bother you?"

He screwed his face up in irritation. "Yes, it bothers me. You're being stubborn."

"Ah-ha!" I pointed my finger in accusation.

He grasped my hand. "*Ah-ha* what?"

"You're giving me the cold shoulder because you're mad at me," I accused.

"I'm not mad at you, Steven, and I didn't mean to give you the cold shoulder."

His hold on my hand turned into a caress with his thumb. I looked down at our connection and watched as his thumb moved back and forth along the back of my hand. He always did that. He loved to turn touches into caresses. It wasn't enough to drape an arm over my shoulder—he had to glide his fingers down my arm. He wasn't content to lay his palm on my knee—he needed to squeeze. He was so tactile... so damn near worshipful when any part of us touched.

I didn't know if I believed he wasn't angry with me, but I decided that to get through this, to get on even footing, I was going to employ the same sensual tactics he used.

"Then why," I whispered, lifting a hand to his chest. "Aren't you…" I squeezed his pec and grazed his nipple. His breathing kicked up. "In my bed right now, fucking me?"

Before he could answer, I ran my hand down to his growing arousal and cupped him firmly. This elicited a moan and a thrust. I wasn't playing fair. Sex wasn't a great way to solve problems, but I was consumed with the need to see him wild for me, for reassurance that he wanted me.

"Why aren't you there," I continued, circling his hardened shaft as best I could through his soft pants. "Naked, sweaty, and pounding this fat dick in my ass, Ken?"

Those words were enough to open the flood gate. Suddenly, Ken became the aggressor, pushing me back against the armrest and taking my mouth in a hard kiss. He pulled my shirt from my waistband and rubbed my stomach, then he set to work on my pants, freeing me from my clothes. I couldn't help the instinctive thrust of my hips as he fondled me. He'd hardly done anything, and I was poised for orgasm. Damn, I'd missed this.

"I missed you," I rasped, as he pushed my shirt up to lick a nipple.

"Me too," he said into my navel. He peppered my belly with wet, hot kisses, moving steadily downward to my cock.

When I felt the warm heat of his mouth enveloping and sucking, my balls tightened, my release hovering near.

"Jesus, Ken," I tapped his shoulder. "That's too good, you have to stop."

He raised his eyes to mine and gave a slow, firm, deliberate lick up the underside of me until he reached the head and swirled his tongue. *Thor have mercy.* I groaned.

"Why?" he asked simply, not breaking eye contact.

"Because I don't want to come until you're balls deep, that's why."

Sharpness came to his gaze and he raised to his feet. "Strip off and get into my bed." He held his hand out and pulled me up from the couch. He grabbed my ass and pulled our pelvises together. "I was waiting for you to invite me in." He grazed a finger along my crack. Softly, he said, "I'm warning you though, I don't get less intense from here, Steven. You have to know you have all of me, for better or worse."

CHAPTER TWENTY-SEVEN

DKM

He came to me.

Steven was here.

I had been tossing and turning, unable to make myself fall asleep, even though I was tired. I was ready to give up and go back to Steven's place, just so I could rest. In a short amount of time, I'd become dependent on him, his company, his body, his voice—to the point that being alone was intolerable.

But I hadn't wanted to make him uncomfortable. I'd been a mess the past few days. Angry, anxious, morose. I saw the looks he'd given me, the questions in his eyes and I knew it wasn't fair that I subjected him to it. I could have confided in him—knew that if I did, he'd make me feel better about the situation. But I didn't want to ever hurt him, and I was sure that telling him about my conversation with my sister would be hurtful. I needed to shoulder this alone.

I also needed to get over it. That's what I'd been telling myself for the past two days. On Tuesday, I'd hear Steven tell a joke or say something sweet and instead of feeling happy or laughing, I'd think, *they don't deserve to know him*, and I'd feel worse.

I thought being alone would help me get some clarity about this. In a way it had. It had become crystal clear that I hated being away from

Steven. Clear that I was in love with him, and clear that if I wanted to get any sleep, I needed his body next to mine.

But no clarity regarding Kari. It didn't matter, though, because he was here.

Naked.

In my bed.

Screw Kari and screw her wedding.

Only Steven mattered.

"Are you going to get in here, DKM, or are you going to stare at me all night?" he asked with a cheeky smirk. He was also squinting, trying to see me without his glasses, which he'd abandoned next to the lamp. I knew I was such a freak for thinking his blindness was cute.

I'd been standing at the threshold of my bedroom watching him settle his beautifully naked self into my rumpled bed, and my chest constricted.

He was mine.

He was perfect and amazing, and I took a moment to recognize that I was staring at the rest of my life—took a long, reverential look at the man who owned me.

When I didn't move, Steven's smirk slipped, his gaze filling with unease.

"I just wanted to burn the sight of you and this moment into my brain," I said, my voice cracking, betraying my emotion. I cleared my throat and walked to the bed.

I stared down at him and rubbed my thumb along the coarse stubble of his jaw. "And I want to be as perfect for you as you are for me," I whispered.

Steven's brow furrowed and he rose up on his knees to meet on my level. "God, Ken, you are. You don't even have to try."

We kissed roughly for long moments until Steven pulled me down onto the bed. He spread his legs and I settled my hips against his. He yanked my shirt over my head, and I groaned over the heated skin-to-skin contact. I loved his heat. He was like a furnace, soothing all the frozen, aching bits of me.

I looked into his eyes as I pumped my hips, rubbing my flannel-covered cock against his. I loved watching his expressive face change with each new sensation. Pausing briefly, I freed myself to allow the slide to resume with more skin contact.

Steven seemed to be onboard with more skin, because he pushed my pants down my ass and massaged firmly. His hands felt so good, so sure and strong. I needed more, so I made quick work of removing the pants and socks the rest of the way and brought myself back to his warm hardness.

Propping up on one forearm, I leaned so that we could see our cocks sliding together, so that I could stroke and squeeze. This went on for a few moments, until Steven, shaking and sweating, demanded I stop.

"I'm about to come, Babe, but not yet, not yet, not yet."

At his words, I scrambled to the nightstand to grab a condom and lube. Steven chuckled at my haste. "Your enthusiasm makes me feel ten feet tall."

I rubbed my hands along the outside of his hairy thighs and said, "*I* feel ten feet tall whenever you look at me."

"God, Ken." He said this like my earnestness was painful. Maybe it was, but I warned him. This is what he was getting. I didn't think I could give less than all anymore.

I reached for him, fondled and stroked for several minutes before I brought my lubricated fingers to his entry. We'd done this before. I knew how much pressure he liked, how many fingers he could take, knew just where to rub and how fast to rub to get him off. But this time, I wasn't going to finger him into oblivion—I was preparing him for me, for us to ride into oblivion together.

I wanted to take it slow, use more care and draw it out, so I slid to my belly and laved his balls and the underside of his dick slowly as I pumped one finger in and out. I kissed the crease of his leg, the inside of his thigh, I lifted his sac and rubbed my tongue firmly along his taint until he was trying to fuck himself with my finger.

"More, please, God. Give me more," he panted.

I slowly added another finger and gave him a deep thrust. He moaned long and loud, grasping his cock in his hand.

"Yeah, Ken, that's it, that's what I need." He pulled on himself and watched me through hooded, pleasure-drunk eyes.

"Is it?" I asked gruffly. "Or do you want something else?"

"I want all of you," he choked out as I sped up my thrusting.

With a hiss, he let go of his dick and demanded, "Now. Fuck me now, no more playing."

I separated from him slowly and made short work of the condom, lubricating myself generously. I wanted this to feel incredible for him.

Steven spread his legs wide and raised them a bit to give me better access. It was another view, another scene I wanted burned into my memory—more lurid, filthy, and desperate than the last, but just as significant. His hair was mussed, his eyes were full of tenderness, his pale, hair-dusted skin aglow in the lamplight, and his most private and vulnerable parts laid out on display, offered to me so trustingly, so eagerly. He was everything I wanted.

I poised my head at his opening and gave a slow push, testing the give of his muscles. There was little resistance and as I continued, I watched Steven's face morph from intense concentration to rapturous pleasure.

I tried to stay mindful of him and his reactions, but as soon as I saw his bliss, I let myself get caught up in the act. He was so tight and the slide of my body into his was more delicious than I ever thought it could be. Our bodies moved instinctively, it seemed like both a beautiful dance and a rude, inelegant race.

Breathing roughly, we held gazes for long moments, communicating wordlessly all the lust and reverence we had for the act and each other.

Long before I wanted, I felt my pleasure spiking—my hips began to pound wildly. I finally spoke, huffing, "Steven, I need you to come, I want to see it all over you."

He reached down to pull furiously on himself. "I'm there, I'm there, I'm there," he chanted as his neck arched and his seed spurted.

The sight of him quaking with completion, the feel of his ass clenching me impossibly tight, tore my own hovering ejaculation from me.

It took long moments for us to come back to reality. I felt like my bones were liquid, like my heart was galloping from my chest. Steven's grip on my shoulder relaxed, as did his legs. I felt him become soft and slack under me as he recovered.

Once I cleaned up and disposed of the condom, I rejoined him in my bed. His sleepiness reminded me of my own exhaustion. The orgasm combined with several nights of poor sleep made me tired. I knew I'd sleep well tonight, because I was next to Steven. My lover, my furnace, my comfort.

My everything.

CHAPTER TWENTY-EIGHT

STEVEN

An angry, stupid alarm woke me from the best sleep of my life. I didn't know where it was coming from, and as much as I wanted it to stop, I couldn't make my muscles move or my eyes open.

I was warm and comfy, pressed against Ken's hard, naked body, his arm crooked around my middle and up my torso. I really didn't want to get up.

But that devil's sound needed to cease, so I gave his arm a shake.

"The alarm is going off."

"Hmm?" he hummed sleepily.

"That gawd awful noise is telling us to get up."

Ken moved behind me and inhaled deeply. I felt the loss of his hard heat immediately as he rolled away. He shut the alarm off, but, thankfully, resettled himself against me. This time, he kissed my shoulder and gave a small grind of his hips, presenting the evidence of his morning wood.

His hard-on made me aware of the slight soreness I was sporting. I loved it. I loved every minute of the night before. It had been so hot having his beautiful, smooth body over me, inside of me—watching him come apart from the feel of me surrounding him. Yeah, it had been the hottest sex of my life, with the hottest man I'd ever met.

But what made it unlike anything I'd ever experienced, was the level of emotion I was feeling—and that Ken had obviously been feeling, too. He was worshipful in his attentions. His gaze, his voice—they held so much leashed emotion, I thought for a moment he might cry. When he said he wanted to be perfect for me, I had a stinging sensation behind my eyes that warned I was close to an emotional upheaval, too.

Ken gave me another poke of his erection and growled. "I have to get up," he said. "I have never wanted to stay in bed this badly, and that's really saying something, considering I've had to get up and fight blizzards to get my ass to the hospital." He gave my shoulder a nip and a kiss and rose from bed.

I resented reality intruding on our cozy love nest, but I needed to get up as well. Time wasn't going to stand still for us.

"If you'd like to shower with me, you're welcomed to, but…" he let the sentence hang, seeming reluctant to finish his thought.

"But what? Is it gross? Growing mold?" I joked.

"No, it's just *a lot* smaller than yours."

"Pshaw." I waved away his concern. "Don't think for a minute I'd mind all the 'accidental' bumping uglies we'd do. Sounds like fun."

Ken's face went slack.

"Did you just…*air quote?*" He sounded disgusted and I laughed. Finger air quotes were obviously an anathema to him. "It's a good thing I'm in love with you, you know."

I stopped laughing, the seriousness of his words hitting me squarely in the chest.

"You love me?" I asked quietly.

He nodded, watching me carefully. There was a long silence, then he said, "Enough to overlook air quotes."

Just like that, the mood was lightened, and I barked out a laugh. "Shut up," I teased. "I seem to remember you air quoting once." I tossed a pillow at him, but he deflected it.

"Never speak of that again, it brings me shame," he said with fake solemnity. "Now, let's have that shower."

Ken hadn't been joking when he said it was smaller. We were very cramped and had a difficult time moving around each other to rinse, but, as I predicted, there was a lot of fun, inadvertent rubbing of the cocks.

We were both wearing dopey grins by the time we dried off. Seeing him that happy after the week we'd had, was a relief.

"I like seeing that smile back on your face, McPretty."

It dimmed fractionally, but he said, "It feels good to wear it again."

"I guess my magic ass made it all better," I joked, trying to keep the mood jovial.

"You make everything better."

He said it so matter-of-factly, it hit me hard. My Adam's apple bobbed in my throat as I tried to swallow the sudden emotion. *Mighty Thor*, Ken was going to kill me with his heart.

As we dressed and ate a quick breakfast, I thought about King and how Ken said I was being stubborn. I didn't think I was being stubborn. Quinn—and now Dan—had their plates full, and I wasn't going to add to their burden, especially considering there wasn't any immediate need. But I did have to admit that I was being uncharacteristically passive. There was no reason why I couldn't utilize the resources I had available without dragging Quinn or Dan into it.

If anyone could help me *and* be discreet, it was Alex. This slow-moving, absurd situation needed to be resolved and it didn't look like I had too much hope of King just going away. After each interaction, each contact, I tried to tell myself that there probably wouldn't be a next time—that he'd get the message and go away.

But he'd approached me last week. Pushed his body to mine. Said things that let me know he wasn't through with whatever crazy shit he was doing. It *was* past time for me to be proactive, and maybe if I promised I'd be more proactive, make an effort to deal with the situation instead of pretending it would go away, then Ken would be happier.

"Listen, DKM," I said stopping him before he could open the front door. "I really am sorry about King and the worry. I promise you, I'll enlist some help, okay? *Not* Quinn and *not* Dan," I clarified. "But I'll talk to our information officer today and see if there's anything we can do."

Ken stood still, watching me, oddly expressionless. I thought I'd see relief on his face, but instead, he looked like the powered-down cyborg again.

"What's that look about?" I asked. "Don't you want me to involve someone? Hasn't that been your beef?"

"I do." He nodded. "I'm very glad you'll talk to your information guy."

He reached for the knob again, so I put my palm to the door and stuck my face close to his. "But? Don't leave me in the dark wondering how I'm screwing up. As much as I'd like you to believe I'm Nostradamus, I really don't have a clue what's going on in your head. Help me out."

He seemed to war with himself. He opened his mouth to speak, only to close it again. He growled, huffed, and started rubbing his hair and neck. Something was very wrong.

Alarmed, I said sharply, "Ken, what is it?"

"I'm sorry," he blurted. He looked like he was going to confess a crime and my stomach flipped.

"Sorry for what?"

"I'm sorry I made you believe that King was my problem. I'm sorry you felt guilt over that. I'm an asshole."

He said this all in a rush and it took a second to comprehend that there was something other than King that kept him away. Something he didn't want to tell me.

"Tell me what the real problem is," I encouraged, trying to modulate my voice to conceal the mild panic I was feeling.

"I will," he promised. "But not right now. I have to get to work and this conversation requires more time than we've got."

My face must have told him I couldn't bear the suspense, because he added, "It's nothing you need to worry about, okay. It's family problems."

It was at that moment, when the agonizing tension melted from me, that I knew I was the most selfish person on Earth. Once I knew it was about family, my gut relaxed, my heart started beating to a natural rhythm and I knew it was going to be okay—for me. I knew I could wait out the day to hear the story. It made me a dick. I knew it did. I didn't want Ken hurting, but if he was going to make me wait to talk, it was a relief knowing it wasn't going to be a talk that ruined our relationship or changed us.

I requested a cab, walked him to his bus stop and gave him a kiss, making him promise he'd join me at home after work.

Once I got to the residence, I went up to my floor, but instead of going into my apartment, I knocked on Alex and Sandra's door. Alex answered almost immediately.

"Oh, you're ready for Wally now?"

I blinked. I'd forgotten he and I were sharing Wally duties while Dan was in London.

"Y-yes. All ready."

Wally was standing behind Alex, snorting and whining, trying to get between his legs to greet me.

"I'll get his things," he said, opening the door wider and retreating into the apartment. Wally came out into the hall and did a dance around me.

"Hey, bud." I gave the dog a head scratch and flank pat, waiting for Alex to return. When he did, he was carrying Wally's leash and bed. "No food or bowls?" I asked.

"I have some of my own stuff for him here, just not a bed or leash yet, so his bowls and food are at Dan's." When Dan's schedule stopped being crazy, I was going to feel bad for Alex. He seemed to be attached to Wally and vice versa. I hoped he and Sandra would adopt a pup of their own, Alex was good with dogs.

"Thanks." I paused for a moment then asked, "Are you available today to help me with something?" I glanced away from his intense gaze, uncomfortable with revealing my need for help.

"Is this *something* why you changed your phone number?" he asked knowingly.

Jesus, this kid. Was there anything he didn't know? "Yes."

He nodded. "I'll be down in the center at eight." He started to back into the apartment, but then added, "I walked Wally at six-thirty, so he's good for a while."

* * *

After changing clothes and taking the dog back to Dan's, I met up with Alex down in the data center.

I didn't exactly know what I needed from him, or what I wanted to divulge. I supposed that first and foremost, I wanted to know King's real name and whether or not he had a criminal record. Perhaps the facial recognition software could find out both of those things with a simple scan.

Or maybe that was wishful thinking. I didn't understand how any of it worked, nor did I know if private companies like Cipher could access databases. But, if anyone could, it was Alex Greene.

When I walked in, Alex spoke without looking away from one of the many monitors along the wall. "Do you have a name for me, or is that what we're going to figure out?"

I took a deep breath and said, "I don't know this guy's real or last name, only that he said he was 'King.'"

Alex swiveled his chair to face me, his face free of reaction. He didn't ask another question, instead, letting his silence encourage me to continue.

"I was hoping maybe you could use the facial recognition software to find out what his name is and if he has a criminal record."

"You have a picture of him?" he asked.

"No, no. Well, I mean, I have one of his torso and one of his penis." My face heated at the admission.

Why did you say that, Thompson, you idiot?!

Look at his face, I argued to myself. *He's been taking lessons from Sandra on how to pull secrets from people!*

Don't let it happen again, man! Buck up! Pertinent info only!

"Unfortunately, there's no penis database from which I could glean the information."

I barked out a laugh. "I meant using the software on the cameras in the building."

"He was here? What date?" Alex spun his chair around to a computer and started typing.

"You can do this?" I asked, relieved. "I was worried it was a big ask, I don't know how this works, what databases you can use, et cetera."

He snorted. "*Legally*, we're not supposed to be doing this. Illinois requires companies to obtain consent before scanning faces. I'm not overly concerned with that, though. As for the databases," he shrugged. "*I* can access them all."

No wonder Quinn likes him so much. Alex's casual disregard for legality reminded me somewhat of Quinn's own ends-justify-the-means vigilante code.

When justice fails, he finds a way to make people pay. When he found me as an internal auditor, we worked together to bring down a CEO and CFO for fraudulent reporting. What we had done hadn't been strictly legal, but it was necessary. He offered me a position in his young company, and I hadn't needed any time to think it over.

It didn't matter to me that his methods weren't above-board. This was a man who knew how to find the bad guys and make them go down hard. I respected that, I wanted in on it. I supposed I had my own warped moral code where technical honesty and the ends justifying the means was a perfectly right and correct way to move in the world. I also supposed Quinn saw this in me, like maybe he had Alex and knew there was a place for us with Cipher.

Since Janie had come into his life, Quinn had kept the vigilantism to a minimum, preferring to work within the bounds of the law. It was for the best, really. Janie was too smart to not catch on to his dealings eventually, and she would have never condoned it or accepted the risk. My opinion was that, either way, I was happy to work for Quinn Sullivan.

"Steven," Alex said, reclaiming my attention. "What was the date?"

"Oh, right, yes. It was June twenty-third. No, wait, it was after midnight, so the twenty-fourth," I corrected.

Alex pressed a few more buttons and footage from one of the lobby cameras appeared on screen. The timestamp said 12:00 AM. I could see the front door clearly, the video quality surprisingly crisp.

"What time do you think you came in?"

"I'm not sure. 1:15ish," I guessed. "Possibly earlier."

Alex skipped forward until the video showed me crossing the threshold of the entry. He slowed the playback, and we watched, frame by frame as I entered, followed closely by King. For several frames, he had his head tilted down, like he was looking at the floor. I worried we weren't going to have anything usable—at least from this camera—but then he looked up to the ceiling and for a moment, straight into the camera. Bingo.

Alex froze the video, zoomed in on King and asked, "This your guy?" I nodded.

Within minutes, Alex had given me a name and an address. Jacob Kingston Moore. He lived in North Park, and further digging resulted in an arrest record. Criminal threats, breaking and entering, criminal trespass, and assault were what he had been charged with in the past, but charges of criminal threats *and* assault had both been dropped. Separate arrests, months apart. The B&E charge and criminal trespass somehow were misdemeanors and the only penalty had been fines.

"What the hell?" I said softly, deeply disappointed in what I saw before me.

Alex looked at the information and said, "He's been lucky."

"Yeah, I was hoping this guy was on parole or something." I pasted on a smile for Alex and said, "Well, thanks for looking him up for me. At least I know his name now."

Alex looked at me for a long moment, his blue eyes piercing. "What did he do?"

I shook my head. "Nothing anyone could do anything about."

CHAPTER TWENTY-NINE

B y 7:00 PM, when Ken arrived at my apartment, the morning's disappointment regarding King had faded.

I told myself that I wasn't at square one, I knew his name and his address, so I did have something to give to the authorities if the situation escalated. But seeing his arrest record had been chilling. Seeing his lack of convictions had been frustrating. I supposed I hoped he was hanging by a thread as far as the law went, possibly on strike two of the three strikes. I didn't know if three strikes was a thing anymore—I just wanted leverage or hope that I could make him stop. As it was now, I didn't have anything. The police would shrug if I made a report. Pictures of me? So what? A picture of his penis? They wouldn't care. I didn't have proof that he'd put his hands on me or intimated that he'd retaliate if I hurt him. Looking at this from the outside, I recognized that I had nothing—nothing against him and no recourse.

I shook it off, knowing I was in a much better position and frame of mind than I had been two days ago. Two days ago, I didn't know if Ken was on the verge of dumping me, didn't know who King was, and didn't know if I was going to have to marry my best girl friend to save her from her evil cousin and his nefarious scheme to take over the world.

Now? Now I knew Ken was in love with me, knew his troubles weren't about me or King, and Daniel O'Malley had stepped up to save Kat and the world. Things were looking up for Steven Thompson, yes indeed.

Once Alex had come back to collect Wally, I decided to order Chinese for dinner. When Ken walked in, I met him with a sound kiss.

"Hey there, sexy thing," I greeted.

He dropped his gym bag on the floor of the entry and squeezed my waist. "You're in a great mood tonight, I see." He dipped his head to nuzzle my ear with his nose and whispered, "Rub some of that off on me."

"Ooh, gladly." I gave him another kiss but kept him from deepening it. I wanted to have our talk before we started yanking our clothes off.

I took him by the hand, led him into the kitchen and announced, "Ta-da!" with a flourish. I had the countertop littered with boxes and boxes of take-out. "It's the same food from our date. I figured we could have a little do-over, but this time, I'd be clued into the fact that I could get a little action at the end of the night." I gave him a wink, making him laugh. "We'll have lots of leftovers that you'll help me with this time."

He shook his head and smiled widely, like I was crazy in the best way. "You've made my day a thousand times better, just by being you."

I swear, this guy…his candor and heart were going to kill me. "You do the same for me," I admitted. "I've never felt like this before. It's addicting. *You're* addicting." Deciding that was enough mushy stuff, I interrupted the mood, "Load up your plate, let's go eat!"

After we got settled, I asked, "Did you have a hard day at the hospital, or are you stressed out because we're going to have that talk?"

He chewed and bobbed his head back and forth. "A little of both, actually," he said once he'd swallowed.

"Well, don't stress over me," I insisted. "I'm here to support you, not make your life harder."

He stared, his brow scrunched. After a moment, he sighed, and it was hard to interpret. Could a sigh be dreamy and frustrated at the same time?

"That's what I'm talking about," he shook his head. "Right there."

"Right where? What *are* you talking about?"

Instead of answering, he said, "I told Kari about you on Sunday."

My body stilled. This wasn't going to be good. "Okay," I said slowly.

"She didn't take it…very well."

I nodded my head and repeated, "Okay," encouraging him to continue, but my face was starting to lose blood. Dread filled me. He hadn't been completely honest when he said it wasn't about me—that it was only family problems. This was absolutely about me.

"She said some nasty shit," he said in a rush. "And I asked her if I was disinvited from the wedding if I brought you as my guest. She said we needed to cool down and talk later."

I exhaled deeply and closed my eyes. "You hadn't come out to your family until now?" I didn't like this. I didn't like the idea that I was the wedge, that I was the bombshell in the family. Suddenly, I felt a whole lot less secure.

"That's just it!" he bellowed, then seemed to check himself and continued more calmly. "They've known for years. I guess I didn't realize that Kari had her head in the sand this whole time. It hurt." His jaw clenched. "And it made me angry. So angry."

I felt a small sliver of relief at that—knowing his sexuality was not new information to his family. But I was afraid of what this meant for us. I scooted closer to him and laid my hand on his. "I'm sorry you had to go through that, but I have to ask…" I couldn't keep the worry from my voice, though I tried mightily. "Were you thinking of breaking up with me this week?"

"No!" he insisted. "*Hell* no." He grabbed the sides of my face and brought our foreheads together, making my glasses shift. His vehemence erased some of my tension and I sagged in relief. "Not for one second, do you hear me? I love you."

I love you. I let the words wash over me and I tried to soak up the comfort and reassurance, but they didn't quite have the same impact they'd had this morning. *He loves his family, too.* I didn't know if loving me and loving his family was going to be compatible in the long run. *Eventually...*

I pulled away and sat up straight. Ken examined my face then continued, "I just needed time to get over the sadness of losing Kari, too."

I frowned, not understanding what he meant. "Too? And what do you mean, 'losing?' You guys are going to talk it out. Emotions are running high, but you'll work it out."

He was shaking his head before I finished speaking. "No, she said things I can't forget, Steven. I expected more from her. Kari, my dad, hell, maybe even my mom..." He sneered in contempt. "My relationships with them apparently come with some high expectations and strings. I didn't realize that until college—didn't think it was the case with Kari at all."

His use of the word, 'expectation,' reminded me of our conversations about his family. Knowing Ken's personality like I did, I thought I was starting to see what was happening.

"Babe," I said gently. "I know I don't know much about the dynamics of your family, but I do know that you and your sister can both lose your cool when people don't stick to the imagined script. It sounds like each of you went into that conversation with different expectations and came out of it angry and hurt."

He gave a small, reluctant nod of his head. "Yes, but she knows how strained my relationship is with our dad—and why. She said things that brought that betrayal back to the fore." Eyebrows raised he shook his head bewildered. "What did she think? That I'd hold on to hard feelings this long over nothing?!"

I knew I was missing part of this story. It sounded like something similar had happened in college with his dad and Kari hadn't learned a lesson from that. Selfishly, this realization helped my own inner turmoil. He had issues with his family years before I'd come along, and I wasn't as afraid that he'd resent me over it.

Gently, I encouraged him to tell me the story. He painted a picture of an idyllic childhood and family—his parents happily married, his father, the judge, an important and wise man, Ken's own desire to emulate them and to be passionate about things that mattered and make things that mattered a priority.

He said of his dad, "He had a passion for law and a passion for people. He never wanted to let anyone down. It never crossed my mind that he'd ever let me down. But he did."

I listened with quiet consolation as he told me about the night his dad caught him with a guy at school—how his dad tore into him, berated him, tried to make him think he was screwing up his whole life.

"I didn't think he'd let me down," he said again, his eyes filled with sadness. "And I didn't think I'd ever disappoint him. But we both did those exact things by simply being ourselves, I guess. We assumed things about each other, things we thought we knew, then got upset when the other didn't…"

"Stick to the script," I supplied softly. "I'm seeing a genetic pattern here, Ken."

He let out a huff of reluctant amusement. "Ya think?"

I thought about his dad. I thought about his relationship with his sister and what I knew about it. Ken didn't have many people in his life who he loved, who were his cheerleaders. The idea that he was losing one of them broke my heart. He loved his sister and she loved him. I knew she did. Maybe they just needed to fight the pull of their DNA that wanted to write people off who disappointed them. I wanted Ken to be happy and losing his relationship with his sister wasn't going to make him happy.

"Do you want my advice, even though we've established that no one takes or has any use for good advice?"

He was frowning, probably anticipating what I was going to say. Still, he said, "Sure."

"I don't know about your dad—you guys have let a lot of years go by. But Kari is a big part of your life and you love her. Right?" I asked pointedly.

He nodded stiffly.

"You love her," I repeated. "So be the bigger man here, Ken. Go to the wedding without me. Help make her day fairytale perfect." The look on his face was pure incredulity. He opened his mouth, no doubt to argue, but I held my hand up to silence him. "I know, I know," I assured him, and squeezed his knee. "She was awful. I know it, you know, *she* knows it.

"This wedding is happening soon. It's important to her. When you guys make up—and you will—you'll both look back at the wedding pictures and be sad that you were absent. It will be a reminder of a very sad time for both of you. This way, you can avoid that regret and, honestly"—I gave him a conspiratorial, somewhat evil grin—"take some satisfaction in knowing you're the bigger Miles. She's petty and you're not."

"B-but," he sputtered. "It's the principle of the thing! Why should I go and celebrate her and her love, when I can't even show up with the person I love?"

"Because you love her," I said quietly. "And I'm right here. The wedding isn't about me or you or us. It's about her and what's-his-name."

"I don't like this," he muttered. "Are you trying to turn me into a good person or something?"

"You're already a good person. I'm just trying to look after that soft heart of yours." *Somebody has to.* "Go. Fulfill your family duties. If you guys haven't patched things up by Thanksgiving, take me home with you and we can set fire to the holidays. We'll ruin all the holidays for years to come."

His face lit up at that. "Promise?"

"Oh, Thor give me strength. Yes, yes, I promise."

We finished eating our cold Chinese, then Ken announced that he was going to email Kari to tell her that he'd be in Cleveland for a fitting on the sixteenth.

"Sounds good. I'm going to watch some DWTS." We'd been together long enough for him to know that DWTS meant *Dancing with the Stars*. We'd also been together long enough for me to know he disliked the show.

He gave a rueful twist of his lips, but said, "I've got a book in my bag, so go crazy." He pulled his phone out of his pocket and started typing.

I scooted down to recline on the armrest and turned on the DVR to get the show going, but my eyes kept straying to Ken who seemed to be concentrating hard on whatever he was writing. Once, he huffed and said, "No. Delete," and started again.

This witch...

Pride and principle were important to Ken. Extending this olive branch, letting her have her way was difficult for him. But he was tenderhearted under his crust, and I suspected he was relieved that I was encouraging him to do this.

I hoped his sister took this opportunity to make things right with him, because if she didn't, I was sure Ken wouldn't be giving her another chance.

His phone chimed with a text. I glanced over to see him exhale shakily. When he connected eyes to mine, I could see his were shimmering with moisture.

"What did she say?"

He cleared his throat. "Just *I love you.*"

"Oh," I replied. "That's good. That's a good start."

He set his phone on the table and swatted his hand in the air. "She's just saying that because she's getting her way." The words were gruff, but he wore a smile. He came toward me, so I started to rise from my reclined position, but he stopped me.

"Don't get up." He lifted my legs and settled himself underneath them, draping my limbs over his lap.

"You okay?"

"I think I will be, thanks to you."

"I didn't do anything," I said, waving my hand in dismissal.

He caught my hand mid-swipe and brought my knuckles to his lips. "You did everything," he said, relief and gratitude etched on his features. I paused the playback on the TV, anticipating a serious conversation about what came next, but he surprised me when he affected a comically horrified expression. "You *DVR* this show?"

Ah, I *loved* when Ken became playful.

I played along, fighting my smile. "Yes, I do, McPretty. Don't judge me. The new season is starting next week, so I thought I'd re-watch the last finale."

His eyebrows lifted in surprise. "Wait. This is old? You've been watching reruns? You already know who wins?" His voice was infused with exaggerated incredulousness, underscoring how crazy he thought it was.

I felt my lips twitch, but I held fast to my composure. "What?" I shrugged, pretending to be oblivious.

"I don't know how I feel about this." He dropped my hand like I had leprosy. "Movies are one thing, but re-watching *contests*? *Dance contests?*"

I couldn't hold back, I burst into laughter. He was too freaking adorable.

He continued to fight his smile and muttered, "You think you know somebody…then he uses air quotes and records dance contests." He shook his head like the situation was completely tragic.

I scrambled up, removing my legs from his lap. "What do you have against dancing?"

"I don't enjoy it," he replied baldly.

I straddled his lap, brought my face close to his and whispered, "There's nothing about bodies moving in sync that stimulates you at all, Ken?" I lowered my groin to his and gave a tight, controlled grind.

He hissed out a breath, bringing his hands to my hips. "I under-stand *wanting* to dance, enjoying the act as a participant—like Paulie does. But watching others dance, viewing it as art holds no appeal for me."

I gave another thrust, pulling a moan from him.

"Do you like participating? In dances? What about a lap dance? Do you see the value in that?" I asked softly, my lips just above his.

With my next grind, he was un-bucking my belt.

"Steven," he said, breath shallow. "If we were the participants in a recorded lap dance, I would re-watch the hell out of it."

CHAPTER THIRTY

STEVEN

A week later, I had the distinct pleasure of witnessing Dan and Kat's marriage ceremony at the courthouse. It was satisfying to see my friends finally embark on the relationship I always knew they were destined for—not to mention it was also a huge relief to hear the *I dos* that signaled I was officially off the hook for helping Kat out of her predicament.

Bonus: I was in possession of one hilarious wedding video of my friends macking on each other with complete abandon. It was going to come in handy the next time I wanted to bust Dan's balls. After the macaron bomb prank, he had it coming.

The next day, after a reportedly long, difficult labor, Janie and Quinn welcomed baby Desmond. Once word got out, all the staff in the residence were wearing happy smiles and talking excitedly about the baby.

On our way into the building, Charles, our doorman, asked, "Are they bringing him home tomorrow, Mr. Thompson?"

I didn't know.

As we passed the desk Larry said, "I bought him a teddy bear. Do you think the baby will like teddy bears, Mr. Thompson?"

I didn't know.

In the elevator, I wondered aloud how many days old a baby was before they opened their eyes. Ken said babies weren't kittens and, *oh my God*, wasn't I an uncle, how did I not know this?

One thing I did know: Ken was so fun to mess with.

Dan left for his Australia trip that night, and Kat moved into his apartment. We spent several hours together over the next week. And though she'd tried fishing for information about the mystery man I was seeing, I still resisted telling her about him. It wasn't normal, and I didn't understand why—besides it being a habit to keep people out of my business—I kept up the secrecy. Checking the hallway before we left the apartment and exiting the elevator first to scan the lobby was becoming tedious. The longer we were together, the more ridiculous my efforts seemed. I needed to just rip the Band-Aid off and let everyone know we were a couple. But, honestly, the unveiling of Ken to Ernesto didn't exactly go well. I was still annoyed and avoiding him, and I didn't need more of that same judgment from anyone else. Maybe it *was* for the best that I kept Ken under wraps for a bit longer.

On Friday, I went up to the penthouse with Kat and Stan to see Janie and the baby. Quinn let us in, and since it was the first time I'd seen him since Desmond's arrival, I shook his hand and congratulated him. He gave me a terse, *thank you*, then stalked back to stand by Janie's side. I didn't know why I was disappointed, but I was. Quinn had never been given to chitchat or small talk, and he looked haggard, to be honest. I got it. He was tired, probably unsure and slightly nervous about having a tiny human to take care of. And, I bet my bonus, he wasn't keen on visitors coming in to gawk at the baby or tiring Janie. Still, he gave Kat a tiny smile and later, pulled Stan aside for a conversation.

Elizabeth was also there, and she kept giving me…looks. Knowing looks. Squinty-eyed, suspicious looks. Those looks turned devilish when she said, "So, Steven, what have you been…*doing*…lately?"

Ken would have been so proud of me, my face was *blank*—not one muscle betraying anything when I answered, "You know, stuff and things."

"*Stuffing things*?" she asked wryly, cupping her hand around her ear like she was hard of hearing.

I glared at her, but it was completely ruined by the small smile playing on my lips. I gave my head a little shake and turned back to Janie, who was cradling her son. The baby had been sleeping since before we arrived, so I hadn't had a chance to see his eyes. That thought spurred me to pull my phone out and send Ken a text.

ME: This kid hasn't opened his eyes once. He's six days old. I think you need to go back to medical school. :P

I didn't get a text back until almost seven, long after I'd escaped the penthouse and Elizabeth's gaze.

DKM: Shh, my degree is in veterinary medicine. They haven't caught on yet.

I smiled at his goofy response. Who said DKM wasn't funny? He was a riot.

DKM: I just picked up my race packet. I need to be out the door by 4:30 tomorrow morning to catch the shuttle, so no sexy time tonight. I need to conserve my energy.

The half-marathon he was running was the next day. He'd been excited about it all week. I understood his excitement and competitiveness, but *no sex*? This was crazy talk.

ME: Sure, sure. But wouldn't a blow job relax you and help you get to sleep faster? I mean, if you'd rather do your breathing exercises, that's fine too...

His response was almost immediate.

DKM: You make a compelling argument...
DKM: I'll be home soon.

By 8:30, Ken was out like a light, dreaming sweet dreams. I, however, was restless, so I got up and watched television for a while, checked my email and opened my physical mail.

I had two brightly colored envelopes in the pile that looked like greeting cards or birthday cards. My birthday wasn't for a few more months, so I was curious. No return address on either and my name written in the same handwriting wasn't a good sign. I had my suspicions about the sender before I opened them.

The first card, in a pink envelope, showed a photo of a lipstick-wearing gorilla smiling widely, displaying impressively scary, yellow teeth and fangs. The smile looked deranged, and even though nothing about this situation was funny, I laughed.

Above the gorilla were the words, "IT WOULD BE TOTALLY BANANAS..." When I opened the card, the printed message ended with "...IF YOU WERE MY VALENTINE."

"He's a lunatic," I whispered. Did this guy have unused Valentine's Day cards hanging around his house? Did he stock up in February so he could woo men year-round?

"ROSES ARE RED

VILETS ARE BLUE

LOSE THE GUY

OR I'M GONNA HURT YOU"

Crazy and stupid, what a combo...

I grabbed the next card. It was in a neon orange envelope, with a drawn picture of a corgi under a word bubble with the phrase, "HEY CORGEOUS" printed in shiny block letters.

Inside, the handwritten note started on the left side, in decent handwriting, but as it got closer to the bottom, the words became sloppy.

"I'm sorry, come back to the Male and we can talk about it. I didn't mean to make you mad. Forgive me. I love you. Why do you want to make me jealous? I'm not nice when I'm jealous. Ditch him and we can start over. I promise I'll be better. I won't hurt you I promise. I won't hurt you unless you try to hurt me again. If I see you with him again, I'll know you are trying to fuck me up and I'll fuck *you* up, do you understand? I'LL FUCK YOU UP SO HARD NO ONE WILL RECOGNIZE YOU! Meet at our place on Saturday. I love you."

The pain behind my eye was coming back. Every time things started to seem like they were settling down, King had to pop up. Maybe this was going to be his *modus operandi*. Maybe I'd get cards or letters or pictures every few weeks until he got bored. I hoped he got bored very soon, because this was getting old.

I had to hide the cards. If Ken saw them, he'd go to Quinn. I knew he would. He said he would. But...Quinn wasn't in a particularly generous and understanding mood lately, nor was I his favorite person on staff. If he found out I'd let a nutcase into his building—the same building where his wife slept, he'd be furious.

I told Ken he'd murder me and throw me into the lake, but that wasn't the worst thing he could do, honestly.

He could fire me.

Quinn had never warmed to me. I knew it, I felt it. But he'd put a lot of trust and faith in me and that had been enough.

I looked around at the apartment. It was luxurious, no doubt. But it was also home. This apartment, this building, it felt like home in a way no place had since childhood. Cipher Systems wasn't just my source of income, it was a career that fulfilled me. My coworkers were my friends, neighbors, family. If he fired me, I'd lose everything.

With these thoughts swimming in my head, I took the cards and stuffed them into a magazine then tucked the magazine into the bottom drawer of my desk in the spare room. I wanted to throw them away, tear them to pieces, but part of me knew that the day might come when I needed them as evidence. I hoped that day would never come, but I had to be smart about it. I'd deal with this when I could, when I needed to.

I still didn't have anything law enforcement would care about, so what was the point in making a stink? There wasn't one.

Ken wouldn't see it that way.

* * *

Just to prove my point that Cipher Systems was a kick-ass, awesome family to be a part of, I got to be in a *posse* on Tuesday evening.

A posse in a showdown with the enemy, Caleb Tyson.

Ken arrived home after going to the gym and headed straight for the shower. I forgot to pick up my mail from Larry on my way up and decided to dash down and grab it to make sure there were no new greeting cards from King.

When I approached the concierge desk, Lawrence handed me the mail.

"Here you are, Mr.—" He cut his sentence short, glancing quickly at the entrance of the building. A flash of worry crossed his features, but he quickly masked it as he swept up the handset of the desk phone and dialed.

I stiffened when I saw the large group coming through the glass doors.

A man in a bespoke suit entered and was immediately flanked by two uniformed police officers. Behind them were ten identically dressed men, all muscled and watchful in a manner that was a dead giveaway they were security.

Their presence was conspicuous and alarming. I had a bad, bad feeling about this.

Before the group could reach the concierge desk, Damon intercepted the leader.

"What can I do for you gentlemen this evening?"

"You can start by getting out of my way," the man said, glaring up at Damon. "We're here on official police business, and I have to speak to someone who isn't a mindless goon."

"Hey, asshole!" I took exception to his treatment of Damon. Whoever this person was, he wasn't going to get far in here with that attitude. *Fuck this guy.*

I heard Larry place the handset of the phone down on the receiver and clear his throat. "Officers, maybe I can be of service to you." He flicked his eyes to Damon, and I saw him issue a subtle nod.

Damon stepped back and allowed the group to proceed to the desk. I stayed rooted to the spot directly in front of Larry, unwilling to concede any space to the man. It was deliberately antagonistic, but he'd pissed me off.

"I demand you release—" he started to say to Larry but stopped when he realized I wasn't getting out of his way. He looked to me and snarled, "Move."

Instead of stepping out of his way, I leaned into the counter, draping my arm along it, making sure I was taking up as much room as I could. "So, this is *police business*, huh?" I asked. "Are you a detective?" I swept my eyes down his form, in an obvious perusal. "That looks like a suit a detective might wear."

Oh, and didn't *that* just piss him off. I smirked, knowing he'd take offense. His suit was tailor-made and of the finest quality. There was no way a Chicago detective could ever afford what he was wearing. Insinuating that his suit looked cheap got him right in the ego.

"I'm not a detective," he replied stiffly. "I'm the CEO of—"

"But I thought you said this was police business," I interrupted. "If you're not the police, who are you to make any demands?"

He wasn't a lawyer, wasn't the head of a government agency. The way I figured it, cooperating with him wasn't necessary. If these police officers wanted something, they were going to have to speak up.

"I have a court order!" he snapped.

"For what, exactly?"

One of the officers side-stepped me and gestured for Larry to move down the counter.

"I don't see how that's any of your business," the man said, deliberately pushing his cuffs back to look at his watch. It was a Rolex, and he made sure I saw it.

Behind me, I heard the officer say *Kathleen Caravel-Tyson.*

I whirled around, startled. The cop looked at me curiously, so I wiped my face of expression.

Kat.

They were here for Kat, and this slimy, entitled asshole was Caleb Tyson. I should have made the connection. Over the years I'd seen a few pictures of him, but, *boy oh boy,* those snapshots had no way of conveying the sheer and immediate repugnancy of his aura. He was *Vile Level: Mr. Burns Meets Patrick Bateman.*

Kat's 'Uncle' Eugene hadn't been overstating this clusterfuck, obviously, because here her cousin stood, prepared with a court order, police backup, and his own hired muscle.

Kat and Dan had their certificate—had irrefutable proof of their marriage—but I still didn't want Kat to have to be a part of this or be afraid. The spectacle of security-overkill and police presence was meant to be intimidating. It would be for the best if Dan could handle

Caleb alone. I knew he was back from Australia but had no idea if he was in the building.

Please say Kat's not here, Larry, I begged silently. *Please, Please.*

"There is no one in the building by that name, officer," the concierge replied smoothly.

"That's impossible!" Caleb said, pushing by me to get in Larry's face. "I have a witness! What about Kat Tanner?"

Unperturbed, Larry repeated, "There's no one in the building by that name."

Caleb pounded his fist. "Bullshit!"

The officer raised his voice to interrupt whatever tantrum Tyson was about to unleash and asked, "Is there a lease or tenant registry you can search?"

"Yes, sir, but I can tell you, you won't find any Tanners or Caravels on the list. And the only Tyson is a seventy-year-old widower."

Damn, Larry was good. I wanted to reach over and give him a big kiss on his weathered cheek. Feeling cheered, I leaned close to Caleb and said, "Looks like you're shit outta luck, Detective Douche."

"Steven," Quinn said abruptly, approaching the desk.

I straightened, took in his stony expression, and stepped away from Caleb.

"A word." The order was accompanied by a tilt of his head toward the seating area.

We stood by the settee and Quinn's eyes surveilled the room, taking in Caleb's watchful security personnel. His jaw ticked, a telltale signal of his leashed anger. "Don't try to help," he said under his breath, making sure he wasn't overheard. "You might do more harm than good, so don't say anything."

Without waiting for a response, he walked back to the concierge desk.

"*Don't say anything*, he says," I muttered to myself, peevishly. What made him think I would say anything? I was a motherfucking *vault* and he knew it. And, *don't try to help*? What the hell was that about? I was the only one in this room who witnessed the marriage. I was selected precisely to be *the* designated helper. I had video recording—on my person—that would shut this shit down in no time flat.

Whatever. Quinn was the boss. Stan was guarding Kat when Dan was gone, so that made this his concern. I agreed that the less said now, the better. We all had to have our stories straight and let Kat and Dan lead this show. Did I know what date Dan had finagled to have put on their official marriage license? No, I did not. Therefore, I wasn't going to say jack shit.

Quinn didn't need to pull me aside and verbalize the importance of playing it close to the vest. It was a given. At least, I thought it was. If he was worried about my discretion, then there was trouble. Discretion, confidentiality—these were paramount when working for Cipher. Not for the first time, I doubted his trust in me.

"I have a witness that says my cousin lives here, and I demand you produce her now, Mr. Sullivan."

Tyson's raised voice broke through my ruminations. This situation was becoming volatile. The longer Quinn prevaricated the more frustrated Caleb became.

I heard a voice come over a radio saying, "I have eyes on the target, over," and Quinn's posture went rigid. Caleb smirked.

One of the officers spoke into his radio, "Secure target and hold position. We'll be right out, over."

Kat was here. If luck was on our side, then Dan was too. If he wasn't, then I was going to have to stand up and vouch for her marital status. I looked around the room to gauge the tension level. Damon was standing at his post near the elevator. His eyes were watchful, but other than his eerie stillness, he betrayed no hint of stress.

A message came through that Kat was married, and Caleb's smug face morphed into outrage. He reached over and yanked on the radio at the officer's shoulder. "She's not married, she's crazy. You can't believe a word she says."

"Target doesn't look crazy to me, sir," the static-crackled voice replied. "Nor does her husband..."

I relaxed my shoulders at this news. Dan was here. He'd no doubt have documentation to back up their story, and there was no way in hell he'd let her be taken into custody—not Caleb's and not the Chicago PD's.

As Caleb yelled into the radio, arguing with another officer, Quinn shook his head, casting looks at the police and security as if to say, *can you believe this guy?*

I smiled in spite of my earlier irritation with him. He let Caleb dig his own grave by thwarting and frustrating him until he let his emotions reveal himself to the police for what he was. It worked. The policemen were sighing and moving around like they were at the end of their patience with him too.

Quinn was such a badass. A jerk, yeah, but still a badass.

Finally, the officer whose radio had been commandeered by Caleb, wrested the handset from him and pulled him aside for what seemed to be a heated exchange. In the end, Kat's cousin appeared to win the argument because he shouted, "Court order!" again, turned toward the door, and led his group outside.

I heard steps to my right and found eight more of our security personnel entering the lobby. The other guards, Damon included, moved forward toward Quinn, awaiting instruction. Voices came from the elevator and Alex emerged, making a beeline for Quinn. He was followed by his wife Sandra, Nico, Ashley Winston, and a giant of a man I knew, based on descriptive gossip, had to be Ashley's mountain-man boyfriend, Drew.

As soon as Alex stepped next to Quinn, Quinn looked to the dozen men and said, "Let's go."

The rest of us let security proceed, but as soon as we were clear to exit, Sandra looked to me, pushed up her shirt sleeves and said, "I guess this *ya-hoo* didn't get the memo that knitters have posses. Let's go get our girl."

CHAPTER THIRTY-ONE

DKM

When I got out of the shower, Steven was nowhere to be found. I'd started cooking dinner, thinking wherever he'd gone to, he wouldn't be gone long. When he hadn't returned by the time I finished up and plated the food, I decided to text him.

ME: Where did you go? Everything okay?
STEVEN: I'm in the lobby. Be right back.

I breathed a sigh of relief when I read his message and rubbed the soreness in my chest.

Anxiety.

That's what this was. I'd been living with a slightly paranoid feeling since we had the run-in with King last month. Given Steven's information that the man had an arrest record, I thought I was justified in my worry. But I didn't need to know about his arrest record to know he wasn't harmless. His behavior here in this apartment was enough to worry me.

I feared for his safety, mostly when we were apart, and it had begun to have subtle effects on my life.

Over the weekend, right before I began the half-marathon, I kissed Steven and told him I'd see him in eighty minutes—because I was determined to keep pace at just over six minutes per mile the entire race. But after I'd started, I thought about him standing at the finish line, waiting by himself in the crowd of strangers, and how King could possibly approach him. Those worries unconsciously made me pick up my pace and I finished in 76.25. Even though it didn't get me placed in the top ten, it was my personal best for a long run.

Yeah, it was great that I made good time, but living with near-constant worry wasn't.

"Oh my God, Ken, you will not believe what just happened!" Steven said, walking through the door.

I met him at the threshold of the living room

"What?" I asked, alarmed. "Is King here?"

He waved the hand holding his mail. "No, no. It's my friend Kat. Remember the woman from the wedding video?"

I nodded, thinking of the pretty, dark-haired woman who married the tattooed guard.

When Steven showed me the video, I'd been surprised to learn that the Dan I'd heard so much about from Steven, was the same man assigned to Elizabeth when she'd been attacked. Seeing him brought up vivid memories and bitter feelings I was holding on to. Dan had left Elizabeth alone in the doctor's lounge of Chicago General to go investigate a bogus stalker-sighting. That poor decision made Elizabeth vulnerable, and her stalker took advantage of the moment. If I hadn't come into the lounge when I did—interrupted the woman holding Elizabeth at gunpoint—I doubt she'd be alive right now.

Still feel bad for shooting Menayda, Ken?

I asked myself this every time I was forced to think about King and the possible risks to Steven. More and more I found I was able to forgive myself for the shooting—and for the way I'd bungled the situation. The truth was, we were all alive. No one had to die that day, and I needed to realize that. Though I could have done several things differently to make the outcome better, in the moment—in the end—I stopped a woman from killing Elizabeth.

And Dan, he no doubt had his own regrets for that day. I'd clearly seen the remorse stamped on his face in the aftermath. I heard the concern and gentleness in his voice when he comforted her.

Initially, I hadn't felt upset about it—only relieved Elizabeth and I hadn't ended up full of bullets. But as the adrenaline wore off—as my own guilt surfaced, I felt bitter and blamed them. Blamed Nico for bringing this into her life. Blamed Elizabeth for making Nico's problems my problem. Blamed the guard for not doing his sole duty.

Now? Now I understood—*truly* understood—that Elizabeth, Nico, Dan and I were just doing the best we could in a situation that wasn't our fault.

And we were okay. Everyone was okay.

Based on the wedding video Steven was talking about, Dan seemed pretty okay in life too.

"Well, Kat's evil-ass cousin showed up in the lobby tonight with police and security demanding he take her into custody."

"What?!" I could feel my face scrunch up, betraying the surprise and incredulity I felt.

"Right?!" His eyes were wide behind his glasses. He seemed edgy and excitable, gesturing with his hands and swinging the mail around. "Dan and Kat showed up outside and this *ghoul* took his hired guys and the police and went outside thinking he's going to take her away. Quinn gathered all the security in the building and marched out, so the rest of us, we all went outside to stand behind Dan and shield Kat in a show of support."

He took a deep breath, finding his momentum again. "Anyway," he gave another swipe of the mail. "All of us went out there to support them and Dan and Kat give enough proof to the police that they're married, and that Caleb had no legal right to take her. Then—and this is funny—Nico starts shaking hands and giving autographs and telling jokes. The police and even Caleb's own security are all like, *Ooh, Nico Moretti,*" Steven said this in falsetto and pretended to swoon.

Freaking Nico. I didn't understand what the big deal was. He wasn't *that* funny.

"We were all getting a big kick out of it, because, *fuck this guy,* right? Then he dropped the bombshell that Kat's dad has had a major stroke." He shook his head, disgusted. "Her cousin is straight-up evil. Man, I'm so glad I didn't marry her. Dan's got a heap of shit on his plate now that her dad's fail—"

"What do mean, *glad you didn't marry her*?" I interrupted sharply. This story was already making no sense, but the idea that Steven would marry Kat was baffling. "Were you together?"

"Uh…" Steven's body had gone still, arms dropping to his side. By the smoothness in his expression, I could tell he'd said something he hadn't meant to say. This couldn't be good.

"Steven…" I raised my eyebrows expectantly, waiting.

His eyes blinked rapidly, and he sputtered for a moment. "I…No… We…" He seemed to get frustrated with himself and growled. "No. It's nothing. Not even a blip, okay. She needed to get married, and she asked me. But Dan stepped up because they have a *thing*. No big deal."

"She asked you," I said robotically. "And you said what?"

"I told her to ask Dan!" His voice raised in annoyance. He was getting angry, like he resented having to answer my questions. I could have dropped it then. Kat asked, Steven said to ask Dan, she married Dan. Resolved. Except his whole attitude reeked of guilt. Of secrecy.

Steven always has secrets.

Secrets kept from friends. *I'm a secret.*

From bosses. *King's a secret.*

From me. *Kat's a secret.*

"That's not a 'no' though, is it? Were you going to marry her? If Dan didn't?" I demanded.

"But he did!" He scrubbed his free hand through his hair. "I *knew* he would. *She* knew he would."

Intellectually, I knew marriage to his friend was not something he would have wanted—it would have been something he felt he needed to do to be helpful. But my heart didn't see it that way.

Thinking of all the times he'd check the hall before we left, and all the times I'd said *I love you* without hearing it in return—I didn't feel like he was as invested in this relationship as I was.

And it hurt.

To know he'd considered marrying someone without discussing it with me—just made something snap in my heart.

"Please don't look at me like that," he begged, his body sagging. "You don't understand, she needed—"

"I don't want to know what she needed!" I cut in. "Not only do I not care about your friend, I suspect a lot about this situation isn't exactly legal, so spare me." My pain was bleeding into anger now, all my built-up frustration and hurt needing to vent.

"Why are you so mad?" he asked, in surprise. He shook his head like I was unreasonable. Just that simple, affected bewilderment enraged me. He was going to act like this was nothing? *That* was how he was going to play this?

Not with me, he wasn't.

This could not stand.

"Why am I here tonight, Steven?" He wrinkled his brow, opened his mouth to respond, but I plowed ahead. "It's because I all but begged you to let me come over during the week. You were fine with weekends. Why haven't I met Kat? Or Dan? Or the couple across the hall? Why did you want to keep me from meeting Ernesto and Paulie?"

Why won't you say you love me?

I wouldn't let myself ask the question. I didn't think I could handle the answer.

Steven wasn't looking at me anymore. His eyes were focused on some point in the distance off to the right of me, but his jaw was ticking with furious, rhythmic clenches.

"You always do this," he gritted out, bringing his eyes back to mine. "You take everything personally. It's not always about you, you know." He gestured angrily with his hands, shaking the mail close to my face.

It pissed me off—everything he said pissed me off, so I grabbed the mail and pulled, intent on getting it out of my way. But he wouldn't let go.

"Stop!" he said and pulled against me. "Let go of the mail!"

The tug of war was bizarre, and his voice rose—had a distinct thread of panic in it. Instinctively, I knew I needed to see the mail, so I pulled as hard as I could and managed to wrench the papers loose.

I had two—what looked to be cards—and a sales circular from a furniture chain store.

He looked at my hands, blood draining from his face.

"No!"

CHAPTER THIRTY-TWO

STEVEN

Ken was holding two cards from King. And he was looking at me like I'd betrayed him.

"More secrets?" he asked, shaking the mail.

I didn't know how it had happened, but I'd rapidly lost all control over this situation. He didn't want to hear me out—to understand that marrying Kat was never something I thought would come to pass. No, he wanted to make this about another issue—use it as a catalyst to fight over some imagined slight.

Three nights a week together wasn't nothing. I wasn't an unreasonable, mean person because his approach to relationships was all or nothing. Someone here needed to be sane and have regard for the inevitable future.

I wanted to fight with him about it. The look in his eye—the hurt and disappointment—those bothered me. But the gleam of righteous indignation was infuriating. I wanted to tell him he needed another reality check. Tell him to pull out a calendar and take a good look at the weeks. Who did he think he was making demands on me? Pushing me?

God, how I wanted to tear him up.

But I stopped myself. I stopped myself because he was holding two cards from King.

I needed to get those away from him.

"Ken," I modulated my voice to sound calm.

His eyes narrowed in suspicion.

"What's really bothering you? Huh?" I was hoping to direct his attention away from the envelopes with my softly voiced question. "This isn't anything to worry about. For a few minutes, Kat needed me to help solve her problem. I told her to find another solution because I was seeing you."

Ken blinked, "You did?" The hand holding the cards sagged a bit.

I sighed. "Yes. Yes, of course, I did."

His hands dropped to his side, relief suffusing him. I stepped into him, put a hand to his hip and met his lips with mine for a quick kiss. "Now, McPretty, I smell dinner." I brought my free hand to the mail. "Let's go eat." I gave a tug on the papers, but he tightened his hold.

"What are you doing?" He jerked back. "I can't believe this," he said shaking his head. In four rapid strides, he crossed the room and tore into one envelope.

"Don't—" I protested, but it was too late, he was already flipping the card open. I noticed today's offering had a bunch of brightly colored ice cream cones with sprinkles. I could only imagine what Ken was seeing inside of the card.

"*You think you're better than me?*" Ken read through clenched teeth. "*I'll show you. I love you.*" He looked at me, accusation in his eyes. "How many of these have you gotten?"

"A few." In addition to the two I received Friday night, there'd been one in Saturday's mail and two in Monday's.

He let out a huff of a laugh. "You don't take anything seriously, do you? Nothing except your secrets."

"It's not—"

"*It is!*" he boomed. "Don't you dare try to tell me this isn't a big deal. Don't say there's nothing you can do about this!" He flung the mail onto the floor. "You work for a *security* company. Did it occur to you for one second that they might know exactly how to handle this?"

He scraped his fingers through his curls, face taut with agitation. "You're just too afraid to admit you need help. You're not in this situation because you're weak or stupid. This could happen to anyone. But I'll tell you what does make you weak and stupid—not reaching out for the help that's right in front of you. Fucking stupid."

I closed my eyes and took a deep breath, readying to tell him what an insufferable dick he was being when he launched into a full-blown tirade.

"You know what?" He gave a derisive shrug. "Maybe you're not afraid. And I know you're not a complete moron. Maybe what's happening here is that you don't want your company to solve this for you. Maybe what you want is high drama all the time. We both know you love being front and center in wild scenarios." Ken's already loud voice was verging on shouting and with every word, my own rage built higher and higher.

He emitted a disgusted scoff. "I mean, look, you came in here practically *erect* from whatever soap opera went on downstairs."

His accusation made my blood boil. It was so far off the mark, but such an easy insult to hurl. In the past, many of my decisions where men were concerned were made from boredom or fear of boredom. Ken knew this, I'd admitted it to him, confessed it. He was using it against me in anger and I felt like it was a low, low blow. Especially about Kat and Dan's situation. I hadn't been happy about it. Sure, Quinn, Dan, and Nico had been totally kick-ass, and I derived a lot of pleasure from seeing Caleb cut down, but it had been a touchy, scary situation with real, impactful possible outcomes. Add to the fact that Kat was probably now on her way to Boston to say her final goodbyes to her estranged father—and I was sickened by Ken's implication that I was getting off from the tumult.

"But you know what?" he continued, shaking his head. "This isn't something I'm going to let you flirt with anymore. Lies and secrets have got to stop. I'm calling Quinn Sull—"

"No, you're not." I said icily. Ken's tongue was sharp, and he could wield it expertly, but he had no idea the level I could stoop to when pushed. He was about to find out, because I'd just been pushed into not caring what damage I did.

Vision red, I plowed ahead. "Accusations of lies and drama from *you*? The man in his *thirties* who waits until his sister gets married to create his own coming-out fiasco? What in the hell is that about?" I took a step closer to him. "I don't blame your sister for doubting you. Your timing was suspect and, what, your sexuality non-existent for a decade?"

Ken's nostrils flared. This was his chink. This was the vulnerable part in his armor—and I was going to stick my sword in as deep as I could go.

He thought he was going to come into my life and lay a bunch of landmines to destroy it? Hell no. His sense of entitlement was unreal. His bulldozing into my life had to be squelched. His lack of self-aware-ness needed to be brought to light.

"What kind of guy—who looks like you—doesn't go out and get laid at every opportunity? I get that you have some personality defects, but that never stopped anyone."

His body stilled—all except for the clenching of his jaw. "Do. Not," he gritted out in warning.

I ignored him. "My best guess is that you're either a coward or you're completely confused."

If there was anything Ken hated more, it was for his bisexuality to be called confusion. I knew exactly where to strike to cause the most damage. At that moment, I wanted to cause damage. He was going to jeopardize my career? Call me stupid? Call me a drama queen? Well, I wasn't going to let him dole out this hurt to me today and sit back and take it. If he wanted to kick me, I was going to kick back harder.

His face had gone pale. A little voice in my head—my good sense, the one that usually ruled—whispered that I shouldn't take this any further, that I was going to say something Ken could never forgive.

I told that voice to piss off.

"I see you, Ken. I know what's really happening. You don't expend energy into anything or anyone unless the payoff is big. Which is why you're clinging to this 'bi' label so hard." I used angry air quotes, intentionally, provokingly. "It's selfish, is what it is. You want all your options open, but when it's said and done..." *Eventually.* "You'll end up with a wife and six kids because permanence and payoff are what you crave, right?"

Tapping into my own insecurities didn't just fuel my anger, it was taking over. Those words weren't calculated, they'd been dragged out of me with little forethought. Thinking of my strained relationship with Ernesto over his concerns, thinking of Ken going to Quinn and upending my life when he, most likely, was going to be a transient presence in it—made me wild. I wanted this shaky, sick, violent feeling in my stomach out and the only way to do that was to spew it all at Ken. Spew it right in his face.

"I thought I could have it with you!" He shook his head, his shoulders slumping. "Do you think I'm going to leave you and pretend like I never felt this way about you?" He shook his head again, like he was trying to dislodge the offending thoughts from his brain. "No. No, you don't. You know me better than that. This is bullshit."

"Please!" I rolled my eyes. "As soon as you get bored of this, you'll be gone. Not just gone but pretending like dick doesn't get you off."

Ken's mouth twisted into a bitter smile. "I'm not the one who gets bored. That's your MO and I should have seen the signs."

I was silent for a moment, then asked a question that had floated through my mind from time to time.

"Answer me this, Ken. When you were with Angie, did you tell her you were bi? Did you tell her why you and your father weren't close? Hmm?"

Ken closed his eyes and I knew. He hadn't. He'd had a long-term relationship with a woman and hadn't discussed his sexuality with her.

"I—" he began, then closed his mouth.

"Oops!" I put my hand over my mouth in mock chagrin. "You didn't want me to know that, did you? Why? Because it means you're a *liar.*" I walked close and put my hand on his shoulder, as if to comfort him. "I don't think you're confused, babe. I just can't trust you, that's all."

"Fuck this!" he said, pushing my arm roughly from his shoulder. He turned and scooped up his gym bag from the hall. Slinging it to his shoulder, he faced me and said, "Fuck you, too."

His lack of an intelligent response was in its own way gratifying. He was on the ropes and lashing out because what I said resonated with him in some way. "Who was it with all the secrets and lies, now?" I smirked.

He walked toward the door and grabbed his wallet from the table. "Oh! You're leaving? Cutting me out?" I accused with feigned surprise, my voice dripping with sarcasm. "I'm not sticking to your script, so you're gone!"

With his back to me, he stood at the door, his hand on the knob. His slight pause, the bunching of his shoulders was almost enough for my good sense to try and assert itself again. My heart started to pound, and my gut twisted into a sickening knot.

As he opened the door and passed through, I yelled, "You're not the only one with a script, asshole!"

CHAPTER THIRTY-THREE

DKM

As soon as I slammed the door behind me, I knew it was over, but I didn't let the hurt set in.

I stalked to the elevator, fueled by my anger.

I was done. I wasn't going to beg and plead with someone who didn't give a shit about me or went out of his way to invent reasons to push me away.

He didn't even care about *himself* enough to reach out for help.

Well, screw that.

I cared about him. I worried about him.

And I warned him.

I roughly pushed the down button on the elevator and cobbled an immediate plan on my way to the lobby.

He's left me no choice.

I wasn't going to be here to check up on him and I couldn't bear the thought of him exposed, endangered and alone.

I warned him.

The concierge, Lawrence, was at the desk. I wiped my expression clear as best as I could and approached.

"Good evening, Lawrence," I greeted.

"Good evening, Dr. Miles. What can I do for you?"

"I was wondering if it would be possible for me to talk with Quinn Sullivan—either via phone or a meeting here. Would you be able to contact him for me?"

"Yes, sir. May I know what this is regarding?"

"Security concerns," I said flatly.

"Very well, I'll ring the penthouse." He lifted the phone handset, then pointed to a seating area. "Please, have a seat while you wait."

I situated myself on a sleek settee facing the desk and watched as Lawrence spoke into the phone. I wondered if the man would meet me. From what Steven had told me, his boss was big, mean-looking, and under a lot of stress from his wife's complicated pregnancy. They'd welcomed their son two weeks ago, but that didn't mean this guy's mood was going to be any more receptive to me. Also, the confrontation he'd had earlier in the evening with the police and Kat's cousin sounded like a difficult situation. I'm sure the last thing he wanted was for me to interrupt his evening to alert him to Steven's problem.

The thing was, I really didn't give a shit.

He could come down here and glare at me all he wanted to as long as he listened to me. As long as he gave me assurances that his company could and would do the work they specialized in. As long as he protected Steven, I didn't care if he had his guys throw my ass out into the gutter of Randolph.

I just hoped he'd listen.

I was agitated, too amped up on adrenaline and anger to sit still. As soon as Lawrence hung up the phone, I stood and walked back to the desk.

"What did he say?" I demanded.

Lawrence furrowed his brow at my snappishness and replied, "He'll be down in a few moments."

I watched the elevator intently. A few moments later, the doors opened to reveal a tall—and surprisingly young—man, exiting with purpose. I don't know why I was surprised by his age. I knew he was a new father, but something about Steven's references had my imagination painting him as a paunchy, curmudgeonly father-figure with a young, hot wife. Not this towering, icy-gazed, relatively youthful man. If he were as old as forty, I'd be shocked. It also didn't escape my notice that he was strikingly handsome, which irked me for some reason. His handsomeness was combined with a hint of thuggishness—his body fit and large, his expression fixed to mask any look other than cool disdain.

He wasn't the only one with a mask, I thought, and fixed my own expression.

As he approached, he gestured to the settee I'd vacated. "Have a seat, Dr. Miles."

As soon as I sat, I said, "Thank you for meeting with me. Steven needs your help, but he won't ask for it."

He raised a brow at me but didn't reply. He sat down on the chair opposite from the settee and leaned forward. His black T-shirt fit tight across his shoulders and his eyes were piercing. The severity of his appearance was tempered somewhat by the evidence of baby vomit on his shoulder. I doubted he even knew it was there.

If I hadn't been heartsick and angry, I might have smiled.

"He's being stalked by a man who tried to assault him on a date," I continued. "He doesn't think anything can be done about it, but the guy is making contact more frequently—sending cards in the mail. Maybe more, I don't know."

His expression didn't alter, but he sat up straighter in the chair.

"He talked to your information guy and found out who the man was, but that's all. Nothing further was done to stop him. I want you," I continued, "to make sure nothing happens to Steven. Give him help, even if he's kicking and screaming the whole time."

He was quiet a moment before he asked, "What about you?"

"I won't be around. I don't matter." I meant that to mean I was no longer involved in this situation, but another meaning, the one that meant I didn't matter to Steven anymore, struck me suddenly and my breath hitched.

I didn't think I could continue this conversation running on adrenaline. The adrenaline was rapidly being replaced with sadness.

I had to get out of there.

I stood up and held out my hand for a shake. Sullivan stood and met my hand firmly.

"Take care of him, Mr. Sullivan." Without waiting for a reply, I turned on my heel and left.

CHAPTER THIRTY-FOUR

DKM

Oscar Wilde said, "Hearts are made to be broken."

The quote had been repeating in my mind like a litany. It would crop up when I would start to feel ill and play on a loop until I felt a measure of calm.

Perhaps I needed to help myself believe what was happening to my brain—the violent despair and agonizing pain—were simply a rite of passage. I had a heart, therefore, it must break.

But mostly I knew the inaudible chanting was just another repetitive, self-soothing act which was showing signs of some effectiveness.

All I really knew was that it was helping me to not throw up.

I was glad for Mr. Wilde and his short, succinct words of wisdom, and I was also glad for my trip to Cleveland. It may have seemed strange that I'd be happy to be flying home to face my sister—with whom I'd been at odds—so soon after having my heart torn from my chest. But I was. Something I excelled at was focused avoidance. When I had a job to do, a task to complete, my brain allowed me to shut out my troubles and fears and buckle down into work.

At the moment, my brain wanted to fixate on Steven, wanted to replay his words. But when I landed and had a part to play and a job to complete, I'd have no trouble putting Steven out of my mind. I needed that. I wanted it.

I arrived early for my flight, which proved to be torturous. I found myself unable to sit still, unable to quiet my mind. *Hearts are made to be broken. Hearts are made to be broken.* I chanted these words over and over as I chewed gum and walked around the periphery of my gate.

It didn't help. Not really. Tuesday's scene wasn't easy to ignore or forget. Flashes of Steven's angry countenance, his calculated vitriol, his singular determination to wound me as deeply as he could, would come upon me and leave me breathless and panicked. I'd been blind-sided. I hadn't known he was capable of it.

Even *I* wasn't capable of that level of verbal attack—and my tongue was notoriously uncensored when I became angry. My temper flared often and hot, but it cooled quickly. Steven seemed to never lose his cool. Looking back, his phone messages to me were really the only time I'd sensed he'd been unintentionally reactive. But even that wasn't much—nothing compared to the dozens of times he'd seen me irritated.

I ruminated on this during the flight, letting my brain obsess—not bothering to attempt to mitigate the fixation. I promised myself I'd get my shit together when I landed, but in that moment, I needed to think about Steven.

It killed me to think he'd been harboring those doubts and feelings about me all this time—that my bisexuality was a point of concern, that he'd secretly hated what I was. If that was true, if he did, then there was no hope. No amount of love I had for him was going to change it.

The alternative was that he said what he had because he wanted to hurt me, and he knew me well enough to know exactly what would break me.

Either scenario was abhorrent. In one, he fundamentally distrusted me and there was nothing I could do to change it. In the other, he wanted to hurt me enough to drive me away. Where was the hope? I had none. Whatever Steven was feeling for me, it was negative enough to push me away.

Why? I wondered. Did he not feel what I felt? We were so good together. There was so much affection—physical and emotional affection. I refused to believe I was the only one moved, the only one whose world had been irrevocably changed, the only one whose heart was made full by our time together. But what else could I think?

He threw me away, I thought, my throat closing on a silent sob. I felt a tear trickle down my face, and I turned my body into the window, unwilling to let the women in my row see my emotional struggle. I was sweating with the effort of keeping it inside, keeping it silent.

I cursed myself for not giving over to this earlier. Once I'd left his building, once the cool night air hit me like a slap, I bottled up my sadness with a cork of righteous anger. But compartmentalizing, bottling, and focused avoidance was only resulting in a public meltdown. I refused to let it happen. I never cried, and if I did, it sure as hell wasn't in public.

Hearts are made to be broken. Hearts are made to be broken. Hearts are made to be broken.

Screw you, Wilde. The heart was made to pump blood. Aside from a temporary increase in pulse rate, it was functioning just fine. My brain, on the other hand, was sending out distress signals: tears, nausea, sweat. Anguished sounds wanted to burst forth, and I had a compulsion to run. Literally run. I promised myself when I returned to Chicago, I was going to run the lakefront as long and as hard as I could until I was exhausted. Maybe then I'd sleep. And if I slept, maybe my brain could rest and stop sending out distress signals to my organ systems.

By the time the plane had landed, I'd composed myself. I turned my phone back on while I was waiting to disembark. There were a few missed calls and texts.

None were from Steven.

All were from Kari.

Without listening to the messages or reading the texts, I disembarked, eager to get this day over with. I was going to fake the hell out of this day or maybe even have a huge screaming match with my sister. Either way, I wanted it over. And to get through it, I was going to fixate on that run. I'd imagine the rhythmic pounding of my feet on the paved path, the rhythm of my audible breaths and it would soothe me. *Stride, stride, stride, stride.*

It was much more effective and pleasant than Oscar Wilde.

Walking down the jet-bridge, my phone rang. It was Kari.

"Hello."

"Has your plane landed? Are you here? I came to pick you up." *Dammit.* I told her yesterday not to pick me up. I wanted to show up at the tailor's, do my duty, and be off with as little stressful interaction as possible. But now that plan was toast.

"I'm walking into the airport as we speak," I replied. "Where are you?"

She gave me directions and I found her. She was smiling, but there was a hesitancy about it. The hesitancy made me feel better somehow, as if it gave me permission to not be a total liar for the afternoon. We didn't have to pretend everything was fine. I breathed a sigh and relaxed a measure.

"Hey there," she said, embracing me in a hug. I gave her an extra, indulgent squeeze before releasing her, enjoying the brief contact. *I needed a hug*, I thought, then chastised myself. *Buck up, man, you're mad at her.*

She was dressed casually in faded jeans and a fitted blouse. She was also wearing her signature Chucks. Her job as her school district's superintendent, required her to dress professionally. She maintained that when she was off the clock, she was wearing comfortable shoes.

"Well, Dr. Miles," she said with a small grin. "You are looking very handsome with your shaggy hair."

I touched my over-grown hair and realized my slight waves were probably askew and ridiculous. I hadn't combed it before I left the apartment. I didn't think I'd so much as glanced at myself in the mirror. I'd also been running my hands through it all morning, so I was sure it was a mess.

"Time for a cut then?" I asked.

Her grin fell as she realized I wasn't going to harass her about her EdD. I didn't feel up to espousing the superiority of my degrees compared with hers, I just didn't have it in me to joke.

"Eh, it looks cute. You'd look cute bald," she said somewhat grumpily.

I snorted. "Come on, let's get this fitting over." I headed to the exit, then followed her to her car.

We didn't speak until she maneuvered onto the freeway.

"When is your flight today?"

"Four-thirty." It was nearing eleven and I realized I had to spend around four hours with her. I desperately wanted to get out of it. "But don't worry, I can take a cab from the shop and see myself off," I assured her, hoping she'd take the out I was handing her. "You don't need to babysit me or chauffeur me around."

She shot me an irritated glance. "I can take you to the airport, Ken. And I think we should talk. Let's have lunch or go to my place when we're done."

Fan-fucking-tastic. Not only was she refusing to take the out, she was apparently going to make the day a thousand times more unpleasant.

When we arrived at the shop, she stopped the car and looked at me. She still wore the hesitant, sadness-tinged smile. "How was your marathon?"

"It was a half marathon, and I made good time," I shrugged. "It was fine." I didn't want to think about the race because thinking about the race meant thinking about Steven waiting for me at the finish line, Steven doting on me and massaging me. I shut my eyes against the memory.

He was going to invade my brain today whether I wanted him to or not. I'd already let twinges of worry set in over King—let myself wonder if Quinn Sullivan was going to honor my request and heed my warning. What if he'd shrugged it off? What if he'd gone to Steven and let him downplay it? What if right now, Steven was outside alone, being followed and menaced? My stomach hurt to think about it, and my heart hurt to know I wasn't allowed to be there for him anymore.

Kari lapsed into silence and simply stared at me. No doubt trying to read whatever the hell was going on with my face. The quiet of the car and her perusal pissed me off so I snapped, "Can we just get this finished, please?"

"Yeah," she nodded. "Let's go."

CHAPTER THIRTY-FIVE

DKM

The fitting took almost no time and before I knew it, we were back in the car, headed to the house she shared with Brandon.

I don't want to do this today, I thought, sulking out the window.

"Too bad. We're having this conversation." I realized I'd spoken aloud and cursed myself. Her tone brooked no refusals and she wore a determined expression.

It annoyed me.

"Are you sure that's wise?" I snapped. "I just had my fitting, I'm participating in this wedding, you're getting your way. Do you really want to rock the boat right now?" I felt like the emotional precipice I was on was a dangerous place, especially for her. She didn't know it, but I was on the razor's edge of backing out. Only Steven's voice warning me that I'd regret it in the long run kept me from unleashing on her.

Regret, I snorted at the thought. I wondered if Steven had regrets. I wondered if he even *thought* about calling me. He set us on fire with an ease that was nearly pathological. I guess I understood that. I was ready to do it with Kari.

The more she quietly seethed at my comment, the more mellow I felt. I was probably sick in some way from finding my sibling's turmoil gratifying.

When we arrived, she didn't speak to me until we'd entered the house. Her body was taut and tense and she threw her purse onto the kitchen counter with force.

Turning to me she said, "I'm not fine with an uneasy truce, Ken. I want this settled. I want to know we're okay."

I folded my arms across my chest. "So, talk." As far as I was concerned, I'd said my piece *and* extended the olive branch. Any further effort needed to be hers. But I knew her, she was going to start by going on the defensive and justifying her shittiness. What I needed was some heartfelt apologies, acknowledgment, and validation. Not demands for me to see it her way.

I was in no mood to hear it.

She inhaled deeply and blurted, "I'm a huge bitch," her body deflating with the announcement.

A booming laugh erupted from me. I hadn't been expecting it, and her words struck me as hilarious. I mean, she said it like it was a deep, dark secret that needed confessing—like it was a huge relief to admit— like it was something I didn't already know.

"I'm serious here, Ken," she asserted loudly—and angrily—over my laughter.

My humor tapered. "Please, continue," I prompted once I'd composed myself.

"That wasn't funny. Why are you laughing? Why did you laugh? I'm trying to be serious, jackass."

I pressed my lips together, trying to hold in another bout of laughter. She was pissed. It wasn't easy for us Miles to apologize, or to keep our tempers in check while we issued those apologies. It was kind of ridiculous. She was ridiculous. *I* was ridiculous. Was this what Steven saw when he looked at me? Someone who took themselves way too seriously? Someone who took everything too personally and was too reactionary? No wonder he said I had *personality defects*. He probably felt like having a conversation with me was the mental equivalent to whiplash. Nice, pissy. Contrite, pissy. How had he tolerated it? *Oh, wait, he didn't,* I reminded myself.

With those thoughts, my humor fled. "We had to come all the way to your house for you to tell me something I already know?" I snapped. *Yep, I'm a dick.*

"Argh!" She threw her hands up in frustration. "What I mean to say is that I'm sorry, okay? I'm sorry for saying the awful shit I said." She reached one hand out as if to touch me, but she didn't make the connection. "I'm sorry I made you feel like you couldn't confide in me or be yourself with me or that I need you to live your life a certain way to suit me." She paused only long enough to draw a breath and bring that hovering hand to her chest. "And I'm so sorry I said you'd be a spectacle." She rolled her lips in and flinched, closing her eyes tight. After a second, she smoothed out her features, looking me in the eye earnestly. "That was beyond horrible. No one who is going to be at that wedding is more important to me than you. If everybody talks, they talk. As long as you're standing up with us, I'm happy. As long as you are happy, I'm happy. Bring Steven next weekend, let's meet—"

"Wow!" I cut her off, halting talk of meetings. "Okay, hold on, calm down." Kari's eyes were welling with tears and I could feel the emotion and sadness rolling off her. As much as I wanted to be bitter and hang on to my anger, I hated to see her cry. I pulled her into a hug and held her for a moment before I heard a car door shut.

"Brandon's home, I guess," I said, releasing her.

She wiped her eyes and sniffled. "Uhhhmmmm…" a distinctly guilty look crossed her features and I had a bad, bad feeling.

I peeked out her front window to see my parents and my grandmother exiting my mom's BMW.

"*Nana*?!" I asked, nearly baring my teeth in a snarl. "You're ambushing me with them *and* Nana?" I stalked toward her, all good feeling forgotten. "What kind of sadistic she-devil are you? You're diabolical, you know that?"

"We need to air this out!" she shouted.

"Do they know why they're here, or are you ambushing them too?"

I ran both of my hands through my hair, panic beginning to set in. My sister wasn't a she-devil, she was *the* devil.

"They know," she replied, her chin jutting defiantly. "They want to talk to you, too."

Without a knock or a ring, they came through the front door, my Nana leading the charge. She was a short woman, nearing eighty, but neither of those things made her less commanding. She had a sharp mind and took absolutely no shit from anyone. Don't get me wrong, she was my Nana and she was sweet to me, but I didn't want to be on her bad side.

"Nana!" I greeted, stooping down for a hug.

"Oh, my, Kenny. It's been too damn long since I've seen you." She patted my face with her soft, wrinkled hand and smiled at me. "But now, honey," she smacked me lightly on the cheek and her smile dropped. "You and your sister need to sit your keisters down on that Chesterfield so we can get this mess sorted."

"Yes, ma'am." I turned from Nana, not sparing my parents a glance. I did, however, give Kari a withering glare—a silent promise of retribution.

As the two of us sat on her loveseat together, I whispered, "You're dead to me."

Kari held back a laugh, but a snort came through and Nana honed on it. "Is anything funny about this situation to you, young lady?"

I nudged Kari's leg with my own, letting her know I was enjoying watching her get reprimanded by our grandmother. She nudged me back harder.

"No, ma'am," Kari retorted confidently, unfazed by Nana's sharp tone. "If you recall, this intervention was my plan. I know how serious this is."

"Dead. To. Me," I whispered again, this time in earnest. The word *intervention* made me angry. It implied I was doing something I shouldn't and needed to be taken to task for it—which was complete horseshit.

I looked to my mother to gauge her demeanor. She was standing apart from my dad, arms crossed over her chest. Her brows were

STICKING TO THE SCRIPT

furrowed, and her mouth drawn in a severe frown. My stomach plummeted with the realization that my mother was angry. I'd held out some hope that maybe her feelings about me weren't as negative as Dad's or Kari's had been, but she seemed just as upset.

For his part, Dad looked a little...beleaguered. He appeared a lot older than he had the last time I saw him—which had been at Christmastime—and his hair, still thick and dark, was practically standing on end, like he'd not combed it in days. His eyes were tired, and his slightly slumped posture made him seem deflated or subdued.

My parents were clearly not themselves today.

"Well, then, maybe you should start us off." Nana crossed to the couch and settled herself in the middle. She made a sweeping gesture to my parents to join her. Dad moved to sit, but Mom stayed standing.

"I think Robert should be the one to start, since this is all *his* fault."

My mother's words, said with such venom, shocked me. I realized her anger wasn't aimed at me—she was furious with my dad. I didn't think I'd ever seen such a thing before. She was looking at him like he was a piece of poop on her shoe and he was looking at the floor to avoid facing her censure.

Part of me thought I should be taking pleasure from the situation—that seeing my dad brought low by my mother's anger on my behalf ought to have given me some satisfaction...but it didn't. I didn't enjoy seeing their discord, didn't enjoy knowing I was a party to unhappiness.

My grandmother huffed out a sigh. "Or you can start, Julia. That works, too."

Mom took a seat next to Nana but didn't speak.

There was a lengthy silence, so I spoke up. "How about *I* start. I don't have all day to hash this out, and frankly, I don't care to. You're all here, but no one is saying anything, so maybe you don't care to either. That's fine. Kari and I have started to work things out. I'm not disrupting the wedding plans or anything, so there's no need to worry." I was watching my mother as I said this, and her face, which had smoothed out, pursed up again as if what I said infuriated her.

She turned in her seat and leaned over Nana, putting her face close to Dad's. "Do you hear that, Robert?" she ground out. "Ken doesn't want you to worry. How does it feel knowing your son thinks your only concern is the *disruption of plans?*"

This time Dad did meet her gaze and they had a stare-off until Nana pushed Mom back to her side of the couch.

"Yes," Nana added. "I'd like to know the answer to that, too, Robert."

I swear, in that moment, I felt sorry for my old man. In all my life, he'd never been anything but confident and articulate. But there he was, speechless and cowed by the shame these two women were making him feel. It was a surreal moment, and damn painful to witness.

Kari leaned over and whispered, "Mom kicked him out on Tuesday. He's been sleeping in the guest house."

"What?" I asked loudly, bringing everyone's attention back to me.

"It feels bad," Dad said suddenly, his voice brusque and gravelly. "It feels bad and I feel like a failure as a parent." He cleared his throat and met my eyes. "As soon as I left your dorm, I regretted everything I said, but I was too stubborn to go back and say it to you, to ask for your forgiveness. I was wrong to say the things that I said, but the worst thing was not apologizing for it." He shook his head. "We have not had one conversation in almost ten years that wasn't banal *chitchat,*" he spat the words like *chitchat* was abhorrent or disgusting. "Every conversation about the weather in Chicago or hospital resident shift rotation or Cubs stats was like a knife in my heart. And it was my own fault. I didn't know how to fix it." He shook his head again, sadly, slowly. "I still don't. There's nothing I can say that can turn back time or make the hurt go away. All I can say is that I'm sorry. And I pray you can forgive me."

Mom had started weeping during my dad's speech and I found myself reflexively swallowing and blinking to thwart my own emotional upheaval. *Stride, stride, stride, stride.* I didn't want to lose my control there, not in front of everyone. I knew once I started, I wouldn't stop until I was wrung dry. Steven, Kari, Mom, Dad, Nana... they were the only people in my life who could turn me into a wreck, and they were all doing it in the same week. My psyche wasn't going to be able to handle it, I was sure. It was too much all at once. A man couldn't flip from robotic stoicism to hysterical shambles in such a short amount of time without some adverse effects on his mental health.

I wanted out. I didn't want this. I wanted away from their eyes and expectant expressions. I didn't know how I was feeling, didn't know what anyone needed from me in that moment. *Stride, stride, stride, stride*. I started to jiggle my leg. Every sound my mother made, increased my anxiety.

I couldn't stand to hold my father's eyes and see the pain and hope there, so I looked to Nana. Her eyes were fixed on me with intent. She raised her eyebrows and issued me a pointed stare. *Step up, Kenny*, the look said. *Say what you need to say.*

I took a deep breath and focused on my feelings. What did I want to say? What did I want to know? How did I feel? This was a time for honesty, so I checked in with myself and found my balls.

"Why did you say it in the first place?" My voice came across sure and strong, despite my inner turmoil. *This* was what I wanted to know. Had it been the shock, or was he a raging homophobe? I knew Nana's look was right. This was my moment to own it all, understand it all, and draw my line in the sand. "Those thoughts and feelings had to come from somewhere. Maybe you were sorry for saying them, but maybe also, they were the truth of what you thought and felt about me."

He nodded. "You know why I said them. I told you then I wanted the best for you, that I didn't want you to have unnecessary hurdles or roadblocks." He scrubbed his face roughly with both hands and sighed. "Part of it was seeing you and that boy together, I think. I was stunned and embarrassed and angry."

"Why angry?" I asked. I only had eyes for my dad, but I realized that the women were uncharacteristically silent. My mom's weeping had stopped, and I didn't think Kari was breathing. Nana had leaned back against the couch, allowing Dad to have the stage.

"Because I had no idea," he replied softly. "You and I were always close. As a kid, you were my shadow when I was home. In temperament, you were just like me. Hell, if it weren't for your mother's hair, I'd swear you were my clone. I...I didn't see it. I never imagined it. I was mad that you had this side to you that I didn't know—that you didn't tell me. A side I had to accidentally see—in living color—instead of being told by you. You should have told us."

The slight accusation in his voice ramped up my irritation. I heard him. I understood what he was saying. He'd been blindsided and felt slighted that he hadn't known everything about me. I got that. I knew it had been a lot in that moment, but I didn't miss or appreciate the subtle shift of blame at the end of his explanation.

Neither did my mother, it seemed. "Robert." It was a warning.

"Julia..." my grandmother issued her own warning. "Let the boys handle this," she said softly, almost in a whisper.

"That's bull. I was twenty-two, Dad," I defended. "My sex life, as far as you were concerned, was a need-to-know type of thing. I would have told you when I felt you needed to know. A person should be able to come out how and when they want." I resented that he felt he was owed knowledge of every aspect of my life. I felt like I should be allowed to have parts of myself that were private without feeling like I was a sneak or a liar. But an image of Steven's sneering face as he told me he couldn't trust me, flashed in my mind.

I hadn't told Angie. I'd kept certain things need-to-know with her as well. Steven thought that was lying. And, in a way, I could see that now. I didn't think it meant I was untrustworthy, but I did omit an important truth about myself.

Bisexuality wasn't just about sex. If it were, I could justify keeping it to myself. But it was an important part of who I was—a part that shapes my relationships and my future. Relationships and a future that are to be shared with people I love.

I hadn't told Angie. Would I have told my parents or Kari if Dad hadn't caught me with Harry Deluca all those years ago? When would *need-to-know* have ever cropped up? Until Steven, I hadn't had a real boyfriend. If things had been different, would I have been only now having the *Surprise, I'm bi, I have a boyfriend* talk?

For all my internal pep-talks about being comfortable and confident and unashamed of my sexuality, I wondered if there was a part of me that felt I needed to pretend for other people that it wasn't there.

I closeted myself. The realization jolted me. All this time I thought I was open and living my life on my own terms, but the people who meant the most to me had been in the dark. My mother hadn't known. Kari figured it was a passing phase. Angie never knew. Once the dust settled after my fight with Dad, I never spoke of my sexuality again—until Steven. And even then, I hadn't been explicit. I'd approached him with such a casualness that he hadn't recognized I was interested in a romantic or sexual way. I wasn't living out-and-proud, no matter what I'd told myself.

"I'm bisexual," I announced suddenly.

Dad blinked and Kari snorted a laugh. "Uh, yeah, we know. That's why we're here," she said sarcastically.

I twisted to include her in my next statement.

"Listen to me. What I mean is that I'm not a straight man when I'm in a relationship with a woman, or a gay man when I'm in a relation-ship with a guy. That's not how it works. I don't want to pretend that it is. I don't want to have to say all this again down the road someday when you've tried to convince yourself I'm straight. But I will. I'll say it as many times as I need to get it through your heads. I'm. Bi."

"Ooookay…" Kari said warily.

I looked to my father. "When it comes to relationships, I'm not going to take the easy road. If I'm with a woman, it's because I want to be with her and no one else. The same goes for men. I'm sorry you had to find out like you did, Dad. It's not how I wanted you to find out. But I'm not going to ever compromise my happiness to make other people more comfortable about me. I work hard at everything I put my mind to, but I never put my mind to people-pleasing. You know this. If someone is going to misjudge me as indecisive or selfish or deviant, that's their problem. I can't and won't do anything to change it. I am who I am."

"I'm sorry I said those things." He shook his head sadly. "I don't want you to live your life for other people. We didn't raise you that way. I had no right to make you feel like you should or that there's anything wrong with being who you are."

There was a long silence. I didn't know what to say to him. I never gave a lot of thought to it, but my dad had damaged more than our relationship that night. I went from being gregarious and confident to being withdrawn and uptight. I ceased feeling comfortable in my own skin, and it was terrible not feeling at peace with myself. I didn't know if I could forgive and forget so easily—erase ten years of hurt and betrayal with one hour of conversation. But I did know I wanted to try. I loved my family, wanted them to love me as I was, wanted them to love whomever I eventually married.

"This boy, Steven," mom piped in. "Kari says you're in love with him."

She paused, waiting for confirmation, I supposed, so I said, "Yes." I did love Steven, but I didn't want to talk about him—not with our situation as it was. I wasn't about to discuss my broken relationship with them.

"Then you're bringing him to the wedding," Nana demanded.

"Um, uh, no, Nana," I protested, but she cut me off.

"It's perfect. Everyone we know can get all their gum-flapping and gossiping out in one day and have done with it. You can show everyone you care for him and we will be there with you showing our solidarity."

"It's not a good id—"

"Yes, it is," she insisted. "Go home, speak to him about it and convince him to brave the family. I expect him there."

Nana used my dad's shoulder to heft herself up from the couch and announced, "Robert and Julia, take me home. Kenny's got to fly back to Chicago and think about things."

Mom and Dad both stood, and we said our goodbyes. My mother gave me a tight hug and whispered, "I'm so proud of you, baby. I love you."

"I love you, too, Mom." My eyes watered, but I refused to let the tears fall. I let go of her and approached my dad.

"Thank you for coming here and saying those things. I needed to hear it."

"I should have said them years ago," he replied.

As soon as they left, I turned to Kari.

"I'm not bringing Steven to the wedding."

CHAPTER THIRTY-SIX

STEVEN

Something startled me awake. At first, I thought it was my own snore because I heard and felt the sharp, vibrating gasp as awareness dawned.

I was lying on my couch, fully clothed, and disoriented by the dimness of the apartment. The faint light from the windows could have been early evening or early morning.

How long had I slept?

It felt as if I'd only just closed my eyes. I had a vague memory of pillowing my head on the armrest and thinking I'd take myself to bed in a few moments. Obviously, I'd never managed.

A knock at the door came then, as I surfaced from sleep. *The knocking.* It had been knocking that woke me, I realized.

I flailed my hand to the coffee table, found my glasses and slipped them on. When I rose from the couch, my hip twinged and creaked, protesting my choice of bed. "Oof."

I hastened to answer the door and standing in the hall was Elizabeth—looking fresh and happy and holding two familiar paper coffee cups.

"Good morning!" she said cheerfully.

If it was indeed morning, it was really, freaking early.

"Huh?" I asked, still somewhat disoriented from my short nap. I doubted I slept a full day—though god knew I probably need to. So that meant I'd only been sleeping—at maximum—two or three hours. The last time I looked at a clock it had been after three.

Adding to the disorientation was Elizabeth's expectant expression. She didn't seem to acknowledge or believe that a pre-six AM visit was completely weird, so I had to search my brain for what I could possibly be missing.

"Is the building on fire?"

"What? No. I was up early and thought I'd get you some Buzzy's before we go. We have a little bit of time and Nico's still getting packed."

She handed me a coffee and walked through to the living room. I followed her and flipped on the overhead light. The sunlight, though filtering in more and more, was still too weak to illuminate the room.

I shook my head. "What are you talking about?"

Elizabeth narrowed her eyes and took in my wrinkled shirt and pants. "You're not going to Boston?"

"Was I supposed to go to Boston today?" I asked skeptically. I knew I had been slightly deprived of sleep the past couple of weeks, but I didn't think I'd forget a trip.

"To see Kat. Quinn said we were all going—"

"Quinn said I was going too?" I interrupted her, jumping on the mention of Quinn. He and I hadn't spoken in a week and our interactions up to then had been noticeably strained. I wasn't feeling very secure where he was concerned. Maybe this was a good sign. If he'd included me in the travel plans, I'd feel more like the strain was probably all in my head.

I blamed it on Ken.

I wouldn't have this guilty, shitty, paranoid feeling all the time if it weren't for him. I kept seeing his face, so full of accusation and incredulity. It was disillusionment and disappointment too and it fueled my feelings of being undeserving of what I had, strengthened my worry that the jig was up, and my whole world was coming down around my ears.

"Well, no," she admitted. "I just assumed. Because, well, it's *Kat.*"

I sighed, disappointment deflating my bubble of hope. It was a fair assumption on Elizabeth's part. She knew Kat and I were close. And with Shiva—the Jewish mourning period—finished, it was reasonable that her friends would visit her now to help lift her spirits. Between her father passing away, Caleb being a nuisance, and the stress of her inheritance, she presumably needed as much support as possible.

Thinking of Kat and all that she was going through and how I hadn't been a good friend to her in these past weeks, filled me with guilt.

I blamed it on Ken.

Kat's father had died the day after we broke up. And though I'd kept in sparse contact with her via text, all my mental energy had been sucked up by him. Thinking about Ken, wallowing in misery over Ken…blaming Ken.

If he hadn't done what he'd done on that Tuesday, I'd have enough energy to be there for my friend in her time of need. But no. Instead, I'd hardly thought of her.

I was a selfish asshole and it was all Ken's fault.

"There's still time to pack if you wanted to tag along," Elizabeth offered.

I snorted. *Tag along.* Sure, tag along, uninvited, when it was clear I was excluded intentionally? Not happening.

"No thanks," I said, bitterness lacing my words. "I'll go see Kat on my own some other time." I didn't need Quinn and Manuel to visit Kat. I could go whenever I felt like it. Maybe I'd even take some vacation days. Whatever I did, I didn't need an invitation from Quinn.

"Is everything okay?" she asked, surprise evident in her tone. I wasn't doing a very good job of putting on a happy face. My only excuse was that she'd caught me at a strange moment. It wasn't easy to get my shit together while I was depressed and sleep-deprived. Still, I needed to buck up—if only to get her to wipe that concern off her face.

I swatted the air. "I'm fine, sugar, just tired. It's way too early." I held up the coffee she'd given me. "But this will help." I looked at the cup and said, "Just what the doctor ordered."

I took a big swig from the paper cup and watched as Elizabeth's face morphed from concern to suspicion—eyes narrowing, head tilting slightly as if she were trying to focus on hearing some far-off sound. *Damn it.*

She gestured with her free hand at my rumpled clothing. "Does *this* have anything to do with Dr. Ken Miles?"

I'd suspected she'd known about Ken based on her pointed question that day at Janie's, but I wasn't going to offer her information, so I asked, "What do you know about Ken?"

"I know that for several Wednesday mornings I'd see him leaving the building very early, wearing scrubs and carrying a tote on his shoulder."

Stupid Tuesday nights.

I shrugged, having no response for her. I wasn't going to lie, but I also sure as hell wasn't going to spill my guts out to her.

"I've been leaving at the same time, but I haven't seen him in a couple of weeks." She stared at me for a moment, then continued, "I was surprised at first. I was just getting into the car in the circle, when I closed the door, looked out the window and saw Dr. Ken Miles strutting out of our doors at five AM. It took a second for the dots to connect, but I realized he had to be here with you."

"Not necessarily," I argued. "A lot of people live in this building." I'd tried my best to wipe my face of expression, unwilling to betray any of my feelings to her. Ken was gone. It hurt. It hurt a lot and I didn't want to think about it, let alone talk about it.

"Oh my God." Elizabeth shook her head. "You're even doing that thing he does!" She pointed at my face and twirled her finger. "It's like the hamster in the wheel stopped running." She tapped her temple in emphasis.

Reluctantly, I chuckled. "See, I thought it was more like an unplugged robot."

She smiled, but it quickly faded as she asked quietly, "Did you break up?"

Inexplicably, the quiet softness of her question made my throat close. I tried to swallow the offending emotions that were threatening to surface. Elizabeth read the answer in my silent struggle and she tsked. Apology and compassion filling her face. "Oh, Steven, I'm sorry." She gave my arm a comforting caress. "Do you want to talk about it?"

I cleared my throat. "Nah, I'm good. You know me, I don't do long-term. It's no big deal." I couldn't cope with her pity or gentle consolation. It was going to make me feel things I'd been trying not to feel for two weeks. I hated to make light of what I felt for Ken, but I had to in order to just get through it.

She nodded her head thoughtfully. "I get the feeling he's kind of a clingy and demanding guy. I don't imagine you loved that. On paper, Ken's great. Smart...has his shit together. Very pretty. But really, give him any encouragement and he gets pushy."

Pushy. It was the same complaint of Ken I'd said to myself repeatedly since he left. He pushed for another night together each week and he insinuated himself into my business with King and Quinn. He made plans for us months in advance. I wanted to call that high-handed and agree with Elizabeth. I thought I should give her something and say, *Girl, he wanted to adopt a dog together!* We'd laugh, share in some commiserate berating of Ken, then she'd leave.

But...I couldn't do it. I couldn't agree. As a matter of fact, my heart rebelled at her words. All he'd done was show me how much he wanted to be with me. Aloof, standoffish, coy...these were not qualities of Ken's, and honestly, I was glad for it. He never half-assed anything—he put effort and sincerity into his commitments, and I loved it about him. It felt good—maybe in an uncomfortable, foreign, itchy way—to be the recipient of his attentions and to rank high on his priorities. But he wasn't what I'd exactly call *clingy*.

"And, let's face it," she continued, "you're such a thoughtful, nice person. Ken's *rude*. His condescension and nit-picking..." She shook her head. "So annoying."

Okay, I didn't like that. Did I think he was a rude asshole sometimes? Yes. But he was *my* rude asshole, not hers. *My* condescending, nit-picking weirdo, not hers. I didn't enjoy this bubbling defensiveness, either. How many times had I sat here thinking about how terrible he was for tearing open my mail—threatening my livelihood? I should be happy my friend was unquestioningly on my side in this—should be happy she was acknowledging how tough I had it in my relationship with Ken. But instead, I was biting my tongue to keep from lashing out at her. What was wrong with me?

I needed her to get out. I couldn't think about him anymore. "Well," I began, about to steer the conversation into, *Thanks for the coffee, have fun in Boston, give Kat my love, yada, yada, yada.* But she wasn't done with Ken.

"Oh man, did he ever call you stupid? He called Meg stupid once. Made her cry. It was great. I mean, having a chief resident calling other residents stupid isn't great. But, in fairness to him, she *was* stupid and had it coming. She had no business being a doctor."

I had no idea what she was yammering on about, but I closed my eyes and sighed, replaying Ken's words in my head. *I'll tell you what does make you weak and stupid—not reaching out for the help that's right in front of you. Fucking stupid.*

Those had been the words that had taken me from being on the defensive to being on the offensive—from trying to appease him, to trying to hurt him. I hated it—hated that we'd said those things. I hated that I'd gone so low.

"Oh, honey," Elizabeth moaned, reading the pain in my face. She squeezed my hand in support and said, "You don't need that negativity in your life. He's wrapped up in a sparkly, dazzling package, I know, but he's just a snooty grouch."

"Stop!" I let go of her hand and stepped away from her, thoroughly irritated. She was trying to make me feel better, but I couldn't listen to her insult Ken. He wasn't a snooty grouch and he was so much more than a sparkly package. His pretty outside couldn't hold a candle to his inside. He had a wide, open heart and a wealth of love dying to be reciprocated. He needed someone to dig beyond his crusty attitude and revel in the hidden passion and sweetness he held inside. I should have been that person. I could have been that person. I *was* that person… until I screwed it up.

Elizabeth was looking at me like I'd grown another head, but I didn't have the energy to fake it. All these big emotions were floating on the surface and with each passing day, they were getting harder to suppress. I thought it would get easier, not harder. Elizabeth's pep talk wasn't helping me to stay in control—it was having the opposite effect.

"Listen, sugar...I appreciate this, I do. But I don't want to talk to you about Ken. You think you know him, but you don't. He's beautiful inside and out. I lo—" *I love him.* I stopped myself before confessing this to her—unwilling to admit it to her before I'd truly processed it myself. *I love him.*

I cleared my throat and continued, hoping she didn't catch the almost-confession. "We might not be together, but that doesn't mean I want to hear anything bad being said about him." I gave her an apologetic look, knowing I was coming off slightly harsh. "I'd like to be able to cope with our break-up without help, okay? I don't want to talk about it."

She looked stricken and I felt wretched about it. I couldn't help that I didn't want to subject myself to post-break-up analysis or share my deepest feelings on the matter. I might occasionally offer to be a sounding board or a strong shoulder for others, but I didn't want it or need it.

Elizabeth, however, wasn't a shrinking violet or easily swayed, so instead of dropping the subject, she asked, "Do you ever talk to anyone, Steven? Maybe you need to."

I gave a small shake of my head, frustrated. I didn't want to hear this.

"Well, you should. I think you need to get it all out. Talk to Sandra." She pointed in the direction of Alex and Sandra's apartment across the hall. "Talk to Ernesto or Kat. They both love you and would help you if you needed it. You just need to reach out."

I'll tell you what does make you weak and stupid—not reaching out for the help that's right in front of you.

I shut my eyes against the words.

"I have to go," she said glancing at her watch. "Are you sure you don't want to come to Boston with us?"

"I'm sure. Thank you for the coffee."

I walked her to the door and said goodbye. But before I could shut the door behind her, she said, "You're right. I don't know Ken, not really. But I bet if you did something you regret, he'll forgive you. He's not a fool."

After Elizabeth left, I took my coffee and sat back on the couch, ruminating on her words.

Ken wasn't a fool; she was right about that. But he didn't forgive easily. When he fought with his sister, he'd imagined their relationship was obliterated—not seeing that work could be done to salvage it. Somehow, I doubted he could forgive my intentional cruelty so easily. I didn't know if I could forgive myself.

Elizabeth was right about something else, too.

I needed to talk to someone. There was a relationship I needed to put work into salvaging.

Grabbing my phone from the table, I typed out a quick text and said a little prayer to Thor that it got a positive response.

Can we meet somewhere to talk?

Within thirty seconds, I had my answer.

Yes! Come over.

* * *

"He's changed his outfit three times this morning," Paulie said as he ushered me inside.

Ernesto and Paulie lived in a tenth-floor condo overlooking Washington Square. It was modestly sized, but Ernesto had used his artistic eye to maximize the space and make it elegantly modern. Every time I stepped inside, I was awed by his talent and creativity.

Today though, I wasn't paying attention to my surroundings. I was here on a mission.

I needed Ern.

I'd lost Ken. My relationship with Quinn was off. Kat was gone and dealing with more problems than anyone should have to deal with. I didn't feel like I had any control over my life anymore and that was scaring me. It had been scaring me for weeks.

I didn't know what to do about Quinn. There was nothing I could do to help Kat right now. And Ken? I pretty much put the nail in the coffin of that relationship.

That left Ern.

I could fix things with Ernesto. I didn't want to smooth things over with him because I needed a sympathetic ear—as a matter of fact, I still didn't want to have any big heart-to-heart discussions. No, I wanted to smooth things over because I cared about him and owed him an apology. We'd been friends for going on ten years and I'd let my annoyance with him turn into avoidance. He deserved better than that and I needed to have my friend back.

So here I was, looking into Paulie's face, expecting some anger on behalf of his husband, but instead, he looked amused.

"Why is he changing clothes?" I asked.

Paulie snorted. "He's anxious. I told him he doesn't need to be. It's you. You're not coming here to fight or anything." He issued me a pointed look. "Are you?"

There it was. Paulie answered the door because he wanted to assess the situation before Ernesto. It was a sweet, protective gesture, and not for the first time, I felt a twinge of jealousy over their relationship. Paulie always had Ernesto's back.

Ken had your back, too, asshole, remember? I batted those thoughts away. Right now, I wasn't here to think about Ken, I was here for Ern.

"No." I sighed. "Tell him to come out here, I want to talk. I don't want to fight."

The bedroom door burst open. "Oh, Steven! I don't want to fight either! I'm so sorry!" Ernesto barreled forward, his arms wide. He grabbed me in a bear hug that trapped my arms at my side.

I laughed and could only use my fingers to give him a few awkward, soft taps on his hips.

"Okay, yeah, hi there."

I started to pull away, but Ernesto tightened his hold. "We're not done with the hug. Just a little bit longer."

"Okay," I agreed, letting him have the connection. I stayed stiff for a moment, then let myself relax. It felt nice, I realized. Really nice.

I needed a hug.

The thought made tears unexpectedly prick my eyes. *Oh no.* I didn't want to get emotional, didn't want to let the dam break. I was here to patch things up with my friend, not unload my turmoil all over him. But the longer the hug went on, the more my eyes and nose stung. Before I knew it, I was sniffling.

Ernesto heard my struggle and pulled back to look in my face. "Oh, my. You need to sit down. Let's talk about it."

He led me to the dining room table which was set for breakfast. I realized then that the apartment smelled heavenly.

"Paulie made us breakfast. Sit."

As soon as I sat, Ern rushed out, "I'm sorry. I shouldn't have said that to you. It was terrible. You guys looked so happy and I threw cold water all over you. I don't blame you one bit for leaving and not talking to me."

"Thank you for apologizing but blowing you off for a month was inexcusable. My only defense is that…" I paused, debating about how honest I should be.

Lies and secrets have to stop.

Ken's voice rang in my head again. He wouldn't leave me alone today. But he was right. I needed to start being honest and stop hiding everything that was even slightly unpleasant. I acted like I could handle anything, but really, I could barely stand any discord or bad feelings. I'd avoided dealing with what Ernesto had made me feel, I avoided letting King upset Quinn, I avoided facing all my fears about Ken. What had this given me except a feeling of being completely alone?

I cleared my throat and continued, "My only defense is that what you said scared me. I was already feeling insecure with Ken. I was falling in love with him and starting to get my hopes up when I knew I shouldn't."

Paulie set plates of pancakes, bacon, and fruit in front of us, and made a tsking sound as he did it. It didn't sound like a sympathetic tsk, either. I glanced at his face and found him glowering. Without comment, he turned back to the kitchen.

"Oh, no. No, no, no," Ernesto chanted. "That was all my issue and I shouldn't have put it on you. I had a really shitty thing with a bi guy in high school. We were young and he was freaked out, I think." He shook his head. "But that's not Ken's fault. I want to look out for you because I know you've had it rough lately, but I just unloaded all my garbage on to you instead. I'm a mess. You know I am. Ask Paulie. Paulie!" he shouted—as if Paulie couldn't hear every word we were saying anyway. "Tell Steven I'm a mess."

Paulie walked in holding his own stacked plate, his glower still affixed to his handsome face. He sat down across from me and just stared for a moment.

He opened his mouth, then closed it. Ern and I sat poised for whatever Paulie was going to say. He was like some wise monk who sat in silence—only speaking when there was sage advice to impart. Paulie raised his fork, pointed at me. "You." He angled his fork to Ern. "And you...Fools. Both of you are fools."

My shoulders sagged and Ernesto growled, "That's constructive."

Paulie stabbed a piece of kiwi and popped it in his mouth, the crease in his brow deepening. "This is the same shit that kept us fighting." He looked at me and said, "While you were at the bar, Ken talked about you like he really liked you. And I could tell he did. He brushed those other guys off without a glance. He's not going anywhere."

He bit into a piece of bacon and sat back with a sigh, like he was exhausted by the topic.

"I'm sure you think you know what you're talking about," I said. "But I think both of you are projecting your problems onto me. You're wrong. Ken's gone. He left," I announced.

Ern inhaled sharply, in shocked sympathy. But Paulie, he barked a bitter laugh. "Did he leave, or did you run him off?"

I don't think you're confused, babe. I just can't trust you, that's all.

I cringed at the remembrance of my viciousness. I'd exploited his sore spot and fed into my insecurities to deliver a crippling blow. For what?

To run him off.

Paulie saw my cringe and nodded knowingly. It chafed. This wasn't simply a matter of feeling less-than and driving him away. There were *circumstances*. There was a backstory, for Thor's sake.

"It's not like that, Paulie," I protested. "He's not blameless. You don't know the whole story."

"So, tell us the whole story. You *just* said you were falling in love with him. If that's true and not hyperbole, then you need to think about what kind of work you're willing to put into love, because it ain't easy. If you want it, you have to get uncomfortable sometimes."

He looked at Ern then and his face softened. Their smiles were knowing—maybe even a little sad as they shared some unspoken memory of rougher times. Again, I felt that twinge of jealousy and hated myself for it. It seemed like the two of them had gone through a lot of hardships to get to the level of trust and intimacy they shared.

I had no right to be jealous of it. They earned it. What had I done to earn anything like that? Doubting? Lying? Sneaking? What did I think I was going to get?

"Tell us," Paulie encouraged.

So, I did.

I capitulated, gave in and gave up, because I didn't want to carry all of this by myself anymore. And there was something about Paulie's quiet wisdom that made me feel like he'd give me whatever it was that I needed. Maybe not what I thought I wanted, but what I needed. Ern, Elizabeth…they might have been too biased in my favor and told me I was right and correct and justified in all that I'd done. Paulie wasn't, though. He'd give it to me straight and probably even see things through Ken's eyes. I liked that. Part of me wanted someone to be on Team McPretty and tell me what a huge prick I'd been.

Even though I was spilling my guts, I still made sure to edit Kat's business out of the retelling. It wasn't central to my story, and Ken's anger over it, I realized, was about feeling like I didn't care about him or value our relationship in the same way he did.

Instead, I told them about King and Quinn and Ken's argument with his sister. I admitted that I'd felt scared of how intense Ken was and how intensely I felt for him and that he'd said he loved me, and I never reciprocated.

When I got to the part where I admitted I'd been hiding mail from King and Ken threatened to tell Quinn, Ernesto broke his silence. "I hope to hell he did! What are you thinking? You're insane!"

Paulie tapped Ern's hand as if to calm him, but looked to me and said, "Why would you do that?"

"He was going to tell Quinn," I said simply, shrugging. With matching expressions, their faces conveyed exasperation and irritation. "What?" I asked, my own irritation growing. "You don't understand. Quinn's had a hard time lately. He's stressed. And he's been short with me. Angry, almost. I won the goddamned lottery when he found me, and I work hard to be the asset he thinks I am. If he knew I was bringing this shit into his house…" I shook my head. "He'd lose respect for me. And if he loses respect for me, he's going to fire me eventually. I have too much of my life wrapped up in Cipher Systems to risk having it all disappear."

"You make a lot of assumptions about people," Paulie remarked. "I see how this went down." He nodded sagely. "You figured Ken wasn't going to be a permanent fixture anyway, so you sacrificed him to keep your secrets from Quinn."

I sat silent, unable to deny Paulie's accusation.

"Did you even think to talk to him about it? Explain exactly how you felt?" Ernesto asked.

"Of *course*, he didn't," Paulie interjected. "Because he knew if he did, Ken would have been understanding." He locked his eyes with mine as he said to Ernesto, "And then he wouldn't have such a neat and tidy excuse to sabotage the relationship."

His words felt like a punch in the gut. *Sabotage.*

I wanted to rebel against the accusation. After all, I wasn't keeping King from Quinn to stir up trouble with Ken. I felt real fear when Ken said, *I'm calling Quinn.* But Paulie was right that I took it further than it needed to go.

All those things I said to him…they weren't true. I was cornered, insecure, and afraid so I lashed out. I turned savage and made sure I came out the victor.

The thing was… I didn't feel victorious. Not in the moment, not in those first, ominously silent minutes after he'd left, and certainly not now. Now I had to live with this carnage.

Carnage that was brought about because I was afraid.

Ken wasn't a liar. He wasn't ashamed of himself or of me. He'd been committed and happy. He consistently showed me that I mattered —that what I wanted and how I felt was important to him. No man had ever done any of that for me. Not even close.

He'd told me he loved me…and I believe it was true.

He'd told me he loved me…and I'd never said it back to him.

I brutalized the heart of the man I loved as a preemptive strike. *What a fucking coward.*

Shakily I asked, "What am I going to do, Ern?"

"It seems to me that the only thing to do is to finally tell the truth," he said gently, grasping my hand in his. "Tell Quinn, tell Ken. Tell them everything and let the cards fall where they will. If the sky starts falling, Paulie and I will be here for you."

CHAPTER THIRTY-SEVEN

DKM

I was pounding out the miles. Pushing myself harder and farther than I had since before the half-marathon. I was after the endorphin high.

Not only did I want the high, I wanted the pain and soreness that would linger afterward. I wasn't a masochist, far from it. I just took pleasure in feeling the resultant microscopic tears in my muscle fibers that I knew would heal and make me stronger for it. I liked knowing my pain was building me up.

That which does not kill us makes us stronger. I wasn't much for philosophy, but I had to admit, Nietzsche knew what he was talking about. I was going to be a stronger man for my pain and experience.

At least my body was going to be strong. I needed to shore up my emotional strength. And as much as my runs were helping me feel physically stronger, they were also meditative. Some days I'd clear my mind of everything but the rhythm of my steps, the sound of my breathing or the beating of my pulse. Those were the days I could feel more at peace with the state of my life. Other times, my runs would pass in the blink of an eye because I had spent the duration mentally replaying scenes in my head—sometimes finding my way through my confusing feelings to a solution or acceptance. If it weren't for my runs, I thought I'd probably be a basket case.

Today, I was thinking about my mother. She'd called me the night before wanting to know about Steven, wanting to set up a meeting, offering to spend a weekend in Chicago so she could get to know him. I put her off by trying to steer the conversation to her and Dad, but she wasn't having any of it. She only said that they were figuring out what comes next—which didn't tell me a damn thing.

I knew from Kari that when she'd gone to Mom and Dad to explain what happened between us, the whole story from a decade ago was revealed to Mom and she'd been livid. Kari said she yelled at both of them, then blamed herself for being out of touch with her own children.

I felt bad. I knew I had no control over my mother's reactions or emotions, nor had I any control over my dad's. Not then, not now. But I'd always been inspired by my parent's love for each other. The way they were together was the model I had for my imagined, perfect relationship. I supposed my ideal image of them was one that was childish and naive—blinded to reality. Obviously, if my dad couldn't talk to her about his relationship with me, then all was not perfect in the Miles household. Maybe it never had been.

I put my mother off and ended our conversation noncommittally. I couldn't bring myself to admit we weren't together—didn't want those words said until I was convinced of the truth of them.

I wanted to reach out. I wanted to see how he felt now that the dust had settled. I wanted to know if there was a chance for us.

But every time I started, I stopped myself with the reminder that *he'd* pushed me away and he hadn't bothered to call me. Calling him smacked of begging.

Had he shown me, besides letting me sleep with him a few times a week, any signs of being committed? He hadn't said he loved me, he wanted me gone, and hadn't called to try to make up. So why did I hold on to hope?

Because you know he cared, idiot, a voice in my head reasoned.

I've never felt like this before. It's addicting. You're *addicting*.

I remembered Steven's words to me and the expression of wonder and happiness across his face. The memory felt like a physical blow. I had to acknowledge that Steven had felt more for me beyond lust. But was it love or a desire for long-term commitment?

If you guys haven't patched things up by Thanksgiving, take me home with you and we can set fire to the holidays. We'll ruin all the holidays for years to come.

I burst into unexpected laughter at the memory. He promised long-term with an offer of mischief and mayhem. God, I loved him. I missed his smile, his calm, his body, and his cute blindness.

It felt good to smile, but it was bittersweet. I hadn't intended for the run to turn into a self-therapy session or an excuse to indulge in my fixation with Steven. I'd put my earbuds in and set out to let the music be the only soundtrack to my steps. Up until now, the music had largely been ignored.

"Closer" by Nine Inch Nails began and the synth beat matched my strides, the chords stirred me into an angry determination, the lyrics mirroring the dark, obsessive part of me that was mostly quiet and secret—the part of me that felt like something was wrong with me and Steven was the answer to making me better—less strange, less rigid. Making me better by taking me into his body and accepting, erasing all that was uncomfortable and awkward, letting me see myself through his eyes.

I hated it. I hated the feelings the song evoked. There was nothing wrong with me. My existence wasn't made valid by Steven's acceptance.

But wasn't love so addicting? Didn't the absence of it, once experienced, leave a putrid, festering hole?

It *was* an addiction. My body and my psyche had been fine without that love, but then I had it, enjoyed it, relied on it and now was ill and suffering, worse off than I was before because it was gone.

These were dark thoughts—ones I wasn't going to indulge, so I slowed my steps to skip to the next track on the playlist on my phone. I had been making my way south from the river and was now at Monroe Harbor, approaching my usual entrance and exit to the trail on East

Monroe and Lake Shore which meant it was nearing time for my cool-down anyway.

I'd made excellent time despite the coolness of the strong wind coming off the lake. Autumn had begun, schools were back in session, so even though this was a Sunday, I hadn't passed as many people as I usually did during my early runs. It was a signal that the weather changes were happening soon, and I'd have to switch to doing all my cardio at the gym.

The thought made me depressed.

In the quiet moment between songs, I heard a faint call—made more faint by the whooshing gusts of wind. My periphery was compromised by the sweatshirt hood I had pulled up and before I could ascertain the sound's origin, I was rammed forcefully from behind.

Someone large plowed into me, causing me to fall. I braced, doing my best to take the impact on my side and roll. My phone clattered to the pavement and my buds fell from my ears. I tore my hood off angrily as soon as I sprung up from my tumble.

The blindsiding blow enraged me. "You limp-dicked motherfu—" I began, but stopped when I saw my assailant.

King whirled toward me and backtracked from the momentum of his sprint. I had only a second to comprehend this was a calculated attack and steel myself for violent aggression when he reached behind him and removed something from his back pocket.

I flinched thinking, *gun*, but with a flick of his wrist, a metal baton expanded from the handle.

When I'd registered the weapon, I felt that choking, paralyzing fear disappear, allowing me to react swiftly, jumping back far enough to avoid his intended blow.

He grunted as he swung wildly again, and I scrambled further out of his reach.

"I'm going to—" Swing. "Break—" Swing. "Every bone in your face!" He said the last words with a guttural grunt of rage and exertion.

He kept advancing and I kept retreating, each swing missing me by mere inches. I knew I couldn't allow him to keep swinging. I knew eventually, he'd hit his mark and a blow from the baton, with the force he was using, would be devastating no matter where it landed.

I jumped back as far as I could on the next swing, hoping it was enough space to create my own momentum. I waited for another swing and as soon as the baton cleared its arc, I rushed him, attacking before he could wind up for another. My fist smashed into his face. I felt and heard the fracturing in his nose. He let out an agonized yell as our bodies collided and fell to the pavement. His body took the brunt of the hard fall and it rendered him momentarily winded and stunned. I used this advantage to wrest control of the weapon from his right hand.

Just as I pulled it away, he recovered, and pain exploded in the side of my face as his fist connected soundly. The force of it moved me enough to allow him to dislodge my body from his.

I held fast to the baton and rolled quickly to the side, trying to get to a standing position before he could. My head throbbed, but I managed to regain my feet and hold the baton up, poised in defense.

He lumbered to his feet, his mouth open and emitting a pained wail. Blood was flowing from his nose so copiously; it was dripping to the pavement below. But despite the obvious pain he was in, he surprised me by stepping forward.

I backed up, and nearly stumbled as my feet stepped off the concrete path onto grass. The near-fall made me angry with myself. What was I doing by retreating? *I* had the weapon, *I* had the advantage, yet he was advancing, and I was cowering away.

What was the endgame here? Fend him off until someone noticed and called the police? If he was intent on violence, then I wasn't going to be able to avoid it.

I knew what the wild look on his face meant. He didn't care that I had the weapon, he was singular in his rage and his mission. I'd seen this before and it had been frightening.

Crack his fucking skull open.

My hand tightened on the baton and I stopped backing away. I pulled back to swing as he neared, and he roared as he lunged forward.

I let out a shout as I brought the weapon forward. But at the last possible moment, I pulled back and whirled to the side, dodging his attack and avoiding striking his head. I spun around and delivered a hard blow into the backs of his legs.

Pain shot through my hands and arms from the force of the strike, and I nearly dropped the baton.

King fell, screaming, face first into the grass.

I turned to look for my phone, and found a jogger sprinting up to me. I opened my mouth to ask him to call 911, but he leaped to straddle King's hips, and began restraining his hands with zip ties.

When he finished, he stood up, faced me and panted out, "Dr. Miles, my name is Amid and I work for Cipher Systems."

CHAPTER THIRTY-EIGHT

STEVEN

K en's Sunday routine was predictable, and that gave me several options for my ambushing plans.

I knew I could get up at five-thirty and wait for him to arrive at the Monument around six. This plan was good because it meant I could settle things earlier, rather than later—and if for some reason he didn't run today, I'd realize it without too much standing around and waiting.

The downside was that it would be pre-run. Post-run Ken was more agreeable. I felt like I might have had a better shot at forgiveness if I let him have his exercise first.

Another option was hanging out in Buzzy's until he came in for his coffee. This idea had merit because waiting in a busy coffee shop was a heck of a lot safer than the Monument at dawn. But I'd had to reject this idea because he didn't *always* stop at Buzzy's, and I couldn't risk missing him.

I decided that waiting at the fountain for him to finish was what I was going to do. This allowed me to arrive once the sun had come up, at least. Now that it was October, sunrise was later than it had been back in the summer, and even though there were still very few people out here at this time, I felt safer in the daylight. King or no King, I wouldn't have felt great standing alone in the dark at the park, anyway.

Unfortunately, waiting for Ken to finish meant I had to stand here for possibly up to two hours, depending on the length of his run, before I'd give up and go home. For all the thought I'd put into *when* I was going to do this, I'd neglected to dress appropriately and was in a thin, long-sleeved V-neck T-shirt and jeans. My only excuse was that I'd been nervous when I was getting ready and started sweating. Added warmth hadn't crossed my mind. The clothes selection was entirely based on the one time Ken said my shoulders looked great in this shirt.

So, here I was—bringing my shoulder A-game, trying to shield myself from the breeze by standing just behind the planter below the first pillars of the monument. Rather than being worried about being accosted by criminals, I was starting to worry I'd be mistaken for one. I was sure I looked suspicious and strange skulking behind the stone monument. I could just imagine having to explain what I was doing.

Well, you see, officer, I'm just waiting here in the crisp, early hours hoping to ambush my ex-boyfriend in the hopes he'll take me back. Totally normal behavior. Nothing to worry about.

It's fine.

I'm fine.

It's fine. Over and over, I repeated it to myself. I wanted to believe it—tried to be optimistic—but I had resolved to go *way* outside my comfort zone and face my fears by confessing everything to Ken and Quinn. It was hard for me to believe that by doing all the things I was too afraid to do before I'd end up with a positive result.

Paulie was sure Ken would forgive me.

Ernesto was sure Quinn wouldn't fire me.

All I knew was that I couldn't keep going the way I was.

I needed Ken back in my life.

I needed to feel like I was on solid footing again.

I needed to be honest.

Quinn was coming back from Boston tomorrow. I was going to tell him everything—from the first scuffle in the apartment, to enlisting Alex's help investigating, to the unhinged greeting cards I'd been receiving. I had to give this burden over and ask for help.

I hadn't gotten any cards in the mail since Ken and I had split, and all last night I'd fought with myself over it. I was tempted to take the lack of communication as a sign that King's torment was ending—and therefore no need to involve anyone. But I'd used that excuse several times before and it always started again. I also knew that if I wanted Ken back in my life, I was going to have to do it.

At some point I realized I wasn't going to tell Quinn about King just to appease Ken. I was going to tell him because I needed to do it for my own peace of mind. It had taken a toll on me, this secrecy and fear.

I just hoped my relationship with Quinn would weather it. If not, I hoped I had Ken by my side to support and love me. If not…well, Paulie and Ern might have a sad, lost squatter sleeping on their couch for a while.

After a time, I got lost in thoughts of Ken, wondering how he was doing, wondering if his trip to Cleveland was stressful, wondering if he missed me, wondering if he still loved me.

And I wondered what his reaction was going to be when he found me here waiting for him. Would he turn on his heel and walk away? Would he tell me to leave him alone?

I didn't have any idea, and that worried me.

My attention was snagged by a large figure emerging from the trees to the left. The way the man stepped forward with purpose and swiftness, immediately set me on edge. He was walking toward me, and it was difficult to make out much detail because the sun was behind him, casting his front in shadow. I could tell by his tall build, he wasn't King, but that didn't mean he wasn't a threat.

Just as I readied myself for a confrontation, the man held up his hand and called out to me. "Steven!"

I recognized the voice as Damon's and held up my hand to shield my eyes against the sun to try to see his face more clearly. "Damon?"

The guard loped up to me, a concerned expression on his face. "There's a car coming for us in a minute. Dr. Miles was just attacked."

* * *

"How far down is he?" I asked, scanning the trail as Josh turned the SUV onto Lake Shore.

"Amid said they're a quarter-mile north of Monroe," Damon replied from the backseat.

As soon as the words left his mouth, I saw Ken. I saw his blond mop blowing in the breeze as he sat on a bench near the harbor. "Stop!" I pointed to the right. "Park in the grass, park in the grass."

Josh turned and drove over the curb to maneuver the car between two trees in the sloping, grassy area separating the highway from the trail. Before he could come to a full stop, I was opening my door and hopping out.

"Ken!" I yelled. He stood up from the bench and relief suffused me. He really was okay. I hadn't believed Damon when he tried to assure me—the word *attack* evoking all sorts of horrendous images and ideas.

But as I got closer to him, I saw the swollen state of his eye and the cut on his cheek. "Oh, no. No, no, no!" I grabbed up his hands in mine, afraid to hug him in case he was bruised anywhere else, and he let out a little hiss of pain at the contact.

I looked down and saw his right hand was also bruising.

I dropped it. "Shit, I'm sorry, I'm sorry," I apologized frantically. "Where else are you hurt? Is it just your face and hand? Are you okay? Your cheek is bleeding! I'm calling an ambulance—you need to see a doctor. I know you're a doctor," I rambled as I pulled my phone from my pants. "But you still need to go. Even doctors need doctors, right?"

"Steven," he interjected. "I've called for emergency services already. They're on their way."

"Oh, yeah, of course." I slid the phone back into my pocket and stared at him.

He raised his left hand to stroke my cheek with his knuckle. "Why are you so cold?"

"Because of my shoulders," I replied absently, examining his face. The small cut on his cheek and the swelling that was making his right eye puff up looked painful and I suspected it was going to be one hell of a shiner.

His brow furrowed. "What?"

I waved my hand dismissively, unconcerned with talk of my temperature. I wanted to examine him more—find out if he was hurt elsewhere. I looked over his body, from his shoulders to his feet and said, "I was waiting at the Monument for you."

"You were?"

Underneath the obvious surprise in his tone, I heard a pitch change that sounded like happiness. Or maybe hope. Either way, it made my eyes snap back to his to gauge his expression.

His eyes—well, the one good eye—was soft and he was wearing a small smile. "No jacket?"

Shrugging I said, "I forgot."

He removed his phone and earbuds from the front pocket of his pullover and put them in his sweatpants pocket. "Here," he said, reaching behind to remove his hoodie.

"What are you doing? Leave your clothes on," I demanded. He was the one who was hurt and needed warmth, not me.

He ignored me and held the shirt out. "It might be a little sweaty, but you should put it on, it will keep the wind off of you."

I felt my face bunch up. There was no way I was letting him give it to me. He had on a long-sleeve compression shirt, and I imagined the sweat being cooled by the breeze had to feel nippy. As a matter of fact, I could see those homicidal, sexy nipples poking out, and I wasn't going to let the poor things get exposed to the elements. "Are you crazy? I'm not taking that from you. You'll freeze! You've had an *ordeal*!"

His nostrils flared. "Well, you either put it on and get warmer, or we both stand here cold because I'll be damned if I put it back on!" he groused. I saw him wince, and he touched his cheek lightly as if it pained him.

"Harrumph," I said, reluctantly taking the sweatshirt from him. "Good to know your hair-trigger pissyness didn't disappear since last I saw you." I removed my glasses and set them on the bench so I could slip into the shirt.

As soon as I had it on and adjusted the hood, Ken grabbed the front of it in his fist and pulled me to him, slamming our mouths together. And, by the mighty tool of Thor, my whole body lit up at the contact.

He wrapped his arms around my waist and pulled me in tight. I matched his hunger—all the terror and aching releasing into passion and relief.

He was here in my arms. Safe. Safe, and kissing me like he missed me, like he wanted me, like he loved me.

Normally, I'd let this ride—let the sex do all the talking for me, or let the sex distract from the talking. But I couldn't do that this time.

As much as I hated to do it, I pulled away from him. He started to protest, but the sound of approaching sirens diverted our attention to the road.

Two police SUVs and an ambulance arrived, and I remembered King. My attention had so wholly been on Ken, I'd forgot to examine the scene. I put my glasses back on and looked to the group.

Surrounded by Amid, Josh, and Damon, King was belly-down in the grass, his hands restrained behind his back and his head turned toward the trail. The lower half of his face was covered in drying blood. It looked ghastly.

Gingerly, I grasped Ken's right hand and looked at his swelling knuckles. "Did you do that to him?"

He nodded. "Yes. He has a nasal fracture, but I'm almost certain I didn't break his femur. He'll be fine."

There seemed to be an underlying importance to his words I didn't understand. Any damage Ken did to him to protect himself, King had coming.

"Thank you," I said, lifting his knuckle to my lips. Seeing my tormentor bleeding, broken, bested, and demoralized was a surreal experience. I didn't know whether I wanted to crow or cry. It was over. Finally, over.

"What are you thanking me for?"

There was a flurry of activity around us, police officers and EMT, voices in conversation, King yelling obscenities, but my attention was entirely on Ken.

What was I thanking him for? For being smart and brave when I wasn't. For ending this nightmare once and for all. For having integrity and self-respect. If he'd allowed me to have my way and run roughshod over him, where would we be now? With one of us dead? Critically injured?

"For everything." My voice betrayed me by cracking. I didn't think I could articulate all the guilt, relief, sadness and admiration I was feeling. But Ken honed-in on the crack, his one good eye narrowing. I knew he wasn't going to ignore it—knew he wasn't going to let me get away with not articulating it.

He squeezed my hand. "Why did you wait at the Monument?"

"To ta—" I began, but stopped myself. I was going to say *to talk to you*, but he knew that much. He was asking something else. Instead of taking the scenic route and making him pull it from me, I decided I needed to say it all.

I took a deep breath then bit my lip when I felt it begin to quiver.

He squeezed my hand again in silent support, causing my eyes to well with unshed tears.

"I'm tired." A tear slipped down my cheek and I swiped at it, willing the rest to stay put or dry up. I didn't think this was a great sign —losing my composure so early in the conversation. There was so much I needed to say to him, but I was verging on becoming a sobbing mess at any moment.

Taking another deep breath, I continued. "I'm tired of being afraid of everything. Tired of worrying about my job, of King, of juggling secrets. Tired of missing you."

Ken released a shaky sigh, but didn't reply, so I continued. "I was going to tell you that I had every intention of going to Quinn tomorrow when he came back from his trip, so that you'd know I was serious about this. But now..." I let the sentence hang, slightly dejected that I didn't have any offering for Ken to prove my sincerity. Action always spoke louder than words, and after my treatment of him, I felt like he deserved more than promises.

But now, that was all I had for him.

He gave an insolent shrug of his shoulder. "I warned you."

Our eyes connected for a protracted moment and I imagined he was restraining himself from blasting me with all the obvious *I told you sos*. I appreciated his control. I already felt terrible for bringing this into his life and putting him in danger, I didn't think I could take it if he went on the attack right now.

"You did," I agreed. "And it scared me. It scared me so much that I lashed out."

He let go of my hand, a look of angry bewilderment crossing his battered face. "What do you mean? *That's* what set you off?"

"I didn't want Quinn angry," I defended. "This job means the world to me. I have a lot of seniority there—a lot of responsibility. I couldn't imagine there was a future for me that didn't include Cipher Systems. I thought there was a very good chance you were going to ruin it all for me."

He shook his head and cursed under his breath. "Instead of *talking* to me about it, you picked a fight?" He shook his head again, this time more forcefully. "Nope. Not buying it. You know I would have bent over backward to help you. If you explained it to me, we would have come up with another way that didn't involve your boss."

He put his hands on his hips, dipping his head closer to me. "What you said to me...you said because you wanted me gone forever—not just to make me keep my mouth shut. Do you really think I'm a liar? Think I'm a coward? Because if you do, there's no point in talking about this anymore."

Before I could respond, he barreled on, his voice rising, "I'll admit that I haven't always been forthcoming about my sexuality. I've let my interest speak for itself without explanation. But with you, I haven't held *anything* back—not my feelings for you or my past. I didn't hold back because I wanted everything. Saying you don't trust me means you're basing those feelings off things I can't control. That's insurmountable. I can't fight that! I couldn't have done anything different." Ken lifted his face to the sky and took a deep breath. When he brought his eyes back to mine, his expression told me he wasn't going to accept anything less than the unvarnished truth. "So, let me ask you again. Why did you wait at the Monument?"

"Because *I* was a liar and coward!" I shouted. "Because these secrets are suffocating me, and I needed to tell you everything. I didn't think you'd stay with me—didn't think you'd want me for long, so I used every excuse and weapon I had to drive you away." Tears were spilling onto my cheeks then, all the shame and buried feelings of inadequacy surfacing.

"*Didn't think I'd want you for long*? Because of women?" he asked gruffly. "That's why?"

"Women! Men! Anyone who's better looking than I am—anyone who doesn't have this clusterfuck baggage of King on their shoulders. Look at you, for God's sake!" I swirled my hand around his head. "Look at me." I jabbed my index finger at my nose. "It's—we're—" I cut myself off, unwilling to continue this pitiful line of self-deprecation. I raised my hand to lightly touch his face. "And, I've been a nightmare for you, bringing a psycho into your life and acting like a crazy person myself, when you didn't deserve any of it. All you did was love me and support me and I was too scared to rely on you. I don't deserve you or your forgiveness, but you need to know I'm so sorry, I'm sorry for everything."

Ken didn't speak for a long moment. I watched as his throat worked and his eyes shimmered with unshed tears. Finally, he cleared his throat and said, "Forgiving you is easy because it's what I want to do." He brought his hands to my hips, holding me in a way that could have been an embrace, or could have been a precursor to pushing me away. "But the secrets, Steven. What else don't I know?" His lips screwed up into a sneer. "Got any other big bombshells I need to know about?"

"Yes, I do," I admitted quietly. "There's one big secret I never told you. It's the scariest one."

Understanding dawned. His face changed then—the cynical twist of his mouth relaxing, his eye widening from its watchful squint. "You should have trusted me with that secret. I trusted you with mine."

A bitter laugh escaped my lips. "Yeah and look where that got you.

At the first sign of trouble, I eviscerated you. You gave me so much power, and when I felt helpless, I wielded that power ruthlessly." I squeezed my eyes shut tightly, shame and revulsion washing over me.

Ken gave my hips a jostle and ordered, "Look at me."

Just as I opened my eyes, I caught sight of an EMT and uniformed police officer approaching. "Dr. Miles," the officer began.

Ken stiffened, and without looking to them, he cocked his head and raised his hand in a *halt* gesture to the duo behind him. "Stop. You need to give us a minute," he said loudly.

His tone, so full of authority and irritation, had the desired effect and the men stopped in their tracks, issuing each other confused looks.

I smiled, finding the moment comical in spite of the tears on my cheeks and pounding of my heart. "Did you really just give a member of the Chicago Police Department an order?"

"You're damn right I did. You were just about to confess your love and they are *not* screwing this up for me."

I laughed softly, but Ken's expression didn't change. "No more secrets," he said gruffly.

Sobering, I promised, "No more secrets."

"You need to trust me," he demanded, sliding his arms around my middle, pulling my body flush with his. "And you need to give up your last secret. Tell me now. Give me the same power I'm giving you."

"Yes! Have it! Have the power. There's no one else I'd want holding my heart, Ken." I grasped his cheeks in my hands, careful not to hurt his sore eye as I finally admitted what was in my heart.

"I love you. I love you in a way that's completely terrifying but wholly necessary. I can't be without you. I don't want to be without you. I feel like I waited my whole life for this love and even one more minute without it might actually kill me, I'm sure of it."

Ken smiled. "Well," he began thickly, then cleared his throat. "We can't afford to waste one minute."

He met my lips with his own. I could feel the relief and love and forgiveness in him and hoped he could feel my own full capitulation to him. I was his. He had me completely. He was my soft place to land and I was going to be his.

"Um…" the officer said from behind us. "Dr. Miles?"

I huffed a laugh against Ken's lips and soothed, "It's okay, McGrumpy. We have all the time in the world for kissing."

He pulled away slowly. His good eye was narrowed in exaggerated frustration, but his mouth was slanted with an impish grin. "You promise?"

"I promise."

CHAPTER THIRTY-NINE

"I'm sure it is awful and terrible, Lambchop," I said into the phone. "But, my god, you look absolutely gorgeous in these photos."

Kat scoffed.

"I'm looking at one now where Dan is giving off major smolder, too. The camera loves both of you."

I couldn't resist grabbing the tabloid this morning when I saw their picture under the headline, PHARMA HEIRESS TAKES CONTROL! It was surreal. And if the situation hadn't been so serious, I'd be busting Dan's balls 24/7.

In the couple of weeks since King's attack, Kat and Dan's life had gone completely batshit crazy. It had been discovered that her cousin Caleb had been acquiring the rights to drugs manufactured to treat rare diseases and marking their price up by 500% in some cases. He'd been defrauding shareholders, and even went so far as to kidnap and ransom Dan in a desperate attempt to fund his own company.

The media was rabid for the story—and any glimpse of the sexy power-couple at the heart of it.

"That could have been you," Ken said to me once the story broke.

"See, I told you Dan was a hero and a saint. You should send him some macarons."

"Maybe I will." He nodded.

"Nah, better not do that," I cautioned. "We don't want Dan to know he was her second-choice husband."

"Yeah." Ken's voice dripped with sarcasm. "I remember how torn up over you she looked in her wedding video."

McPretty was still a riot.

"He's got plenty of smolder," Kat agreed, her voice taking on a dreamy quality.

"Aren't you glad I didn't marry you?" I teased.

"You would have made a fine husband, Steven," she said matter-of-factly. Her pitch rose as she continued. "But I was calling to ask you for another big favor."

"My seed? Done. I can't wait to see little mini-mes running around your mansion."

"Oh my God, no." She laughed. "Not that."

"I'm hurt! Offer rescinded."

"I'm not after your seed, I'm after your brain."

"I can't put that in a cup for you, sugar."

"But could you come work for me? For Caravel?"

Well...that was unexpected. I sat in stunned silence for a moment, my mouth agape.

"After the fraud, after the way Caleb has tanked production, I just don't know who I can trust. I need you to be the head of finance. I know you have a boyfriend to think about—"

"Ken," I spoke up. "His name is Ken."

"Discuss it with him, and don't worry about Quinn—he's already given me the green light to offer you the position."

My ears buzzed at this. Kat's voice took on a faraway quality as the blood drained from my face. *Quinn's passing me on.*

"...Don't answer yet," she continued. "Just promise me you'll think about it, okay?" I was silent until she said louder, "Steven?"

"I-I'll think about it and get back to you," I promised.

After we disconnected, I sat staring at my office walls. On one hand, I was shocked. I couldn't believe he'd do it. But on the other...

well, it was my fear made into reality. Hadn't I worried this day was creeping up? Hadn't I felt it coming?

After Quinn had come back from Boston the Monday after King attacked, he called Alex and I to the penthouse for a debriefing. Even though he'd just spent a few days embroiled in the kidnapping of his best friend, his mood seemed…normal. By normal, I meant terse and abrupt, but not angry.

By this point, I knew Ken had been the one to prompt Quinn to utilize protection against King, and I expected some sort of tongue-lashing from Quinn…but it never came.

Maybe instead of taking that as a good sign, I should have known then Quinn didn't give a shit—didn't think we had a relationship beyond Cipher spreadsheets.

The debriefing had been enlightening. Alex had continued investigating King after I left him that morning in the data center. What he'd found—by hacking my phone and then King's phones—was that I was not the only man being tormented.

Once Alex discovered it, had proof to show Quinn, he'd involved him. When Ken had gone to Quinn…he'd already known. Ken's talk with him did result in my mail from King being intercepted. When I thought communication had stopped, it was escalating, both in number and in vitriol and threat.

"We've encouraged these two men to come forward, press charges and present evidence. We're going to make sure he goes away this time," Quinn announced.

Many times over the years I'd felt lucky to be working for Quinn—but never more than at that moment.

Now? Now it looked like it was all coming to an end.

If I went to work for Caravel, I'd likely find satisfaction in taking the chaos there and setting it to rights. I'd have Kat—and probably Dan to some extent, so it wouldn't be a complete tragedy.

But…Ken. Ken loved his position at BKC Memorial—loved life in Chicago. I knew I couldn't take this job in Boston without his whole-hearted agreement to come with me. Neither one of us was going to be satisfied with a long-distance relationship.

If we moved—if I still had Ken and Dan and Kat and a challenging workload—I still wouldn't have Cipher. Janie, Alex, *Quinn*. God, for all my griping, I loved working for the grump.

I stewed on this for a long time, staring out my office window at the Chicago skyline. I went through stages of grief in those moments, but when I got down and dirty into anger, I decided Quinn needed to hear some of this.

No one ever told Quinn Sullivan off, and it was high time someone did.

Might as well be me.

Screw it.

I marched out of my office and made a beeline to Quinn's, garnering strange looks from a few of my co-workers. I rounded the corner and bypassed Betty's desk without announcing myself. I heard her say, "Steven—" but I ignored her (I'd apologize later because Betty was an angel from heaven and didn't deserve attitude from me or anyone else). I opened Quinn's door to find him sliding his arms into his coat sleeves.

"Kat said you gave her your blessing to send me on to Boston." Not a question, an accusation.

"Yes," he replied stonily.

I let out a bitter huff. "Jesus, you are a cold bastard, aren't you?"

It was barely perceptible, but his eyes widened a fraction with what looked to be...hurt? Surprise? Whatever the emotion, it was very quickly replaced by annoyance. I recognized it easily enough, since it had been his default these past months. I pressed on.

"Six years! After everything I've done and everything you've trusted me with, you're just sending me along like it's nothing!" I was yelling now, and vaguely aware that in my periphery Betty was closing the door for some added privacy. Like I said, *angel*.

"What was I supposed to do, Steven?" he responded—annoyingly, at a modulated volume. "Should I have made decisions for you? *That* would have gone over like a lead balloon," he sneered.

He wasn't completely wrong, but I was hurt and angry, not ready to make any concessions.

"You didn't have any such qualms when it came to King. You seem to know what's best for everybody, huh?"

Okay, I was an ungrateful dick for that comment, and I knew it. But, again, hurt and angry and not giving many shits.

"Oh, you want to talk about King? If there's so much trust between us, why in the hell did I have to hear about your stalker from Alex? It seems to me that I trust you more than you trust me. I had to consider that maybe you'd *rather* go to Boston."

Quinn's words took the wind right out of my sails.

I hadn't imagined he might feel slighted. I only worried about his anger and how his anger would affect me. I didn't get the chance to tell Quinn about King—didn't have to open myself up to that, but there *was* something else I needed to tell him. I valued him, cared about him, so I had to be honest.

"I owe you an apology," I said solemnly. "I'm sorry I didn't come to you months ago. I tried to hide it from you because I thought you'd lose respect for me. Thought you'd fire me for being reckless and stupid."

Quinn stood still, his only motion, three, slow, deliberate blinks. This wasn't a good sign.

After a moment he asked, "You thought my reaction to you being assaulted and stalked would be judgment and not concern?"

"Um…" *Shit.* My apology wasn't making things better. Far from it. It looked like I was digging my own grave. But this was the way it had to be. Clean slate. Clean conscience. I owed it to Quinn. I owed it to myself. "When you say it like that, it sounds bad, but I truly didn't want to upset you. Not when you were so worried about Janie and the baby."

"Would you have advised Betty to keep the stalking under wraps if she were in your position?"

"What? No! That's insane."

"Why?"

"Because she's…" I began but stopped once I saw the *gotcha* gleam in his eye. *Because she's a woman.* He knew what I was going to say and had intentionally backed me into a corner.

I gave an exasperated sigh and said robotically, "Because she's a woman."

"Men get hurt too, Steven," Quinn said with uncharacteristic gentleness. "It doesn't mean they're weak or that they deserve it. I take Nico's safety seriously and I take *your* safety seriously."

His voice lost some of its gentleness when he twisted his lips in a snide smile and said, "Just because you have the *worst* taste in men doesn't mean you should have to endure abuse and torment."

"Hey!" I clutched my chest, pretending to take offense, but his words put me at ease. "I found a good one in the end," I added. "The *best* one." Thinking of Ken brought a smile to my face.

Quinn shrugged. "If you say so. But if this ever happens again, you come to me," he ordered, his voice authoritative. "Not Alex, not Dan. Me."

"You...don't want to force me out then?" I asked, my voice tinged with wary hope.

He sighed, and leaned forward, resting his palms on the shiny desktop. His posture indicated a weariness with the topic. "What Kat wants with you...the position in a company as big and profitable as Caravel...the *money*..." He paused and looked me dead in the eye. "You think you like flying around in Manuel? Just wait, Caravel will have bigger and better at your disposal."

He said *Manuel*. An involuntary grin sprang up on my face, completely spoiling the seriousness of the conversation. He actually said *Manuel*.

"Yes, she needs help," he continued, ignoring my smile. "But also, I can't take an opportunity like this away from you, no matter how *pissed* it makes me."

I jumped on it. "You're pissed?" *Tell me more, Boss Man.*

"You're goddamned right I'm pissed! What the hell am I supposed to do when you leave? Give your work to a *junior accountant*?" He spat the word with such venom and derision, I kind of felt sorry for our juniors.

"Janie's not here, and Dan's going to be in Boston." He closed his eyes, shaking his head. "But it's more than that." He opened his eyes.

"It's more than the workload. I poached you because I saw in you someone I could rely on. Someone I could trust to help me take Cipher Systems where I wanted it to be."

His next words—so un-Quinn-like—had to be the result of baby hormones. That was a thing, right? New dads getting hormonal? It had to be, because there was no other excuse for it—no other reason why Quinn would give me the exact words I needed to hear in that moment.

"Losing you would be a blow. Both personally and professionally."

EPILOGUE

STEVEN

"So, Steven..." Ken's grandmother said, pulling my attention reluctantly away from him. He was dancing with Kari, smiling from ear to ear as they swayed to-and-fro. He was dressed in a finely made gray suit and yellow tie. At some point, he'd shucked the jacket and was currently in a vest and rolled shirt sleeves. His golden waves had been gelled to the side hours before but had begun to show signs of resistance by kinking up. He was happy. He was stunning. So beautiful my heart hurt.

"Are you and my Kenny going to be the next to wed?"

I chuckled at her bold question. The woman was a complete hoot. I'd been able to spend several hours in her company since Ken and I arrived on Mackinac Island late Thursday evening. She'd been game to spend Friday accompanying the wedding party all over the island for photo shoots. She'd posed for some, but mostly had been content to watch the activity from the horse-drawn carriage, tucked under a thick blanket to shield her from the cold, autumn breeze.

Friday's photo shoot had been a day-long endeavor. Everyone dressed in sweaters and knit hats and traversed a bit of the beautiful wooded area of the island, posing next to fallen logs amid brightly colored foliage—brilliant oranges, reds, and yellows dotting the ground and treetops.

We visited the quaint Victorian-era downtown, posed in front of a shop proclaiming it to be "America's oldest grocery store," and pretended to look over wooden crates full of Michigan apples, pumpkins, and jellies. We meandered around the old fort, made our way down to the rocky beach, and even rode the ferry around the strait.

As Ken's SO (as Kari referred to me), I was encouraged to participate in most of the staged shots, but there were times when only the wedding party had been required. In those times, I'd been summoned by Nana to keep her company. I enjoyed her humor and her seemingly filter-less conversation. The woman said exactly what she wanted to say—and with no remorse. I loved her. At one point I asked her to tell me something about Ken as a little kid, and, of course, she went straight to something embarrassing. *Oh, my little Kenny…from the time he was a toddler to when he was about ten or eleven, would stick his finger in his nose whenever he was tired or stressed. Julia didn't know how to break him of it, but he finally gave it up. Kari used to call him Booger Boy.*

I had been *this* close to spitting apple cider all over Nana. *Booger Boy.* If I didn't love that weirdo so much, I'd use it to bust his balls until the end of time.

Now, seated in the reception, Nana's bluntness was getting her in trouble. "Mother…" Julia began, chastising her for her intrusiveness.

"What?" she asked, feigning obliviousness. "Kenny's my last unwed grandchild and I'm not getting any younger."

Despite herself, Julia laughed and shook her head at her mother. "You're impossible," she said, then turned toward me, her face shining with happiness. "Please ignore her, Steven, you don't have to let her put you on the spot like that."

"I could die tomorrow. I don't want to depart this world not knowing," Nana harrumphed, garnering a unified chorus of scoffs around the table.

We were in the Grand Hotel—the festivities beginning to wind down. I was seated at a table designated for the immediate families of the bride and groom, but had to be separated from Ken throughout dinner, as he'd been required to sit at the wedding party's long table at the front of the room. The situation caused Ken a bit of anxiety at first. He worried I'd feel uncomfortable being stuck alone with his parents, grandmother, and Brandon's parents and step-parents. But it had been fine. Lovely, in fact.

The whole weekend had gone perfectly. Ken and his father spent time together working toward building their relationship, his parents seemed cordial—if not loving—toward each other, and I could discern no overt curiosity or judgment aimed my way from the other guests. Kari had been especially lovely. Even with the stress of the weekend and moments of snappishness toward some of the party and staff, she'd gone out of her way to make me feel welcome. Not only had she included me in activities, she'd also pulled me aside for a sincere apology for the things she'd said. Looking into those sapphire eyes, so like Ken's, I couldn't help but be charmed by her.

I hadn't precisely known what to expect with Ken this weekend but found myself surprised by his easy cheerfulness. He hadn't avoided physical contact with me—he'd been as demonstrative as he'd have been in Chicago—nor had he avoided conversations or introductions, either. He embraced the celebration and duties and was happier and more relaxed than I'd ever seen him. Truly, it had been a beautiful weekend.

As for me, I'd been trying to work toward earning Ken's forgiveness. I knew it meant time, proving oneself couldn't happen overnight. But I was all-in, ready to play the long game. I didn't imagine it was always going to be easy. I had to admit to myself that I let deep-seated insecurities erode my trust in Ken and myself. I'd had to acknowledge that I wasn't as confident as I thought I was, that I had doubts about my desirability as a permanent partner for someone who was as handsome as Ken—and for someone who had an endless selection of potential lovers. It was all on me, and I needed to work on myself because Ken was amazing and didn't need the burden of having to constantly reassure me. He deserved to be trusted—judged by his own actions and words and not be tainted by factors he couldn't control.

Ken wanted to be known. He wanted me to know the entirety of him and still love him. Didn't we all want that? Wasn't that vital to having a pure love? I wanted it. I wanted to wake up sure that Ken knew every flaw and vulnerability I had and still loved me unconditionally. Hiding was exhausting. Living up or down to expectations wasn't sustainable. Being raw and naked was scary, but it was honest. We couldn't be known without being honest.

Since the King attack, we'd been nearly inseparable. Ken had unofficially moved in with me—that is to say, as of now he still had his apartment, but most of his personal belongings had made their way to my place, and the only nights we'd spent apart were nights I'd been in Boston with Kat.

After Kat had offered me the job eleven days ago, we'd worked out a schedule where I was going to fly to Boston on Sunday nights and return to Chicago late on Tuesdays. I'd do as much remotely as I could while keeping up with my Cipher projects. Caravel Pharmaceuticals was in a mess but would weather it.

"What are we talking about?" Ken asked from behind me, his hand coming down to rest on my shoulder. He seated himself next to me and draped one arm across the top of my chair. "Not Nana's impending death again, I hope. Don't fall for it, Steven."

The table erupted into laughter. Even Nana reluctantly chuckled.

Ken reached over, plucked my wine glass and took a drink. He choked when his dad, smiling devilishly said, "Your grandmother only wanted to know when you and Steven were tying the knot."

I worried momentarily that Ken would take exception to his family asking me such things, but he recovered quickly and laughed, his eyes twinkling.

"When we do, you can bet we're not doing this," he gestured behind his shoulder at the lavish reception. "We'll elope, thanks. No need to hide your wallet. I won't do that to you."

I was stunned. I couldn't believe he'd said it so plainly and confidently. My face must have displayed my shock because his smile grew wider as he winked at me, rubbing the back of my neck comfortingly.

"That's not what I was...I didn't mean...I wasn't worried about—" his dad sputtered, brows furrowed.

Everyone laughed again, this time at Robert's expense. I could clearly see Ken and his temperament in his father. The resemblance was uncanny.

I leaned close to Ken and asked quietly, "We're eloping, huh?"

Impossibly, his grin grew wider, teeth glinting in the soft ambient light. "Well, it's my preference, but we should compare scripts and then decide." He kissed me softly, uncaring of our audience, his attention wholly on me. "But if the only way I can make it happen is by sticking to your script, then that's what I'll do, because I want forever with you."

Tears pricked my eyes and I was momentarily choked with emotion. "Forever sounds perfect."

I loved him and I couldn't believe sometimes that he was in my life. I'd come so far in this year. From despair to hope, from friendship to love, from doubt to surety—and it was all because of Ken. Ken and his steadfast, open, beautiful heart. I wanted everything with him. I wanted to write my script with him on every page.

The End.

ACKNOWLEDGMENTS

In addition to those beautiful ladies, Linda and Brooke, to whom this book is dedicated, there are a multitude of others who were integral to not only getting this book published, but to my heart.

Steve, my husband, my love, you are in every part of this book. You're the inspiration, you're the backbone, and you are the reason I understand what love is. Thank you for being my rock and my muse.

My sweet teens, thank you for always giving me a reason to keep going. Thank you for being encouraging and most of all, thank you for not asking to read what Mommy was writing.

Mom, thank you for your unwavering enthusiasm and support. You smiled and cheered for me, even when you were struggling. This book will always remind me of the summer we held each other and cried and laughed and reminisced. Thank you, also, for not asking to read what I was writing.

Dad, I don't know if there's a heaven, but if it's real, then surely you are there. You gave me so much in life that it seems greedy to ask for one more thing now. But, I'm your child—always needing, always asking. Visit in my dreams if you can. I'd love to see you one more time.

Crissy, I love you. I'm so blessed and grateful to walk through life with you as my sister.

Brynne Asher, you were my first editor, my first mentor and helped me build the confidence I needed to share my work. I'm so thankful for your friendship and wisdom.

To my fellow Smartypantsers: WE DID IT! I'm so fortunate to have been selected to take this journey with the sweetest, funniest and most generous women around. Everything about this experience was amazing and uplifting. Piper, Nora, Ellie, Elsie, I've loved all our chats and appreciate all the pep talks and commiseration. Can you believe this is real life?!

Last but not least, the two biggest smartypants of them all: Fiona Fischer and Penny Reid.

Fiona, you are the single hardest working woman in romance. I don't know how you managed to wrangle all of us cats (lovely, sweet, brilliant ones for sure), get everything organized so beautifully and do it all with boundless humor and otherworldly calmness (seriously, I think you might be an Angel…or an Alien. I haven't decided which yet). Thank you for working so hard for all of us and for making this experience the highlight of my life.

Penny. Ah, Penny. So, the thing is, I wrote this because I love you. You—your books, your Sharks of Awesome—came along when I was feeling low. You made me laugh, you made me eager for what was to come, and you gave me a community of friends around the world who were always there to talk. Some of these friends I will have forever. Not only did you hand me quality entertainment and a kind of social life I was missing, but you inspired my own creativity. I wrote this to pay you back, make the Sharks happy, and give love to a couple of your characters I thought deserved it. But now here you are… still *giving* to me. I don't know what the heck I did to deserve being in your sphere and having my dreams handed to me, but… here I am. There's nothing in this world I could ever do to repay all your generosity, nothing I could say that would come close to conveying how profoundly you've changed my life. Thank you for giving me my dream.

ABOUT THE AUTHOR

Stella Weaver is a reader, writer, sloppy crafter and family woman. She's a native of coastal northern California who now lives on the Texas Gulf coast. She was a finalist in Love Notes from Purgatory's 2017 Teeny Tiny Romance Contest and has won the much-coveted #1 Mom of the Year Award (she has the coffee mug to prove it, too).

COME FIND ME
Facebook: https://www.facebook.com/stellarweaving/
Instagram: https://www.instagram.com/stellarweaving/
Goodreads: https://www.goodreads.com/stellarweaving
Blog: https://stellarweavings.blogspot.com/
Twitter: https://twitter.com/stellarweaving
Email: stellaweaver123@gmail.com

Find Smartypants Romance online:
Website: www.smartypantsromance.com
Facebook: www.facebook.com/smartypantsromance/
Goodreads: www.goodreads.com/smartypantsromance
Twitter: @smartypantsrom
Instagram: @smartypantsromance

Made in the
USA
Monee, IL